SIMON of CYRENE

The Man Who Carried the Cross of Christ

CHRISTIAN EPICS

SIMON of CYRENE

The Man Who Carried the Cross of Christ

FRANS VENTER

EDITED AND INTRODUCED BY JAMES S. BELL, JR.

MOODY PRESS
CHICAGO

To my daughter Rosheen

Though the cross may get heavy and painful sometimes,
don't be afraid to pick it up anyway
and follow Him.

About the Author

Frans Venter was a farmer in the Karroo flatlands of South Africa as well as a best-selling author.

James S. Bell, Jr. (B.A., College of the Holy Cross; M.A., University College, Dublin) is editorial director at Moody Press. He is the former director of religious publishing at Doubleday and the former executive director of Bridge Publishing. He, his wife, and four children live in West Chicago, Illinois.

Preface

Most of us have at least heard of the name of Simon of Cyrene. He played a "bit part" as a very minor actor in the greatest cosmic drama of all time—the crucifixion of Jesus of Nazareth. Here is the Son of God, King of the Universe, too weak to carry this Roman instrument of execution. The soldiers scan the crowd for an able-bodied male to shoulder the heavy cross long enough for Jesus to regain strength, only to later endure the agony of being nailed to its wood. An innocent observer named Simon is forced to comply, to aid the effort to brutally punish another innocent man—the only man who never deserved to die.

Here is a story filled with irony and paradox. Who was this man from North Africa, and why was he in Jerusalem at the Passover? Was he there to mock or to sympathize with Jesus? As a child hearing this story, I pictured Simon as a wayfarer, traveling to another land, inadvertently caught up in a violent mob scene— a victim of unusual circumstances. Yet how could he not be profoundly affected by his participation—relieving the Savior's pain and yet sealing His doom?

Author Frans Venter weaves a convincing and gripping tale of the man from Cyrene. He reveals the passions and strong ideals he is willing to fight for—his hatred of the Roman oppressors, love of chosen Israel, and deep yearning for the Messiah-King, who will deliver them. Around Simon swirl a number of unforgettable characters—his loving, supportive wife, Deborah; his two sons, Rufus and Alexander (also mentioned in the Scriptures), so different, and yet each seeking truth in his own way.

We see other more familiar characters in a whole new light —through the eyes of Simon, the typical devout Jew who cannot, because of his tradition, understand the strange teachings of the carpenter from Nazareth. In this way, we gain an entirely new and important perspective on the apostle Peter, Judas Iscariot, Joseph of Arimathea, Lazarus, Mary and Martha, and Barabbas. Their weaknesses blend with their dreams under the influence of divine grace.

As the story opens in the wheat fields of Cyrene there is a profound sense of foreboding as well as expectant hope. The Roman yoke is becoming a stench to the Jews and insurrection is simmering. At the same time, a carpenter from Galilee is performing numerous miraculous signs and speaking of a new heavenly kingdom for Israel. Simon, lover of the soil, instigates a rebellion against the Romans, who take his crops as he flees to Jerusalem to manage the groves of Joseph of Arimathea.

Simon is overjoyed with the thought of a new life for his family with the produce from oil and wine. Yet beliefs concerning Christ have divided his family. The more he scorns this would-be Messiah, the more His haunting presence confronts him. Simon is there at the vortex of this great cosmic struggle between good and evil—at the cross and even as the temple curtain is torn in two.

He is a God-fearing man, strong-willed, with a stubborn integrity, and he must confront a Truth that shatters all of his presuppositions. From Cyrene to Jerusalem, to the mines of Mesopotamia, and to Nero's Rome, Simon struggles with his own heart and, more important, the hearts of his beloved Deborah, Rufus, and Alexander. Finally, back in Cyrene, the place of his roots and identity, he comes "full circle" and discovers the meaning and purpose of his life.

Simon Niger, as he was called, felt that he needed to protect, defend, and fight for his family, his nation, and his religion. Yet he learned that he was living in a world of shadows and the full meaning of what he longed for was not what he had expected. Surprisingly, as a result of his experiences of loss, he found himself to be a different person—one willing to let go, surrender, and lay down his life for what mattered most.

Did he follow Christ? I'll let you, the reader, discover this. Though he was forced to carry Christ's cross for a short time, we must volunteer to pick up ours daily and follow Him.

To some of the characters in this book, that prospect brought great joy. Yet to others, the pain involved in following this alleged Messiah was not worth the price.

Simon of Cyrene may not have the stature of classics such as *Quo Vadis* or *Ben Hur,* but it is a rare and precious find for the Christian Epic series. I hope you will enjoy and be edified by it as I have.

JAMES S. BELL, JR.

Part One

1

On a headland of Africa, just above the sea, lay Cyrene, pearl-white city, built by the Greeks while Rome was still a child. In the hot glare of summer its roofs flashed and its spires glittered, while the arcades of its temples lay in cool, enticing shadows.

On either side of the city, all along the sea, stretched the fertile regions; to the south, the desert that Rome herself could not subdue. Far away to the north the sea licked at the very feet of Rome, and to the east it lapped beside the temples of Alexandria, the papyrus fields of Egypt, and Palestine's faded coastline.

The palace of the Roman governor reared high and massive above the wide expanse of flat-topped houses and their court-yards crowned with date palms and mulberry trees. An arch triumphantly proclaimed a victory of the legions. High on a basilica tower, a turtledove preened its feathers.

Life stood still in Cyrene at this hour. No loaded wagons clattered through the streets; no Roman soldiers threw their dice on the cobbles; no hawkers led their burdened mules; no women came bearing heavy pitchers on their heads. From the smithies came no sound of hammer blows, and no caravans made their caterpillar progress toward the market places.

This was the hour of relaxation in the white city, as it dozed beneath a haze. The blinding sun beat down, driving the people to the cool and shaded colonnades, to the groves, to the canvas shelters in the market places. Time sifted by in talk, or slumber, or reflection.

Nearer the sea, in the forum, sat the scribes in their white togas with parchment unrolled and spread out by sweating hands. Patricians sauntered in the spacious precincts of the marble baths. The deserted amphitheater baked and shimmered in the sun. Only the trampled arena told of recent contests . . . the blood of a bull . . . the paw marks of a lion that had died. . . .

It was siesta time in Cyrene, but on the terraces, where leaves moved in the sunlight, work was being done. There a wind came from the sea and, reaching the land, sighed through the olive trees. It was a wind from Rome.

Cyrene, like a temple, stood with steps descending to the sea. These steps were not of Grecian marble, but were terraces cut from the dark earth of Africa—fertile levels bearing olive orchards, vineyards, and fields of wheat, nourished by the silt-stained waters from the aqueduct that Caesar Augustus had built.

On the terraces no one relaxed or sought the shade. The golden cloud of harvest hovered over the orchards and the stub-bled fields. On the threshing floors men sweated and drove animals ruthlessly round and round. As each bundle of wheat was threshed, shoulders bent and wooden pitchforks were swung high. The wind, seizing the chaff, carried it up into the Cyrenian sky.

Wheat grains fell rustling in ever-growing heaps.

Heavy wooden spades slid under the heaps of wheat and, turning over, filled the sacks. Eyes glittered in faces masked with the dust of wheat. There was a ceaseless hum and bustle as on the busy terraces the sons of Cyrene gathered the harvest for Rome.

Simon the Jew gently combed his winnowing fan over his heap, sorting the bent straws to one side. He did it deftly, separating every fragment—for he sought perfection. He found toil in the sun a joy and every new mound of wheat a victory. He was a son of the soil, and to him its fruits were as a blessing.

He was big, this Jew—bigger than most men, his shoulders like a yoke; not clumsy, but lithe and powerful, with hands that could break a large animal's neck, arms that could swing two sacks of wheat with rhythmic grace, and a neck like the trunk of a rising cypress tree.

His dark face was broad and strong and friendly. When he laughed, as he often did, loudly and freely, his pitch-black beard parted as he threw back his massive head. His heart was spacious—though a wrong word might cause his eyes to flame and his hands to tremble with resentful anger. They called him Simon Niger (pronounced *Nee-jair'*).

His eyes were calm, but deep within them lurked rebellion. His mouth was relaxed, but sometimes it could compress to a thin and angry line and his jaws clamp as if he were forcing far back within himself something that he dare not liberate.

He was barely forty. But his face was marked with crisscross lines, for he had known suffering—more of the body than of the spirit. He was a patriot who had been trodden beneath the heel of the Empire. He was a son of Israel, who, under Tiberius, was forced to breathe the poisoned air of Rome.

And now his mound of wheat was clean. He glanced at Ezekiel, the aged Jew who had traveled far with him under the stars, and at Juba, the powerful Numidian, his faithful slave. He saw that they had almost finished the last sweeping of their threshing. Ezekiel and Juba: good workers, both.

Simon Niger leaned on his winnowing fan, looked out over the terraces descending to the sea called *mare nostrum* by the Romans, and the old bitterness stirred again within him.

But his mood succumbed to the beauty of the world that lay before him: the green luster of vineyards in the sun; the olive orchards, cool and dark; the bundles of straw exploding in the sunlight where other men were harvesting. He stared out over the scene that stretched off to where the ancient Greek columns of Cyrene shone in the sunlight. Lest the old bitterness take hold of him again, he looked once more at the bright expanse of sea, the sea that touched the terraces below him, the distant shores of Rome . . . and Palestine's far-off coast.

Simon Niger loved to watch the sea. His gaze was always expectant, always searching, always deeply yearning.

Suddenly his eyes became fixed. This afternoon the sea was not empty. A heavy galley was gliding into the bay of Cyrene. The mainsail stood out high and white, and from where he stood he could distinguish the sign of the fasces—an ax blade projecting from a bundle of rods, the emblem of Roman authority. The prow rode proudly above the white spray that fell away before it on either side. He watched the galley slaves lift their long, glittering oars from the water and dip them once again under the white manes of the waves.

Rage flickered in Simon. His eyes narrowed and became

15

hard, his jaws compressed as he stared at the galley. But only for a moment. Then his heart filled again with the old longing, which made him sigh and wipe his face with nervous hands. Alexander . . . his first-born, where could he be? The young man with the same black beard as his own, the same shoulders, and the eyes. His first-born whom he had named Alexander—in his foolish days when he had believed that Rome and Athens were greater than Jerusalem.

"That's the grain ship from Ostia," said Ezekiel, as he leaned on his pitchfork. Simon saw the contempt in his eyes. "See how they ride the sea as if it were their own. One day they will claim the sky and sun too."

Then the light in Ezekiel's eyes changed as he added: "It may be that Alexander is on that ship."

Simon flung his winnowing fan down in silence—almost in anger—and strode off through his vineyards to where his few mules stood nibbling at the straw. He took them to their drinking place at the ditch, and they lowered their muzzles to the water. "Drink, my animals," he said, "drink of the water of Rome; drink from the aqueduct of the great Augustus."

He turned around and watched the grain ship again as, far below the vineyards and the orchards of fruit and olive trees, below the neatly ordered vegetable plots, it slid closer to the shore. He stepped forward, threw himself down on his stomach and scooped water from the ditch onto his hot forehead. He washed his face and neck with vigor and drank deeply of the water.

When Simon stood erect, the grain ship had disappeared behind the line of olive trees that grew on the third terrace above the sea.

The noon sun burned down, bleaching the world below, and the white columns of Cyrene glistened. From where he stood, the pillared halls of the Roman governor looked cool and dark.

Simon led his animals back to the shining hay and turned toward the mighty olive tree whose seed must have risen in the early years of the Roman domination. He sat down sighing in its shade, and the earth was warm and dark and friendly. He loosened the coarse working clothes from his chest, unwound the hot turban, and let the cool sea breeze caress his beard.

He closed his eyes against the wind and sun, and leaned back against the trunk.

"You are growing old, Simon Niger. Once you always had to wait for me, but, now, it is I who wait for you."

He opened his eyes with pleasure. There she stood before him, eyes sparkling, thick black hair gleaming, tall and supple, as she had been in her youth.

A smile split his beard, and fine wrinkles showed where time and sun had touched him. "As long as you are with me, I never shall grow old," he said, stretching out his hand. She came closer and put down the basket that she had woven from the reeds growing beside a fissure in Augustus's ditch. She sank down beside him. Putting out his hand, he softly touched her throat: "You will never grow old, my Deborah," he said, and his voice trembled slightly. She touched his beard with her fingertips, and she felt as she did that day when first she met him in an orchard beside a canal in Alexandria. He was a caravan trader then, moving between Alexandria and Cyrene. Simon drew her toward him and caressed her hair with his lips.

For a moment she leaned against him to feel the warmth of his strong body. Then she placed the basket before them and removed its covering cloth. He peered into it, and his eyes sparkled.

"A veritable feast, my wife!"

There was a fresh griddlecake, baked of his own wheat ground by her hands; there was roast meat, figs from his trees, honey from his hives, and a small wicker flask of the wine he had laid down the previous year. There were fat brown dates from the Nile, and there was Deborah's own goat's milk cheese.

"This is no ordinary day," she said, and her voice was warm and musical. "Is it not the last day of harvest? And is not the harvest good?"

He chewed a fig, his beard moving up and down. She saw the tension in his eyes as he stared into the sun, off in the direction where the roofs of Jerusalem should rise, far across the sea.

"Yes, this is the last day of the harvest," he said and flicked away the stalk of the fig in a slight gesture of impatience. "The harvest is overflowing, abundant. Soon the gluttons of Rome will gorge themselves on the wheat of Simon Niger."

"Simon . . ." Her hands stirred restlessly. She frowned. "You mustn't talk like that."

"But it is true, my wife. Another grain ship has arrived. The harvest has hardly been brought in before they come to take it away to Rome."

"A grain ship? A large one?" She leaned forward, and he saw the expectancy in her eyes.

His work-roughened hand caressed her chin. Looking gravely into her eyes he said, "You must not worry about Alexander so. He'll return one day. You will grow old before your time if you fret so about the children. And I don't want you to grow old." He laughed but could not quite suppress the longing in his eyes.

Deborah took a fig she had peeled for him and put it tenderly into his mouth, as if to reconcile him. "When Rufus comes home again, we must keep him here," she said cheerfully, but he knew that she was seeking to hide her own sadness.

"Rufus . . ." Simon said. "He studies Latin and Greek while his father labors at cleaning wheat. He places the godless city of Alexandria before Cyrene."

"He sits at the feet of the great Philo Judaeus, husband. One day, our Rufus may be a great man too."

"A great man. Where? In the heathen temples of Rome? All he needs to know is the law and the prophets; all he needs to do is to work as I do. On the soil, which knows no sin."

She looked out over the shimmering orchards at a vision far beyond—farther than the sea, farther than the horizon, where the haze of the sky seemed to touch the green curve of the earth.

"If he studies hard, he may be able to serve the Nazarene," she said, without looking at her husband.

The hands of Simon Niger shook as he broke a piece from the griddlecake. He did not eat it immediately. Sitting there with the piece of cake in his hand, he struggled with a vast unknown, tried to break through the realm of sunlit space to the veiled place above, where truth and certainty lay concealed.

But almost immediately he returned from those far regions, with the door still closed to him.

He put the piece of cake in his mouth, gave Deborah a side-long glance, and said teasingly: "You are indeed a faithful Jewess, my wife. Every summer, with the coming of the swallows, we learn of a new master who will deliver Israel, who will make Jerusalem great."

"I have a feeling that this Galilean is the Messiah. . . . I can't help it."

Simon almost choked. "The Messiah! He is as little the Messiah as John the Baptist was!" he exclaimed. The leaves seemed to tremble at the violence of his voice. "We believed the Baptist was the Messiah—and Herod had him beheaded! No, I have heard enough of this Galilean to know that He is not the Deliverer."

"But this man is different. Rufus says that thousands follow Him."

"See how they followed the Baptist! What is so different about this new man? He is but a carpenter who has a crew of fishermen by the ears. Once you even said that Simon of Samaria was the Messiah."

"But this man works miracles. They say He preaches only love."

"Simon of Samaria also works miracles. He is a sorcerer. This man is but a carpenter, and He left His work to make fine talk."

"Do you not wish to see the coming of the Messiah, husband?"

He turned his massive head and gave her so stern a look that her hands moved uncomfortably in her lap. "Woman," he said clearly, his eyes wide in dead earnestness, "I yearn for Him just as Israel yearned for Canaan—you know that. But He will not be a carpenter who shuts His eyes to Rome. He must be great. He must destroy the temples of Rome and bring power to Jerusalem. He must deliver Israel and free the world from Tiberius. He must be greater even than Isaiah. He must be a prince—not a wretched carpenter." Passion clenched his fist. "He must break the yoke of Rome."

"He must be a prophet, husband, a priest."

"A ruler first, and then a priest."

Wordlessly she lay on her back staring up through the green leaves at the empty sky. She wished some mighty hand would write there, on this side of the stars. Then she would know with absolute certainty that He was greater than Isaiah.

"They say He is the son of David. They say . . . they say He is the Lamb of God."

Simon shrank back as if her words had flashed a blinding light into his eyes. There was dread and piety in his voice as he spoke.

"Do not sin, Deborah! Do not take the name of your God in vain! The thought alone can destroy you. It is blasphemy . . . blasphemy against God."

She stood up quickly, frightened. "I do not want to sin. I want only to believe. Why, they say even His birth was different."

"Shepherds' talk! They do not even know where He was born. Some say Bethlehem, some say Nazareth. I have heard it told that even His own kin, His own blood, do not believe in Him."

"But all those other—"

"A small group of Galilean fishermen! They believe anything, everything. When there is a ring around the moon, they believe the fish will rise. How is it that the learned men of Jerusalem do not believe in Him? Why does Philo of Alexandria not believe? It is only the gullible fools of Galilee who believe, because they have nothing else to do."

He glanced at her quickly and felt triumphant at the doubt in her troubled eyes.

He leaned over and put his face close to hers. "If He is the Messiah, why does He tolerate Pontius Pilate? This Roman villain has defiled Jerusalem with Roman emblems. Have you forgotten? If He is the Messiah, why does He allow tribute to Tiberius? Does the law not say that tribute is due to God alone?"

His wife looked toward the faint haze that lay upon the sea. Her eyes mourned for the dream he had shattered within her. She felt frail and quite alone, her joyous vision faded and her heart's hope gone.

"Will He still come—the Messiah?"

Simon pointed to the city that the Greeks had built when Athens was still free. "Do you see those shining pillars erected by the Greeks? Do you see their colonnades?" His voice sounded sharp in its certainty. His hand made a wide sweep. "Do you see here, before you, the sea of Rome? As certainly as you know that all the things you see before you have reality, as certain as you are that the sun is shining, so can you be sure of the coming of the Messiah, because the prophets have said it. But He will be no carpenter in fear of Rome. He will be a prince who will cause the sun to shine only for Jerusalem. He will liberate us, magnify us, according to the Word." The veins stood out on his neck, and his clutching hands trembled as if intent on crushing.

She gazed gratefully at him. Although he had destroyed her latest dream, he had, here in this place, revived the old one.

Then both were silent, and, gazing through the sunlight, they saw two birds flying eastward toward Egypt, the land where men had held them sacred. "I wish I were one of those birds," she said wistfully. "I should be with Rufus tomorrow."

He sipped the wine and tried its coolness on his tongue. "Rufus and Alexander," he said with his old cheerfulness. "You think of them only. Am I so old that I mean nothing to you?"

She laughed. "You will never be old, Simon Niger." Her tenderness soothed his heart. She stood up. "I must go," she said. "I have work to do. Will you bring me a bushel of wheat to grind for bread?"

"Will you fry me a piece of mutton? This evening I want to rest and eat and talk with you, for the harvest is finished . . . and even Rome must pay me for it."

She glanced at Ezekiel and Juba, who were frying a fish under another tree, saw the heaped up wheat, the bags already filled, and an old uneasiness stirred in her. "You must be careful, my husband," she said, and looked at him with pleading eyes.

He stood up, and his bulk seemed to fill the shade. "I ask my price for the work I have done," he said and stretched until his fists touched the olive leaves.

"You know this governor—

"I know that barrel Quirinius."

"He is not unreasonable, but he is strict. Remember, Simon, he takes his orders from Rome."

"He is a Roman." Simon said it contemptuously.

"Why do you fight the system? You will only bring difficulty upon us."

"Must I then fatten the idle nobles of Rome for a pittance?"

With a sigh she turned and walked away. He watched her

graceful progress through the sunlight, then moved from the shadow of the tree and walked among his sunlit vines.

On the edge of his lands he stopped and watched a slave with a ball and chain fastened to his leg tilling an open piece of land. The man, big and black, seemed to be a Syrian. He swung the long-handled hoe slowly, and laboriously dragged the iron ball after him as he moved.

Simon watched the man for a while with narrowed eyes. "Slavery, oppression, and violence—that is Rome," he whispered. "Enslaver of the nations. I would rather die than become a slave like this Syrian. A slave of Rome is an animal."

He turned abruptly away and walked back to his threshing floor. He picked up the winnowing fan and again combed lightly over his heap, flicking here and there at the small stalks still remaining.

Ezekiel and Juba had finished eating. They returned to toss the last heaps with their pitchforks.

It was then that Ezekiel saw a rider coming briskly through the vineyard that Simon and he had laid out only the year before.

Ezekiel's pitchfork stayed its motion in the air. He glanced quickly at Simon, who was still busily working.

"A Roman comes," he said and saw how Simon stiffened, winnowing fan in hand. Juba stood to one side, submissive and afraid.

Simon Niger stared at the Roman, whose white garment was flapping in a light breeze. He looked at the two soldiers who followed. Their red helmet plumes waved with the movement of their horses.

He took three paces in their direction, his tread making no sound on the dense chaff. Then he said, into the wind, "It's that scoundrel Vitellius, Quirinius's assessor."

"No doubt he's coming to tell us how much of your wheat must go to swell the bellies of Tiberius's beggars," Ezekiel said with a short laugh. His laugh made something deep within Simon shudder. The handle of the fan shook in his hands.

Vitellius and the two soldiers came riding across the threshing floor and pulled up sharply close to Simon.

"Why do you trample my vineyard? " Simon asked in grating tones. "There is a road across the terraces."

"I go where I please," replied the fat Roman. "I come to see how much clean wheat you have. The grain ship is here."

"This is my vineyard."

"The great and august Tiberius owns you, vineyard and all." Vitellius laughed out of his great belly. "You are a Jew, and you irrigate your lands with water graciously provided by Caesar Augustus."

"This is my land."

Vitellius dug his heels into his horse. The animal whinnied and reared, and its front hooves swept past Simon's face. The Roman roared with laughter. "If you don't take care, we may even take your land and make a galley slave out of you. You have good shoulders for the oars."

The two soldiers drew their swords from their scabbards. It was then that Simon struck Vitellius with the handle of his winnowing fan. It was a swift and savage blow. The handle of the winnowing fan flashed in the sun.

Ezekiel gasped with shock and fright. For Simon was a Jew, and Vitellius a Roman.

2

Simon's blow almost unhorsed Vitellius, but the assessor succeeded in retaining his seat, though his horse reared up with fright. As one of the soldiers spurred forward with raised sword, the shining teeth of Ezekiel's pitchfork caught him under his shoulder blade and hurled him screaming from the saddle. At the same moment Simon thrust the handle of his fan into the groin of the other soldier's horse. The animal snorted, arched its back, and flung its rider against the mound of wheat.

Leaping up, the two soldiers charged at Simon and Ezekiel with swords raised. But Vitellius, his fleshy face gleaming with sweat, screamed, "Don't kill the dogs now. We will hand them over to the vengeance of Quirinius. The sword is too sweet a weapon. It is long since someone was crucified in Cyrene."

"Set your foot on my land again, Lucius Vitellius, and you'll have a pitchfork through your bottom," Simon shouted and came menacingly closer.

"There won't be time for that, Simon Niger," Vitellius said contemptuously. "I am informing Quirinius immediately that his assessor and two of his soldiers were set upon by Jewish dogs. Have you forgotten the penalty for attacking a Roman?"

Simon stood silent, trembling too much with anger to utter a word.

"By sunset," Vitellius said, "all the wheat must be in bags. Tonight it has to be loaded on board. The price is one and a half denarii a bag."

"*Two* denarii," Simon said. "I shall not sell for less. Tell that to Quirinius; tell it to the doddering Tiberius if you so desire."

Fury flushed Vitellius's face, and the soldiers gripped their swords.

"The price has been fixed by the chief wheat officer in Rome,

Cornelius Marsus. Not a penny more or less. The wheat must be loaded by tonight."

Vitellius wheeled his horse and, followed by the soldiers, galloped away through Simon's vineyard. The leaves and young shoots whipped against the hooves. Simon sat down slowly on a bag of wheat, and his whole being felt burned out by his anger.

"You've made a big mistake, Simon," Ezekiel said and threw his pitchfork down. "Vitellius is Quirinius's lackey. They will break us."

"One and a half denarii a bag!" Simon groaned, as if he had not heard Ezekiel speak. "I'd rather burn it all than sell it at that price."

He stared away toward the white temples of Cyrene, the triumphal arch, and, farther, the gleaming palace of Quirinius.

"One and a half denarii," Simon muttered again as he stood up, and points of light glinted on his damp neck. He clenched his fists as he looked at the swath cut through his vineyard.

"It is the fixed price," Ezekiel said fearfully.

"You speak like a slave!" Simon Niger shouted and swung around. "Would you have me be a slave and sell at their price? Have you heard how many tramps and drunkards there are in Rome? Five hundred thousand! They keep them happy so Tiberius may remain Caesar and live in luxury on Capreae. And I, Simon Niger, must sell my wheat, my wine, everything, for the price of dirt. And on top of this I must pay their taxes—a tenth here, a fifth there . . ."

"Caesar is Caesar," Ezekiel said warningly and wiped his mouth with his hand.

"There is but one Caesar, and that is the Almighty!" Simon thundered. "To Him and Him alone does Israel owe anything; she owes nothing to this brute creature who thinks only of women, wine, and blood."

Simon took a few steps, gripped a bag of wheat, lifted it, threw it down again. The effort seemed to drain him of his anger.

For a few minutes they stood relaxed and silent in the sunlight with heads bowed, for the tension had been broken and there was emptiness in them. Ezekiel gave a frightened glance at the dent in the wheat heap made by the Roman soldier.

Then Simon lifted the wooden shovel and stood it in the wheat. "I am sorry I spoke so harshly," he said penitently. His dark eyes looked out mildly at Ezekiel, who for so many years had helped him till the ground. "If there should be trouble, the blame will be mine. I struck first."

"I love my life," Ezekiel said with a weak smile, "and my freedom. Of what use is it to lift one's hand against Rome? They send you to the salt mines on the other side of Jordan, or they make you a soldier in Gaul, or perhaps they send you to break stones on the Alexandria road; or you get the treatment that fellow over there got." Ezekiel nodded in the direction of the slave working in the open lands.

"Bring the bags, Juba!" Simon called to the Numidian and pulled the spade from the mound of wheat. He moved with a nervous haste, for Ezekiel's words had jarred him; he knew how true they were.

For one bitter moment, with the sun in his eyes, he thought of Deborah and of everything he had built up in this place.

They began to fill the bags. Simon worked with eager movements of his broad shoulders. Work always gave him pleasure, no matter what his mood. Juba held the mouth of a bag open, Simon filled it, and Ezekiel tied it up.

"What do you think of this new man who is preaching in Galilee?" Simon asked casually, as if it were a matter of no moment. From under his bushy eyebrows, he watched Ezekiel's busy hands.

"Which one? The one from Nazareth?" Ezekiel asked without looking up from his work.

"Yes, that carpenter."

"He's a ne'er-do-well—too lazy to put His hand to labor. He's been full of fine talk ever since He was a child—and now tries to measure words with the scribes and Pharisees."

"And they say He has many followers," Simon said regretfully.

"That sorry crew in Galilee would follow anybody. If I went there and said I was Moses, they'd believe me too. A herd of fishermen, tanners, wretched shepherds."

"They say He works miracles . . . heals the sick."

"Now what's so strange about that? Simon of Samaria does the same—he too works miracles."

"That's what I told Deborah just now," Simon replied gratefully.

"Mark my words, Simon Niger, this carpenter will cause trouble—just like that other Galilean, Judas, who led the revolt. He too set himself up above others. And what happened? The Romans crushed our people as they would flies."

"Yes, many were crucified."

"If this Nazarene had any worth, why did He not save the Baptist from Herod?"

"That is what I said," Simon agreed, without pausing in his work. He felt as sound and sure as a newly made cedar cask. "If He were the Messiah, He could have saved the Baptist. Where were His miracles then? Moses brought forth water from a rock, but this man could not even save the head of the Baptist!"

Ezekiel shook with laughter.

"Yes, that is so. They say a young Pharisee in the temple confused Him so with his questions that He fled back to the country, to Galilee where there are only fishermen to preach to. I hear His lieutenant is that fisher fellow from the lake of Galilee—Peter."

"The tall man with the auburn beard?"

"Yes, that's the one. He is your namesake—he's also called Simon. You sent him reeling across a tanning vat one evening. Do you not remember? That was the time when we were returning from Damascus with a load of skins."

Simon remembered the days when youth was his.

"Yes. He was tall and sturdy, but as clumsy as a Roman senator."

Ezekiel wiped the perspiration from his upper lip and stood upright. He leaned backward, looking at the terraces that stepped down to the sea. He deliberately remained silent, for he wished to say something of importance.

"But that's nothing," he said at last. "Who follows after Him is no concern of ours, but did you hear about that Matthew?"

"Matthew? What Matthew?" asked Simon as he worked. "Is he a fisherman—or just another fashioner of wood?"

"No, this Matthew is neither a fisherman nor a carpenter. He's a tax collector." Ezekiel's voice came clearly through the warm stillness. "The Nazarene has even eaten at his house, so I have heard."

Simon gave such a start that he tossed his spadeful of wheat completely past the mouth of the bag. For a moment he stood as if a heavy blow had bowed his back.

Then he slowly stood erect and his big shadow stretched out far before him. He stared broodingly at Ezekiel, and his hands were slack on the handle of the spade. His eyes were puckered, as if he were gazing into the sun.

"A tax collector?" He spat the word. "A tax collector . . . a villain . . . a traitor . . . a lackey of Rome? Such a man is one of His followers?"

Ezekiel raised his eyebrows, pleased to have revealed so shattering a secret.

"Did you not know that, Simon Niger?"

Simon shook his heavy head and looked in confusion at his hairy hands.

"But . . . but then He cannot be a Jew—He is nothing but a traitor," he whispered at last and sat down heavily on a bag of wheat. "A man who consorts with a tax collector is a traitor to Israel, a betrayer of the people! That is why we shall never be freed! We have too many weaklings like this man." Simon looked up into Ezekiel's eyes. There he saw what Ezekiel left unsaid.

"Like my two sons. Why don't you say it? That's what you're thinking, Ezekiel, and it's true!"

Ezekiel looked away quickly at the trees swaying in the wind.

"The one is a tool of Rome, and the other follows Roman dogma instead of studying the prophets."

Ezekiel said nothing. His silence, the sympathy in his eyes that had seen so much, struck Simon harder than condemnation.

The big man sat limply, with head bowed. When he spoke, his voice was listless. "Let us finish," said Simon. "The sun is already touching the horizon."

Swiftly they shoveled the remaining wheat into the bags.

"What of Vitellius . . . if he reports to Quirinius that we have attacked them?" Ezekiel asked as they finished their task.

Simon looked away; his glance searched the sea. But the sea was like his heart at that moment, wide and empty. He had finished the harvest, but the thought gave him no pleasure.

"You need not fear, Ezekiel. Quirinius will laugh Vitellius out of court when he learns that two Jews as good as trounced him with his two soldiers. We spilled no blood—we only frightened them. And I've told you—I'll take the blame."

He turned and walked toward his home. Ezekiel and Juba also left, each taking his own direction.

Simon walked quickly through his vineyard. This time he did not linger to see the swelling grapes.

"A tax collector follows Him, and still they say He is the Messiah," he muttered. But no one heard, and his words were lost in silence. "I hope Herod cuts off His head—it's worth less than that of the Baptist."

When Simon reached the house that he and Ezekiel had built on the outskirts of Cyrene, he halted, and his eyes lit with pride. It was a low house with a flat roof, on which a man could rest when it was cool. The tapering poplars threw trembling shadows on the walls.

Four Roman horsemen and a number of slaves came riding by from the countryside where they had been hunting, but Simon did not look at them. He crossed the yard and stood in the doorway of Deborah's kitchen. She turned lightly from the hearth.

"So you've finished your task, my husband."

He went inside quickly, took the wine flask from its peg on the wall, and, with head throne back, took deep drafts of the cool wine.

"Yes, the harvest is in. . . . This Messiah of yours has a tax collector as one of His followers. Can you imagine that!"

He expected her to show indignation and revulsion, but her eyes stayed soft and calm. She stood quietly by the table he had fashioned for her from driftwood.

Her voice was placid. "They say He is like that. He said that He came to save sinners—even tax collectors."

"A tax collector is worse than a sinner. He's a traitor! He chokes the coffers of Rome with money bled from his own people. You know that."

She sat down at the table, hands folded in her lap and longing in her eyes. "Sinners and the poor. They say His heart goes out to them." Suddenly there was fervor in her voice. "One day He was preaching on a mountain top. He said that the poor will inherit the kingdom of heaven."

"The poor," Simon said disparagingly as he went to the washtub in the corner. "The poor and the tax collectors—such are His flock."

"We too were poor once, Simon Niger."

"But we were never tax collectors!" he said it with bitter triumph. "We have always been faithful to Israel."

"They say His kingdom is of heaven—not of earth."

He swung around. His eyes glittered. "I will hear no more about this man of Nazareth, do you understand, Deborah? We will discuss Him no longer. Always I drive Him from your mind, as I did this afternoon, but always you go running back to Him. It's been like this a long time, but now it must stop. It has gone on long enough!" His words, harsh and loud, seemed to remain suspended for a moment in the silence between them. Then they faded away into stillness, and only his heavy breathing could be heard.

She looked questioningly into his eyes. "It is *you* who brought Him into our talk this time." She spoke so quietly that he hardly heard her.

Guilty and confused he shied from the implication of her words, and roughly thrust his hands into the washtub. Grunting, he splashed the cool water over his head and beard. His shoulders shook with the vigor of his washing.

When he had finished, he looked at her, drops of water glinting in his beard, his hair dripping wet. The anger had left his eyes. Only respect and humility remained. "I was harsh with you, my wife," he said as he came to her, and he took her face in his wet hands. "It was because of this Nazarene." Her hair was silky to his touch. "Am I forgiven?"

"You are always forgiven, even before you have offended." She smiled softly, and he felt secure. He went to the wall to take down his crook. "I shall bring in the animals now."

But in the doorway he paused. "I had a little trouble this afternoon with Vitellius—gave him a thrashing with the winnowing fan."

"Simon, no!" She stood up quickly. "You are looking for your death."

"Yes, I . . . Ezekiel and I half-killed him and two soldiers." He gave a careless laugh. "He wants to pay me one and a half denarii a bag, as if I were a slave."

"Quirinius will punish you, Simon. Oh, why, why don't you listen?"

"My wheat is my wheat, wife—it does not belong to Vitellius or Quirinius or even Tiberius. They—"

Simon did not finish, for a man stood in the doorway.

His form darkened the room. He was young, but broadly built, with ample shoulders. His beard was black. Simon could only stare at this young man in the dress of a Roman seaman. Before him stood a likeness of himself. It seemed to be himself as a youth that had entered and was smiling at them both.

3

It was Alexander, their son. After all the days of waiting and longing, there he stood, one shoulder bare like a Roman's, a short sword at his side. On his wrists he wore broad bands of red pigskin studded with bronze.

Without a word Simon and Deborah gazed at the scar on his cheek that gave him added years and changed him from the boy he was when he first left them.

Alexander was the first to speak. "Father . . . Mother!" he cried out, laughing. His scarred cheek shone. He gripped Simon round the shoulders and clasped him hard in greeting.

"My son," Simon whispered, "you've come back . . . a man."

Alexander rushed to his mother and for a long time pressed her against his hard body, held her close while she simultaneously laughed and cried. When at last he let her go, she sank down on a chair and looked up at him through tears. "We have watched the ships so often . . . waited so long," she said.

"Come, sit down!" Simon called, while he dragged a stool toward them. "Sit, Alexander, and let us talk." He glanced fleetingly at the bare shoulder and Roman dress, but at this moment it did not matter much to him.

"I am home . . . I'm so happy!" Alexander exclaimed and sat down at the table.

"You're the last one I expected," Deborah said and wiped her eyes.

Simon leaned far over the table. His eyes sparkled. "Three years . . . for three years our eyes have missed you, son. Mother, bring wine," he roared and thumped the table. "Bring wine that we may celebrate." He laughed, his eyes grew moist, and he stroked his beard toward his chin. "Two important events on the same day—I've finished the harvest, and my firstborn comes home again."

Alexander gripped his father's hands and looked at him silently. Then he said, "Three years is a long time. I was happy to see the coast of Cyrene again."

Deborah came and went with busy movements. She fetched the earthenware decanter of wine and the heavy bronze beakers, putting them down noisily on the table. She sniffed happily and kept sending glances at her son. Simon Niger looked at his wife and was moved by her happiness. He struggled not to show it.

"You have become a man, while your mother and I have grown old," he said to Alexander with a smile in his eyes.

"Father," Deborah said as she busied herself, "you must slaughter a fat lamb—we haven't too much meat, and I asked you to bring me a bushel of wheat."

"Your mother is still the master, and I the slave," Simon said, roaring with laughter and putting his hand on that of Alexander. Alexander laughed with him, and in the smiling, tanned face of his firstborn, Simon saw himself as he was before the years had rolled over him. He felt his own blood pulsing in his son's warm hand.

"So I see, Father." Alexander winked at his mother, and that small gesture, so intimate and affectionate, brought a glow to Simon. He felt happy and free from care.

Simon filled the vessels with joyous haste. The wine flowed down the sides, and ruby drops splashed onto the grain of the wood. The big man held his beaker high, in measure with his joy.

"To your return, my son!" Simon said, raising his cup to Alexander. "Mother, to our son's return!"

She seated herself at the table near them, and when Alexander smiled at her and squeezed her hand tightly in his, she longed to touch the scar upon his cheek. To touch it only once—for on the day it happened, when blood lay on his lips, she was not with him.

"This is a great day for me," Alexander said, putting his free hand on Simon's.

"Yes, a great day indeed," Simon said hoarsely and sucked the wine from his beard. "Mother, we must keep him with us now."

"Yes, we have missed him so much."

Alexander stared down into his wine and flushed lightly under his brown skin. "But where . . . where is Rufus?" he asked quickly.

Simon leaned back and put his hand confidentially on his son's shoulder. "Rufus is studying in Alexandria under the great Philo Judaeus. I believe he wants to become a Roman philosopher." His laugh filled the room, a scornful laugh that brought a shadow to Deborah's eyes.

"I would like to see him," Alexander said, somewhat constrained now.

"Yes, he studies under Philo," Simon said seriously. "Why, I do not know. The law of Moses and the words of the prophet are all we need to know."

Alexander moved uncomfortably but did not speak. It was his mother who intervened with a nervous laugh.

"You're too serious, Father. See, Alexander's cup is empty."

"That must not happen," Simon said and refilled the drinking vessels. They toasted each other again.

"I'm happy to find you both so well," Alexander said with shining eyes.

"We are well and blessed by the Almighty. He has blessed our bodies and our work. I have a large vineyard, an olive orchard, fruit trees, and wheat land. And I'm still strong enough to work. Three years." Simon said suddenly. His face tightened. "Three years . . . where have you wandered all these years, Alexander?"

Alexander leaned forward. "I've traveled," he said. "Twice I have been to Spanish ports and sailed through the Pillars of Hercules. There we took on oil, honey hides, and vegetables. A few times I've been to Tyre to take on cedarwood for the villas of the Emperor Tiberius. I've often been to Joppa to load leather from the vats of Jerusalem, and to Alexandria several times a year to load papyrus and tent cloth, linen, silk, and wheat."

Something flickered in Simon's eyes, but he kept silence.

"And often I've been to the ports of the Greek islands—Rhodes and Chios and others. That's where they make those lovely clothes for women—beautiful clothes they are."

Deborah's eyes were round with admiration.

Simon sat and stroked his beard. His eyes were without expression.

Alexander rose suddenly and went outside. He returned immediately with a large bundle, which he placed on the table, with a sly look at his parents.

"I've brought a few things home," he said as he undid the covering. He took out a black walking staff and handed it to Simon. "Every time you go walking, Father, use this and think of me."

Simon looked at the masterpiece admiringly. He slid his roughened hands over it.

"Fashioned in Persia—" Alexander said, "from black ebony out of Africa—and the handle is ivory."

Simon got up and, swinging the walking staff proudly, walked about the room. Deborah gave a maternal smile at her husband's boyishness.

"It's beautiful, Alexander," Simon said, putting his hand on his son's shoulder. "It is strong and heavy. I shall take care of it, and wherever I use it, I shall think of you."

Then Alexander turned to his mother. "And here's something for you, my mother," he said and gave her a broad Roman bracelet of shining yellow copper. She looked appreciatively at the delicate handiwork and the broad serpent's head engraved on it. As Alexander put it on her wrist she caught his hand and kissed it.

"And these I bought in Joppa," Alexander said, "from Simon the tanner—the best tanner and shoemaker in all Judea."

"My son!" Simon said as Alexander put the beautiful sandals in his hands.

"With your new walking staff and sandals, husband, you can pay the governor a visit," teased Deborah.

He gazed at the sandals. "Hardly the governor. We are not on visiting terms," Simon said calmly.

Alexander rummaged in the bundle and brought more presents out: a round water flask, Roman fishing hooks, and a set of broad-bladed Roman knives for Simon; and for his mother, a delicate vase of Roman glass, a small casket of perfumed ointment, a bronze lamp shaped like a swan.

She touched all these things and her eyes shone brightly with pleasure. Simon looked at his new possessions and smiled. He felt once more that Alexander was one of them, that the heart of his eldest son still belonged to them. He felt the knife blade cautiously with his thumb, peered carefully at the fishing hooks, and sniffed at the water flask.

"This I brought for Rufus," Alexander said and took out a gilt harp. Deborah drew in her breath sharply and took the harp from Alexander. "Oh, how beautiful," she said. "I will keep it safe for Rufus." Simon touched the strings, and they sounded softly. "Now you will be able to play to me, Mother, when we are alone," he said.

But Deborah scarcely heard him; she stood lost in wonder, breathless, with her hands held to her cheeks.

"Alexander, child!" was all that she could say.

Alexander's face wrinkled with laughter, and his scar shone brightly. He held his hands high and displayed a thin cloth. It was soft as a summer cloud, transparent, purple as a queen's garment, exquisite as the empress's robe.

"This I bought in Ephesus," Alexander said proudly. "It was made in Phoenicia, and they call the color Tyrian purple; it's for you, Mother."

With a sob Deborah embraced him, hiding her face in his neck. Simon stared at them, breathing deeply, his eyes moist. To hide his emotion he picked up the harp and stared down at the strings.

"I'm . . . I'm glad you didn't forget us," Deborah said. She took the cloth, pressed it to her lips, and buried her face in it, admiring its superb texture.

"Lovely," she whispered.

Through her tears she saw the scar on his cheek tremble. She put out her hands slowly and humbly, laid them on his cheeks tenderly, as if afraid that the scar still gave him pain. "Thank you, Alexander," she said softly. "What you have done makes us one again."

Without intending to, she gently stroked the scar. Alexander could read the question in her eyes.

His face grew taut. Deborah watched him, and she knew a bitter memory lay within him. Alexander looked carefully at Simon. His father was staring at him with such intensity that he knew he had to speak.

When he did speak, his words were cold. "A slave," he said, "a slave struck me—with the blade of an oar. He tore it loose and struck me. The sharp edge caught my cheek. It happened out in the open sea, this side of Crete."

"A slave?" Simon asked sharply. He frowned and seated himself. Alexander too sat down. His hands gripped the wine cup. He stared into his wine.

"Yes, a slave . . . a Syrian brute . . . I . . . I broke his skull."

Deborah's hands lay limp on the table.

"But a slave—what have you to do with slaves?" Simon drew the decanter toward him.

Alexander hesitated a moment, and then he said, "I'm an overseer of slaves on the galley that arrived this afternoon."

Wine splashed over Simon's hands. He let the decanter fall.

He jumped up and pointed a trembling finger at Alexander. "You . . . a slave driver for the Romans?" His voice rose high.

Alexander glanced at his father apprehensively. "There have to be overseers," he said defensively.

"But you're my son! You are a Jew!" Simon stammered.

Rebellion flickered in Alexander's eyes, but he sought self-control, for his father stood over him massively, with furious threatening eyes.

"Father," Alexander said, "Rome rules the world, and Caesar Tiberius is above all. Does it avail us to resist?"

Simon's words contrasted strangely with his trembling body —he spoke softly, in a penetrating voice: "There is but one ruler, and He is God. He rules the world. Rome is master of our lives, but not of our hearts. Those slaves that suffer beneath your whip, they also are His creatures."

"They are criminals."

"They are not. They have been torn from their homes and kin by Tiberius and Germanicus because they refuse to bend their knees to Rome. They are treated like animals. And my son—a whipmaster, a tearer of their flesh . . ."

Simon's hands hung down. Perspiration showed on his forehead as if he himself knew the agony of a galley slave. He turned toward the washtub, bent over, and splashed his burning face with water.

Deborah got up quickly and poked the dying fire. She talked without ceasing. "Father, you talk so much. Please kill a lamb; it is already late. I want to fry a side of ribs. Alexander must be starving. It's three years, three long years, since last he sat at the table with us. I wish Rufus were here—then the whole family would be together. And you haven't brought the wheat. Don't you want to wash too, Alexander, child? We can give you some fresh water."

Simon turned from the tub. He spoke in a low voice, but his words cut clearly through Deborah's chatter. "Alexander," he said, "if you remain a slave driver, never show your face in my house again."

Deborah dropped the basin with a clatter. "Simon, he is our child. You cannot turn him out like that. I am his mother. I won't let you."

Alexander jumped up. His bare shoulder gleamed in the flickering light of the lamp Deborah had lit. He put his hands on his hips, and his eyes challenged Simon.

"Am I, your firstborn, forbidden the house because you hate Rome, Father?"

"You are a slave owner. To me that is as shameful as being a tax collector. The one takes money, the other blood. Both are an abomination in the eyes of Jewish law."

Alexander drew himself up, tall and supple in his strength. His eyes were fearless. "My name is that of a Greek . . . and Rufus has a Roman name. Now you wish to drive me forth. When you named us, were you a good Jew then?"

Simon clenched his fists. He felt a tingling on his neck.

"Alexander, no!" cried Deborah. Her face was white, and her eyes glittered.

Simon spoke softly."Don't remind me of my youthful folly! When Rome gave me a piece of God's earth, I thought her gracious." He seemed suddenly exhausted, drained of strength. "I would give my life if I could change it all!" He looked bitterly at his son. "But why should I, even if I could? Why should I give my sons good Jewish names if they are no longer worthy of being Jews? The one serves Rome, and the other learns from Gentiles, not from the history of the afflictions of Israel or the laws that Moses gave."

There was no longer revulsion or anger in his eyes; only grief remained.

Alexander could not meet his father's eyes. He stared, instead, at the presents on the table—the harp, the purple garment from Ephesus, the ebony walking staff—and none had meaning. He could hear his mother busy at the hearth behind him. He searched for words, words to speak to his father who stood there bowed and silent. But he knew it was of no use. He saw how wide a gulf stretched between a Roman slave driver and a man who ruled his life by the law of Moses.

At last Alexander spoke, more calmly, and his words were penitent. "I . . . I'm sorry if I said what I should not have said. I'm sorry if I've hurt you."

"Why don't you stay with us, my child?" Deborah asked from the hearth, where she was aimlessly moving the pots and pans. She straightened herself and stood with closed eyes, waiting for his answer, waiting and praying.

At her words Alexander closed his hand around the walking staff he had brought his father.

"There is work, and to spare, in Cyrene," she said, her voice strained and uncertain.

Simon came out of his distraction and smoothed his temples where the first gray hair was showing. "Yes, why don't you stay?" It was both a supplication and command. He went to the table, leaning on it with his trembling hands, bending his body forward to bring him closer to his son. He spoke in a low, urgent voice. "I will hand over the olive grove to you alone—and the oil press, too. To you alone. I will keep the vineyard. Your mother and I do not need a great deal anymore . . ."

He fell silent and saw Deborah, who had turned round from the hearth, waiting and expectant. "And I'll give you the wheat lands. I will help—Ezekiel and I—we will help you on the land. The soil is rich and black and fertile. You can make more here than on the sea. Cyrene is a good place!" He made a sweeping gesture with his hand. "Cyrene is well favored. Your mother and I have built ourselves up from nothing, here on this land."

Aimlessly, Alexander plucked at the strings of the harp. A chord sounded through the silence of the room.

"I cannot stay here," Alexander said with his head turned away as if he were trying to shield his eyes from blinding light. He gripped the neck of the wine decanter as if to break it. "Don't ask me to stay here!" he cried out. "You will only hurt me. . . . It's not possible!"

"Why?" Simon asked. "You were born on the land. You used to lead my oxen."

"I went away because I love the sea. I cannot leave the sea. The sea takes hold of you."

Simon stiffened. "Then you want to stay a slave driver?"

"I cannot leave the sea. I may become commander of a ship."

"I see. I understand. Rome has crept into your blood."

"It's not that," Alexander protested and beat the table with his fists. "I love the sea . . ." He looked at his father as if his eyes could make him understand.

But Simon had already left his place at the table. He was standing in the doorway, his body blocking the shadowed light of dusk. He hesitated, looked back at them as if to speak, and then walked away into the twilight. In his yard he stood still, looking back toward the light. Then he walked on slowly, stopping beneath his poplar trees, barely hearing the rustle of their leaves in the cool breeze. He looked up and saw three birds in flight, their bodies somber in the last red of the dying day. And he saw Cyrene, a dark outline against the fading light.

He walked through the trees toward his orchards and wheat fields, and it was as if something within him compelled him to go there.

In the kitchen Alexander rose, went to his mother. Putting his arms around her, he led her to a chair beside the table.

"Perhaps I shouldn't have come," he said as he sat down with her hands in his. "But it's three years, three long years, that I have been away."

"Those years have changed him," Deborah said. "Perhaps it had begun before you left, but the last three years have altered him completely."

"He is so different. . . . He hates Rome."

"There is something else you should know," she said, freeing her hands from his. "We have never spoken about it, but you mentioned it this evening, and now you should be told."

"Alexander . . . Rufus—I wounded him with that comment." Alexander's eyes contracted at the memory.

"Yes, you did hurt him, more deeply than you know. He regrets it."

"Tell me the story of Alexander and Rufus, Mother."

She fingered the purple cloth he had brought her. Alexander saw her eyes grow big with memories.

"When we came to Cyrene from Alexandria after the great rebellion, we were young, poor, and starving. That was the year when nearly the whole of Egypt was in revolt against Rome. Rome blamed the Jews. Many died upon the cross. But we escaped, your father and I. There was a Greek, Alexander Deandros, a merchant, a good man, who lived beside the canal. Your father worked for him, traveled with his caravans—sometimes beyond Damascus, sometimes nearly to the Persian Gulf. Alexander Deandros saved our lives—gave us two camels, good clothes, money. And he gave us timely warning. He was a member of the city government of Alexandria. He knew beforehand of the revolt; he knew what Rome's revenge would be."

"Why did you not escape to Jerusalem?"

She gave her son a long, slow look. "Alexander Deandros sent us to Cyrene. Most of the Jews who went to Jerusalem perished on the way. Later on, your father again worked for Alexander—until he went on his own. This time Alexander gave us five camels. And when you were born, we named you in gratitude after the man who had saved our lives."

"I understand," Alexander said. "Now I understand. And Rufus?"

"It was also through a kind deed that Rufus got his name. When we first arrived in Cyrene there was a Roman centurion here, Cornelius Rufus, a good man. He was strong and serious, anxious to learn." Her eyes stared into distance.

"He and your father became great friends. They often fought together. Your father still has the short cudgel with which he and Cornelius used to fight. And they threw the javelin. Your father always won." She smiled.

41

"They argued often. Your father said that there was one living God, the God of Abraham, Isaac, and Jacob, and he made light of the gods of Cornelius Rufus—soulless Mars and Jupiter and the rest. Until Cornelius came to believe . . ."

"To believe?" Alexander frowned.

"Yes. He began to believe. Your father made him believe. And when Rufus came to believe, he could no longer be a soldier. He could no longer take the oath of loyalty to Tiberius. He bought his discharge from the army and came to live with us."

"I remember him. He was tall, was he not, with a red beard?"

"You were very young, but you remember. He made you a sling and a bow and arrow. He accompanied your father on his caravan journeys—once he saved your father's life when he was attacked by highway robbers. And then came the time when they were hired to catch wild animals for the governor in Egypt. They sought adventure. They went far up the Nile, and it was there that one day a lion charged your father before they could fling the string net over it."

She paused, looking down, and was silent for a moment. "Had it not been for Cornelius Rufus that day, your father would have perished. Cornelius attacked the beast with his spear. He and the lion died together. When your father returned here, your brother was not yet a month old. And so we called him Rufus."

"Strange that he never told us about it. He told us stories about so many other things—his travels, his fights with robbers."

"He doesn't like to speak about it. It grieves him still."

"What changed him so? What made him hate?"

"So many things—taxes, tithes . . . the death of John the Baptist—the murder of that good man infuriated him. To him it was a victory of the oppressor over Israel. He became more and more bitter. Now he curses Rome. Every day he prays for the coming of the Messiah who will break Rome and make Israel great."

Alexander was silent. He tried to feel the same about these things, but could not. He knew then how far apart he and his father really were.

When Simon Niger came out from beneath the poplar trees, he walked slowly over the plowed land. Suddenly he stopped, stood motionless. His breath came slowly. His hands clenched. About him it was dark. The last daylight had faded away behind the palace of Quirinius.

He walked a few steps, then broke into a run. He stumbled over clods and tufts of stubble with eyes fixed on the torches that gleamed in the darkness before him. The tendriled shoot of his vines whipped about his legs. As he ran through the orchard, olive branches struck his face, but he did not feel them.

Short of his threshing floor he stopped, panting, his hands clenched.

By the light of torches men were busy loading his wheat onto Roman wagons.

4

Sextus Quirinius, governor of Cyrene, helped himself to roasted heart of pheasant from the silver dish proffered by a slave. Quirinius was a big man, grown sleek and fat on the produce of Cyrene. He dipped the heart into the thick gravy of a well-browned suckling pig, devoured it, and stretched out his hand for the slave to wipe.

The late afternoon sun touched the silverware on the round table, glowed on the marble mosaic of the palace floor, and lent a richer luminescence to the wine in the silver drinking vessels.

Quirinius, reclining on the carved eating couch beside the table, adjusted his laurel wreath and drew his toga closer about his shoulders while he pensively regarded a silver dish of shrimp. His guest, on the other side of the table, picked at a breast of peacock.

Quirinius sipped the wine that had fermented before the regime of the Emperor Tiberius. He let the nectar from the Tiber Valley gently lave his tongue. His eyes were preoccupied, as one thought filled his mind.

"You're paying too little for wheat this year," Quirinius said. "One and a half denarii a bag is not enough—Cyrene is used to a price of two or more."

Caius Papinius, a slender patrician with hair graying at the temples, wrinkled his worldly eyes.

"That's what Cornelius Marsus will pay," he said. "No more, no less." He spoke with finality.

Quirinius looked fixedly at his guest and thought that Caius Papinius could just as well have been one of those detestable *publicani*—tax collectors with almost unlimited authority—abolished by Julius Caesar.

"Does Caesar know of the new price?" Quirinius asked tentatively, aware of the unfriendly look on the face of Caius Papinius.

"Cornelius Marsus," Papinius said, "is a man of authority —he must feed the Roman masses. He does not need to discuss the price of wheat with Tiberius."

"We can expect trouble," Quirinius said. "We have been free of that here for some time past."

Papinius detached a purple grape from its tight cluster and laughed cynically.

"Rome is no stranger to trouble," he said.

"Why are you paying less this year?" Quirinius asked, watching the play of the fading light on the back of his hand.

"We are still paying for the campaigns of Germanicus. Rome has many mouths to feed. There is overproduction of wheat—here in Cyrene, and in Egypt, the Tiber Valley, Judea, and Galilee as well."

Papinius ignored the slave standing by him and detached a goose wing with his own hand. With narrowed eyes he looked at Quirinius. "Besides," he said, "Cornelius Marsus has a new idea. He says he is not prepared to enrich the people of the provinces at the expense of the treasury any longer."

Annoyance heightened the flush on Quirinius's puffy cheeks. His words rang sharply across the laden table. "You in Rome call the tune, and we in the provinces have to pay the piper. There is already unrest, and now you come with the affliction of this new price."

"There is always unrest in the Empire, Quirinius. The Empire is like a huge cornered reptile—it rears and twists. Given form by blood, by blood it must be nourished."

"You people in Rome do not know the provinces. When to-day you arrived from Ostia with the wheat ship, you set foot in Cyrene for the first time. These people work hard. They want their reward. This new wheat price can cause a conflagration. There are many Jews here. You know the Jews. They are always getting stirred up by one thing or another. In Palestine they seize every opportunity to start a new revolt."

Papinius laughed above his wine. "You've gone soft here in Cyrene. You must keep your hand on the sword like Pilate."

"Pilate is a fool," Quirinius said angrily. "Much of the trouble we have with the Jews is due to him. First he marched into Jerusalem with the Emperor's image displayed on banners, then he used the money from the Jewish temple for an aqueduct. Here in the provinces you have to respect the people's feelings and traditions."

"Pilate has always kept the Jews in their place," Papinius said with careless confidence. "If they cause trouble, he will break them. You must do the same, Quirinius." He looked pointedly at his host. "If I were you, Quirinius, I would be sensible. Cornelius Marsus is a power in Rome. He doesn't look for trouble over the price of wheat, and the Emperor will support him against any provincial governor who chooses to be disloyal."

Sextus Quirinius spat an olive from his mouth, as if he had suddenly lost all taste for it. He glanced first at the marble pillars of the dining hall and then looked long and frowningly at the visitor from Rome.

"Very well, Caius Papinius," Quirinius retorted, "let us discuss loyalty. In the days when you and others pressed for Germanicus to become emperor, I remained faithful to Tiberius." He saw with satisfaction how his shaft had struck home. He raised his drinking cup aloft and said, "To the illustrious Tiberius, Caesar of Rome." Papinius raised his cup uncertainly and repeated the toast.

As he put his cup down, Quirinius said, "I tell you, Papinius, the wheat prices of Cornelius Marsus may start a conflagration."

Papinius was on the point of saying something when his host's chamberlain appeared and stood stiffly at attention.

"Yes, Cassius? " Quirinius asked indifferently.

"Vitellius is outside, Your Excellency. He urgently desires to speak with you."

"Vitellius comes always at the wrong time. I'm in the midst of dinner and conversing with a distinguished guest."

"It has to do with Simon Niger the Jew, Your Excellency."

Quirinius turned to look significantly at Caius Papinius. "Tell Vitellius to enter," he said to the servant.

Vitellius came in, flushed and nervous, his white garment crumpled and his sandals white with dust. He had visited many settlers after Simon. He halted at the dining table, bowed to Quirinius and Papinius, and concealed a longing glance at the food.

"Well, Vitellius?" Quirinius asked.

"It's the Jew, Simon Niger, Your Excellency," Vitellius said, still a bit out of breath. "The one whose land is on the terraces. He attacked me. He and another pulled two of Caesar's soldiers from their horses."

Coolly and speculatively, Quirinius looked at his assessor. A smile compressed the corners of his mouth.

"Did they break any bones, Vitellius?"

The flush on the perspiring face of Vitellius deepened. "He struck me with a staff; he lost his temper because we rode through his vineyard."

"Are the two soldiers dead?" Quirinius asked, with a contemptuous look.

Vitellius stared down at the marble floor and did not speak.

"Cassius," Quirinius said and beckoned his servant to come nearer, "fetch your pen and tablet. I am going to write to the Emperor telling him about this valiant Roman who was put to flight by a Jewish farmer."

Vitellius thrust out his flabby chest. "Simon Niger refuses to accept one and a half denarii a bag," he blurted out.

Quirinius looked quickly at Papinius. Then he swung his legs off his couch and stood upright. "There you have it, Papinius!"

Papinius also rose. "Nail him to a cross—make an example of him, and all your trouble will be over," he said, watching Quirinius out of the corner of his eye.

Quirinius's expression grew cold as he stared straight at the patrician. "Caius Papinius," he said, "I am governor of Cyrene. If punishment is to be meted out, I shall so order it." Then he turned sharply to the bewildered Vitellius. "Simon Niger's wheat is to be loaded the same as everybody else's," he said. "What Cornelius Marsus says seems to be the law of Rome."

Caius Papinius's eyebrows raised at the tone of scorn that threaded Quirinius's words.

Vitellius bowed and moved away toward the marble arch that led out of the colonnade.

"Lucius Vitellius," Quirinius called after him, and Vitellius turned around hopefully. "Beware lest Simon the Jew thrust his pitchfork through your belly." Quirinius and Papinius burst out laughing as Vitellius turned again to leave, his eyes filled with anger.

Quirinius turned and walked to the big window on the eastern side. He looked out over the terraces, fields, and vineyards at white birds flying in patterns against the purple dusk that was stealing along the sea from the far side of Crete. He watched the sunlight flee before the coming darkness, and for a moment his attention was caught by a tall cypress that split the dark background of the sea.

"Unless I am mistaken, Sextus Quirinius, you will have a few crosses to erect," said Papinius from beside the governor.

Quirinius closed his eyes. His lips trembled, but he forced himself to remain calm.

On the bay the fishermen were urging their boats out before darkness fell. Quirinius said, "I have always tried to govern fairly. I have tried to continue the great work begun by Augustus and Tiberius . . . to rule in peace. But now . . ."

"But now you are losing heart for your work, and a Jew like this Simon Niger can refuse to heed the voice of Rome!"

"No, not so. Ever since Tiberius went to Capreae a different spirit has emerged in Rome—a spirit of violence and coercion. Of flippancy and debauchery. The arena and theater count more than the Capitol itself."

Papinius grinned. "You are no longer a Roman, Quirinius. You have been in Africa too long."

"Africa has taught me many things that Rome does not yet understand."

"Such as cowardice in the face of challenge, perhaps?"

The contempt of these words brought a dark flush to the governor's neck. In the dim dusk in which all landmarks and boundary lines were now melting, Quirinius looked up at Papinius. "Just why have you come to Cyrene—to gather wheat or to spy?"

"I enjoy the favor of Cornelius Marsus," Papinius said with meaning. "He has great power now that the Emperor soothes his gathering years with women—and Sejanus is dead."

"That answers my question," Quirinius said dispiritedly. "I will set up the crosses if the need arises."

"That would be wise, Quirinius. Cornelius Marsus detests incompetence. He must feed Rome. He cannot do it with sentimental governors."

"I'm going to bed," Quirinius said abruptly. "I am very tired."

He walked away across the marble floor. A slave had come to light the torches, and his form threw long shadows against the ornamented walls.

The night wind that stirred the green summits of the trees cooled the sweat on the face of Simon Niger. But he did not feel it. All his being centered on a yellow patch of torchlight in a corner of the night and the movement within it as ox wagons were loaded beside his threshing floor.

He took two stumbling steps forward, two steps over land that he had tamed and made fertile with his labor. He put his hand before his eyes as if to shut out the scene—the sight of red plumed soldiers in the torchlight; of men, with angled backs, stumbling under the weight of the sacks they were loading for the dissolute of Rome.

Blood surged in his ears; his breathing slowed and deepened. Dazedly, he moved nearer.

In the outer circle of light he stopped. He saw Vitellius, the fat official who had tried to humble him that afternoon.

And from the edge of the threshing floor, where he stood giving orders, Vitellius saw him too.

To Vitellius, Simon seemed a monster on the edge of the darkness. He looked huge and threatening, with shoulders bent forward like a gladiator awaiting his opponent, arms hanging loosely, feet planted far apart.

The Roman recalled the words Quirinius had uttered that afternoon: "Beware lest Simon the Jew thrust his pitchfork through your belly."

His jaws tightened with vindictiveness and rage. He looked at a soldier who was standing close to him. Then he climbed over the low wall of the threshing floor and approached Simon, step by step, as if walking against a wind.

When he stopped one pace away from Simon, Vitellius felt as if he had reached the fringe of many things he did not fully understand. It was as if an unknown power hovered above him.

"You're stealing my wheat for the scum of Rome."

Simon's accusation was carried trembling on the low murmur of the wind. In the torchlight his face was an angry, gleaming mask.

"I'm not stealing your wheat, Jewish dog; I'm confiscating it," Vitellius lied, in order to provoke the big man to commit some serious offense.

"Confiscate? You are confiscating my wheat?"

"Yes, I am confiscating your wheat. Today Quirinius gave ear to Lucius Vitellius. If you don't take care, we may take away your land."

Simon lifted up his arms, but then he fought back the rebellion within him, for suddenly the rustling of his vineyard came to him as a message. He heard the wind in his olive trees; the scent of fresh hay and the rich earth came to his nostrils. And in one brief moment he lived again the years of sweat and worthy labor, of wresting a living from this dark earth for Deborah and himself.

He lowered his arms, and his resistance faded to a bitter whisper: "The just God of our covenant will punish you, Lucius Vitellius."

The Roman knew now that his victim, for the sake of his land, would offer no resistance.

With the short-handled whip he used on the slaves, he lashed Simon in the face.

The savage blow forced Simon's head back, and when it came forward again, he felt blood upon his lips.

Simon's blow caught Vitellius on the temple and killed him where he stood.

As Vitellius fell, Simon seized him, hoisted him on high, and flung him against a wheel, breaking his back against the hub.

Simon stood motionless, the wind playing with his hair. Very slowly, the realization came to him that he had killed a citizen of Rome, an officer of Quirinius, an underling of Tiberius, a son of the Empire.

The sober realization lasted but a moment. It was driven out by rage, the reckless fury that blinds a man and dulls his senses, that sets free the primitive in him and makes him like an eagle seeking blood.

They were taking from him what he had won from the land through the long years of wind and sun and rain—that was the thought that filled his being.

His land—they would take that too, the land where his and Deborah's youth lay buried—the sweetness of their early days, the vigor of their prime—the land in which his life was centered.

Because Vitellius had died without a sound, none of the others had seen his death. The four soldiers and the slaves were still engaged in loading wheat.

A frenzy drove Simon back into the darkness. He ran to the shed he had built for his wooden plow. For a moment he stood there breathing hard and sweating—one wild moment in which his hatred flared, and his own danger and the need to shield Deborah were quite forgotten: hatred born of the years when he was forced to stifle the revolt in his soul; hatred of the eagle of Rome being flaunted over the Star of David; hated of the oppressor who set up an idol above the God of Abraham.

All the years of bitterness and longing engulfed him and swirled him into a blind and storming folly. Breathing hard, he crouched in a dark corner and searched for an old jar of olive oil he always kept there. His searching fingers touched its round belly. With a cry he swung the jar onto his shoulder and ran out into the night wind.

A startled soldier noticed Simon for the first time as he reached the mound of bags that had not yet been loaded. He saw the big man leap onto the stack and empty the contents of the jar over the wheat.

Before the bewildered soldier could move, Simon flung the heavy jar at a gaping slave who stood there holding a torch. He jumped down from the wheat stack, picked up the torch of the fallen man, and thrust it against the wheat bags, stained dark by the olive oil. Little flames sputtered a moment, then darted up and dimmed the light of the torches as they shot skyward.

When Simon swung around, the soldier, sword held high, was almost on top of him. But the big man jumped aside and thrust the torch into the face of his adversary, so that the man screamed and staggered back.

There was shouting, a trampling to and fro of soldiers and slaves. Simon leaped in among them, swinging his torch in a fiery arc.

The fight was brief. A soldier crept up from behind and with his spear shaft struck Simon a heavy blow on the neck. He staggered forward, tottering, his hands stretched out, his mouth wide open and panting. When a torch wielded by a slave hit between his shoulder blades, his strength broke, and he sank to his knees, sobbing aloud with rage and weakness. He fell and crawled forward groping for the enemy with open hands.

They had conquered him. Another blow on his head made the torchlight blur and fade before his dimming eyes. The good soil, cool and friendly, kissed his trembling lips. In his nostrils was the scent of the golden hay. His fingers groped in the soil he had cherished. He searched for his vanished strength, tried to brace his muscles, to rise and fight, but the earth heaved beneath him like a swelling sea.

Two slaves raised him, held him so he could stand. His head fell backward, and a soldier struck him in the face—once, twice, three times. He tasted blood in the corners of his mouth and tied to clench his fists, but his hands were powerless.

He heard somebody moan, and he remembered that he too had given blows. He heard the crackling fire and saw a red blaze reaching upward to the stars. He knew then that it was his wheat aflame. He sobbed with triumph and joy and felt his strength slowly flowing back to him.

Then he was led away toward the hill where Cyrene shone like a jewel beneath the stars. He shuffled between two slaves and heard the rustling of his vineyard. His bleeding lips moved continuously. "Deborah . . . my Deborah . . . ," he said without pause, almost in prayer, softly, as if her name were holy.

A little later Sextus Quirinius awoke, startled from his slumber on a gilded couch, and looked up into the face of his aide.

"What is it, Cassius? What is so urgent that you should break into my sleep?"

Cassius bowed respectfully. "It has to do with Lucius Vitellius, Your Excellency. He is dead."

Quirinius sat up abruptly. "Dead?"

"Murdered by the Jew, Simon Niger."

Quirinius sank back dismayed onto his pillows. "The fool . . . the poor, blind fool," he said through his clenched teeth. "Had it to do with the wheat?"

"With the wheat, Your Excellency. He set fire to the wheat and struck a soldier in the face with a burning torch. It seems that the man is blinded."

Sextus Quirinius closed his lips tightly. "Where is the Jew now?" he asked in bitter anger.

"In the dungeon of the barracks, Your Excellency."

"Prepare everything for a trial tomorrow morning early. Then I will punish him. That is all, Cassius."

The aide bowed again and turned around. "Oh, Cassius," Quirinius called after him, "tell Marcus Camillus to strengthen the guards and alert the army."

Lucius extinguished the torch he had lit beside the door.

When it was dark again, Quirinius looked at the latticework of his window, black against the light of the stars.

There he saw, clearly defined, a cross.

He closed his eyes, turned over on his side, and waited for slumber to release him.

5

The sun came up from the sea, and its light shone yellow against the dungeon wall. The straw on the floor shimmered and almost seemed to be alive. In this early light the cell looked small and forbidding.

Simon Niger felt the sunlight on his lids and woke completely from the sleep that toward dawn had freed him from his pain and fear. He looked at the stone wall that slaves had built for their Greek masters and saw the granite shining in the sunlight. But he was not conscious of the glory of the dawn. He only saw Deborah, her eyes filled with sad longing. Terror made him breathe more quickly. He sat up but fell back again with a sudden stab of pain. He touched his neck, and shock suffused his eyes. He struggled unsteadily to his feet and touched his face. The place where Vitellius had struck him felt like a wet wound. He tried to rub the dry blood from his swollen lips.

He went to the window, and his hands closed around its cedar bars.

He tried to see his land, his house, Deborah, but the palace, where Quirinius lived, cut off his view. He could only see a sluggish plume of smoke that rose above the sharp roof of the basilica.

All was still. He saw three waterfowl slant down through the air toward the east and the pools along the water furrows—the pools where Deborah picked her reeds for plaiting.

He closed his eyes, and he saw her moving hands, hands delicate but firm; her dark head bowed, her neck soft in the light of the old lamp.

Then he looked again and saw that two Roman guards were standing, straight and still, before the rear gate of the palace, their javelins planted at their sides, their feet apart.

A horn sounded. It cut through the silence and told him that the new day had begun, that Rome was again astir in Cyrene. He turned back from the window with terror gnawing at his heart. He remembered the low hill beyond the stables of the Roman cavalry, to the west of the city, on the near side of the desert, where he had heard men scream and had seen their crosses stand out black against the evening light.

He stared at the wall and watched with horror the silhouetted vision. Suddenly he heard the hinges of the cell door creak. He turned and saw a captain of the Roman army standing in the door: a young man with bright blue eyes, red plumes above his helmet, his breastplate shining brightly. The handle of his short sword gleamed above its scabbard. Two subordinates were behind him.

The captain gestured without speaking. The soldiers came forward and bound Simon. A chain joined the irons around his wrists to those on his ankles. They led him out, and he walked with difficulty over the pavement, the chains jangling, the sun warm on his neck. He looked up only once: to see if Deborah were not standing somewhere in the gateway; but all he could see was the sunlight and the empty morning—empty of all sound or movement, with only a thin haze of smoke hovering somewhere between the buildings and the sea.

As they were crossing the square, the silence was shattered, and it sounded as if a thunderstorm had crashed loose on the world. War chariots came clattering and clanging across the pavement. Sparks flew from under the hooves of black stallions as they swiftly drew the chariots toward the great gateway. The sun flashed on the helmets and breastplates of soldiers who held the reins taut in their hands. Javelins gleamed, and shields glittered.

Birds rose in alarm over the square, then climbed high into the air, slanting over the palace as they fled.

Simon Niger stood still, listening, with his head tilted to one side. He looked at the triumphal arch over the main gateway where towered the great eagle of Rome, with wings spread out and head thrust forward haughtily as befits the conqueror.

And he heard a roaring, a rushing, as when a fierce wind drives a fire through forest trees.

He looked up at the sky where the breeze from the sea was spreading the thin smoke haze toward the desert. He was puzzled that the burning of his modest harvest the night before should have so veiled the sky.

They pushed him roughly, and he walked forward, with a strange hope stirring within him.

Out of the corner of his eye he saw a squadron of the legion marching smartly across the square, moving toward the gateway where the eagle's eyes glinted in the sun.

The guards led him up the steps. Columns towered high above Simon. He was vaguely conscious of soldiers in doorways, their javelins long and deadly, of gleaming white marble, of spaciousness and beauty, of cool peacefulness. He entered a wide hall. He looked at the high vault from which chandeliers were suspended, at the mosaic of the floor, at the ferocious paintings on the walls depicting rearing horses, fighting soldiers, storming chariots, elephants trampling men, lions storming across arenas.

Then he saw the small group in the center of the floor. Behind a gilded table was an ornamental chair with an eagle carved on it. Here a thick-set man was seated, two soldiers standing alert and straight on either side of him. To the left on a low bench a few slaves were sitting, and opposite them some soldiers. Among them was one with bandaged eyes.

The chains clanged in the empty hall as Simon was led closer. And when that ceased, he heard the soft slap of sandals on the marble floor. A swift fluttered high above in the decorated vault from where the image of Jupiter looked coldly down.

Simon felt the clamminess of his hands and the throbbing pain from his neck. The sweat lay cold upon his body.

He stopped in front of Sextus Quirinius. The governor sat bent forward in his gilded chair, his hands motionless on the table before him, his eyes tired and withdrawn.

A voice filled the silence, echoing from wall to wall. "The Jew, Simon Niger, Your Excellency!" the young captain said loudly.

Quirinius did not stir or speak. He stared at the man before him, and his eyes revealed the thoughts behind them. The purple facing of his toga lay carelessly over his upper arms. A soldier rose from the low bench, one of those who had overcome Simon the night before. He told the story of the death of Vitellius at the threshing floor, of the conflict and the torch.

Simon looked at the man with the bandaged eyes, saw him sweating, his hands trembling with pain.

Other soldiers and then some slaves told of what had happened. After that there was silence. Only the scratching of the calamus on the parchment could be heard as a slave recorded what was said.

Sextus Quirinius pushed his toga back, then gripped the sides of the table. His voice was thin, with menace: "You have heard everything, Jew of Cyrene. What have you to say?"

Simon's voice was weak among the high columns. "What has been said is true . . ."

"Why did you do it?" Quirinius's question was sharp.

"It was because . . . because of my wheat."

"Is not the price of wheat fixed by Rome? Who are you to decide how much you will accept or not accept? Is what Rome says not the law?"

Simon looked down, saw the chains that joined his shackles and the links that looked so strong, so lasting. "It . . . it wasn't only the wheat. Vitellius taunted me . . . said he was confiscating my wheat."

He looked up, and his eyes glittered. His mouth trembled, his beard shook. He stretched out his hands to Quirinius and his chains jingled. "It was because of my land too. Vitellius said they would perhaps take that as well." He remained silent for a moment, and then he shouted so that Quirinius's hands jerked with surprise and the soldiers gripped their spears more tightly. "But I still kept silent before Vitellius. I did not speak, kept silent—silent because of my land . . . my house and everything. But then he lashed me here, as if I were a slave." He pointed to the bloody welt that reddened his black beard. "He struck me here," he repeated with a sob. "After that I hit him back . . . I did not know what I was doing."

"What did Vitellius say about the land and the wheat?" Quirinius asked frowning.

"He said he was taking the wheat . . . for nothing. He was seizing it . . . confiscating it. And if I did not take care, he would take the land as well."

Quirinius stared at the prisoner for a long time. He was suddenly grateful that the toadying Vitellius had died for that lie. He looked at the man before him with compassion, realizing how he had been provoked. In truth, the man was innocent. For a brief moment he toyed with the idea that perhaps, because Vitellius had lied, he might release the Jew.

Then he remembered Caius Papinius, the ambassador of Cornelius Marsus. His hands grew clammy at the memory of what had happened to some other governors. His friend Flavius, forced to slash his veins because he had blundered in Thrace—because of a kind deed that in the eyes of Rome was a betrayal of the Empire.

He thought of the consequences of Simon's act, and he knew that there was but one course open to him—one narrow road, the road of Rome.

"The torch you threw last night has set Cyrene ablaze," Quirinius said, without looking at the prisoner. "You've touched off a rebellion."

Quirinius looked straight at him, and for the first time Simon, taut with surprise, saw anger in his eyes.

"Rome has been good to you, Jew of Cyrene," the governor said, bitterly now. "She gave you land and freedom. I have tried to govern in peace. Now you have wrecked my work. Because you threw a torch last night, all that I have accomplished has been consumed in flames. Other settlers have fired their wheat. Cyrene is burning, and blood will flow today. The flames from your threshing floor are now a conflagration."

Simon stood silent, his eyes glittering, the perspiration shining on his forehead. He was staggered by a victory of which he had known nothing. But mounting with his joy was the fear of what lay ahead.

The governor too was silent, deliberating. His thought moved like a pendulum between right and wrong, pardon and punishment; he tried to be compassionate and yet a Roman. He groped for truth and light, searched in his soul for a verdict that would make him secure from remorse and suffering, that would leave his tomorrows as tranquil as his yesterdays. But always he went back to the same irrefutable point: the Empire must triumph.

"You are guilty, Simon Niger," Quirinius said at last, wearily. "Have you anything to say?"

"I am guilty. I ask for mercy. Vitellius drove me to it. I was demented. I ask for mercy."

"Mercy? You have murdered a citizen of the Empire. You have set off a revolt in Cyrene. You have mutilated a soldier of Tiberius. And now you ask for mercy?"

Simon looked at the bandaged soldier with the tight-shut lips and trembling hands. His voice was sorrowful: "I . . . I am sorry that I struck that man. . . . I ask forgiveness."

"Forgiveness! Forgiveness! You blinded me! I am blind!" The man leaped up hysterically, his words rising to a shriek.

"Blind!" the man wailed again as he was led away. "When the sun shrivels you on the cross, I will rejoice, Jew! Rejoice! Rejoice!" His cries echoed through the hall, until it seemed to Simon that they would never die away.

Quirinius swept the toga from his shoulders as if it stifled him. He sank back in his chair, looked upward and closed his eyes. His face contorted as if he were in pain.

"Simon Niger," Sextus Quirinius said in a faltering voice, "I sentence you to perish on the cross. It is what your crime deserves."

Simon took a deep breath, and the fluttering of the swift high above them sounded to him like the roar of a mighty wind. He touched his brow with his knuckles.

He heard the voice of Quirinius again, coming from afar, as if through the sound of rain: "Take him to his cell."

He felt their hands upon his arms, and he stumbled as he turned. His chains seemed to weigh him down, crushing him beneath their weight

Sextus Quirinius rose quickly, with head bent.

"Let the carpenters make the cross," he said to the young captain.

"Only one cross, Your Excellency?"

The governor threw his head up and scorched the captain with a look. Then he turned and walked away, his white robe flapping, his footfall loud in the silence of the hall.

6

When they brought Simon out, the square stood empty in the sun. Confused sounds filled the air. On the first step of the stairs leading to the entrance, Simon paused and listened.

"Cyrene has risen," he said softly, without defiance, only expressing his thought aloud.

One of the guards struck him between the shoulders with the shaft of his javelin, and he staggered forward. When he looked up at them, he saw apprehension in their eyes. They thrust him on in desperate haste to get him to the cells. The captain in the lead walked still more quickly, his eyes darting this way and that, his hands on the hilt of his short sword.

Simon noticed that the palace guards had been increased. They stood in close lines around the palace, the sun glistening on their weapons. The cloud of smoke in the sky had thickened, and it tendrils now swirled about the square.

They brought the smell of burning wheat to Simon's nostrils.

"Cyrene has risen!" he whispered to himself, and closed his eyes.

But stronger than the smell of smoke was the deep rumbling sound, like thunder across the sea. And then there came the beat of horses' hooves, the clash and clang of steel on steel, the yells of struggling men.

"Make haste! They're at the gateway!" the captain shouted, his voice shrill and anxious.

The two guards dragged Simon along more quickly than before. It was true—they were at the gateway. Almost the whole population of Cyrene was bursting like a great wave against the fortress walls. That night, passion had risen in them, just as in Simon Niger. When he put the torch to his wheat the flames did not die; they ignited a ready tinder in thousands of other hearts.

Simon's challenge had become the challenge of all Cyrene.

For when men heard he had been taken to the palace he became a martyr, their champion, a hero to be avenged.

The Roman legion shuddered before the first onslaught of the shrieking crowds. Arrows whistled through the warm air and stuck quivering in shields. Short clubs struck dully on shining helmets. Old swords clashed against the newer steel of Rome.

The war chariots cut broad paths through the crowds spilling out of every street. Roman arrows flew like bright birds toward the throngs, and hands clutched at bleeding breasts. From behind round shields the short swords of the Romans cut down Cyrenians.

Not even the fear of death could quench hatred that had smoldered for so long. Nothing checked these men. Those who died, died screaming defiance, and those who lived vaulted the bodies of the slain and ran fearlessly into the Roman lines.

The guards reached the door to Simon's cell.

As if this were a signal, a light wagon came racing round the corner of the barracks. Drawn by two great stallions, it clattered across the pavement. The driver stood leaning forward, the reins taut in his hands. As he reached Simon, he wrenched at them with such force that the steeds reared up in their harness. Only then did the captain realize what was happening. He leaped forward and dropped with an arrow in his throat. The two guards released Simon and fled across the square. But the flight of arrows was swifter, and the guards died on the sunlit paving stones.

Four men leaped from the wagon, caught hold of Simon and hoisted him up. Rising to his knees, he saw that the driver was Big Micha the blacksmith.

Micha turned the horses and raced back. The wagon thundered across the square, shot through a side gate, and, skirting the fighting crowds, swept toward the heart of Cyrene.

Simon remained kneeling on the wagon floor, tears rolling down into his beard. "God of Israel, you have delivered me!" he said as he pressed his fists to his eyes. He struggled to his feet and stumbled forward. "Big Micha," he said, "you have redeemed me, and my life is yours."

Micha's frizzly, ash-colored hair was dancing in the wind. He was too intent on guiding the horses through the narrow street where fowl and dogs fled before the clattering hooves to look back to Simon.

"If it meant my life, I did not wish to see you hanging on a Roman cross, Simon Niger," Micha shouted over his shoulder. "We had to wait an eternity before they brought you out of the palace."

"And Deborah?" Simon shouted back above the rumble of the wagon.

"She is safe . . . at your house. We're keeping her there."

In front of a low, white building Micha reined in his horses. He helped Simon from the wagon and gripped his shoulders hard. "Thank the Almighty, you are safe," the big blacksmith said. "Ezekiel saw them take you away last night—he and Juba. They came and told me. Ezekiel has managed to get camels for you . . . but first the handcuffs." Micha turned suddenly to the four men who had helped to set Simon free. "Go back and fight!" he shouted.

"God will bless you, Big Micha," Simon whispered gratefully.

Simon knelt before the anvil. Big Micha came hurrying with a sledge hammer and heavy chisel. He began to cut through the heavy shackles. "The whole of Cyrene has risen," he said between hammer strokes. "At sunset, we shall be free!"

"I pray God will grant us that," Simon said, and saw how Micha's hand trembled on the chisel. "You will hurt yourself, Micha. See how your hands are shaking."

"It is from fatigue," Micha said, grunting as he struck. "I was up all night—beating arrow heads, forging spear points, stringing bows, for the day of liberation. You are a hero in Cyrene today, Simon Niger. Today you are greater than Quirinius."

"Strike, Big Micha, strike!" Simon shouted. "Have you a sword for me?"

Micha cut through the last of the irons. He hurled the hammer clattering against the forge, picked up Simon's chains and flung them down on a heap of wheels. "You are not to fight, Simon Niger," the big blacksmith said, and his eyes held a strange light.

"I shall fight!" Simon roared. "Give me a sword . . . a javelin . . . anything. God saved me for this battle!"

Micha gripped his friend's shoulders, his cheeks quivering with determination. "God has saved you for leadership—not to rush in there and die! You must live, and you must lead!"

Simon leaped over to where the coals were glowing red before the bellows, and wrenched out a piece of red-hot steel. He swung it like a scythe. "I began it, and I must help end it!" he shouted and beat the coals with the half-fashioned sword—the sparks flew upward. Micha retreated for a moment before the fury in his eyes. Then the blacksmith approached him, huge shoulders bent forward, hands outstretched.

"I risked my life to save you, Simon Niger. Why must you play the fool? I saved you for Cyrene—not to die. How will it help to gain a victory now, and then lose because we have no leader?"

But Simon did not hear Micha. He stood silent, listening. Above the roar of the battle rose a cry, high and shuddering like the great shout that signified a gladiator's death in the Roman arena.

It rose higher and higher.

"They've gotten through the gate!" Micha rejoiced, running to the entrance. "Cyrene is free!" he shouted, and raised his mighty arms.

Simon came up and stood next to him, the flat steel dangling from his fist. They stood there listening, breathing deeply.

The sound of voices rose higher, until it seemed to quiver against the fleecy clouds that floated in the sky. Shouting came swirling down to them on the light morning breeze beginning to blow in from the desert.

"Big Micha, son of Nathanael, I think Cyrene must be free!" Simon whispered, almost in awe. "They must be celebrating it in the square of the palace." He forced the steel deep into a wagon shaft and left it quivering there.

Micha tore off his leather apron and flung it aside. "Let's go, Simon Niger," he said. "You should be at the palace."

As they went toward the wagon, a dark chestnut horse came trotting down the narrow street. A man lay forward crookedly across its back, a Roman arrow projecting from between his shoulders.

Micha stopped short and whispered, "This . . . this is my horse."

"It's your son—Philippus, your eldest son!" Simon exclaimed.

They ran forward together. Simon seized the bit, and Micha lifted his son from the horse, wiping away the blood that frothed upon his lips. Then he laid him gently down, and, holding his shoulders, stared helplessly at the slender arrow that moved as Philippus fought for breath. Simon squatted near them, looking first at the arrow, then at Micha. But Micha shook his heavy head. "It's gone right through," the blacksmith said. Tears trembled in his eyes.

Philippus moved his bloody lips: "They have defeated the people. . . . Marcus Camillus took the palace guards round the back. . . . The attack is . . . broken."

Simon and Micha stared at one another, their eyes wide with shock.

"And Simeon?" Micha bent low over his dying son.

"He died by my side."

Simon rose and heard the people of Cyrene wailing in their defeat.

Philippus clutched convulsively at the collar of his father's leather jerkin and died, his lips moving with unspoken words.

"It is over," Simon said. "What I've begun cannot be ended." Then he came nearer and helped Big Micha rise—the man's strength had left him.

"You must go away, Simon Niger. There is little time," Micha muttered.

"How can I go while everyone stays to die?"

"We won't all die. Quirinius cannot crucify a city. But you— you will die as surely as I live now."

"I can die for Israel's God!"

"Will you help Israel's God and Cyrene on a cross? And you have a wife, Simon Niger."

Simon closed his eyes and saw Deborah. "I will go if you come with me, Big Micha. We grew up together. We have been like brothers."

"No, I'm staying here. The blood of my sons is in this soil." Big Micha's shoulders, broadened by the anvil and the bellows, shuddered as he embraced Simon. "Go—work for Israel and its God, but not here," he begged. "There is nothing you can do here . . . except die."

He hurried Simon toward the wagon.

The world swam before Simon's eyes as he picked up the reins and urged the horses on down the street. He looked around and saw that Micha had lifted up his dead son and was standing there in the sunlight nursing him in his arms, as if Philippus, by dying, had become a child again.

Simon went on through the empty city, and the slaughter on the hill was now only a soft accompaniment to the rumble of the wagon. He left the city and passed between fields smothered in the blue smoke of burning wheat. He rounded the corner of the house and drew up at the poplars. He saw Ezekiel and Juba busy with the camels, but he did not speak to them.

Deborah looked up as his big figure loomed in the doorway. She rose and stood motionless, and she seemed to have aged overnight. Her face was white, her eyes enlarged, her mouth wide open. Simon went to her and threw his arms about her.

"God heard me—you are safe . . . you are safe," Deborah kept sobbing. She looked up and laid her hands on his face. "I cannot believe it is you . . . that you really are alive."

"I am alive—God be thanked," he said. "Big Micha saved me. But he has lost his sons. And Alexander—where is he?"

She moved away from his embrace and stood beside the hearth where, for so many years, she had watched the dancing flames.

"Alexander," she said hesitantly, "left last night to join his ship. It was when the fires started. Why did you do it, husband? You have brought disaster on Cyrene."

He sank down slowly on a stool, his head bowed. His hands closed round the harp that Alexander had brought. The strings snapped, resounding in the grip of his fingers. He looked up from the broken harp to his wife's slender back, rose, and hurled Alexander's present into a far corner. His words were as harsh as the note of the broken strings.

"Often freedom comes from disaster, just as life is born in pain."

"We have lost everything today—our home, our land, everything we won here in Cyrene—because of half a denarius."

"With half a denarius a man can buy his freedom, or lose it.

We have our freedom still; we have our faith. We have God's mercy—and I still have you. I have the strength to start again."

She turned to face him, her smoldering eyes accusing him: "We were happy here—happy . . . free. . . . You have destroyed that, Simon."

His voice cut through the silence. "They were going to take my wheat, my land—they threatened to crucify me! Because I refused to be a slave."

Deborah's cry of horror filled the room: "Crucify?"

He spoke calmly now, without anger or defiance, for the bitterness of the memory made him meek. "If Big Micha had not risked his life to save me, the nails would have pierced my hands this very night."

She stumbled to the table and leaned against it. "I didn't know about the cross!"

"We must go now, Simon Niger," Ezekiel said from the doorway. "Soon the Romans will be searching here; it is finished on the hill. The camels are waiting. We have packed food, water, and bedding."

Simon gazed at the things that had become part of their lives: the hearth he had built, the wooden dishes he had made, the table, the chairs, the barrels, the goatskin wine sacks against the walls.

He swung around and ran into the bedroom, took his scabbard from a peg on the wall and tied it to his waist, and picked up his long bow and his quiver.

For a moment he stood looking at the possessions now lost to them—these things their hands had made—in order to hold them for a moment, before they were lost forever. He touched the bedstead he had made from Lebanese wood, the bed in which his sons were born.

Then he stirred himself, for he knew that the minutes were becoming as precious as life itself. He put his arm about his wife and gently led her outside. They helped her onto the kneeling camel Ezekiel had brought up. She stared at her house—the open doors and shutters. Two of her ducks stood on the threshold; her pet goat rubbed himself against the wall; two pigeons sat dreaming on her washtub; and near a poplar tree her red heifer lowered its head to graze.

Simon saw the despair in her eyes, but quickly swung himself up onto his camel. Juba and Ezekiel also mounted camels.

"Are you accompanying us?" he asked.

"We go with you, master," said Juba the Numidian.

"I don't know where this journey will end. We go into the unknown. We may get hungry, even die. You can stay here and work. Rome will not harm you."

"Juba and I have served you for many years, Simon Niger," Ezekiel replied. "You have been good to us always. Where you and Deborah go, we go as well."

Simon wished to say more but could not. He jerked his reins and started off so suddenly that Deborah's fowl scattered before him. She followed, and then Ezekiel and Juba.

Simon led the small company past the poplars across the open ground, where a slave looked yearningly after them. At the end of the terrace he waited until Deborah caught up with him. "Ride down the terrace," he said, "then turn right beneath the bridge until you reach the sea. The tide is high, and the sea will cover our tracks."

"And you?"

"I'll follow soon. I want to wait a little to see if the Romans are not following."

For a while he watched Deborah and the other two urging their heavily loaded camels along briskly. Then he turned his animal and trotted back toward his lands.

At the edge of his vineyard he stopped, and everything was there before him. He looked at the clusters of swelling grapes beneath the sheltering leaves. He looked at his olive trees, their leaves shining in the sun, at his few animals grazing on fresh hay. He saw the black patch where his wheat still smoldered, then the field of stubble where, with Ezekiel and Juba, only a few days ago he had cut the heavy wheat. He smelled the moist earth and the hay. And he smelled smoke, smoke from Cyrene's still burning crops.

The tumult of the revolt was borne to him on the light breeze from the desert. He looked toward Cyrene glittering in the sun, and he knew he could not linger. He gave one last conclusive look at everything that had been his. Then he turned and followed after the others.

At the third terrace down, he looked around again, but he could see only the tops of the poplar trees waving a farewell in the midday breeze.

He clenched his jaws and spurred his camel as a new sound broke in upon his senses. It spoke to him with a voice louder than the voice of man; it was the sound of the sea, bearing an unknown message.

He overtook the others, and they urged their animals on still faster. With each swinging stride of the camels' long legs the future became more real. They crossed the beach through the rising surf, and the restless sea smoothed out their tracks behind them.

"These camels move well," Ezekiel said as Simon drew past him. "They are from the stables of Quirinius."

Simon glanced at Ezekiel and saw that this small victory brought laughter to his eyes.

Then he was at Deborah's side. She smiled sadly, and he longed to reach out and touch her. "Where are you taking me, Simon of Cyrene?" she asked, but her eyes thanked him for his presence.

"To the birth of a new day, my Deborah," he said, and his voice rose clear and strong above the sound of the sea. "In Alexandria . . . or perhaps some other place. I will make you happy, as you were in Cyrene."

When the six Roman soldiers drew up at Simon Niger's house, they were met by stillness. Only the poplars rustled in the warm wind of the afternoon. Big Micha's two horses, which Ezekiel had unhitched, were drinking from Deborah's washtub. Simon's red goat lay on the threshold of the open doorway, leisurely chewing its cud.

The soldiers walked through the empty house. One bent down and picked up a broken harp lying in a corner. Another unhooked Simon's leather wine sack and drank deeply.

"The Jew has gone," the centurion said. He felt balked and helpless. With his sword he smashed the neck of the earthen pitcher that Cornelius Rufus had brought for Deborah. He went to the hearth and stood looking down at the barely smoldering coals.

"Come," he said, "we must search for them." They sprang on their horses and looked for tracks across the yard; but the ground had been trampled hard. They went to the hard road running across the terraces—beneath the aqueduct. There they debated whether they should turn left toward the sea or take the road to the right.

The centurion dug his heels into his horse's side and turned into the road to the right, past the city toward the place where the caravan route to Alexandria had its beginning.

On the beach, Simon looked back once more, searching for those who followed. But they had passed the great limestone cliff whose edge touched the sea when the tide was high.

The voice of bleeding Cyrene was heard no longer; there was only the voice of the sea.

The shadows of the fugitives lengthened as they glided over the beach, until they danced in the surge of the waves.

7

Ezekiel reined in his camel suddenly, and the small caravan came to a halt. He pointed to the east.

"Alexandria," he said, wearily but cheerfully. "There lies Alexandria."

Cleopatra's city rode like a white swan upon the blue of the early evening.

Simon looked at Deborah, saw her staring wordlessly, enraptured, her body bowed with the weariness of many days. She gazed at the confusion of spires and domes and at the gleaming highway of the sea where the sails of ships glimmered in the falling dusk.

She looked toward him.

"We are free, Deborah," Simon said huskily. His eyes shone in a face gray with the dust of their lengthy journey.

Deborah's eyes glowed. He pressed her hand, and she felt his old strength in his grip.

"God has brought us here, as He led Israel through the desert of Sinai," he said.

"It took so long," she sighed, still staring at the city where their hearts had first found each other.

"It was many days, wife, long and bitter days."

"Cyrene . . ." He heard sadness and longing in her voice. "It seems so long since we left it—as if the days were years."

He did not answer. They remained motionless, wordlessly watching Alexandria fading in the dusk.

At last Simon slid off his camel. He made Deborah's mount kneel, helped her down, and caught her in his arms.

"It won't be so long before we are with Rufus," she said. "I long for him so much. Will we be able to find him tonight?"

"We will clean up, prepare ourselves, and go into the city when night has fallen," Simon answered.

"Will we be safe? The arm of Rome is long."

"We will be safe. Nobody could have traveled here faster than we did," he said as he released her. "Ezekiel, Juba, let us get ready to go in."

Simon's sandals grated on the stones and sand. He walked some distance away until he stood alone in the enveloping dark. He turned to the west, where light still lingered, and gazed toward where Cyrene lay, lost in the haze of many days of travel. But the long trail they had followed beside the sea, across plateaus, over endless wastes of sand where heat had fissured the face of the earth and made the horizon quiver, had vanished from his mind.

He was back on his land again. He heard the lowing of his cows and the rustling of his vines. He smelled the burning wheat. He saw Big Micha standing in the sunlight, his dead son in his arms.

You are a coward, Simon Niger! The thought throbbed through his mind, but he did not utter it.

He felt himself flush, and knew that he was alone no longer. Deborah was beside him.

"Husband," she said in a firm voice, "what has been, has been. Cyrene is no longer part of us."

"You speak the truth, my wife. Cyrene belongs to the past. We shall build anew. Alexandria is wealthy. There is work to be had, and we shall be with Rufus. I . . . I wandered away to stretch my legs. I have been too long on a camel's back."

"I understand," she said, and in the dim light he did not see her tears. Whenever he tried to mislead her, she read him like a child.

They went back to the camels. They washed themselves in the darkness with water from bags they had filled at the oasis that morning. Then he fetched a pack from the camel, and she dressed herself in the purple gown that Alexander had given her.

Ezekiel and Juba were washing themselves, and Ezekiel called over to him, "Simon Niger, now we can become caravan drivers again and see the world."

"No, not I," Simon said decidedly. "I shall work on the land —where, I know not."

"Perhaps we can go to Jerusalem," Deborah said as she

rubbed her hands with an ointment of fragment myrrh. "Or perhaps we may go further, to Galilee. They say there is rich land in lovely valleys."

"What must we do in Galilee? " Simon asked, standing motionless in the darkness.

"It's far from Cyrene," Deborah said. "We shall be safer there."

"But that's the country of this Nazarene," Simon said in astonishment.

"But, husband, what concern is the Nazarene of ours?" Deborah said, trying to keep her voice casual

It was a few moments before he spoke: "I and my house will never have anything to do with this carpenter. This I swear by the God of Abraham!"

The fierceness of his words made her react "But, husband, this Nazarene has not hurt us. Why take on so about Him? Can't we even go to Galilee just because He is teaching there?"

"He has done *us* no harm, but He will still harm Israel. Have you ever heard that He has spoken a single word against the heathen of Rome, against the godless conquerors of our people, against those who grind the people of David beneath their heel? Israel again bears the yoke of slavery, as in Egypt, but this man is silent. Has He ever once raised His hand for Israel and said, 'Rise against the tyrant! Throw off the yoke!'? No, never has He spoken for Israel's freedom."

"But Israel is so small—how can He lead us against the legions of Rome?" Deborah ventured.

Simon snorted in contempt. "Have you forgotten Gideon's band? That too was small, but Gideon was a warrior, a leader. But I feel sure that this fellow cannot even swing a sword. His weapon is a shepherd's crook. They say He is the Messiah. If He is the Messiah, why does He preach in the backwoods of Galilee? Why does He not go to Jerusalem and raise up Israel?" Breathing hard, he fell silent for a moment. "Judas of Galilee was defeated when he rose against Rome in the time of Augustus, but at least he fought. What has this man achieved? Nothing. Give Israel a Joshua or a David, and she will drive the legions of Tiberius into the sea."

He stopped and looked up at the stars, as if he searched there for the sign of a fiery sword.

"I do not even wish to be near this Nazarene," he said. In the darkness his words seemed to have an added strength and bitterness. "I'd rather cross the Jordan and go to Persia than wander in Galilee. It would endanger my soul to be near that heretic."

"Persia!" Ezekiel said excitedly. "Now there is a good place to go—full of wealth and trade. There we can get rich quickly with precious stones, gold, silk, and furs, Simon."

The black Numidian Juba, who had worked for Simon for so long, stood quietly and looked up at the stars that twinkled in the coal-black sky—without opinion, without passion, with one thought only. He wondered about this strange man who was everybody's friend and who, they said, loved everyone. One day he had heard two Jews in the marketplace of Cyrene talking in subdued and cautious tones about this man as if He were some kind of a scandal. He heard them say how this Jew had healed a Roman's foreman. He did not understand it then, and he did not understand it now, but he knew that it was right and good.

He had never spoken of it, not one word, for he was a slave, a black man, and a black man was different from a man with a pale skin. He knew that it was so.

But he had heard the conversation of the two Jews regarding this strange man, that day while he was guarding his master's heaps of watermelons and muskmelons in the marketplace of Cyrene, and ever since that day he had always listened, eager to hear more concerning Him. He had heard other people talk about Him, sometimes in the fields, sometimes in the marketplace, sometimes at the irrigation furrow that ran across the terraces. He had heard them say that the man had said that all people in His kingdom—Romans, Jews, Greeks, even the Egyptians, the Numidians, and the Persians—all these people were equal.

He wondered where that man's kingdom was—perhaps on the other side of the Jordan where he, his master, and Ezekiel had gone once to fetch some camels. Or perhaps beyond Damascus, far away in the Taurus mountains where robbers would certainly have killed them if his big master hadn't been so handy with the sword. Or perhaps in the green valley of the Euphrates.

He was thinking of what he had heard, now, as he tightened the girth of his camel.

When he looked up at the stars that stretched away to where the Jordan must lie, he felt a strange hope in a corner of his heart. Perhaps he would see this good man if they got to Galilee where the water was cool in the wells.

"What are you waiting for, Juba?" he heard Ezekiel ask. He mounted his camel in confusion. Only then did he realize that the others had risen while he still was searching for the Jordan somewhere on the dark horizon.

Simon led them along the sea again, for they were too close to the caravan routes, and he still dreaded to hear the clatter of Roman horsemen at their heels.

"Do you still remember where he lives?" he asked Deborah as they rode along.

"I remember. I remember where he lives. He is with those pleasant folk further down near the canal, not far from the harbor. Are we going to Rufus now? I can already hear him laugh when he sees us. He's been away from us so long!"

Simon heard the excitement in her voice. He hurried his camel and looked in pleasure at the vague glow over Alexandria, for there his son was, as well as rest for their weary bodies.

They entered the city through the Greek quarter, avoiding the spacious, tree-lined roads. They felt strange and lost. Alexandria had changed much since they were there so many years before.

"The city of great learning," Simon said respectfully. "They say there are more men of learning here than in either Rome or Athens."

"The city where our love was born," Deborah answered him. Her voice sounded young, and he thought of an evening, long ago, when beneath a trellised vine she gave her heart into his keeping.

Simon continued to the left, toward the sea, over the half-moon bridge built by Augustus, and then further down to the canal. He still remembered that part of the city, although it too had changed a great deal.

The houses, hidden behind small gardens, behind fig and date trees, were low and unattractive. Here the only light was the faint glow of the moon, coming up in the east, and the radiance of the stars. "The Jewish quarter," said Simon.

They peered into the gloom, searching for the house. "Rufus wrote that in front of the house there was a fig tree bigger than the others, and a long arbor," Deborah said softly.

"Every second house has a fig tree and arbor," Simon sighed.

Then they saw a man walking ahead, away from the canal, his shoulders bent under a yoke from which two pails of water were suspended. Simon spurred his camel on and overtook him.

"Here, friend!" Simon called, and his voice sounded loudly in the empty street. "I'm looking for the house of the widow Naomi. She lives somewhere in this street at the side of the canal."

The man looked up at Simon in the darkness.

"I said . . . Naomi the widow. Where is her house?" Simon asked again.

Instead of answering, the man swung around and ran, the water splashing from his pails, in the direction of a grove of palms.

Simon went cold with shock. He heard the man's footsteps fade in the distance. For a moment he hesitated. Then he turned toward the others, who had halted their camels beside him. "Go back a ways, turn down toward the canal, and stay there under shelter," he said. "Take mine too," he added, as he dismounted.

"What are you going to do, Simon?" Deborah asked, her voice fearful.

"I'm going to search for the house. There is something strange about this. Ride until you are out of the street."

Before Deborah could protest, Simon slipped into the shadows of some date palms and cypress trees. He walked quickly along the houses, searching. The houses and trees all seemed to be alike. The dark shadows under the trees seemed to menace him.

As he was passing the garden of the third house, he bumped into somebody with unexpected force.

8

Simon leaped to one side and stood waiting for a sign of movement, his hand on the hilt of the short sword by his side.

"It seems that your camel is tired," the man said. At first these words surprised Simon, then he understood.

"You are the man with the water yoke?"

"Are you seeking Mother Naomi?" the stranger asked softly, as if he did not wish to be overheard.

"Yes, I am looking for Mother Naomi."

"You've come a long way?"

Simon realized that there was more to the question than the stranger showed, and answered guardedly: "A long way, yes. Through the desert. The desert was fierce today."

Grasping Simon by the arm, the stranger threw open a wooden gate, and hurried with him beneath the arbor to the front door of a house. They entered quickly, and the man fastened the door behind them.

Simon stood motionless in the dark room, his hand still grasping the hilt of his sword. The hairs on his neck felt as if they were standing erect. The blood pulsed in his throat. He controlled his breathing and listened, trying to penetrate the dark.

Light stole into the room and a golden glow spread slowly on the walls. Suddenly the source of the light was before him. A woman, tiny, gray, but upright, stood in the doorway that led to the back of the house. An Egyptian oil lamp, suspended from a chain, hung motionless from her hand. Old age had shrunk her, but her eyes held authority.

"Simon of Cyrene?" she asked in a trembling voice.

Simon remained silent, on his guard. He looked at the dark-haired youth who had admitted him. His eyes were friendly.

"I am Naomi."

Simon stepped forward, relaxed now, and wiped the sweat from his eyes.

"Naomi the widow?" he asked respectfully. "The second mother of my son Rufus?"

"That is so." Her eyes brightened.

Simon went closer and laid his hands on her frail shoulders. "May God bless you for your kindness to him, Naomi of Alexandria."

"Jesus of Nazareth says we must love our neighbors . . . but Rufus is more to me than a neighbor. He is like my own child."

Her words, spoken with a pride and an assurance that bewildered him, made him feel slightly giddy.

"But come, there is no time now. The Romans are searching for you."

"The Romans?" Simon burst out.

"Yes, the Romans, Simon of Cyrene. Come, we must go where it is open and quiet." She blew the lamp out and guided him through the dark house, out through the back to a thick fig tree. In the darkness Naomi gestured Simon to a bench, on which they both sat down.

"The Romans?" Simon asked unbelievingly. "How can it be that the Romans are looking for me? We hastened from Cyrene, and traveled both by night and by day."

"The wind is swifter than your camels, man of Cyrene. A large galley arrived here just after midday today—a grain ship—"

"A grain ship?" Simon jumped to his feet, and her words rang through his head.

"Sit down, man of Cyrene. You are tired. Let us talk."

"First tell me about my son Rufus."

"Your son Rufus is still safe. I and my Shalom, here, saw to that. Shalom, bring our guest wine to refresh himself. The grain ship came here on wings, as they say. The north wind blew hard for five days. That is why you lost. Besides, they pushed the galley slaves so hard that four men died."

"The galley . . . came from Cyrene?" Simon asked again, and tried to suppress his trembling.

"Yes, from Cyrene. I believe they could not load enough wheat. They say you caused the settlers to burn it all. That's why they've come to Alexandria—to take you captive."

"I burned *my* wheat, it is true. A riot followed."

"So we heard. Many have been crucified. They say the crosses stand thick in Cyrene."

Simon clenched his fists. He tried to see her face in the dark —only her voice seemed real.

"Some of the galley slaves were driven to death?" Simon asked with anguish.

"We heard that four died."

"The slave driver on that ship is my own son . . . my son Alexander." He hoped that the confession would drain his heart of grief and shock.

"I know your sorrow, man of Cyrene," she said without emotion. "One of my sons is a Roman centurion in Galatia. Perhaps the Anointed One will one day touch their hearts—your son's and mine."

"You believe in the Nazarene, Mother Naomi?"

The silence that followed was like that of the desert when the wind has died. Then she spoke.

"I believe in Him as I believe that the sun brings day, for He has simplicity and goodness, and He preaches love. But we cannot discuss Him now. There is no time. Rome seeks your life. The galley had scarcely arrived when a young man came running to Philo to warn him that the Romans were searching for Rufus's parents; he said they were thought to be on their way to Alexandria."

"A young man?"

"Strange, Philo thought he was a Roman sailor. He said he was tall and dark, dressed in seagoing garments, but he wouldn't give his name. There was a scar on his cheek."

Simon leaned against the tree and felt the cool roughness of the trunk. His eyes widened with a new understanding, and his sorrow and fear were destroyed. He wanted to shout: It was Alexander . . . it was Alexander who brought warning. But he repressed the urge.

"Here is the wine," Shalom said in the darkness, and Simon felt for the drinking cup that was held out to him, put it to his lips and drank, rather to toast his happiness than to quench his thirst.

"There was also a Roman of consequence on the ship," Naomi said, "one Caius Papinius, an underling of the wheat chief in

78

Rome. They say he is a vindictive man. We've heard that he urged the prefect here to mete out heavy punishment if you and yours are not given up."

"Heavy punishment?" Simon asked, as he felt the warm glow of the wine rise in his body.

"Unless you are handed over, five Jews will be crucified."

Simon's hand jerked, and wine splashed over his knuckles. He tightened his trembling grip on the vessel.

"Take your water yoke and climb up on the wall of the canal," he heard Naomi tell Shalom. "Go, perhaps you may see something."

"Mother Naomi," Simon said, "I am a simple man. I have worked on the land. But I brought disaster to Cyrene, and now I bring death here. Why must it be? What have I done that God has put a curse upon my handiwork? Why must blood follow wherever I go?"

"I think you are chosen, man of Cyrene. I think you are chosen for something that you have yet to understand."

Her voice was soft and gentle, but she spoke as a prophet.

Simon swallowed and tried to see her, but all he had was the memory of her eyes as he saw them in the lamplight, old and faded, but with a humbling strength.

"I am not chosen for anything," he said bitterly. "I am a coward and a fool."

Tall leaves slapped and rustled in the night wind that had sprung up. Even the tree seemed to whisper condemnation.

"You are too humble, man of Cyrene. You are neither a coward nor a fool."

"Others have died and I am free. More will die, and I may still be free."

"I think the Messiah is guiding you to Jerusalem. That is why I do not fear for your safety."

He spoke, and his voice drowned out the rustling of the leaves: "Why do you too embitter my life with this Nazarene, Mother Naomi? Messiah! May God preserve us from a Messiah like this man. If He is the Messiah, why does He not free Israel from the Roman yoke that has driven me from Cyrene? I have lost everything I had because of Roman tyranny—my land, my vineyards, my livelihood, and my future. I am now a wanderer; there is no-where I can go. When Rome does these things to His people, He remains silent."

"He will return to you more than you have lost," she replied with calm strength.

"He doesn't even know me, and I have no desire to know Him," Simon said more calmly, ashamed of his outburst.

"Yes, He knows you, just as He knew Matthew the tax collec-tor before they met. And although Matthew's sin was greater than yours, he is now a disciple."

"I beg of you not to speak of the Nazarene to me. You are a good woman, Mother Naomi. I do not wish to quarrel. You are wise. Tell me rather what I must do to prevent the spilling of inno-cent blood here. Shall I go to the prefect and give myself up?"

"You have an honest heart, man of Cyrene," Naomi said. "An honest heart is good. And a heart that is good belongs to Him."

"Mother Naomi . . ."

"Very well," she said, and raised a hand in the dark. "I shall not talk about Him anymore. I am only a widow who believes you are chosen: a chosen man who has not yet heard His voice. No, you shall not go to the prefect. You will go to Jerusalem."

"Jerusalem? "

"Yes, to Jerusalem. A Greek merchant ship is leaving tonight for Joppa. Your son Rufus sent word of it. He is waiting at the har-bor."

"Rufus?"

"When the news came that they were looking for you, Philo at once sent Rufus away. He came here for a hurried good-bye. My Shalom knows where he is."

"How can I go to Jerusalem if my flight brings death to the innocent?"

"Man of Cyrene, many will die before the Messiah has estab-lished His kingdom on this earth, before the world can under-stand His teaching. Rome shall fall before He is victorious."

"But others must not die because of me. It was bad enough that Cyrene—"

Simon stopped. His sharpened senses were aware of move-ment in the dark. He sat rigidly, waiting tensely.

Close to them came Shalom's voice. "They are coming along the other side of the canal with torches," he said softly. "They must be Romans. They seem to be searching."

"Go, man of Cyrene," Naomi said quickly. "I knew they would come again. We cannot speak longer. Peace to you and Rufus and all your loved ones. I wish it were I who was going to Jerusalem . . . and perhaps to Galilee."

In the dark, Simon's hands found her thin body that was so strong and full of purpose. He clasped her shoulders. "Peace be to you, Mother Naomi. I know I am a coward, but I wish to live."

"You have no choice but to go. It is destined so."

He was still pondering her words when Shalom said, "Follow at once; time is short."

"Peace be to you, Mother Naomi," Simon said again, swung around, and followed Shalom through the garden.

"Go in peace, man of Cyrene," came the faint voice from the darkness.

Simon and Shalom moved quietly around the back of the house, cut across toward the street, crossed it and hurried along under the trees. Simon whistled softly, and Ezekiel answered. They hastened to where the others were waiting.

"The Romans are searching for us," Simon said. "Come!" They forced the tired camels to rise and moved off beside the canal. Shalom led the way. Simon brought his camel next to Deborah's, reached out and touched his wife's hand. She held his rough hand tightly.

"I thought you were never coming back."

"Woman of little faith! I shall always return to you."

"Rufus." She whispered in the darkness. "Where is Rufus?"

"He is waiting for us."

Then he told her what Naomi had told him and of Alexander's warning. He knew her silence held gratitude and pride.

They heard loud voices behind them, on the opposite side of the canal. "It seems all the rabble of Alexandria is searching for us," Shalom said over his shoulder, and urged his camel on faster. Simon looked around, and in the distance behind them saw torches blossom along the canal wall.

"We must hurry," he hissed. They forced the weary camels into an ungainly trot.

"They are in front of us too," Ezekiel said anxiously. Far ahead of them were more torches.

Shalom made them turn sharply, straight toward the sea through the date palms, and soon the flares on the great wharves of Alexandria came into view. They stopped under the last trees, jumped down, and cut the packs free. Shalom took Deborah's hand and hurried her along the road toward the wharves. Simon, Ezekiel, and Juba seized the packs, threw them on their shoulders, and followed at a run.

Great piles of hides, bales of papyrus, and stacks of sawn timber were lying on the wharves. Men shouted as they worked; the night was alive with the lights of heavy torches. Whips cracked, and slaves, their torsos bare and gleaming, staggered up the gangways with heavy loads.

They came to a high heap of wheat bags arranged for shipment. Shalom stopped behind it and turned around anxiously, waiting for Simon and the others to catch up with Deborah and himself.

A sound made them look up, and they saw a man sliding down the heap of sacks. The next moment Rufus stood before his mother.

With a sob she was in his arms. "It has been a long time, Mother," Rufus said. He held her away and looked at her, his face pale, his eyes bright in the faint light. Then he pressed her to him again.

"We must go," he said. "The ship is already laden. They are waiting for us. I thought you would never come."

He suddenly let go of her and ran to meet Simon. He freed the pack from his father's shoulders. They stood looking wordlessly at each other, with hands clasped. "Father . . . thank God you are safe."

"Rufus . . . my son," the big man faltered.

"Come, there's no time. Come, Ezekiel, Juba. We will talk later. There are torches on the other side of the road."

They bid Shalom a hurried farewell. "You must go, my friend," Rufus said. "This way, past the wharves. Carefully! Greetings to Mother Naomi. Peace to you!"

"Peace be with you all," Shalom said, tears trembling in his eyes.

"May God bless you, Shalom, my son," Simon said as Shalom's body merged into the darkness.

Rufus led them to the ship. "I've only paid for three," he said. "I did not know of Ezekiel and Juba. The great Philo gave me the money."

"I still have money," Deborah said. "We can pay."

Rufus and his mother were in front, followed by Simon and Ezekiel, with Juba in the rear.

Simon looked around. He saw how Juba labored. The slave was bearing the heaviest pack.

And he saw that which struck fear into him. Six or seven Roman soldiers were coming along the quay, holding their torches high. The light gleamed on their helmets.

"The Romans are just behind us!" Simon shouted. He seized Juba's pack.

The Romans spread out, searching between the piles of freight. Deborah and Rufus ran up the gangway, followed by Ezekiel and finally Simon, staggering under his heavy load. They threw down their packs. Four sailors raised the gangplank quickly.

"We very nearly sailed without you, Jew" said one of them.

"I'm going to have a word with the captain, Father," Rufus said and disappeared behind the mast.

Orders were being shouted. Somewhere a whip cracked, and the vessel moved slowly, gliding from the quayside, lazily, as if unwilling to stir.

Breathing quickly, Simon stood with his arms around Deborah who was leaning against him trembling. "We are saved once more, husband," Deborah murmured.

"Where . . . where is Juba?" Ezekiel called out suddenly.

They looked around in consternation. Simon hurried to the railing, Ezekiel by his side.

They looked back toward the quay.

There was Juba, his sword flashing in the light of Roman torches, facing four soldiers. He fought and gave way, then stood, fighting again, his body swaying with repeated thrust and parry.

Simon gripped the railing. "He saw the Romans too," he whispered, "and turned back to fight them off."

One Roman fell crookedly under Juba's sword, and his cry reached them over the water. But the others were forcing Juba backward toward the edge of the wharf. Suddenly he swung around, ducked, and dived in a wide arc from the quay.

Simon and Ezekiel shouted out joyfully as Juba swam with powerful strokes, his arms shining in the faint torchlight.

"Come, Juba, come!" Simon encouraged him with every movement of his arms. but suddenly Juba's body rose in the water, and they heard him scream. On the quay a Roman pulled a second arrow from his quiver.

Juba swam on, but weakly, and the arrow in his back trembled like a bloody feather. Then there was only his hand, lifted in despair over the dark waters. Simon tried to leap into the sea, but Ezekiel held him. They watched Juba's body sink from view.

They stood for a long time and watched the coast of Africa fade and merge into the night. Ezekiel's eyes smarted with his sorrow, and Simon's spirit burned with the intensity of his hatred against Rome. Outlined against the narrow strip of light over Alexandria they saw the silhouette of a Roman galley, its pagan figurehead high and proud upon the prow. It was the wheat ship from Ostia.

"Do you see him?" Simon asked, in the voice of one who talks in a dream.

"Who? Juba? Juba's gone. You saw it happen, Simon Niger."

"No. My Alexander. Do you not see him on that wheat ship?"

"Who can see anything on that vessel now, Simon Niger?"

"I only wondered . . ."

Then he looked up at the lighthouse, which sent a beam far into the night, a shaft of light piercing the darkness.

And in the quiet bay of Alexandria the swishing sound of long oars could be heard as galley slaves propelled a Roman vessel over a Roman sea.

Part Two

9

Two black donkeys trotted along the wide road that the Romans had built. They looked small and of little account in the throng of swift pack animals—fast-moving camels, eating up miles with their long strides, large loads bouncing against their flanks; slower camels, with swaying legs and necks held low; horses, trotting briskly.

The sun shone pale and mild on the road that twisted over hills and valleys where the first green of spring had broken through. Dogs trotted alongside, their pale red tongues drooping from open mouths. Wild flowers of many colors made carpets on the plains.

Loads of wood bounced on the backs of the animals; papyrus bales rocked slowly. There were rolls of cotton, large jars fastened beside the packsaddles, bundles of pungent hides.

Greek drivers urged their camels forward, Persians goaded theirs, Syrians moved shouting up and down the lengths of their caravans, Jews trotted along in front of their pack animals.

Herds of stock animals, bleating and bellowing, were being driven over spring fields still light green and tender before the maturity of summer. A golden light rested on the far height, and the valley approaching Judea's ancient hills seemed cool and hospitable. On a distant ridge the cedars were green slits in the blue sky.

The woman on the lead donkey jogged up and down, peered through her veil, and turned her face aside each time a camel overtook her mount and the driver looked at her contemptuously or perhaps made some unflattering remark.

For a time she watched the flapping ears of the donkey, the swinging shoulders of the young man who led the animal, the quick movement of his sandaled feet on the hard road, the yellow dust that had settled on his turban.

His rough rice-blue garment fluttered about his ankles, and he seemed to be spurred by a deep desire, as if he were racing toward some destination beyond the folded hills. She watched him tenderly, and a smile lit up her eyes. But then she looked into the distance once again, searching the bright horizon for their journey's end. She looked for a green summit, for old walls winding over the hills, for an ancient city.

"When do we reach Jerusalem?" she asked.

"It's still a half-day's journey, Mother," the young man answered cheerfully.

"Still all that traveling?" she said, disappointed, and tried to ease her aching body, for they had moved quickly up from the sea. It felt to her as if the harbor of Joppa was just as far behind them as Cyrene or Alexandria. She recalled the face of the Greek captain who had brought them across the sea from Egypt and the quiet days of sun and skies and ceaseless swells as they sailed toward the coast of Canaan.

Suddenly she heard a decisive voice. "You'd better slow down, Rufus. Jerusalem will not run from us and the donkeys cannot last at this pace."

Deborah looked down at Simon, who had come up beside her. She put out her hand and tried to wipe the dust from his beard. "You look as if you'd been winnowing wheat, husband," she said.

He laid his big hand on her lap. "Are you very tired, my wife?" he asked, his eyes grave and tender.

She nodded and said, "I don't mind—Jerusalem isn't so far anymore."

"No, it's not so far away."

While he spoke, Simon looked up at the sun. It was already low in the sky, hanging between them and Africa. He looked westward at the far horizon, and he thought sadly that the same sun would set that night over his land in Cyrene—over his vineyards and orchard.

"Drink," he said all of a sudden. "You are tired and thirsty."

She took the small wine flask from him. "Wine?" she asked gratefully.

He laughed. "Ezekiel bought it—I don't know where. He is

never at a loss to know where to buy wine."

Deborah looked around at Ezekiel who was leading the other donkey, heavily laden with everything they had saved during half a lifetime, together with some things they had collected during their short stay in Joppa. Joppa had attracted them. They would have liked to stay on there. But there were too many Romans, and too many Roman ships touched there. And there was the past: the bloodshed in Cyrene. Moreover, during Passover they preferred to be in Jerusalem.

"Drink," Ezekiel said cheerfully. "That is good wine; it comes from Galilee—they make good wine there. I bought it from a Syrian; he needed the money and I the wine."

Deborah drank, and the wine was cool, tart, and tingling on the tongue. "Where *is* Galilee?" she asked as she handed the wine flask back to Simon.

He pointed to the north with a staff he had cut in a ravine outside Joppa. "Galilee lies there," he said, "on the other side of Samaria."

"Is it far?"

"Not too far. Why do you ask, Deborah?" There was a frown on Simon's face.

"I only asked," she said, but he knew it was not quite the truth.

"Why must you know about Galilee when we are going to Jerusalem? Who discusses Galilee when he travels to Jerusalem?"

"Galilee is a lovely country," Rufus said. "Full of hills and valleys and springs; there is a beautiful lake."

" . . . and poverty," Simon reminded them.

"One day we must go and see it," Rufus said vaguely, and Simon looked at his son with suspicion. They had had many discussions on the journey—on the ship from Alexandria, on the road from Joppa, when Rufus told them of the wisdom he had gathered from his teacher, Philo, and of how they had investigated the teachings of the prophet from Galilee.

"Where is Nazareth?" Deborah asked, and Simon glanced at her searchingly.

"Near the foot of Tabor, east of Carmel, not too far from the Sea of Galilee," Rufus answered.

"You sound as if you've already been there" Simon said, surprised at the accuracy of his son's knowledge.

"During our investigations in Alexandria we verified the location of Nazareth."

"But why Nazareth? One would think it was important, like Tyre or Sidon . . . or Tarsus," Simon said irritably.

"Because the new prophet was born there," Rufus replied calmly, as if it was the most ordinary thing in the world to say.

"Prophet?" said Simon with profound contempt, striking a stone from the road with his staff. "Prophet?" he repeated, and gave a short laugh. "Why do you keep making so much of this man? Why do you wish to make Him great like Isaiah? What has He prophesied for Israel that you should dub Him prophet? If He were a true prophet, He'd be in Jerusalem teaching the people— not hiding out in Galilee."

"But we really don't know much about this man, Simon," Deborah said. "How can we know everything He said?"

He gripped the mane of the donkey and pulled the animal to a stop. His dark eyes smoldered as he glared at his wife. Rufus halted in surprise, and Ezekiel looked at them, wondering.

"Because I don't choose to discuss this man, I have said nothing till now." Simon's jaws tightened. "But now I shall tell you. It's not necessary to know what this man has said. It is enough to know what He has done."

They waited for him to continue. Deborah turned away from the hatred in his eyes.

"On this road is a caravan driver who is a Galilean. He told me . . ." He struck the ground with his stab and glared at them.

"What did he tell you?" Deborah asked.

"How this so-called prophet desecrated the Sabbath."

"Desecrated it? No!" There was shocked piety in her tone.

"Yes, desecrated it. He and His band of followers walked through a wheat field on the Sabbath. They were alleged to be hungry. He allowed them to pick the grain. That is what this Nazarene has done. Allowed men to gather food on the Sabbath!"

He examined each of them in turn, looking for the shock in their eyes. "That is not all. He was not satisfied with that trans-

90

gression. When He was rebuked for desecrating the Sabbath, He said that He was *above* the Sabbath."

Deborah's head was bowed as she stared at the ground. But Rufus gazed at his father steadily.

"There is your prophet for you, Rufus," Simon said with gravity. "He is master of the Sabbath, the holy day of God, and thus master of the law. He is lord of the holiest thing of Israel, but a slave of Rome. There is your prophet of Nazareth."

He looked at Ezekiel, staring at him round-eyed. "Here, take your Galilean wine," Simon said and flung the flask at Ezekiel, who caught it clumsily. Then he turned, strode aimlessly off into the fields along the road, and busied himself helping a cattle driver round up his animals.

Rufus tugged at the donkey's rope, and the little caravan resumed its journey.

"I shouldn't have brought up the subject," Deborah said, following her husband with her eyes. "It always angers your father. And you shouldn't have said that the Nazarene is a prophet."

"But He *is* a prophet."

"But all this about the Sabbath! How can a holy man of Israel desecrate the Sabbath?"

He shrugged his shoulders. "We do not really know what happened. Perhaps it's just a story, Mother."

Deborah glanced at Ezekiel behind them. She leaned forward. "Rufus, do you think He is the Messiah?" she whispered. "Don't let your father know I asked."

Rufus walked more slowly, and the donkey all but passed him. He stared down at the baked surface of the road. Then he jerked the animal to a stop. He looked up at his mother, and she saw a strange light in his gray eyes. It was as if he were searching for something—as if he sought in her dark eyes that which he himself did not possess.

"I do not know," he murmured. "I do not know."

Deborah gazed for a long time at her son standing beside her slightly bowed, as if sudden fatigue had reached him. His young beard showed rusty red through the layers of dust on his face.

"You have studied under Philo, and you don't know?"

"There are things that even Philo doesn't know," he said

loudly, and began to walk briskly, pulling the donkey along.

She looked down at her hands and for a moment did not even hear the tumult of the passing traffic.

They traveled across the hills, crossed a few narrow valleys. And then quite suddenly, Rufus let go of the donkey, ran forward, and stopped in his tracks. He turned and pointed with his arm. "There lies Jerusalem!" he shouted. He ran forward a few steps, excitedly.

"There lies Jerusalem!" he shouted again, and the caravan drivers looked at him in surprise.

Deborah sat quietly on the donkey and pressed her hands to her mouth when she saw the city. It lay dimly outlined on a distant rise. And beyond the straggling disorder of Jerusalem lay the green hills, one of which must be the Mount of Olives.

"There she rests—the bride of Israel," Simon said, panting as he joined them, for he had been walking behind the herds and talking to the cattle driver. "Jerusalem, city of David!" he said hoarsely and wiped his face.

Ezekiel pulled up his donkey next to Deborah's. She looked down at him and saw his tears.

"I always weep whenever I see Jerusalem," Ezekiel said.

"This is the first time for me," Deborah replied. "I am happy now."

The sun was low in the sky, and though its golden light was gentle, its rays still had sufficient strength to make the city glitter. The four travelers gazed and gazed. The city looked eternal, as everlasting as the hills themselves, as real as the sunlight that caressed it. The city of a thousand years, perhaps of eternity—the fortress of David, Solomon, and all the great ones who had dwelt there.

Simon gripped the donkey's mane, closed his eyes, and lifted his face toward Jerusalem. Then he prayed aloud. "God of Abraham, Isaac, and Jacob, God of David, we thank You for having brought us safely to Jerusalem."

The others bowed their heads. When they lifted their eyes again, they saw the golden light beginning to fade from the ancient city of Solomon.

"Let us go on," Simon said, grasping the head of Deborah's donkey and dragging it forward. He looked laughingly over his shoulder at his wife and met her smile that was showing through her tears. He pointed his staff excitedly toward Jerusalem. "There lies our new Cyrene, wife," he cried.

They traveled so fast down the ridge that Ezekiel and Rufus were obliged to keep prodding the second donkey to keep up with Simon. He kept talking as he walked, pointing his staff, and, with his eyes directed on Jerusalem, tripping and stumbling over stones.

"Do you see the Mount of Olives, Deborah? And there you can see the Valley of Kidron . . . and here on this side is the Damascus Gate. Can you see the temple? There on the hill?"

Before their eyes Jerusalem grew out of the distance, becoming clearer, more distinct. The vast roofs of the temple shone dimly in the setting sun, tall spires coated in a mist of golden light; the old walls that time could not destroy twisted darkly across the hills. The palace of Herod glittered like a great white jewel, new and challenging in the midst of ancient splendors. Simon recognized the tower of Antonia, slender as a needle. For a long time he looked at it, a symbol of Rome's military might in Judea.

Then the sun sank away beyond the Valley of Rephaim, on the other side of the old land of the tribe of Benjamin, beyond the sea, beyond Africa . . . beyond the world.

And it spread a scarlet glow, like the blood of a thousand martyrs, over Jerusalem. It ringed the quiet roofs of the temple with a purple-red, and it touched ominously on palace and temple, on tower and spire and hill.

For a few minutes only. Then it dimmed, and the first darkness drifted down the Valley of Kidron; the Mount of Olives faded slowly in the dusk; the garden of Gethsemane merged into its slopes; the hill of Golgotha, near the main road to the north, to Damascus, to the lake country of Galilee, was like a black pearl above the haze of smoke drifting from the city.

Simon watched it all intensely; then he sighed once, the trance broke, and he looked at Deborah. "We've reached Jerusalem, Mother," he said, and his eyes were moist. "Tomorrow, God willing, we will enter through the Damascus Gate . . . but we'll stop now for the night, at the next water hole."

They made their way farther along the road outside Jerusalem. Where the main routes from Joppa and Caesarea met, they joined the crowd thronging around the water holes. Everybody was busy watering animals and carrying water for drinking or bathing. The twilight overflowed with the lowing and bleating of animals, with the strident voices of drivers and their helpers.

They stopped at the edge of the throng. Simon lifted Deborah from the saddle, supporting her until she could stand without assistance.

"Rufus," ordered Simon, "you fetch firewood. Ezekiel, go and water the donkeys."

They unloaded the packs, and as Ezekiel went off with the donkeys and Rufus disappeared into the bushes to collect wood, Simon came to Deborah where she was seated on a hide mat. He lifted her shawl and ran his fingers through her hair.

"Mother," he said, "I want to ask a question."

She looked up at him—weary, but grateful and contented.

"Is the question important, my husband?" She stretched out her hand, took his big hand in hers and held it to her warm lips, pressing it against her face.

He looked down at the dark of her hair. "I wanted to ask whether you haven't got enough money yet for a slaughter-animal, perhaps a lamb. We've had very little fresh meat since we left Cyrene and tonight is an occasion. We've reached Jerusalem."

She looked up at him, her eyes serious. "If we eat so royally tonight, what of our offering? We have traveled far and safely—we shall have to take a sacrifice to the temple tomorrow."

He breathed deeply and looked away into the twilight. "That is true," he said. "We must keep something for a sacrifice. But we shall only be able to offer something small—a few pigeons perhaps—until I have found work; then we can make the proper sacrifice. I'll go and fetch water for washing." He turned and picked up two large goatskin water bags. She rummaged in her leather pouch. Two small silver pieces lay in her warm hand.

"Simon," she called as he was about to go, and rose to her feet. He came back and stood before her. "This is all we have," she said.

"It is enough to buy pigeons for the offering," he replied. "I'll get the water."

When Simon returned later with the two full water bags and Ezekiel came up with the two donkeys, Rufus had a fire going.

"Tie up the donkeys, Ezekiel," Simon said, and approached the fire.

But at the side of the firelight he stopped in his tracks, frowning, his shoulders bent forward beneath the weight of the two water skins. He gazed at the strange scene around the fire.

Deborah was sitting down kneading dough in a wooden dish. Rufus was tending the fire.

Next to the fire lay a fat, slaughtered lamb.

On the other side of the fire sat a stranger—the most hideous looking human being Simon had ever set eyes upon: a man bereft of his left hand, with sunken face and a dark cavity where his nose had been.

Simon moved a step nearer in surprise and shock.

The stranger squatted by the fire, and in his right hand, which boasted but two fingers, he held a walking staff. Simon knew at once that it was his ebony staff, the one Alexander had given him.

Then the strange man saw him and smiled—and the smile softened his horrible mutilation, almost erasing it.

10

When Deborah saw Simon's surprise, she rose and went to him. She stopped half guiltily before him. "I've managed to get a lamb—bartered for it," she said brightly, and looked him straight in the eye. "I . . . I wanted at first to exchange the purple garment that Alexander gave me for it, but the stranger said it would be of no use to him. I got it for . . . for your stick, the one Alexander gave you. Are you angry with me, my husband?"

He looked at her with a proud smile. "How could I be angry when I know that you have done it for me?" he whispered. "I didn't even know the stick was here."

"I packed it just before we left Cyrene. I didn't do it only for you—all of us are hungry."

"I know. I am grateful. You could always strike a better bargain than I could. Who is the man who has bartered a fat lamb for a stick?"

Deborah took him by the arm and led him to the stranger. "This is my husband, Simon," she said.

"Peace be with you, friend," the stranger said, and his voice, like his ravaged face, repelled, for he had a split palate. The air whistled through his ruined nostrils as he spoke. "My name is Nimrod. Only I am not a great hunter as Nimrod was—I am nothing." With the thumb and forefinger, all that was left of his right hand, he lifted the black ebony wood stick, and it glinted in the glow of the flames.

"I am happy to have this stick," he said. "It will be the first little treasure that I've possessed . . . since I became like this." He pointed to his face.

"We thank you for the fine lamb. I think you've made a bad bargain," Simon said.

Nimrod laughed. "I am content," he answered.

Simon set the two water bags down next to a bush and came to sit at the fire.

"Where do you live, Nimrod . . . my friend?" Simon asked, removing his sandals as he watched Rufus and Ezekiel skin the lamb.

"I live near here," Nimrod replied, and pointed over his shoulder. "I am grazing my master's flocks. I am a shepherd—that's all I'm good for—but I am satisfied." His gray eyes were mirthful under his coarse cap. "I water the animals here each night, and then I bivouac among the bushes. That's where your wife found me."

"Your master—he won't object to our transaction? We are strangers here, and I do not look for trouble."

"Because of a lamb? No, the lamb is mine. I own a few animals."

"I understand," Simon said, relieved. "Besides, I have a good master—a fine man, a devout man."

"Who is he?"

"Joseph of Arimathea—a person of consequence. He sits on the Sanhedrin."

"Indeed?" Simon said, and his eyes widened.

"Yes . . . and wealthy." Nimrod leaned forward in his eagerness to talk about the great man. "Nearly all of Gethsemane belongs to my master—the oil press and the orchard. He also has extensive wheat lands on these plains. But he is humble—like the poor."

He saw Simon staring out into the darkness. "I too am a farmer," Simon said. "I also had a vineyard and an orchard and wheat lands."

"From where do you come, friend?" Nimrod asked.

Simon looked at Nimrod in confusion. He waved his arm vaguely. "I . . . us? From the Nile. I had my fill of Egypt. One year the Nile overflows, and the next year our wheat is killed by drought."

"So now you come to live in Jerusalem?"

Simon nodded. "I'm here to look for work—something to do, for we have nothing except our two donkeys. I want to work on the land. I will be a foreman, a sharecropper—anything, so long as I can work on the land. I don't know anyone here. I am a stranger."

"Go and see my master," Nimrod said immediately. "Perhaps he can help. He employs many men."

"Good, I will try that"

Nimrod rose. "Now I must go back to my place."

"No," Deborah said from the fire, "eat something with us first."

"But I . . . I shouldn't eat your meat."

"There is enough here for everybody—and you have been good to us."

"Thank you," Nimrod said as he sat down again. "It's been a long time since I have eaten with anybody." He sniffed the aroma of the griddlecake and stared at the sheen of Deborah's black hair. He started slightly when Simon spoke.

"You . . . you live alone? You have no family?"

Nimrod shook his head. "How could I marry? I was a leper."

Simon jumped up, staring at Nimrod. Deborah dropped a spoon with a clatter, and Rufus and Ezekiel straightened themselves to gape at the bowed figure sitting before them.

"Leper! " Simon gulped. "You a leper—and sit here?" He spoke harshly. "Do you not know that the law lays down that the leper may not be touched, that he must keep away from others? Do you not know the law that Moses gave to Israel?"

The split mouth and the sunken nose were like dark lesions in Nimrod's graying beard. But his eyes shone with such an inner joy that for a moment Simon thought the man possessed. He searched deep in Nimrod's eyes for any sign of madness, his body trembling.

Nimrod held out the stump of his left arm, lifted the mutilated right hand so that the red light of the fire played clearly upon it.

"I am cured," Nimrod said, as simply as a child tells of his thirst and with the same assurance. He rubbed his mutilated face with his stump of an arm. "See—I am cured!" he laughed.

"Cured?" Simon shouted. "No leper is cured!"

"I *am* cured!" Nimrod insisted. "Look at this. See . . ." And again he held his hand out to the light of the fire.

Simon came a step closer. Rufus and Ezekiel moved to stand

beside the fire. Nimrod looked in turn at the three men, then at Deborah, his eyes pleading.

"Nobody can cure you of leprosy," Simon said in a hoarse voice. "Nobody! Your blood is tainted."

Nimrod looked into the heart of the fire. The black stick lay between his knees, resting against his cheek. His eyes were large, almost ecstatic, as if he saw, through the dancing flames, a vision in the sky in which everything was pure. And when he spoke, his words came from deep down in his throat, like the speech of a child about to cry.

"It was not an ordinary being who cured me," Nimrod said. He closed his eyes and lifted up his face, so that the firelight showed the nature of his scars.

"Jesus of Nazareth healed me," Nimrod said, and his gray beard trembled with the rapture of that memory.

Simon of Cyrene shouted across the fire: "You lie, you leprous dog! Jesus of Nazareth? You lie!"

Deborah stood up in fright, and Rufus and Ezekiel stared in dismay at Simon. He seemed consumed with fury. He bent down swiftly, picked up a stick from the fire, swung it hissing through the air. "Get out, you filth. You and your Jesus of Nazareth! Go, before I mark you further with a brand!"

"Father!" Rufus pleaded, but Simon looked at him with such threatening hostility that he became silent.

Nimrod stood up slowly. There was neither fear nor anger in his eyes—only something like compassion. He almost smiled.

"Peace be with you," he said without looking directly at any of them. Then he became aware of the staff still in his hand. He bent down and, with calm deliberation, laid it on the ground.

"Take it with you!" Simon shouted. "You have defiled it. Take it! And take your animal. I do not eat of flesh proffered by one who is unclean."

Nimrod turned and walked away, without a further word. His spare, bent body dissociated itself slowly from the firelight, became one with the dark night.

Simon turned away, seized the lamb, and flung it far into the bushes. Then he stood still. Above the thudding of his heart he heard Nimrod walking into the darkness. He closed his eyes tightly to erase the memory of the leper's eyes. He walked back to the fire, and he felt unutterably alone. He listened avidly for sounds, trying to destroy the echoes of Nimrod's voice in the fissures of his mind.

The fire had grown smaller. Only erratic flames now flickered on the coals. Deborah stood there with Ezekiel and Rufus. Simon came to them looking ashamed and guilty.

"Why did you do that? He is a good man," Ezekiel said. "He gave us his meat."

Placing his foot beneath the stick that Nimrod had left there, Simon kicked it away into the darkness. The dying firelight played on Deborah's pale face. "He was so defenseless, and you spurned him like a dog," she said.

"Do not berate me about this leper," Simon said loudly. He turned his back on them. "He is a leper, and I a Jew. To me he is untouchable. Or are you Jews no longer? Have you become heathens, knowing nothing of the law?"

"But he is cured," Rufus said.

Simon spun around, his eyes glaring in the light that was dying about them. "Cured? He is not cured. He can never be whole again!" he shouted. "Or do you also believe that this Nazarene healed him? Do you believe that?"

They all looked toward Rufus, who seemed to wilt under his father's question.

"Do you believe it?" Simon repeated, and it was more a challenge than a question.

Rufus knelt down beside the fire, looking at the coals that were glowing more dimly still, at the uncertain flames. He picked up a dry stick, snapped it in his hands, and said, "I do not know what to believe."

Silence fell between them, as if there were nothing to add to the words Rufus had pronounced. When at last Simon spoke, his voice was so hoarse that he sounded like a stranger. "If you do not know what to believe, then you already believe in what the leper said." Rufus looked confusedly up at his father. "The day you believe, on that day you shall find shelter beneath my roof no longer. The day you believe in this carpenter, this consort of tax collectors, of lepers, and of the worthless—"

"Why do you hate Him so? What has He done against you?" Deborah's question came thinly through the darkness.

"I do not hate Him," Simon said softly, calmly, almost cheerfully. "I despise Him."

"We cannot hate, despise, or even love Him, for we do not know Him," Rufus said.

"I have spoken, spoken clearly and with a purpose," Simon replied loudly. "So far as I and my house are concerned, this carpenter is a heretic. For us the law suffices. So it is now, and so it will remain."

"Let us eat," Ezekiel said suddenly. He saw the anger in Simon's eyes, and he was afraid that Rufus might speak again. Rufus had changed. He had become a man in Alexandria. And Simon—he too was a man, big, hard, and unyielding.

They seated themselves around the dying coals and ate griddlecakes with the honey that Ezekiel had found. They drank water.

"Early tomorrow morning I shall go to Jerusalem," Simon said. "I shall look for work. You had better stay here meanwhile. Here there are trees and water."

When they had finished eating, they spread their mats and laid themselves down to sleep, for their journey had been long.

But long after the others had gone to sleep, Rufus lay awake looking up at the stars.

11

It was nearly noon when they saw Simon coming toward them, striding over the level plain with a great jar hanging from the staff over his shoulder. Quails flew up before his feet, and his step was springy. He held his head high and looked as if the world was his. There was happy haste in the rhythm of his stride.

Even from afar, Deborah could see his eyes sparkling with a surprise and his face filled with laughter.

His strides became even longer as he approached the tree. He saw that Deborah had washed some clothes and put them out to dry on flat-topped bushes. Rufus was lying on his back reading from the huge scroll he had brought from Alexandria, which was really about all he had brought with him. Ezekiel was occupied with the shaping of a crook.

Simon slid into the shade of the tree. "You must have thought, my wife, that I'd run off with one of the beauties of Jerusalem," he said as he lowered the staff from his shoulder, the old laughter wrinkles showing about his eyes.

"Are there women in Jerusalem more beautiful than your Deborah?" she asked gaily, for when he was happy, she was too.

He put his hands on her shoulders, bent, and kissed her forehead. "No," he acknowledged, "you are beyond compare!" His fingers tightened on her shoulders.

"Something has happened, my husband," she said. "Jerusalem has done something for you. You are the man I knew before the bad times came."

"Something indeed has happened," he said. "Deborah, I have land. I have land to farm again."

"Land," she cried in surprise and pleasure.

He lowered his head. His hands slipped from her shoulders and hung slackly at his sides. For a moment he could not speak. What had happened to him in Jerusalem was of such overwhelming meaning that he could only gulp and look away.

"Yes, land," he said at last, in a quiet voice, "land on which to work. Vineyards . . . an orchard . . . wheat fields. Now I can turn my hands to labor once more, Deborah. We are no longer wanderers."

"The name of the Almighty be praised, husband. We are not worthy."

"No . . . *I* am not worthy of this. It is a blessing that I don't deserve."

"Land?" asked Rufus, who had risen and was rolling up his scroll. Ezekiel also joined them, his face showing his joy.

"We have land, Ezekiel," Simon said, laughing with shining eyes and pulling off his headdress.

"Now we can work again," Ezekiel exclaimed.

"Like the days of old."

"Tell us everything," Deborah begged, tugging at Simon's garment.

"And you even have a jar of wine," Ezekiel said, caressing the cool earthenware jar.

"Pour us a draft, Ezekiel. Bring beakers, Rufus," Simon ordered, and sat down with his back against the tree trunk. "Let us rejoice. We have a future now."

He took off his sandals while Deborah fetched a bowl of water. She sat down before him and began to bathe his feet.

"Is it your own land?" Rufus asked.

"No, not my own," Simon told them. "But land. I am to cultivate it."

"Whose land is it?" Deborah asked.

Taking the drinking cup from Ezekiel, Simon drank deeply and wiped his beard. "It belongs to Joseph of Arimathea, one of the wealthiest men of Jerusalem."

"Then you followed the leper's advice after all?" Rufus asked.

They all looked at Simon. "I did as the leper advised," he acknowledged softly. "I entered at the Damascus Gate. I followed along the back street till I reached the Street of the Potters. There I asked the way. They took me to this Joseph of Arimathea. A good man. A sincere man. A man with a big heart. It so happened that he needed someone to care for his vineyards, orchards, and fields. The man he had before had vanished—perhaps he ran after this Nazarene. Can you imagine it! He gave me the job. He owns almost the whole of Gethsemane, and vineyards on the Mount of Olives and arable lands in this area. Rich, fertile soil. I went to see it. At Gethsemane there are enormous vats for wine, and an oil press. The place lacks nothing. There is even a house, close to the garden of Gethsemane. We can move in there."

"But it is unbelievable, my husband," Deborah said, as she dried his feet.

"Give me more wine," Simon asked, holding out his beaker to Ezekiel. "Yes, it is almost beyond belief, Mother. It is as if everything had been foreordained for us."

Deborah gazed at him fixedly.

"Why do you look at me like this? Do you not believe me?"

"I believe you, my husband," Deborah said quietly.

"And Joseph of Arimathea said that if my work was good, I might later be able to buy some land. He would like to part with some of it. He is old and does not wish for further wealth." He stared into his cup. "I will work, and I will buy. I want land of my own again, be it ever so little. We will all work. Ezekiel and I . . . and Rufus. We will get land here outside Jerusalem. Land for all of us."

Deborah looked at Rufus, saw that his lips had whitened. She saw him wander away behind the tree trunk, the scroll still in his hand. He stood there uncertainly, his shoulders bowed.

"We will work, from dawn to sunset," Ezekiel said. "We will work as we worked in Cyrene." He combed his graying beard with his gnarled fingers.

"Even harder," Simon said, and swallowed the last of the wine. "My muscles cry for labor," he said joyfully. "Why, we have been living the useless lives of peddlers."

He looked down at his wife. "And you, Mother? Will you care for us as you did in Cyrene? Tell me, are you not pleased?"

Deborah looked at him, lips quivering, bright tears gathering in her eyes. She nodded slowly as she put his sandals on his feet.

When he spoke again, his voice was humble. "Thank you, my Deborah. My feet feel refreshed and cool now." Then he called out, "Ezekiel, bring the donkeys. Rufus, pack up. We must move.

There is much to be done. That useless foreman left things in a sad mess."

Ezekiel walked off into the sunlight, and Rufus gathered their few belongings. Simon took Deborah's hand in his and drew her closer to him. "I am pleased for your sake, Mother. It is I who have dragged you through all this."

"No, it is something greater than ourselves," she whispered, and stroked his beard with her hands. In surprise he stared into her eyes. "It is not you or I who have the say. It is something beyond us that moves us this way or that, often without our knowing why it should be so. Perhaps we were brought here to perform some task—perchance a great one, perchance a little one . . . who can say?"

"You talk almost like the widow Naomi," he said absently, watching some worker bees fly past on their way back to the hive.

"What did she say?"

"She said that I was chosen . . . destined for something."

He felt her hands grip his wrists tightly, and he grew uneasy beneath her intense stare. He laughed, throwing back his head. "Imagine that—chosen! I suppose I'm to become the leading disciple of this Nazarene."

"Simon . . . did Naomi say you were chosen?"

"Yes . . . she said that. It's nonsense, of course." He fumbled under his garment. "Here, I've brought this for you." He handed her a tiny jar.

She opened it and laughed excitedly. "Simon . . . it's Egyptian perfume. And I thought you had no money left," she reproved him.

"I got it in exchange for one of those Roman knives that Alexander brought me," he said gaily.

"My husband," Deborah said, leaning against him. "You are very good to me."

He took the jar, tilted it against his fingers, and gently stroked her hair. Then he ran his finger tenderly over her forehead, noticing the fading bloom of youth on her blushing cheeks. He touched her head with his lips. "Now you are my bride again," he whispered.

"Tell me about Jerusalem," she said, blushing more deeply.

"It is greatly changed since I was there last—new squares,

new streets, new buildings. This Herod has an enormous palace. The whole place teems with people. Many are already here for the Passover—you can easily pick out the pilgrims."

"And the Nazarene . . . what do you hear about Him?"

"Nothing," he said shortly. He remained silent for a moment. And then: "Deborah . . ." His voice was urgent.

"Yes, Simon?"

"You must not let this Nazarene come between us."

"This Joseph of Arimathea . . . is he going to pay you for your work?"

Her deliberate change of subject made him frown.

"I do everything on the basis of half shares. He will help us with money until the harvest."

"Here is Ezekiel with the donkeys," she said, rising, and it seemed to him almost that she was glad for the interruption.

Simon rose also. A spirit of optimism and the will to work possessed him, and his uneasiness and doubt fled.

12

They sat on benches around the rough deal table in the little house near Gethsemane. The swan-shaped lamp, Alexander's gift, flickered cheerfully between them, casting a golden glow over their hands and faces.

They were eating supper early, for they were tired and hungry. Simon had spent the whole afternoon wandering through the richly budding orchards. Walking down to the fields, he had looked with deep satisfaction at the young crops—green, healthy, abundantly promising. He had checked up on the vats, sharpened two scythes, looked over two wooden plows, examined the olive press. Rufus and Ezekiel had cleared all the seeds from around the house, and Deborah had swept up inside with a broom that Simon had made for her of reeds from the Kidron. She had tidied the house and unpacked their things.

They ate griddlecakes with honey, and dates and raisins that Joseph of Arimathea had given them. There was even fresh milk, for Ezekiel had milked some goats that he discovered in the olive grove.

"The wheat is doing well. God willing, we shall have a good harvest," Simon said, dipping his griddlecake in the honey and eating with good appetite. "Joseph will give us half of the crops, even though we didn't sow them. There will be grapes and fruit in abundance—that I can see. But we shall be fully occupied with drying and pressing. The oil press needs repair. The wine vats are cracked and old. Work is not lacking . . . and neither is wine." His eyes twinkled.

"Wine?" Ezekiel asked with interest.

"Near the olive press is a small building where Joseph keeps his wine casks. He keeps it locked, but we may take as much as we want."

"Why is everything so neglected, my husband?" asked Deborah.

"Joseph of Arimathea told me that he has difficulty maintaining this place. He sits in the Sanhedrin and cannot always keep an eye on everything. He has already had a number of foremen, but none has been of any use. And everyone is so full of the coming Passover now that no one wants to work. 'I hope you will work better than they did,' Joseph said to me." Simon gave a deep laugh. "We will show him, Ezekiel, will we not?"

"We know how to work. We'll show him," Ezekiel said smugly.

"In a month's time he won't know this place," Simon said. "But we shall have to bend our backs. In some places the weeds are almost shoulder high. The soil must be loosened around the trees. The presses have to be cleaned, and there are casks with loose staves."

"What do we tackle tomorrow?" Ezekiel asked, full of enthusiasm.

"The trees, first. Rufus and you can begin with that, while I see to the threshing floor. The harvest will soon be upon us. I don't know what wielding a spade is going to do to Rufus's back." Simon and Ezekiel laughed, and both looked at Rufus.

"Will the spade suit you, rabbi?" he mocked lightly, noticing that Rufus's face was very pale. His auburn head was bowed; sweat glittered on his forehead.

Simon brought a date to his lips, but did not eat it. "What is the matter, Rufus? Are you ill? You haven't said a word the whole evening. Are you not thankful that we are back on the land?" Then Simon spoke more sharply. "Or do you long for the lights of Alexandria, for the airless temple galleries where they peddle wisdom?"

Deborah brushed her finger tips quickly over her cheeks.

The lamplight flickered and danced about them. The shadows of father and son on the mud-brick walls were agitated, like those of wrestlers endeavoring to overcome and destroy each other.

"Well, Rufus?"

Rufus's hands fluttered over his plate, toyed with a piece of griddlecake. When he spoke, his voice was flat. "Father, I don't think the land is for me. I—"

"You are not going to work on the land?" Simon leaned forward against the table top. His words rose like a flame between them.

"No, Father."

"But *I* say that you must. Ezekiel and I cannot do everything, and I won't have strangers here. Each one of us will have to work because we are making a new beginning. Everything we ever possessed is in Cyrene."

"Your father needs you, Rufus," Deborah said.

"I know, Mother, but I cannot help it. I am not suited to the land. I won't be much use."

"And what exactly *are* you suited for?" Simon's question was sharp.

Rufus looked up for the first time. Then he stared down reflectively at the wavy grain of the table top, his eyes bright, as if he were hesitating on some brink, as if he were about to give up something that had been precious but was now of little worth. Then he looked straight at Simon: "Father, I want to study further . . . with Gamaliel. I don't want to give up now. I got quite far in Alexandria."

Simon sat back, relieved. He even smiled, and with a careless gesture slammed his hand on the table. "Study further? What more can you learn than you have learned already? You are as clever as a rabbi."

Ezekiel helped himself hastily to a few raisins, quite unnecessarily, for he had finished eating. Deborah put her hands about a small earthenware pitcher filled with wine. Rufus's shoulders were bowed as if he were trying to escape from a blinding light, or from a truth that could cut through bonds and set hearts bleeding.

Simon sat motionless. His hands rested on the table, his nails glittered in the light. He spoke softly, but penetratingly. "There seems to be something you want to say, Rufus. There is something you are keeping back. Why don't you tell us what is in your heart?"

Rufus, disconcerted, looked at his father and read in his eyes the demand for confession. He knew that he had reached the point where nothing but the truth would do. He must risk Simon's wrath.

"I . . . I want to see whether Gamaliel can teach me something about the gospel of the Nazarene," Rufus said courageously.

He saw his father's fingers contract and grip the table top.

"They . . . Philo asked me to do it," he said, and then he felt a coward for the excuse he offered.

"The Nazarene. Always the Nazarene." Simon's eyes were narrow and his mouth a thin line in his beard.

"He has a new doctrine," Rufus said, as matter-of-factly as possible. "We want to make a study of it. That was Philo's last request to me. I owe this to Philo."

Simon spoke very softly, and very intensely. "Yes, He has a new doctrine, this Nazarene. He teaches Israel that the Sabbath can be desecrated, that a commandment can be broken. He teaches Israel that He is the lord of the Sabbath, the holy day of God. He, the carpenter, looks down upon the holy day of Israel. That is His preaching and His text. He teaches us that we can mix with lepers, that we may touch them, though it is forbidden by the law. He has violated the law of Moses. He set himself up to be greater than the law, greater than the holy institutions of Israel. *This* is His doctrine. Israel rejects the tax collectors, but your prophet from Nazareth falls upon their necks, makes them His friends, even His followers. Matthew, the tax collector, is one of His foremost followers, the same Matthew who bled his own people white to fill Rome's coffers. Such is this Nazarene. . . . And now the son of Simon Niger burns to study this man's teaching. What is there to learn about it? I have just told you what His teaching is."

Simon ceased talking suddenly, his neck thick with swollen veins, his forehead covered with sweat. "You are a fool, Rufus. I forbid you to have anything to do with this Nazarene. His teaching is evil, because it is against the highest and holiest institutions of Israel. I shall not allow His teaching to contaminate my house." The table shuddered under the blow of Simon's fist. Ezekiel stood up and walked into the darkness.

"His teaching is evil. I forbid you—"

"He preaches love." Rufus's voice was unsteady, but his hands lay quietly.

Simon did not look at his son. He looked searchingly at Deborah. He always sought an answer in her eyes whenever he had to cope with a crisis. But Deborah's eyes were wide and empty, holding no message for him. Her hands clutched tightly to the pitcher.

"So. His teaching is love?" He said it calmly, but anger surged through his words. "Love or no love, I forbid it. It is enough for me that He has desecrated the Sabbath, that He breaks a commandment."

"You must not forbid me, Father, because I shall have to disobey you."

"I am your father—"

"You are my father and I love you, but there are greater things than that!"

"What I say is law in this house!"

"Some things transcend any law of man."

Silence descended between them, as the shadows flickered on the walls. Simon's body seemed enfeebled by defeat and doubt. Only the muscles in his jaw flexed, and his beard jutted.

When he spoke again, Simon was looking into the lamplight that weaved and writhed from side to side as if there were something in it that he was searching for . . . another, richer life that had evaded him.

"And how long have you been deceiving me—and your mother —about this Nazarene?" Simon's tone was almost casual.

"I have not tried to deceive you."

"But you believe in Him, do you not? Or are you ashamed to admit you believe in a heretic?" Simon's voice was growing harsh.

"I believe in Jesus the Messiah . . . since last night." Rufus leaned forward, his head in his hands. Now that his deepest secret was out, his whole body seemed completely powerless.

Simon rose to his feet without realizing it and kicked the bench so that it fell clattering on the floor behind him.

Deborah also rose, but slowly and helplessly. "The leper?" she asked.

Rufus looked at his mother, begged for her protection with his eyes. "I went to the leper and spoke with him last night. He is healed. He is honest. I believe him. I believe that Jesus healed him. I believe He is the Messiah. I cannot help it. It is in my heart."

"Rufus . . . Rufus . . ." Deborah gasped.

"I forbade you to believe in this man," Simon spoke gratingly,

111

"but you believe in Him. You've shamed your mother and myself. You're taunting us, humiliating us."

"I can't help it, Father. When the leper spoke with me, I realized suddenly that Jesus is the Messiah. He is the Savior."

Simon snatched his knife and hurled it at the beam above the hearth.

"Get out of here before I break your neck!" His passion made his voice low and hoarse. ". . . before you defile this house. You shall live under my roof no more. Go to your Nazarene!" His eyes were turned upward as if he were in a state of ecstasy. "Begone from this house!"

"Simon . . . don't! He is our child!" Deborah warned.

Rufus stood erect. There was now no fear in him. Rather, a strange strength. He looked at his mother, then at his father. "I shall go. I shall pray for you."

"Do not pray for us. We have no need of your prayers. Go, before my temper gets the better of me."

Rufus walked to the door, stopped there, turned and looked at his mother. "My heart is free. I am delivered," he said, and she could see his victory in his eyes.

He turned and walked off into the darkness. They heard his footsteps fading into silence. He walked off under the stars toward the shelter of a haystack that he had seen that afternoon. The black mass of the Mount of Olives loomed up before him, and he smiled to see the torches light the way to Bethany.

Inside the house, in the dim lamplight, Simon turned around slowly. He looked wretchedly at Deborah, then shuffled away to the small window in the rear wall. He threw the shutters open and gazed out, waiting for her to come to him.

But only her voice reached him in his loneliness. "You behaved like a fool tonight, my husband."

"A fool? We have two sons. The one follows Rome, and the other a false prophet."

"They are our children. How can you pluck them from your heart because they don't believe as you do?"

"I am their father. I know what is right."

"And I am their mother. I know they are good, although they differ from us."

"Are you also against me? Am I alone?"

"I am not against you, but neither am I against our children. I am not going to allow you to drive them from our lives. They are our flesh and blood. We love them, and they love us. They have done no wrong."

"Done no wrong?" he asked resentfully. "The one serves a heathen people, and the other dances to the tune of a false prophet who is engaged in undermining the very foundations of Israel."

"No, it's only that they are different. Is that a sin? Even you have changed. Even Jerusalem is different. Everything changes. Youth cannot be the same as middle age."

He looked at the budding mulberry tree, silhouetted by the light shining from the window.

"If you continue to behave as you did this evening, my husband, you will surely be alone, for hate has no companions. Hatred is a lonely traveler on the road to nowhere."

Her words had lashed him into silence. When he turned around at last, the room seemed empty. Standing beside the table, Deborah seemed remote from him. Even Ezekiel, sitting on the threshold whittling a piece of wood, appeared far removed.

He looked at his wife and saw the grief he had brought her. He passed a hand wearily over his eyes, and his voice came falteringly: "My two sons . . . do I lack the wisdom to guide them anymore? Have I no strength to protect them? Have I become so great a sinner that God must break my house about my head? Have the traditions of Israel foundered, and the law lost all is meaning? Did we not rear them in the way Isaac reared his sons?" He motioned helplessly with his hands. "Are we inheriting a new world in which tax collectors and lepers and lawbreakers will be the new elect?"

He fell silent, and his hoarse voice lingered in the silence. He looked at his wife and realized that her eyes were veiled from him—it came to him with fear and suspicion. But he did not try to fathom it, for he was overcome by disillusionment and shock. He felt small in defeat. He looked out into the brooding darkness.

Suddenly she came to him, laid her hands upon his cheeks. "Perhaps we will understand them one day," she whispered. "One day, perhaps, we too will enter into a new world, my husband."

13

Rufus spent the night in the haystack. He slept soundly in the soft straw, though on occasion he was awakened by stray animals nibbling at the fodder.

At last bright daylight came, although the Mount of Olives still cast its dusky shadow. Rufus could see the roofs of the temple shining softly within the walls of Jerusalem.

He sat thinking over the events of the night before. He saw his mother's eyes again, wistful in their sadness, and his father's eyes, fiery in their anger. But he felt no regret, no fear. He gazed at the orchard of Gethsemane, emerging green from the darkness of the night, and looked toward the little house among the distant trees. He thought he saw his father walking in the yard, and his eyes grew tense.

Rufus lay for a while with his hands beneath his head, listening to Israel's city as it stirred to meet the day, exchanging slumber for the sun that rose behind the mountain. Then he turned, knelt in the straw, and prayed, searching in his mind for the presence of Jesus. He prayed with humility and deep gratitude, talking aloud in his lonely state so that a horse turned its head to look at him. He gave thanks that he believed and prayed that his parents and Ezekiel and Alexander would have faith too.

"Let them see Your light as I have seen it," Rufus prayed, and then he felt the warm sun touch his neck. When he opened his eyes, the sunlight was shining bright yellow upon the straw, turning each stalk to gold. He rose to see the city flirting with the sun, free from shadows and the dim legacy of night. The gardens of Gethsemane were green and fresh. Only the cool recesses of the trees remained dim and mysterious.

The young man shook the straw from his clothes and stretched his slender body. As he jumped down from the haystack, he thought of places where he might go. He turned right toward the city, and, when he reached the brook of Kidron below the city walls, he saw a wide gateway before him.

That's where I shall enter, Rufus thought. *I'll go and speak with Gamaliel and arrange to be his student.*

He descended to the stream and seated himself on a stone ridge beside a small pool. Pulling off his sandals, he washed his feet and legs in the cold, stimulating water. He took off his head-cloth and washed his face and neck, gasping as he splashed water over his head and body. Then he took off his outer garment and shook it violently to expel the dirt of many days. He beat it on the stones while the dust arose in clouds, and his muscular body swayed and shone in the sun. At last he spread out the garment to see if it were any cleaner. As he did so, he heard the tapping of little hooves behind him.

He swung around, then quickly donned his garment. On the bank a rider was approaching. Her donkey came at a steady trot, and dust puffed up beneath its hooves.

She was obviously making for a ford across the stream close to where Rufus stood.

Rufus pulled on his sandals. He did so clumsily, his eyes fixed on the rider. The woman sat astride, urging on her mount with a little olive branch. The donkey pricked his ears, flicked his tail, but maintained his even pace. The woman's garment was a dull grayish-brown, but her shawl was white.

As the donkey trotted into the stream, Rufus jumped up and ran toward it, jumping from stone to stone. When he caught up with the donkey and its rider in the middle of the stony ford, he took hold of the bit to halt the animal.

"I would like to ask you something, please," he said, speaking quickly so that the woman would not think that he meant to rob her or attack her.

The woman was young, though a little older than himself. Her eyes were emerald with a lively spirit in their depths. The beauty of her face, noble and serene, astonished him. Her hair was heavy and held the light of polished bronze. She looked at him so calmly that he felt abashed.

"I am rather in a hurry, stranger," she said. Her voice was as deep and as gentle as her appearance.

He let go of the bit and put his hand to his chin. "I am strange here," he confessed, and smiled uncertainly. "I wanted to know where Gamaliel lives, the great teacher in Jerusalem."

"Gamaliel?" she asked, and he saw surprise flicker in her eyes.

He nodded. "I wish to study under him. I come from Alexandria, where I was a student of Philo Judaeus."

She moved her lips as if about to speak, but then stayed silent, looking into his eyes. He shifted his feet awkwardly.

Finally she spoke. "Gamaliel lives in the shadow of the temple, close to the Tower of Antonia where the Romans house their soldiers." It seemed to him that contempt lay beneath the words.

He frowned, but before he could say more, she started off again. Rufus kept beside her, stumbling and slipping over stones.

"May I accompany you? I am a stranger, as I said. It will be hard to find my way about—I've never been to Jerusalem before." He smiled, watching her face eagerly. "Perhaps you could show me more easily once we're through the gate."

"As I told you, I am in a hurry," she said shortly. "We have illness at home."

"Illness?" He quickened his pace, half-running, for she was urging on the donkey with little cries. "Are you fetching a doctor? Where do you live?"

With the branch she pointed vaguely behind her. "We live in Bethany, beyond the Mount of Olives."

"What is wrong?" he asked. Giving her a sidelong glance, he saw her blink her eyes and turn away her head. But when she spoke her voice was calm.

"It is my brother. The sun has stricken him, and he is feverish."

"Is it serious?"

She nodded, looking down. "We all love him very much. He is good and gentle."

"What does he do?"

"He is a potter. That's why we live in Bethany. There is good clay there." She pointed with her olive branch to a line of women who, with pitchers on their heads, were walking toward the city gate. "Many of those pitchers were probably made by my brother. Almost everyone in Jerusalem knows him."

"What is his name?"

"Lazarus."

Rufus stared down at footprints and stones worn down by many hooves. Lazarus. The name meant nothing to him.

"There must surely be a doctor you know—somebody who can reduce the fever?"

She flicked the donkey again and tugged the reins.

"I am not calling a doctor."

"Indeed?"

"I am looking for someone to send to Jesus of Nazareth."

Rufus, who was holding the bridle of the donkey, jerked the animal to a halt so suddenly that the young woman almost toppled forward. He gaped at her with wide eyes.

"Jesus? Jesus, the Nazarene?"

She nodded.

"The man who preaches in Galilee?"

"There is but one Jesus of Nazareth." For the first time a smile lit up her eyes.

"I don't understand . . ."

"He is a friend of our family. Jesus always stays with us. Only He can cure my brother. We must send someone to fetch Him. I know someone in Jerusalem. We can't send just anybody."

Rufus stared at her with narrowed eyes. His mouth was dry, and suddenly his legs felt weak. He moved closer to her, so that the scent of myrrh on her hair came to his nostrils. He licked his lips and said hoarsely, "Someone in Jerusalem? Why can't I go? I will go . . . I will fetch Him . . . now . . . at once!"

She stared at him for a long time. "But I don't know you at all. I don't even know whether you believe in Him."

He gripped her hand with sudden impulse. He pressed it so tightly that she flinched.

"I believe," he said softly. "I believe in Him. I believe in the power of His works: I have seen a leper He healed."

"Simon of Bethany?"

"No, Nimrod, the shepherd of Joseph of Arimathea."

He saw her eyes soften and knew that he had been accepted.

"May I go?" he asked again.

Gazing at him, she said, "You may go, stranger, although I don't even know your name."

"Rufus . . . Rufus of Cyrene."

"Cyrene?"

Alarmed, he bowed his head and shook it in denial. "No, not Cyrene—Alexandria. What is your name?"

"Mary."

"It is a worthy name."

She did not answer. She looked at his weatherworn garment, at his square shoulders, at the youthful vigor of his neck.

"Where is Jesus?" he asked.

"We hear He is in Perea, beyond the Jordan."

"How far is that?"

"About one day's journey."

"I will go." He seized the bit of the donkey, turned him around, and they crossed the ford over the brook of Kidron. He tugged at the animal's head. Soon he was running alongside with long, swinging strides, as the donkey bore Mary in the direction of Bethany.

Even before Rufus had seen the sunlight gild the roofs of the temple, Simon and Ezekiel were up and stirring. With an old spade he had found under a tree, Ezekiel busied himself cleaning out furrows and strengthening the walls. Simon went down to the Kidron, cut a bunch of reeds, fashioned it into a broom, and with vigorous strokes began to scrub out the big wine press. Deborah too had left the house. She went to the big drying racks and busied herself removing broken rungs for Simon to replace before the drying time.

When Simon had swept the press and examined it for cracks, he visited the drying racks. He wanted to be with Deborah. He peered through the trees half expecting to see Rufus returning down the shaded path, but it was empty.

"How is the rack, Mother? Shall we be able to dry on it?"

"Many rungs have to be removed. You will have to put in new ones, Father."

"Are you going to dry a lot of fruit?" His eyes smiled.

118

"I mean to," she said, and for just a moment the sorrow vanished from her eyes.

"We shall be kept busy," he said enthusiastically. "Pressing grapes and olives and harvesting wheat. I already feel the stir of summer, and we are short of help."

She sensed the reproach in his voice. "I will help," she offered.

"I can't accept your offer," he said emphatically. "Two grownup sons, and you, a woman, work on the land! I won't allow it." He pulled out a rotten rung and flung it aside. "I will mend it for you, Mother, long before the figs have ripened. I am going to see what Ezekiel is doing." He turned, then halted, looking over his shoulder at her. "Do you think he will come back?"

"He will return," she said with certainty. "You were cruel last night, my husband. If he returns, you must not reject him. He is our child, and still so young."

"But he doesn't believe as we do. He doesn't believe as a Jew ought to believe. His mind has been twisted by those people in Alexandria."

"To believe in God is enough—and he believes. We cannot tell him what his heart must hold."

"To believe in God is not enough. You must also believe in what is right . . . you must follow Israel."

"When he returns, you must not spurn him."

Simon walked quickly toward Ezekiel, and Deborah gazed after him, her heart filled with love for him . . . and pity, for she knew how he yearned to have his sons with him on the land.

They worked in the orchard until noon, when Ezekiel and Simon went back once again to the big wine press. Simon had his old sword and Ezekiel the blade of an old scythe. They scratched the cracks clean, preparatory to plastering them in readiness for the time of pressing.

"Your joints are getting stiff, good Israelite," Simon gibed. "You must be getting old."

"We are both getting old," Ezekiel said, looking at Deborah, who had come to see how they were doing.

"A man is riding this way on a donkey," Deborah told them.

Simon stopped work and peered over the edge of the press. "Oh, it must be Joseph of Arimathea," he said, "coming to see whether his hirelings are busy."

Joseph reached the press and pulled up his mount. "Ah, you're in a hurry with the vat," he said. "The grapes have scarcely started swelling and you're nearly ready for the pressing."

"What is done, is done," Simon remarked. "We still have to put in a lot of work on the olive press. It is inclined to leak, and a number of bungs have worked loose. It will be quite a task to fix it. . . . Joseph of Arimathea, this is my wife, Deborah, and this is my faithful helper, Ezekiel."

"Peace be with you, Deborah," Joseph said, and his eyes were kindly above his graying beard. "I have brought you a bag of meal and salt and other necessities. I thought they might come in handy now."

"Peace, Joseph of Arimathea," Deborah said. "I am very grateful—we are not overburdened with supplies."

"Simon," Joseph continued, "you must send your servant to fetch a sacrificial animal from Nimrod, my shepherd. His place is near the water holes on the Joppa road."

"I know of him," Simon said quickly, almost indifferently.

Joseph went over to the donkey and relieved it of its load. "How are the vats?" he asked while he was doing this.

"A number of staves are broken," Simon replied.

"I'll see to it that you get new ones by next week. You are an energetic man, Simon. It is the first time that Gethsemane has known such labor."

Joseph returned to the press. "I just came to bring you these few things. Now I must leave."

"Why be in such a hurry?" Deborah asked. "I was just going to fetch a little refreshment."

"Good woman," Joseph replied, "I should have liked to linger here, for it pleases me to watch busy men at work, but I must return. Caiaphas, the high priest, wishes to see me. I understand this Nazarene is returning to Jerusalem, this Jesus—"

Simon's busy hands stopped moving as he looked up at the landowner.

"Jesus?" Deborah asked, and gave her husband a quick glance.

"Yes, whenever He comes here, there is trouble. We had a lot of bother the last time—the Jews here wanted to stone Him. He overturned the temple tables and used a whip on some priests and buyers. If the Romans hadn't intervened, the temple guards would certainly have killed Him."

"What does He want here now?" Simon asked.

Joseph shrugged his shoulders. "I gather that a man named Lazarus of Bethany is seriously ill, and his sisters have sent for Jesus. But in any case, He would have been here for the Passover. When He comes to Jerusalem we must be on our guard. Strange man, this Jesus. Many follow Him, and many hate Him. . . . But now I must go. Caiaphas doesn't like to be kept waiting. Peace be with you."

"Peace be with you, Joseph of Arimathea," all three said, and they gazed after the old man as he mounted his donkey and rode away.

14

The dawn was red when Rufus returned to the little house in Bethany. He pulled up under the big fig tree and slid from the horse that had been lent to him for his journey to Perea. His legs trembled under him, for he was not used to riding. His head felt dull and his eyes confused from the things he had seen on his journey.

There were many people around the house. Some were standing talking in the first faint light; others were resting against the walls of the cottage. He glanced at the shed that Lazarus used for his work, and he could vaguely see the shapes of pitchers, of vases, of large clay bowls that awaited baking in the oven. But the oven was black and cold, and round about were scattered shards of vessels that had been broken before completion.

Some of the people looked at him, but none greeted him, for he was a stranger. Rufus led his horse, its flanks heaving and flecked with foam, and tied it to a branch. Then he went to a tub that stood at one side of the shed, thrust in his hands and washed his face and arms. As he straightened up, head aching and eyes throbbing, he noticed the light growing brighter in the east. In the shed a faint luminosity dwelt on the handiwork of Lazarus.

He walked to the house and then stood still. The thumping of his heart grew louder, and he listened intently, his head to one side. Then he hesitated no longer. He went in quickly but halted in the doorway at the aromatic smell of balsam. He hesitated uncertainly, for gloom dwelt inside the house. A smoking oil lamp stood upon a table.

Through a curtain Rufus could see a dim light burning in the room beyond. He walked toward it, parted the curtains, and stopped in the doorway.

He stood and stared upon death. Lazarus lay with face upturned on a low bedstead against the wall. His hands, crossed on his breast, gleamed oddly in the light of the tall candle placed before the bed. His cheeks were sunken, and the cheekbones deeply shadowed. His eyes were caverns, his lips twisted, as if in pain.

Rufus gazed for a long time at the man who, only the morning before, he had seen living, panting with fever and tossing restlessly. Then he looked at the girl who lay on a mat under the window at the foot of the bed. It was Martha, Mary's sister. She was fast asleep.

He glanced at her only for a moment, for a figure was sitting at the bedside, bowed and weeping, seemingly more overwhelmed by death than the lifeless corpse itself. Her hair shone in the candlelight, and her head was low on her crossed arms.

Rufus stood there uncertainly, not knowing if he should turn and leave. He gripped the soft folds of the curtains, watching her heartbreak and despair. He heard her low, unrestrained moans. She sat in an attitude of surrender, twisting her hands into the coarse sheet.

Rufus moved in the doorway, prepared himself to speak, but suppressed all speech, looking with deep compassion at her heaving shoulders and contorted hands. He noticed with gladness how the candlelight was dying before the onslaught of the sun, which seemed to pierce the walls. It brought an answering glimmer from the slits of the dead man's eyes.

At last Mary rose, pulled the white sheet higher over his chest, and laid her hand on his forehead as if to feel if he had fever. She felt his hands and touched his cheek with the tips of her fingers, tenderly.

"Mary."

Rufus spoke her name gently, but in the silence it sounded loud enough to cause the candlelight to waver.

She turned slowly from beside her brother's body. Her dark hair was disheveled. Her eyes were dull, swollen with fatigue and tears; her face was tense and white. She stared at him as at a stranger.

"Mary, I . . . I saw Jesus at a fountain near Bethabara in Perea. He was spending the night there with His disciples. I found them there last night."

His words brought life to Mary. A sob broke from her. She came toward him, slowly at first, but then she ran and grasped his shoulders.

"Jesus—did you see Him?"

"He is coming. I saw Him. I told Him of your brother Lazarus."

"What did He say?"

"He said, 'Come, let us go again to Judea. Lazarus, our friend, sleeps, but I will go to wake him.'"

"Did he say that?" Mary asked, clutching his garment fiercely.

"That is what He said. The disciples said He should not return again, that the Jews were going to stone Him in Jerusalem. But He said that He would come."

"When? Why didn't you bring Him with you?"

"He is coming on His own. I don't know when."

Mary pressed her head against his chest. "Then it is too late . . . too late," she whispered. "If He had been here, Lazarus would not have died. He died soon after you left here, Rufus."

Rufus stroked her hair gently from her face and clasped her tightly against him, just as if they had known each other for many years. "Mary," he said, "I think Jesus knows that Lazarus is dead."

"He knows? How can He know?"

"I'm sure He knows. That's why He said Lazarus was sleeping and He must come to wake him."

She looked around at her brother and then again at Rufus, her eyes wide. "Do you think He knows? Do you really think so? Are you sure?"

"I do think so . . . I am certain. When I told Him about Lazarus, He grew quite pale. I think He was deeply grieved. He rose, walked some distance, and then returned. It was then that He told His disciples they must come here."

"Can He have such power that He knew Lazarus was dead?"

"I think so," Rufus whispered. "It was the first time I had ever seen Him, but I think that with Him all things are possible."

She clutched Rufus's cloak and pressed it to her face, leaning against him. He held her and let her cry.

"Come, Mary," he said at last. He held her off and looked into her eyes. "It is time you were out of here. Let us go out to the daylight."

She saw him look at the sleeping Martha. "She sat up with Lazarus for the first part of the night. She is exhausted," Mary said.

Rufus blew out the candles.

He put his arm around her and led her to the kitchen, where he made up the fire on the hearth. She seated herself on a low bench and laid her hand on a big water pitcher that Lazarus had made.

As Rufus blew the old coals to a blaze and fed the fire with fresh wood, he heard Mary say, "We must put him in the sepulcher this morning."

He turned from the hearth. "Put him away? Before Jesus comes?"

"We must. He died yesterday."

"Where is his resting place?"

"In the cave in the rocky hill behind the garden. . . . I was there yesterday. There is no better place."

"But what . . . what about when Jesus comes?" he asked.

"We cannot leave him here. When Jesus comes, He can see him in the cave."

"I should like to see the cave."

They walked out past the people who waited silently, and through the garden, listening to the birds rejoicing that the sun had risen once again. Mary paused at an old bench beneath a tree and touched the rough wood. "He often sat here and talked to Jesus when first we came to know Him. Jesus sat there—on this side. Martha and I very often washed His feet—here, beneath this tree. It was here that He said to Lazarus, 'I shall not build a kingdom of this world. My kingdom will be in the heart of man.'" Rufus looked at her intently.

They reached the cave, entered, and stood in its cool dimness, full of moist earth, dripping wet rocks, and old straw.

"Once during the winter, Jesus was with us, and Lazarus let some of His disciples sleep here—on the straw."

Rufus regarded her in the silence of the cave.

"This will be a suitable resting place for him," she said softly. "It was here that he hid Jesus once—after He had overturned the temple tables and when the Pharisees were trying to kill Him. I think His spirit is still here . . . it hasn't faded yet."

"I think His spirit is everywhere," Rufus said, awed, looking about him in the cave. "Here, in the sky, on the sea, and beneath the earth—it is everywhere."

"You are a good man, Rufus. You are a stranger, and yet you are a friend. I feel as if I have known you a long time, though I saw you for the first time yesterday," Mary said.

He turned and looked about him. "I will get this cave in order," he said. "I will heap up stones to form a bier for Lazarus. Is there a spade I could use?" He walked to the entrance, but stopped when he heard her words.

"You are young and alone, Rufus. Did you come here on your own?"

"I am not alone. My parents are here too. They are in Gethsemane. My father works in the gardens of Joseph of Arimathea. My father . . . does not believe in Jesus of Nazareth."

She had seated herself on a stone, but now she rose quickly to her feet. She did not speak, but he knew what he must say. "My father drove me from the house because I do."

He left the cave, and, when she followed him to the entrance, she saw him going down the hill rapidly, stumbling and swaying. He was looking in the direction of Jerusalem, but the green bulk of the Mount of Olives hid it from his view.

The first sunlight was just touching the crown of Zion when Simon and Ezekiel entered Jerusalem with their black donkey through the East Gate. A load of firewood dangled from each side of the animal.

Eagerly they entered the awakening city. Ezekiel led the donkey and Simon urged it on with his rough staff. Each was clothed in a garment with a hood that concealed his face.

"We look like a pair of scoundrels this morning," Ezekiel said when they were through the gate.

Simon stepped around a puddle of water. That night rain had fallen from the north. "It is better this way," he said. "If we were recognized, it would be our end."

"Do you think we'll be able to sell this wood?" Ezekiel asked.

"I think so. There are many pilgrims here for the Passover. And in a city there is always call for firewood."

They walked along, looking around, through the holy city, for it was many years since the time of their visit there together, and Simon had kept to the side streets the day he sought out Joseph of Arimathea.

They turned into the Road of the Tanners. "I think this is where most of the money is," Simon said, "unless, perhaps, in the merchants' quarter."

The leather workers were preparing for the day—removing barricades from their shops, carrying skins to tanning vats, taking down strips of leather from the walls, spreading prepared skins on the tables in readiness for cutting, lifting half-completed harnesses from hooks to do further work on them, sharpening their awls.

Simon thought of what Deborah had said the day before: "When are we going to make a thank offering, husband? We haven't done so yet."

"What can we offer?" he had asked.

"We still have enough money for two pigeons," Deborah replied. But it was Ezekiel who had come forward with the plan. "Why don't we sell some firewood and buy an offering with the money that we make? We have cut out a great deal of dead wood."

A burly harness maker beckoned to them, and they turned toward him gratefully. He was busy fastening a large red leather apron around his waist as they halted the donkey in front of him.

"Is that wood for sale?" he asked in a harsh voice.

"Yes, we've brought it here to sell," Simon said cheerfully, pleased to have found a buyer so quickly.

"How much?"

"Four shekels for the two bundles."

"Too much. I will pay three shekels for the load."

"But . . ." Simon could not continue, for just then the temple trumpets sounded. The harness maker bowed his head; his lips moved as he prayed to the God of the covenant. Simon and Ezekiel did likewise. They knew the trumpets meant that the priests were laying the first sacrifice of the day on the consuming fire. It was a sacred moment.

"Three shekels," the harness maker said quickly as he ceased praying and the trumpets died away.

"Very well," Simon answered. He lifted the wood from the donkey's back, and the harness maker carried it inside.

"You sold much too cheaply," Ezekiel complained. "We should have gotten four shekels."

Simon looked at him strangely. "God has been good to us," he said. "He brought us safely to His city. What does it matter whether we offer one shekel or ten? It comes from our hearts. We give out of gratitude. We shall not quibble over the price of wood, Ezekiel. Sometimes the offering of a dove is of more account than that of a yearling calf."

The harness maker returned and slipped the money into Simon's hand.

"Are there any more in this street who'll take my firewood?" Simon asked.

"You'll be able to sell all you have in this street," said the man with a rumbling laugh. "The tanners and harness makers are full of money. There are hundreds of pilgrims here, and each one of them has brought hides for tanning and wants harnesses or other articles made."

Simon and Ezekiel moved off, tied the donkey to a tree at the side of the street, and walked toward the temple. Simon pulled the hood of his garment more completely over his face and walked with head bowed. He raised it only when he saw the line of Roman soldiers stationed at the entrance to the temple grounds. He stopped short. "What are they doing here? They don't belong . . . this is a holy place," he muttered.

"I don't think they are actually guarding it. I think they are here so that the Jews will remember that Rome is present in Jerusalem," Ezekiel said.

"It must be that," Simon agreed.

They were filled with emotion as they gazed up at the massive stone walls of the temple, at the mighty doors, at the roofs that glittered in the sunlight

"Let us make our offering," Simon said as they passed through the gate into the Court of the Gentiles. They were lost in the mass of pilgrims and worshipers who were exchanging Roman money for shekels to make their offerings, or buying pigeons, lambs, or calves for sacrifice. They stood absorbed in the noise and bustle of haggling men, jingling coins, conversing priests; they stood in the prayerful attitude of pilgrims awe-struck and humble at their first sight of the temple.

Simon and Ezekiel ascended the fifteen marble steps into the Court of the Israelites. They could see into the Court of Priests, where only the priests could go, and beyond, higher up, the short staircase that led to the temple proper. Within this structure, closed off by a veil, was the most holy region of the temple, where very few could enter. Simon looked at it and whispered to Ezekiel, "In there is the Holy of Holies . . . the place of the ark of the covenant."

Ezekiel scarcely breathed. The noise around them did not reach their ears as they stared toward the place where the most sacred possession of Israel, long lost, was hallowed by the dark emptiness of the room.

They turned then and sought out a priest. Simon closed his eyes and, handing over his coins one by one, gave thanks to God for bringing them all safely to Jerusalem.

Leaving the inner court after they had offered, they noticed a great throng of people in one corner of the Court of the Gentiles. They moved toward it and saw that someone was preaching, a young-looking Pharisee, making motions with his arms. He was small, with crooked legs and a raucous voice.

"Did God not give the law to Moses after he had led Israel from Egypt?" shouted the little man, and his eyes glared. "That is the law of Israel, and there is no other, for it is the law of the God of Abraham. Who is this Jesus to break our law?"

"He is a heretic," the crowd screamed in reply.

The Pharisee raised his hands for silence. His voice was low: "Have you heard how He has broken the Sabbath? The Sabbath of the Lord? The day of rest and prayer?"

"Tell us!" they yelled.

"Yes, that is what He did. On the Sabbath He allowed His men to gather food, to pluck the ears of wheat."

A furious muttering swept the crowd.

Simon and Ezekiel saw how people stood on tiptoe to see the speaker. Ezekiel himself craned his neck in order to see the man with the glaring eyes.

"He consorts with lepers," the speaker said, seeming to spit out the words. "What does the law say regarding this?"

He closed his eyes and waited for the answer. And the crowd shouted it back at him. "The leper is untouchable. He must not be touched!"

"So it is, my people," the little man said, and his eyes glittered with triumph. "That is what the law of Israel says. But this carpenter holds communion with lepers."

"And what of that tax collector, Matthew?" a man yelled.

"Yes, a tax collector is one of His disciples—one of the tools of Rome, one of the betrayers of Israel."

A shudder passed through the crowd. They milled about as if their anger could no longer be supported. "He must die," one shouted. And then all roared it out together. "He must die!"

They calmed down again and listened. "Let the Romans make a cross for Him," one called out, and a gale of laughter swept across the Court of the Gentiles.

The orator held up his hands, again compelling silence. "He incites the people," he cried. "He pretends to be king. What will Rome do, do you think? Do we want blood to flow and flames to ravage Israel once again?"

"No!" one shouted. "Not blood and crosses once again as when Judas of Galilee rose."

"As Judas of Galilee misled the people, so this man misleads them. Have you heard what happened in African Cyrene?"

Simon stiffened. Ezekiel looked at him quickly with fear in his eyes. There was deep silence in the courtyard. Even the money changers ceased their babble.

"Nearly two thousand died in Cyrene, Jews and Greeks. The hand of Rome raised crosses there. Crosses stood thick upon a hill, because one Jew rose against Rome."

Simon stared at the ground, closed his eyes, and his neck felt damp with sweat. Cyrene . . . and Alexandria. What might have happened in Alexandria?

"Blood will flow here as in Cyrene," the speaker shouted.

"We want no blood!" the crowd screamed in reply.

"There will certainly be blood if Jesus continues," the Pharisee assured them. "Blood as in Africa. Jerusalem will bleed as

Cyrene bled. This Nazarene pretends innocence, but He represents Himself to be the new king of the Jews." The speaker flung out his arm. "Look toward the entrance to our temple, there outside the gates!" he shouted. "There stand the soldiers of Rome. Do you see them? Look, and you will know what gifts this man will bring you."

Everybody looked toward it, as did Simon and Ezekiel. They saw the broad points of the spears glinting in the sun, the breastplates and the shields.

"If He were the true king, if He were the savior of Israel, as He says, then we should shed our blood to achieve our freedom. Then we would offer up our lives. Then we should not fear Rome. But He is not. He is a seducer, like Judas of Galilee who perished on the cross." He was silent for a moment. "Are we to bleed for this Nazarene? "

"No!" they roared. "We won't shed our blood for a carpenter!"

"He will come to the Passover," someone shouted. "Then He will fall into our hands."

Simon tugged at Ezekiel's garment, and they made their way through the crowd toward the gate. They heard the people shout "Saul! Saul!"

Looking back, they saw the crowds swarming around the speaker, hoisting him and carrying him aloft, praising him enthusiastically.

They reached the gate. Just outside the temple grounds, Simon stopped. He looked at the red plume of a Roman soldier and said, "When I drove Rufus away, in your heart you blamed me. Now you have heard, Ezekiel. You yourself have heard the wise words of this learned man concerning the Nazarene."

"It is the truth," Ezekiel conceded. "What you did was right, Simon of Cyrene." The foreman spoke softly as they went out onto the street. The air outside was fresh and chilly, and although they did not say it, they felt in their bones that the winter lingered still.

15

It was noon, two days after Simon and Ezekiel had listened to the young man at the temple. But they were not thinking of the eloquence of the Pharisee. They were far too busy. They had caulked every crack and crevice in the wine press, and now it was ready for the treading of the grapes.

"We have finished, Mother," Simon said excitedly as Deborah appeared with their lunch. "As tight as a gourd," he added, admiring their handiwork.

"All we need are the grapes," Ezekiel laughed.

"The grapes will come in their due season," Simon said cheerfully, taking the food basket from Deborah. "This vineyard will be full of them."

"You have worked quickly, husband," Deborah said. "What are you going to do next?"

"We are going to turn up the soil under all the trees. This must be finished before the rain. The threshing floor is badly broken up, and must be replastered. After that we will start on the olive press."

"Here comes a rider. I'll be going," Deborah said.

Simon peered over the edge of the press. "Just the man we want to see," he said. "Joseph of Arimathea. Now he can see again how his new employees work."

Joseph pulled up his donkey nearby and dismounted with difficulty, for age had stiffened his limbs.

"Peace be with you, Joseph of Arimathea," Simon said. "Your wine press is watertight once more."

"Mercy, but you work quickly," said the old man. "Now we can press again. Our vats must be empty." He shook his shoulders. "Winter is loathe to leave us."

The old man looked up at the trees where the first green quivered, walked up to one, and flicked his whip against its trunk.

Then he cracked his whip with such force that the donkey jerked up in head in fright. He seemed to have forgotten about the wine press. He looked at Simon and Ezekiel, then at the Mount of Olives, then up toward the sky, like one who searches.

All at once he sat down on an old cask. With an embarrassed expression he said, "I like coming here when I'm worried or have a problem to solve. It is quiet . . . here in the gardens of Gethsemane." He pulled his loose garment closer about his shoulders and nervously fingered his beard.

Simon climbed from the wine press and sat down on a stone opposite his employer. He gave a light laugh. "What problems can Joseph of Arimathea have? You are a rich man and have no cares."

"There are troubles that wealth is unable to dispel," Joseph said, looking at them sharply and then relapsing into silence.

"There seems to be something on your mind, Joseph of Arimathea," said Simon. "Is it something we should know?"

"Perhaps that's why I came here—to talk," Joseph said, almost apologetically. "There are things one must talk about . . . here, where it's restful and there are good people like yourselves." He rose, took a few quick steps, and stopped with his back to Simon. His head was raised, and for a moment he seemed almost in a trance. His voice was high and quavering. "I have seen something. . . . Today something happened . . . something beyond belief."

Ezekiel began to untie the cloth that covered the basket.

"Something beyond belief?" Simon asked.

Joseph of Arimathea turned toward them. "The Nazarene . . ." he said, his words coming faster, "He raised a man from the dead.

Simon looked at the old man from under knitted brows. A short laugh shook him. Then he looked down at the dark brown earth and pityingly shook his head.

The words broke the tension in Joseph. He came back slowly and sat down on the cask again. He passed his hand over his face. "This man Lazarus, a potter of Bethany—the Nazarene raised him from the dead. He had been dead for nearly four days. We had laid him away in a cave. They said the Nazarene stood before the cave and called out Lazarus's name . . . and then Lazarus came forth, still covered in his winding sheet, with the shroud over his face. Many people saw it. Lazarus is alive."

Sweat ran down Joseph's forehead. He pulled back his head-cloth and wiped his brow.

Simon smiled grimly at Joseph. "Joseph of Arimathea," he said, "you are an elder of the people; you are a leading citizen of Jerusalem; you sit on the Sanhedrin. You mustn't say such things. I am a simple man, but I tell you, I do not believe that."

"The day will come when you will believe, for I know it is true."

"How can it be true when the man has been dead for four whole days? Nobody can be raised from the dead after four days."

"It was done. The Nazarene did it, today—this morning."

"It can't be true. It is blasphemy, for death is in the hands of God."

"Today death has been conquered—in Bethany."

"Nobody can conquer death."

"I saw it with my own eyes," Joseph insisted. "I know that Lazarus was dead. I helped place him in his tomb. He has done much work for me, and I know him and his family well. He was dead when we laid him away. Everybody knew that he was dead."

"What concern is it of mine if he was dead?" Simon said, wiping the perspiration from his eyes.

"I am telling you what happened. Early this morning I was in Bethany. And Lazarus was alive. He is still alive. I talked to him. I know him. I have known him for years. I'm telling you, he lives. The Nazarene raised him, and he lives."

Simon bent down, gripped an old keg, and flung it against the trunk of a mulberry see, smashing it to pieces and scattering the stones.

"Why am I pursued with this Nazarene?" he shouted, lurching toward Joseph. "Why do you bring Him back into my life again? I have nothing to do with Him. I don't want to hear about Him, for I know He will destroy Israel. I don't want to know about Him . . . I don't want to hear!" The big man looked as if he were about to crush the frail form of Joseph in his hands. "He destroyed my house—because of Him I cast my son away."

He gasped for breath, then slowly composed himself and

stood bowed before Joseph. He made a helpless gesture with his hands. "I am a simple man. At the temple I gave ear to Saul. He put things in a way that I cannot—how this Nazarene breaks the law, desecrates the Sabbath. How He betrays Israel."

He looked pleadingly at Joseph.

"All I want is to work in peace on the land and go to the temple with my offering," Simon said evenly. "But time and again, over and over, people plague me with this Nazarene, break up my life, make my heart beat as if it is on the point of bursting. I don't believe in Him, but always there is someone to torture me with Him." He clenched his fists and pressed his arms fiercely to his chest. "Why? In God's name, why?"

"Why such a tumult about this Nazarene, man from Africa?" Joseph asked calmly. "If you don't believe, you don't believe. That's all. I merely came to tell you what I have seen."

"Please stop. . . . I don't want to hear any more. I don't want to call you, an elder of Jerusalem, a liar, for you are an old man and you have been good to me. Please say no more."

Simon walked over to the tree against which he had broken the keg, and leaned against the trunk pressing his hands against his eyes. Only when Joseph of Arimathea spoke again did he remember the presence of the old man.

"I did not come here to make you angry. I didn't know about your son. Does he believe in the Nazarene?"

"He believes. I cast him out. That is bad. I miss him, and my Deborah longs for him. . . . I would keep my house unbroken."

"I only came to converse with you, for there are things too big to keep to one's self—like a vat that overflows."

Simon turned his head and looked at Joseph, who was standing there smiling at him. "I'm sorry for the way I spoke, Joseph of Arimathea," he confessed. "But in Africa I saw what Rome does to quell rebellion. And according to Saul the same thing might happen in Jerusalem because of this carpenter."

"I don't think He will have much opportunity to cause that," Joseph said confidentially, flicking at a dry twig with his whip.

"What do you mean?"

"When it became known that Lazarus had risen, the Sanhedrin called a meeting—an emergency meeting. It was . . . well, it was decided that an end be put to His career."

"It is not for me to counsel the Sanhedrin, but the time is long overdue when something should be done. What has this . . . this Lazarus to do with it?"

Joseph looked carefully at Simon. But he saw that the big man was calm, leaning lightly against the tree trunk.

"Today's happening is a great miracle, man from Africa. I don't ask you to believe it—I am only telling you what is said. I was specially sent by the Sanhedrin to see whether it was true. I found Lazarus alive, and I came back and reported to the Sanhedrin. Then Caiaphas said that it would be better for the Nazarene to die before the whole nation perished in a Roman persecution. The Sanhedrin knows that this miracle can cause a revolution in Israel. From today Jesus will be looked on as the leader of the Jews. There is no preventing that. This deed raised Him above everything and everybody, above all who have gone before, perhaps even above Moses. At least in the eyes of the Jews who believe in Him. And revolution is in the air, like the bite of winter."

"What do you think of this Nazarene, Joseph of Arimathea?"

Joseph shrugged his shoulders and sat down with his back to Simon, his face toward Jerusalem. "I am an old man—what does it matter what I believe?"

"You are an important man." Simon looked at his narrow shoulders, at the jutting beard.

"I have no desire to see blood spilled again," Joseph said. "I had my fill of that when Judas of Galilee rebelled. Rome gives you the rope, then hangs you with it. You may wish to fly, provided you do not soar as high as the Roman eagle. You can be free as long as you rest content with the freedom of a slave. The day when Rome considers that this man of Galilee has gone too far, that day blood will flow in Israel. The day He appears to overshadow Tiberius, even in Galilee, that day Rome unsheaths her sword. So Caiaphas says: 'Rather the blood of one man than that of a whole people.'"

"And what do you say, Joseph of Arimathea?"

"What does it matter what I say?" Joseph asked. "I might well ask: What do you say, Simon? It's a question we both must answer."

"You are an elder of the people, I a lowly laborer."

"Your soul has the same worth as mine. You owe yourself as much as I owe to myself."

They remained silent for a long time in the glow of afternoon. Then Joseph rose slowly, bent and tired. He turned toward Simon, who was still leaning motionless against the tree. "After today thousands more will believe in Him, man from Africa," Joseph said. "That is one side of the balance. On the other is the temple and the Pharisees—like that young Saul who is inciting the people against Him. Just now I saw a vision of blood in the sky above Jerusalem. And yet, this Nazarene has no taste for bloodshed. He is a man of peace."

Joseph looked at Simon and, shaking his head, took out a Roman coin and looked at the image of the Emperor upon it. "Strange man, this Nazarene! His love for humanity is so profound that He cannot hate Rome herself. Some days ago they asked Him whether taxes should be paid to the Emperor. He replied that the Emperor must be paid that which is his due."

Simon's eyes dilated and his beard jutted as he thrust out his jaw. "And this is the Messiah who is supposed to liberate Israel! He says we must pay the oppressor! The Redeemer, who tells us to pay the enemy his due!" Simon shook his head with cynicism. "Instead of bringing us fiery swords, He pleads for Rome; instead of leading Israel to uproot the temples of Rome, He overturns the tables in our own. There is your incomparable Messiah, Joseph of Arimathea!"

Joseph shook his gray head slowly. "Man from Africa," he said, "do you not also long for the Messiah?"

"How can you ask such a thing?" Simon asked, momentarily bewildered by the question. "Am I not a Jew who suffers with Israel? Am I not a slave of Rome as well? Did Rome not destroy everything I possessed in Africa?"

He slid down against the tree trunk, squatted there, and looked up into the wide and empty sky. He closed his eyes as if in prayer. "Yes, I long for the Messiah," he said softly. "But He must be the Messiah, not a carpenter of no account. His sword shall reach up into the skies and stretch beyond the oceans. His words will come from the highest mountain summit, and His voice will be heard from the Lebanon to Sinai. He will say: 'Israel, your garment is once again your garment and your dwelling place your own; your hills and your valleys are cleansed of the oppressor. Go forth and rejoice in the morning; lift your face to the healing rain of liberation. Canaan is your country and the enemy your footstool.'

"For His fiery chariot will lead the soldiers of Israel to the destruction of Rome. His white steed will lead the hosts of Israel to the place of victory where Pilate's legions will be overthrown beneath the swords of the risen people.

"He will return to Jerusalem and the trumpet will proclaim His glory. He will dwell in the palaces of Israel—and not seek shelter overnight in a potter's house like this Nazarene. His throne will stand on high for all Israel to see it shining, and His word will be law through the length and breadth of the land."

Simon looked at Joseph, his eyes glittering in fierce ecstasy. "He will be a prince," he said with dry lips. "He will be as mighty as David, as wise as Solomon, and as brave as Saul. Not a wandering preacher teaching to those who will never learn, while the shadow of the eagle obscures the temple of Jerusalem."

"I know," Joseph whispered, moved. "We are looking for a man who will break Rome as Saul destroyed his enemies, a man like David who made Israel unconquerable, a Solomon who brought glory to Jerusalem. We look for victory and for greatness. We seek a golden temple to glow against the sky. But what about today?" he asked. "What about Lazarus? Doesn't this make the Nazarene greater than Solomon or even Moses? Is victory over death not greater than victory over swords?"

Joseph, seeing Simon's bewilderment, smiled gently, almost supplicatingly. "It is no concern of mine what you believe, Simon. You are a good Jew. You follow the beliefs of those before you. But what I told you about Lazarus is the truth. This you must believe, even if you believe nothing else."

Simon looked at Joseph a long time, unblinkingly. "Joseph of Arimathea, I think you believe in this Nazarene."

Joseph looked down at the ground. Then he turned and walked off to his donkey, flicking at the ground with his whip.

As he mounted, Simon came to stand next to the donkey. "What I told you about Lazarus is true," Joseph said again, but Simon did not seem to hear him.

"This carpenter—where is he now?" Simon asked.

Joseph regarded him briefly before answering, trying to decipher the expression in Simon's eyes. He looked at the cask that lay in fragments, he remembered the violence in Simon's angry voice, and he thought of the strength that had plucked up the cask and broken it against the tree.

Joseph said vaguely, "He has gone. He left after midday for the desert in the south. He had been warned."

Joseph turned his donkey, spurred it with his heels, and, his garment flapping behind him, rode away through the trees. Simon stood staring after him with suspicion in his eyes.

After a long time, he went off through the trees, and when he reached the brook of Kidron, he stood looking at the dried-up pools. Then he passed along the valley, turned away, and walked toward the cottage, toward his wife, Deborah. With long strides he climbed the slope through the orchards; on the way he broke a branch from a fig tree, swung it, and flung it away.

When he stood in the doorway, Deborah looked up in surprise from the hearth. "What is it, my husband? I thought you were still working. Who was the rider?"

He entered, drank water from a flask, went to the table, played with a wooden spoon; then he came to her.

"I have stopped work for a while," he said without looking at her. He stroked his beard, because he could think of nothing else to do. "The rider was Joseph of Arimathea."

"What did he say? Is he pleased because the press is ready?"

Simon turned toward the door. "He said they were going to seize this Nazarene. They fear an uprising."

"An uprising?"

Simon gestured in his agitation and gripped the doorframe, hard. "He is inciting the people, and the Romans . . . the Romans will not tolerate that."

"When are they going to seize Him?"

"I do not know. He has fled again. I believe He was near here, but He has gone into the desert. The Messiah is afraid of being caught," he added scornfully.

"Was He near here?" He heard her voice right behind him. "Where was He?"

"Somewhere . . . I really do not know."

He walked out and stood before the door, and she looked at him in surprise. His head jerked nervously, his hands moved as if he were trying to grasp something but continually changed his mind. "I'm going now. I'm going to look at the wheat. . . . I haven't been there yet today."

Simon waved to her and then made for the shelter of the trees. He passed along the foot of the Mount of Olives, looking back to see whether he was being followed or whether Ezekiel perhaps was observing him.

Deborah stayed standing in the doorway. She was greatly puzzled. She had never seen him so restless. Her eyes followed him until he vanished in the trees.

When he was hidden by the olive orchard that clothed the foot of the mountain, he felt more at his ease, not so apprehensive of being seen or followed.

For Simon Niger did not want Deborah or Ezekiel to learn that he was on his way to Bethany.

16

Simon easily found the house of Lazarus. In the distance he could see the black chimney of the pottery kiln. He saw the tapering mound of clay next to it, dried out before it had been used. He saw people constantly coming and going.

The house was neat and compact, with a warm and friendly air. The walls of white plaster were surrounded by tall poplars and cypresses. At the back was a pleasant and extensive garden, with apricot blooms showing white amid the early green of olives, figs, and almonds. In the front of the house was a hedge of jasmine, rampant in yellow bloom.

Simon crossed the yard hesitantly, as one who, intruding, dare not venture further. The sun cast its dying light over the ridge of the mountain, crowning the dark summits of the trees with banners of shining light.

Simon walked around the back of the house, picking his way past old vases, jars, and pitchers, between small groups of people who were talking in awed voices but in tense attitudes—as if they were discussing ominous news, like heavy rains, or floods, or a fresh massacre by the Romans. Although they talked in half-whispers, Simon could hear quite clearly what they said.

They were talking about Lazarus. And they were discussing Jesus. Simon stopped and listened, close to a small group of elderly Jews who, leaning on their sticks, were gesturing with gnarled fingers or cupping their hands behind their ears in order to hear.

"I was present when his sister Martha embalmed him," said one old man in a husky voice. His beard trembled with his intentness in the telling. One or two moved closer to hear him better.

"You were there?"

"I was there. . . . I held the balsam flask."

"But was he dead? Did you see that he was dead?"

"I felt for his pulse. There was no life; his heart was still."

They shook their ancient heads, stroked their white beards, while excitement lit their eyes. And one, whose head trembled continuously from some nervous state, asked in a hoarse voice: "His pulse was still, eh?"

"Cold and dead as a nail—no life at all. As dead as . . . as that stone you see over there. As God is my witness, he was dead. We embalmed him lightly only. . . . I was present when they laid him away . . . in the cavern."

The little gray man who was telling the story looked about him, leaned further forward, and spoke even more confidentially. "He was smelling already when we put him away."

"What?"

"Yes, smelling. It wasn't cold then. The air changed last night only."

"Yes . . . yes . . . indeed," they murmured.

"The winter came back last night," one said.

An old man with a bowed back pushed forward. "And were you . . . were you there when it happened . . . when Lazarus rose, when he came out?" He waggled his cane back and forth.

The storyteller looked down at the cool earth, where winter was dying and summer stirred. Simon kept on peering at him from a short distance away, listening intently to their talk.

The old man adjusted his headcloth just as if he was about to approach something sacred. "I was . . . there," he said slowly. "He came, and He was weary, for He had trudged from the other side of the Jordan. His disciples were with Him, and the two sisters, Mary and Martha, ran to meet Him. He went to stand in front of the cave . . . there on the other side of the garden." He looked quickly at each in turn, his gray head pushed far forward and large tears trembling in his eyes. "And He wept just as I would or one of you. He uttered prayers with the others who were standing there. He shed tears.

"Then He called out loudly: 'Lazarus, come forth!'" The old Jew covered his eyes with his hand, and the others looked at him in bewilderment. "And then I saw Lazarus raise himself and look at us. He got up slowly and came stumbling out, and his sisters rushed to grasp his hands."

"He is the Messiah," one whispered.

"He is the Messiah," they whispered all together. They looked at one another, glanced at the house, looked away through the fading afternoon, and did not stir, but stood here quietly, overwhelmed with joy and wonder.

Simon felt an inward trembling. He walked to the back door, and suddenly he felt lonely, as one rejected and cast out. At the door a stranger stopped him.

"You cannot enter there," he said.

"I want to see this man Lazarus."

"You cannot see him; he is resting. He is weak. Too many people have come here."

"I want to see the man Lazarus," Simon's eyes hardened and grew cold.

"And I say you cannot see him."

"He hasn't died again, has he?" A mocking smile twisted Simon's lips.

"Do you mock the work of Jesus?"

"If he lives, I mean to see him." Simon moved toward the threshold. The stranger gripped his shoulders and tried to force him backwards. Simon put out his hands and flung the man aside.

The next moment he found himself in a cool, dark room in which the smell of myrrh hung heavily. His hands were trembling, his mouth was dry.

Before him stood a young woman, dark-haired, slender. She looked at him gravely.

"We can't allow people in the house now," she said softly. "It will overtax him. He needs rest."

"I must see him."

"Is it so urgent, then?"

"Not so very urgent, but I want to see him."

"But he is resting on the roof where the air is fresh. He is not strong. He was four days dead."

"I shall not speak. I only want to look at him."

"You do not believe that Jesus raised him?"

Simon gripped his beard, twisted it in his fingers. "No, I don't believe it."

The young woman faced him with so strange a look that it

143

made him ill at ease. He did not know whether it was pity that he saw or sad contempt.

"I am Martha, sister of Lazarus." she said. "Follow me. You may sit with him for a few minutes."

She went quickly up the stone stairs to the roof, and he followed her, his knees weak, his hands clammy.

A cool breeze was blowing in from the Mount of Olives as they reached the top. She paused but did not speak. For a moment she glanced at Simon, and then she turned her head toward the bed that stood in the middle of the roof. Her eyes were proud, triumphant.

Simon saw the man lying on his back on the bed. His hair stirred in the breeze.

Simon's heart thudded in his throat. He took one step forward and then stopped. He did not see the dark hulk of the mountain. He did not feel the wind upon his cheeks. He did not know that the young woman had left him to go down the stairs.

He felt that he had floated to a great height where he stood alone with this man, where there was neither sound nor movement; it was as if he were enveloped in a cloud in which nothing, not even the wind, not even shining drops of rain, could ever touch him.

His eyes saw nothing but the face of Lazarus. It was not the face of death. It was the face of life. There was a faint color on his cheeks and an almost infantile youthfulness. The face was thin but firm; the brow shone slightly.

Simon moved closer, seeking the traits of the dead, but he saw none. Joy lived in him for a single moment. This man—was he not dead? Death, he knew, could summon youth again. Death could restore the damage of the years. He had seen it happen.

He glanced quickly, hopefully, at the chest. But there he saw life, real and naked. Lazarus's chest rose and fell with his gentle, peaceful breathing. He bent down suddenly and took the slender wrist between his fingers. He could feel the pulse beating, evenly and steadily.

When he straightened up again, he was looking into the eyes of Lazarus. They were gentle, smiling eyes. Simon took a backward step, as if detected in a crime.

"It is strange," Lazarus said as if thinking aloud, "how many refuse to believe that I am living. Do they wish to see me dead then?"

He reached across and felt his own wrist. "My wrist hurts from so much prodding. Everyone feels my pulse."

Suddenly Simon felt uncertain whether he himself was living, whether he had not died and reawakened to a new, dim world where he found himself together with this man. He shook his heavy head and emerged from the strange abyss. And suddenly he heard loudly the noise of leaves in the wind.

Through the rustling of the leaves in the newly arisen wind, Lazarus was speaking. "I am alive," he said. "I can see the Mount of Olives." He turned his head on the pillow. Simon stood there, silent and ashamed. "I am thankful to be able to see the Mount again." The last light from the west was reflected in his eyes. "What . . . what are they saying in Jerusalem about this miracle of Jesus?"

Only the song of the shifting leaves answered Lazarus's question.

"He has already done great things, but this is the greatest of them. I am glad He has been able to use me, to bring belief to all. After today everybody can have faith. He has vanquished death. . . . Isn't that true, stranger? I am alive. Feel my hands . . . feel them. They are warm; feel my pulse." He smiled and held out his hand.

But Lazarus might well have held out his hand to the lonely wind. He smiled again at the Mount that was now merging with the night. And only the leaves murmured at his question.

For the big stranger was no longer there.

Simon Niger had rushed away blindly toward the parapet, checked himself, looked around, turned, and walked back to the steps. He had descended the stairs in a rush. He did not reply when Martha asked him something.

When he came out-of-doors, he stood motionless. The small group that had been waiting there on his arrival had grown into a crowd, a noisy multitude, talking, thronging, thrusting forward.

He edged along the wall, trying to evade them, but they blocked his passage, pressing around him insistently.

145

"Did you see him?" "Is he alive?" "Did you touch him?" "Did he speak?" "How does he look?" "Is he as weak as they say?"

Simon struggled. Clinging, clutching hands held him, tried to hold him back. He felt the hot breath from many mouths in his face.

One seized his beard and pulled him forward. "Talk!" the man shouted. It stirred the savage in Simon. With a hoarse cry, he jerked his body forward and sprang in among them, striking, kicking, and struggling with such violence that he burst through the milling mob.

Then he was free. He began to run. His garment was in shreds. He had lost a sandal. His headcloth had been torn away. He felt blood on his temple where somebody had scratched him.

But he was free. He ran into the wind, and night overtook him from the east. He ran stumbling over shrubs and stones, avoiding the road to Jerusalem where moving torchlights gleamed —the procession of those who came to verify this strange denial of death.

When he had escaped, he stood in a decayed orchard and struggled for breath. Only then did he realize that it had become completely dark. He looked behind him and saw the torchlight moving into a blazing circle, revealing where Lazarus lay living, the man with the gentle eyes in which shone truth and no deceit.

He sat down with his back against a crooked trunk that had known many winters more than he. The wind sighed among the trees. He touched the cut above his eye and felt the blood congealing.

"Lord God of Israel, what is the truth and what is false?" he groaned aloud, looking up toward the stars, which ducked in and out behind the clouds as if to taunt him. The wind caught his question and scattered it among the trees.

Looking about him, he gazed into the darkness.

Then he rose, pulled his torn garment closer about him, and, feeling forward with bare feet in the dark, he struggled homeward, for his prime need now was to be at Deborah's side.

17

Deborah and Ezekiel looked up to see Simon standing in the doorway. Deborah pressed her hands to her mouth, and her eyes showed her dismay. Ezekiel jumped up from his seat beside the table.

"Simon, husband," Deborah cried and ran into his arms.

"What has happened, Simon of Cyrene?" Ezekiel asked excitedly, staring at the blood on Simon's beard, at his torn garment, and at his bare foot scratched and bleeding.

Simon held Deborah tightly against himself, closed his eyes, and felt peace flowing back again. After all that he had borne that day, her nearness comforted him and brought back his confidence in himself.

But suddenly he moved out of her embrace, entered the room, and stood for a moment before the hearth where flames were dancing merrily. Then he turned and burst out laughing. Deborah and Ezekiel looked at him in bewilderment, and Ezekiel leaned forward across the table. "What has happened to you, Simon?" he asked.

"I thought I was old," Simon said laughingly, "but I am younger than I thought." He waved his right hand carelessly. "Just down there in the Valley of Kidron, if you please, a few ruffians set on me this evening."

Deborah make a quick movement toward him. "Ruffians?"

"Yes, think of it—jumped on me." He walked to the table and broke off a piece of bread. Chewing, he walked over to the wine bag against the wall to slake his thirst.

"And then?" Ezekiel asked impatiently.

Simon thrust the rest of the bread into his mouth, bent down, and with flying arms and fists portrayed the battle. "What do you think? What do you think happened? I took care of the whole outfit. They tackled me, even pulled my sandal off, tore my garment,

147

but when I left the place, they all were lying fat on their backs."

"Well done!" Ezekiel cried. "I wish I had been there."

"Just think, husband," Deborah said admiringly, "you knocked them all down!"

Simon nervously pulled off his upper garment and threw it against the wall. "I knocked them flat!" he affirmed and laughed briefly with averted eyes. He seized a handful of dates with trembling hands and gulped them down too quickly. He turned toward the back window, pushed the shutters open, and looked through the trees at the lambent light of Jerusalem.

"I wish I had been there," Ezekiel said again, while Deborah began filling a wooden basin with water.

"Come, let me bathe your injured foot. Then you can wash and eat, my husband. Why did they attack you, the rabble?"

"They must have thought I had money," Simon said loudly and laughed so strangely that both Deborah and Ezekiel looked at him. He sat down on the low wooden stool and pulled off his one sandal. "But tomorrow their heads will be sore. I pounded them thoroughly."

Simon dipped his sore foot into the water. He grimaced as Deborah's hands touched the sore spots on his body soothingly.

Ezekiel picked up Simon's outer garment from the floor. "I've been meaning to ask you," he said. "What do you think of this story that Joseph of Arimathea was telling?"

Simon knew that Deborah was looking at him intensely and expectantly. He shrugged his shoulders, flung his hands up. "Nonsense, Ezekiel," he said, "utter nonsense! If He raised Lazarus from the dead, why does He not raise Moses and Jeremiah and David and Saul as well?" He clapped his hands on his knees. "What do you say, Ezekiel?"

"Yes, why not?" Ezekiel asked, his small eyes lighting up.

"If He is such an expert raiser of the dead, why does He not raise all the fallen hosts of Israel so that we can really bring old Tiberius down into the dust? What say you to that, Ezekiel?" Simon's body shook with laughter, and Ezekiel followed suit.

But Deborah saw that although her husband's face and eyes were laughing, deep within him there was a solemnity. Only part of him was mirthful.

And then she noticed that his eyes were slightly glazed and that he was not in complete control of his words.

Ezekiel wandered over to the door, looked around at Simon, then down at the ground. "I don't know," he said, "this business of Lazarus is a little too deep for me."

Simon pulled a flask of wine closer, lifted it to his mouth, and drank so greedily that the wine ran from the corners of his mouth. He slammed the flask down, smacked his lips, and wiped his beard. "I'll tell you what, Ezekiel—we two will fetch this Nazarene and take Him to the grave of Samson so that He can resurrect Him too. Then we'll turn Samson loose in Rome . . . among the gluttons and rogues. I'll wager you old Tiberius won't stop running until he's in the sea!" Simon threw his head back and laughed again, and the tears ran down his cheeks.

"Well, I think I'll go to bed," Ezekiel said, and disappeared through the door.

Simon looked from the empty door to the small circle of light made by the lamp in the darkness, and then down at the bowed neck of his wife. She was washing his uninjured foot. He bent down and lightly kissed her hair. "You have the dearest hands in Israel, my wife," he whispered. "Why is it that you always make me feel at peace? Why is it that I always turn to you whenever darkness threatens?"

Deborah did not look up. "You did not tell me anything about this Lazarus," she said, and in her voice he could detect a note of faint rebuke.

"Oh, that!" he said, turning his face away from her. "Just old wives' tales. . . . Must I repeat the gossip?"

"You never used to keep anything—trivial or otherwise—from me."

He shifted his body uneasily. "I detest talking about this carpenter; you know that." His voice had suddenly become hard.

She stood up, moistened a cloth with the cool water, and began to wipe the blood from his face. "You've had too much to drink . . . it's not like you."

"I was tired . . . after the fight. I found myself passing the casks . . . I was thirsty. I suppose I took a little too much."

"That which is said about Lazarus—don't you believe it at all?"

He snorted, slapped his hand hard on his knee. "Street gossip. He was no more dead than I am."

"But Joseph of Arimathea—he said it was true. Ezekiel said that Joseph believed in the truth of it. Joseph is an elder."

"Elder or not, it's a mass of lies."

"I think Ezekiel believes. . . . I think he believes that the Nazarene did raise Lazarus from the dead."

He pushed her hands away. "Ezekiel?" he asked slowly.

She nodded.

"What do *you* believe?" he asked, blowing on his bruised knuckles, fighting the numbness that the wine was bringing to his body.

She did not speak; he waited, and the silence rang in his ears. Her fingers stroked his hair. The shame of his deception made him flush and twist his fingers.

After a while Deborah said: "I believe in you, Simon of Cyrene. What you believe, that is my belief. I think we are completely one . . . even our hearts."

He turned his head slowly and looked up at her with humble eyes. He grasped her hands. "I am grateful," he said. "I was no longer sure. . . . Now I am sure again."

"You were not sure . . . of me?"

"I thought I was alone . . . without you."

"Are you then so terrified of this Nazarene?"

He stared at her as if she had spoken in a foreign tongue. He rose, changed the water into the washtub, and washed his face. When he had finished, he pressed his hands against the wall and rested his head on his extended arms. "No, I do not fear Him. I do not fear this carpenter. I was afraid that He had taken my whole house—you . . . Ezekiel—just as He has taken Rufus. I felt alone. I felt that you were no longer at my side. Now, I do not fear any more. Now, I am sure of you."

His voice came slowly. "This man . . . this carpenter. I feel trapped, encircled. . . . Sometimes I feel that He is surrounding me with an invisible force. Sometimes I feel He is pointing His finger directly at me, saying, 'Simon Niger, it is I who brought you out of Africa. Why do you reject Me? Why do you reject Me? Why will you not believe?'"

Simon turned to her, wild-eyed. "Why must it be like this, Deborah? Why?" He moved closer, his hands imploring.

She stood quietly beyond the lamplight, and her voice was calm: "It is because everyone is talking about Him, my husband. It is because He is always in your thoughts. He touched our hearts when He took Rufus away from us. . . . That is the reason."

Into his eyes came a new understanding as he listened to her words. "That is true," he said. He sat down at the table. "It is the truth."

She still stood without moving. She recalled a day in Cyrene when she saw him standing noble under an olive tree, and she thought of how he now appeared, sitting there. Then, he was like a green oak, tall and shining; now like a cedar whose roots were dying.

His fingers stirred on the table. He looked at them. "This man from Nazareth—how do you understand Him?" he whispered. "Some run after Him, but Caiaphas will have none of Him—the high priest. Saul does not believe in Him. Saul, the clever Pharisee. Rufus believes in Him; but the man is no Messiah, for He cannot set Israel free."

"He healed that leper."

"Yes . . . yes, I think perhaps the leper was healed. But can we believe it in our hearts?"

"And there is Lazarus."

"I don't know. I can't believe it. And still, Lazarus is alive. I heard him speaking."

He looked up in agitation and she came to him quickly. He put his hands up to her. "Come, sit beside me, my wife, so that I may talk to you," Simon said. She sat down close to him, and he held her tightly. "I lied to you—there was no fight. I was in Bethany." He gazed deep into her eyes. "The lie lay like a thorn in my flesh. I would not have been able to sleep tonight if my deception lay between us."

"Oh, Simon . . . I knew there was something . . . something."

He then told her everything as it happened.

"And do you believe now? Do you believe that Lazarus has

been raised from the dead?" she asked when he had finished.

He looked at her with helpless eyes. "I do not know. Simon of Samaria also achieved wonders."

"He never raised anyone from the dead." Deborah laid her hand on his. "Is it not perhaps that the God of Israel is using this carpenter for this one great deed . . . just to show the people that He has not deserted them, that He is still almighty?"

"That is what it is, Deborah," he said, with sudden decision brightening his eyes. "It is the Lord God who is testifying through this man. It is long since Israel has witnessed a miracle. . . . But it still does not make this Nazarene the Messiah."

He rose suddenly, his shoulders squared, his movement sure. He went outside, took deep breaths of the night air, and returned. He stood in the doorway fingering his beard. "Mother," he said to his wife, who still was sitting beside the table, "my beard is growing a little wild. You must trim it for me. I have a longing tonight for the touch of your hands." He came to her, raised her to her feet, and held her tightly against him. "Your heart is a ruby, woman of Israel," he said.

Early the next morning, as the morning star rose bravely above the Mount of Olives, Simon dressed himself. He stood for a moment listening to Deborah's quiet breathing, and he wished that he could sleep like that—from dark to dawn, so deeply and so peacefully. Then he went outside to the yard. The cool air of morning was damp with heavy dew, and he inhaled the scent of grass and fallen leaves.

As he touched the neat edges of his beard, he thought of what they had decided upon the previous night. Then he looked again at the somber world about him, at the dark gardens, at sleeping Jerusalem. What had seemed indisputable last night did not appear so now. Why should the God of Israel use a carpenter to demonstrate His works to Israel? Why not use Caiaphas, or Saul, or even Joseph of Arimathea? And why use a leper and a potter?

Simon went to the brook of Kidron. There he lingered with silence about him, and as he walked along the bank, a ribbon of light above the dark crown of the Mount of Olives proclaimed the birth of day. He looked at his fingers and saw his shining nails.

When he reached Ezekiel's lean-to shed, he found it empty. The bedding had not been slept on and was lying in a corner. In the growing light of morning Simon searched the area, but he could not find him anywhere. He rubbed his hands together and wrapped his garment more closely about him, for the air was almost wintry.

It was then that he heard the voices. He crossed the yard and went past his house to the avenue of fig sees that extended to the olive press.

There were three people walking toward the house, their forms and faces visible in the brightening light of day.

Ezekiel, Rufus—Rufus himself—and a woman unknown to him.

Simon stared with narrowed eyes. Ezekiel was taking hurried steps with his awkward, bandy legs. The woman moved with the ease and grace of youth. Rufus walked unhurriedly, the way his mother walked.

The big man's first impulse was to retreat behind the fig trees, but shame restrained him and he stood waiting quietly beside the mulberry tree. Apparently they did not see him. They passed on their way to the house, and when they reached it, he saw Ezekiel slip stealthily around the back.

Rufus and the woman stopped before the door and lowered the package they were carrying. He saw Rufus go to the threshold. His son peered inside the house, then turned again uncertainly and rejoined the woman. It was then that Rufus saw his father.

They approached each other as if impelled by a force stronger than themselves.

"Good morning, Father," Rufus said humbly.

Simon swallowed and said, "Good morning, Rufus. . . . Have you come back?"

"I did not go far—only to Bethany."

"Bethany?"

"To Lazarus and his sisters."

"You know them?"

"I am living there at present."

"I thought you were studying with Gamaliel."

"I don't think Gamaliel can teach me anything I want to know, Father."

"I'm pleased you've come. . . . You're up and about early."

"I had to come. I missed you."

"I am glad. Your mother will be happy too. . . . We should not be parted. To be parted is not good."

"Father, I heard that you were with Lazarus last night."

Simon looked at his son intently. "You heard that?"

"Lazarus's sister told me about the stranger who had been there. From her description I knew it was you."

Simon looked quickly down at the ground. "I noticed many people going to Bethany. I was curious. I went to see for myself. One hears so many stories."

He felt his son's gaze on him, pleading, questioning. But he refrained from saying more and went to where the young woman was standing in front of the house. Rufus followed him.

"This is Mary, a sister of Lazarus," Rufus said. She glanced shyly up at Simon's big frame and piercing eyes that were scrutinizing her. After a long silence, he put his hands on her shoulders. "I think you are a good woman," Simon said. "It shines out of your eyes. I know you are good to my son."

"He is good to *us*," Mary replied and smiled shyly.

Simon looked into her green eyes and saw there a light he knew, for it was the same light he had known in Deborah's eyes when they were young, something a woman cannot hide, which reveals her inner being at moments when she is unaware.

He stood not knowing quite what to do. He looked down at Rufus's feet, then at his hands, and finally, his face. "Let us go and wake your mother," he said at last. "She has missed you greatly, though she did not say a word. When she is silent, I know her thoughts even better than when she speaks."

He turned and walked toward the door. On the threshold he stopped and looked back over his shoulder. Rufus and Mary had not moved. Simon swung around quickly and looked fixedly at his son. Neither spoke a word.

"Do you fear my house?" Simon asked at last.

"No, Father, we are not afraid," his son said, "but the other evening you gave a certain order."

Simon kicked against a large stone that lay outside the threshold. "Do you want me to say I am sorry that I hardened my heart? Do you claim the victory?"

Rufus came forward. "No, no, it is not so. I do not seek either victory or revenge, for you are my father. It is just that I . . . I am uncertain."

When Simon spoke again, he did not look at Rufus, but at Mary. "Daughter of Israel," he said, "have you ever seen one sunrise that is precisely like another, or two trees identically the same, or two clouds that are twins?"

"Such things cannot be," she said, shaking her head.

"Then how can a heart always be the same? One day there is anger, and another there is peace. One day there is sorrow, and another there is joy—is that not so? Why should I be the same this morning as I was the other evening?"

"That is true, Father Simon," Mary said softly. "A heart changes by the day."

He smiled in gratitude. "You are a wise young woman, Mary. Life has taught you more than my son has learned from all his parchments."

"And you are a wise man, Father Simon. You know that if the same heart can differ, then two hearts can differ even more. One cloud does not destroy the other just because they are different, and one tree does not smother another tree because their fruits are different."

Her words struck home, and he stood there feeling guilty without knowing what to say. Then he turned, walked to the doorway, and beckoned them to come inside.

"Mother," he called loudly, "Rufus is here."

Deborah was dressed, and when Rufus and Mary entered she was standing in the doorway of her room. Rufus gazed at his mother; then he went to her and kissed her, and she buried her face in his shoulder.

He led his mother toward Mary. "And this is Mary of Bethany," he said.

"Peace be with you, Mary of Bethany," Deborah said and knew in an instant what Simon had already seen.

"Peace be with you, Mother Deborah."

"You are the sister of the man who was raised from the dead?"

Rufus glanced at his father when Mary nodded to Deborah. But Simon was busy at the grate, blowing fiercely on a log that still retained the spark of the previous night, and adding twigs to make a fire.

Deborah looked at the packages that Rufus and Mary had set down on the table. Rufus began to open them. "We brought this for you, Mother." There was flour, dried meat, jars of honey, brown dates, dried figs, a few huge pomegranates with glossy red skins, butter, soap, and a flask of olive oil.

"Is all that for me?" Deborah asked.

"All for you, Mother Deborah," Mary said.

Deborah embraced her. "The Almighty bless you, daughter of Jerusalem," she said. "Your heart is kind."

"It is only a little."

"Father, look at all the things we have received—even olive oil," Deborah said, examining the present with delight.

Simon came nearer and looked at Mary gratefully. "The Almighty bless you," he repeated. Then he spoke gaily to Deborah: "Mother, prepare food. The sun has already risen. Let the two children eat with us. We are happy that they are here."

Deborah hurried around the table and gripped Simon's hands in hers. Then she stood on tiptoe and whispered in his ear: "Thank you for bringing our child back beneath our roof."

He gave a short laugh. "A heart is like a cloud, Mother— never the same. And two hearts are like two clouds, even less the same. Mary taught me that."

Ezekiel had come in noiselessly, like a timid child. He looked at Simon guiltily.

"You wander around by night, Ezekiel," the big man said, and could not keep a note of accusation from entering his voice.

Ezekiel squatted hastily next to the wall and brushed his hand nervously over his mouth. "For the life of me, I couldn't fall asleep last night," he said, and waved his arms. "I think I had too much to eat. Then I saw the torches going across the valley and I made my way . . . to Bethany. . . . Just to see . . . just to have a look. Why should a man try to sleep when he is wakeful?"

Simon took his staff from the corner and went out beneath the trees.

"You must not go away again, my child," Deborah said to Rufus. "Your father does not say anything, but it grieves him deeply. You . . . and Alexander . . . he wants you with him."

Rufus sat down on a small stool next to the washtub. "Mother, I have come to say good-bye."

"To say good-bye?"

"I am going to follow Jesus . . . to the north—to Ephraim, in the country bordering on the desert."

"They won't be absent long," Mary said quickly as she readied things on the hearth.

Deborah leaned on her hands against the table. The things she wished to say, she could not utter. She felt Mary's hands on her shoulders.

18

Simon changed during the days that followed; Ezekiel as well. Simon withdrew into himself and rarely spoke. Ezekiel became quite talkative. He talked so much that Simon often lost his temper with him. "Your words outnumber the desert sands of Sinai," he said one day.

Ezekiel never uttered the name of Jesus, to avoid offending Simon; but he continually voiced his wonder at the strange things they had seen since their coming to Jerusalem and advanced theories to explain them.

Sometimes Deborah watched her husband sitting silently and staring at his hands. Occasionally when she spoke to him, he would look up in surprise. She knew that he could not sleep at night and that he rose in the mornings long before she had awakened. Every now and again he would wander off up the Mount of Olives or to the wheat fields; or else he would spend his time sitting beside the olive or wine press.

When Joseph of Arimathea visited them, Simon talked to him absentmindedly, and frequently Joseph could not find him in the fields or in the orchard or at the presses. Very often he would be sitting inside the house or in the shade of the mulberry tree or on a boulder in the avenue of fig trees.

Mary paid them regular visits and helped Deborah with one or another of her many tasks, or in the evenings when they gathered around the lamp, she would play to them on her harp. As she played, a longing that only Deborah could understand glowed in her eyes.

"What do you hear from Rufus?" Simon would ask with feigned nonchalance.

"He is following Jesus through Samaria and Galilee," Mary answered. "We will see them again one of these days, Father Simon, when they come to Jerusalem for the next Passover."

Every time she said that, Simon got up and strolled away to where Ezekiel was working busily. He would lend a hand, but with little enthusiasm. For Simon seemed to have lost his former desire for work these days, and Deborah wondered at it. He would take up a spade and loosen the soil a little but soon put it down again. He would hold the plow handles while Ezekiel pulled it with the help of a poor lad from Jerusalem. Then in the middle of a furrow he would suddenly release the plow and walk away to the water holes, or to the cattle pastures that lay beside the main road to Joppa.

Whenever they were alone together, Deborah and Mary opened their hearts to each other. Often Deborah saw Mary's hands grow still upon the harp strings and a look of longing come into her eyes.

One day Mary brought Lazarus along, and Deborah could not keep her eyes away from the young man whose eyes held the glow of health and whose walk was so assured. But when Simon saw them coming through the trees, he slipped in behind Ezekiel's hut, walked quickly to the Kidron and continued until he reached the Damascus Gate. There he stood watching the beggars and the travelers streaming into the city. He did not wish to see this Lazarus ever again if he could help it—or to talk to him.

While he stood at the gate, he saw a procession coming from the north.

"What is that approaching?" Simon asked a man standing close to him.

"It must be Pontius Pilate and his crowd of thugs," the Jew said and spat in the dust.

Simon gazed at the approaching procession for a long time and then again at the pilgrims moving through the gateway—a stream of men, women, and children, mounted on donkeys or on camels, or on foot: the elderly progressing with the aid of sticks, young men and women treading lightly. It looked as if the whole of Israel was on the road toward Jerusalem that day.

A blare of trumpet directed Simon's eyes to the approaching Roman horsemen. They came with red cloaks flying, their horses sleek and shining. They cleared the way, driving the pilgrims off the road. Behind them rode others: heralds with their trumpets first, followed by four horsemen holding high the insignia of Rome. Then came the soldiers clustered around the carriage—a great gilded carriage drawn by two snow-white stallions. Prancing and tossing their heads, the horses swiftly drew the carriage toward Jerusalem.

Simon withdrew to a spot farther from the gate and sat on a boulder to observe the colorful Roman procession approaching along the road from Caesarea. In front of him lay a loose stone. He picked it up and weighed it in his hand as he watched the crude insolence of the horsemen who forced the pilgrims from the road.

Getting up suddenly, he flung the stone into a bush, turned and walked away. Behind him he heard Pilate's carriage rumble through the gateway.

When he at last reached home, dusk had fallen. Mary and Lazarus had already gone.

In the week that followed his glimpse of Pontius Pilate, the governor of Judea, entering the Damascus Gate, Simon did hardly any work. The excitement of the approaching Passover was too much for him. Ezekiel too neglected all his work. He was almost always in the city moving around among the pilgrims.

Rufus returned as well. He and Mary pleaded with Simon and Deborah to accompany them to Bethany to see Jesus. He had arrived for the Passover and was staying there after walking from Jericho. But Simon would have none of it, and Deborah, although she longed to see the Nazarene, refused to go without him.

Simon would sit in front of the little storehouse where Joseph's wine casks were kept. There were many pilgrims who were eager to buy wine, and he hoped to empty the vats before they would be needed for the wine of a new harvest.

Deborah had gone to the city one morning with Ezekiel. With money made from selling wine and firewood to the pilgrims, Deborah was buying the things they needed for the Passover.

Simon sat whittling a piece of wood that he had picked up near the olive press and gazing over toward the big encampment of pilgrims on the other side of the Kidron outside the city gate.

He saw a dark man approaching. He was short, with an enormous beard and bandy legs. His middle finger was curled round the ear of a big jar that hung from his shoulder. As he reached Simon he swung the jar easily from his shoulder and said, "Peace be with you."

"Peace be with you," Simon answered, intrigued by the man's dark, restless eyes.

"I've come to fetch wine."

"I have an abundance, and I see that your vessel is spacious."

"But first I need to slake my own thirst," the dark man said. "I am thirsty . . . and tired also." He sat down against the wall of the storehouse, and the sunlight sloping from the west lit up his somber face. He seemed a man who had lived long with some affliction, a grievance that pained his heart.

Simon unhooked the wine mug that hung from a branch, filled it, and gave it to the stranger. He was surprised at his mode of drinking—he swallowed in big gulps and emptied the mug without pause, as if its content were water. Then he held it out to be refilled.

"More wine?" Simon asked.

The stranger nodded. He smote his fists together, stood up, and walked around in a circle. "I must drink," he said, "I *must* . . . I am tired." He seemed to be so agitated by an inner turmoil that it was impossible for him to be still. He had the habit of involuntarily winking one eye; his hands and fingers moved continually, and Simon saw that his neck twitched strangely.

Simon gave him another cup of wine and his hand trembled as he took it.

"Who sent you?" Simon asked.

The black eyes of the stranger glistened over the edge of the cup. "Who sent me? Nobody. I know everything—especially where wine is to be had. I know the wine of Joseph of Arimathea—it is good. Much better than the wine one buys in the marketplace." He spoke with a peculiar smile and Simon asked no further questions. He went to a vat and filled the jar. While he was doing so the stranger came up with the mug and filled it to the brim beneath the trickling wine. Simon began to feel annoyed with the forward fellow.

161

"Where do you come from?" Simon asked, keeping his eyes on the jar.

"Where do I come from?" the stranger repeated, and stopped his drinking. "I come from nowhere. I am a wanderer . . . a wanderer!" he shouted and shot the remainder of the wine into a pomegranate bush. "The foxes have their holes and the birds their nests, but I have no place to rest my head." He gave a loud, ugly laugh. Simon saw that the man's eyes were glazed. This could not have been the first time that he had imbibed that day.

"Who was it who said that?" asked the stranger, sucking the wine from his beard.

Simon looked at him blankly and listened to the gurgle of wine entering the jar.

"You do not know?" The stranger flung his head back and laughed. "I shall tell you—the great Jesus of Nazareth said it."

Simon straightened in surprise, looking through the soft afternoon light at the man who had again put the empty beaker to his lips, his head well back to capture the last drops. He did not see that the jar was now full and the wine was flowing over its lip into the dry earth. The dark-eyed stranger held his mug under the flow and then closed the wooden tap.

"Jesus of Nazareth?" Simon stammered.

"Yes, Jesus of Nazareth," the stranger said. "This wine is for Jesus of Nazareth," he said as he bent down to lift the jar from the ground.

Simon sprang forward so quickly that the man could not evade him. He caught the stranger's garment and pulled him close. The mug dropped from his hands. For the first time his eyes were quiet—fear had stilled them. His neck did not twitch, nor did he blink his eye.

"How do you know that I will sell wine to this Nazarene? How do you know? If He desires wine, why does He not come to fetch it? Who are you? Speak! What is your name?"

Simon pushed the man away so fiercely that he staggered backward and stumbled over the threshold to fall heavily on his back. The big man advanced, trampling the jar and knocking it over. He glared down at the stranger lying in the dust. "Who are you?" Simon asked again with menace in his voice.

The stranger struggled to his knees.

"I am one of His disciples," he said with eyes averted.

"One of His disciples?"

"I am Judas."

"Which Judas?"

"They call me Iscariot."

"Judas Iscariot," Simon sneered. "A disciple of the Nazarene." He breathed heavily through his nose. "You buy wine for Him while the Sanhedrin seeks His blood."

Judas struggled up and stood swaying. "The Sanhedrin?"

"Do you not even know, Iscariot? If He sets foot in Jerusalem again, the Sanhedrin will deal with Him." He said it evenly, without emotion.

Judas wiped his mouth with the back of his hand. He came nearer. All his fear had left him; only bewilderment remained. His mouth dribbled, and his eyelids almost covered his sluggish eyes. "You . . . you don't believe in Jesus?" he said, thrusting his fingers out toward Simon.

"How can I believe in a man who favors a disciple like you? A drunkard and a scoundrel! I know you are drunk, and I can see you are a scoundrel." Simon shook his head and laughed softly. "Jesus the Nazarene . . . Judas Iscariot . . . Matthew the tax collector . . . Peter the fisherman. A carpenter, a scoundrel, a publican, and a fisherman." He smacked the wine vat with his hands, lowered his head, and laughed till his shoulders shook. "And you are the ones who are to liberate Israel."

Through his laughter he heard the voice of Judas Iscariot, thick and heavy.

"I don't believe in Him either anymore."

Simon stopped laughing. He turned his head and looked at Judas. Then he straightened himself. "What is that? You are His disciple and you don't believe in Him?"

"No, I don't believe anymore." There was a strange sadness in the words of the drunken disciple.

"I must drink to that," Simon said, picking up the mug and filling it. He sat with his back against the storehouse, but Judas remained standing in the afternoon sun. He suddenly swung round, swaying on his feet, and pulled down his cloak. "Look at my back," Judas said.

Simon's eyes narrowed as he looked at the man's lacerated back. It was crisscrossed with the gleaming welts and scars of old whippings.

"That's how the Romans thrashed me in Caesarea—years ago when I struck a centurion."

Simon did not speak. He shuddered and stared sympathetically at the pathetic back, and all at once Iscariot was no longer a scoundrel, but simply a Jew who had suffered.

"I hate Rome," Judas said, drawing his cloak over his shoulders again. "I thought the Nazarene would be our liberator, the man who would lead Israel to revenge upon Rome. And what does He say now? He says His kingdom is not of this world." Judas threw his hands up in despair. "I followed Him . . . all these years, hoped and prayed that He would lead the revolt. But now I am weary of wandering!" he said loudly, his head jerking in company with the twitching of his neck. "Weary, weary, weary, weary of trudging along. Weary of begging, of wandering, of sleeping in the cold like a dog that crawls under a bush for shelter. Where shall we eat tomorrow, where do we go tomorrow, where will be our resting place? I am sick of it all."

He dashed to the jar that Simon had kicked over, picked it up, uncorked it, and drank quickly. As he bent to put it down, he was pulled forward by the jar and almost landed on his head. He swayed toward Simon, unsteadily, with hands half-clenched. "They made a slave of me—all of them. 'Judas, go fetch water.' 'Judas, go fetch wine.' 'Judas, go and buy the fish.' 'Judas, find a place to sleep.' Judas this, Judas that." He waved his arms about so violently that he almost toppled over.

And then, suddenly, he sobbed. Tears shone in his eyes, and he rubbed them angrily and sniffed.

"And the others?" he said more calmly as he stared at Simon. "They are the elect. Why, those two sons of Zebedee want to sit on either side of the Nazarene in heaven. That Peter—oh, he's the great man and the favorite. And what of Judas Iscariot? He is nothing, nothing but a slave. The first thing when we get here, I'm sent to fetch wine. Peter and that John sent me. The Nazarene bade us prepare for the Passover feast, so they send me to get wine. Always Judas, Judas."

Simon looked at his worn sandals, the threadbare garment, the roughened hands, the beard grown long and straggling. The disciple took a few uneasy paces and then sat down again. He rubbed his shaking hands together. His bleary eyes watched Simon put the mug to his lips. "Do you know Zacchaeus of Jericho?"

"I know no Zacchaeus," Simon answered.

Judas snatched the mug from Simon's hands and drank. "He is the head of the tax collectors there. My father used to be a trader in Jericho—Zacchaeus ruined him. So we became caravan drivers. Today Zacchaeus is one of the richest men in Judea."

Judas drained the mug of its last dregs. Then his face twisted in a contemptuous smile. "When we passed through Jericho on our way here, the Nazarene had a meal at the house of Zacchaeus. Zacchaeus is now a follower," he said bitterly. "Zacchaeus is now more than Judas Iscariot." He spat on the ground at his feet. "In Zacchaeus's hall I saw the big cedar chest that my father bought in Tyre once for my mother. And the large painted pitcher that he once brought home from Damascus." He tossed the mug into the air and watched it fall to earth.

Simon had gotten to his feet. Judas clutched the hem of his garment, then moved his hands up higher, drew himself up, and breathed the fumes of wine into Simon's face. "Do you understand why I'm full of hatred?" he shouted, and pulled clumsily at Simon's shoulders.

Simon loosened Judas's clutching hands from his cloak and pushed him away. "Why do you tell me these things?" he asked.

"Because I can no longer keep them hidden in my heart." Judas came closer, rocking on his feet. He spoke softly and confidingly, concentrating on his words. "I must talk to somebody because I'm afraid there will be bloodshed in Jerusalem. This man will destroy the temple. The Jews who follow Him will think the time is ripe to rise against Rome. There are thousands of pilgrims here. And the Jews who hate Him will think the time has come to destroy Him before he destroys Jerusalem."

The words of Joseph of Arimathea flashed quickly through Simon's mind. Joseph had said the same. A chill moved along Simon's back.

Judas dropped his head. "It is like a dark night in a forest of Lebanon. Go this way or that, but always you walk into a tree."

There was silence for a long time. Then Judas, looking thoughtful and seeming quite sober, turned away toward a cypress, touched the bark, looked up into its branches. He walked back toward Simon. He held out his hands to see their trembling, then dropped them at his sides.

"That is why," said Judas Iscariot, "I believe it is better that He should die than that Jerusalem should perish."

Simon stared at the footprints that Judas had made upon the ground. Then at length he spoke: "If what you say is true, that He draws pictures of a kingdom that is not of the earth, then He must die. There is but one heavenly kingdom: the kingdom of the God of Israel. If He has claimed this kingdom, then He has blasphemed against God, and for this reason He must perish." Simon's voice was calm, without emotion, as if he were stating a fact as true as the shining of the sun upon the earth.

"That is what He talks about. He does so every time we ask Him why He does not break Israel's chains." Judas's voice was now more certain.

"Is he still in Bethany?"

"He is still there. He will enter Jerusalem this evening. And do you know," Judas said, his head thrust forward, "He broke bread in the house of Simon of Bethany, a leper."

"Always lepers and publicans," Simon said fiercely.

"He stays at the house of a man named Lazarus."

Lazarus. . . . Strange, that name no longer raised any doubt or wonderment in Simon. He now moved in certainty. No longer did he try to fathom Lazarus's resurrection or ask questions of himself.

Judas suddenly glanced up at the sky. Night was not far distant. "How much is the wine?" he asked.

"It costs nothing." Simon made a wide sweep with his hand and slapped his sides. "The wine costs nothing."

"Thank you. Then I will go. I must see if they have prepared the eating place. They can do nothing without Judas," he said importantly.

"Where are you going?"

"To the house where . . . we will eat our Passover meal. And after that I am going to . . . to . . . to Caiaphas."

"Are you going to hand the Nazarene over?"

"I am going to save Jerusalem." Judas thrust out his chest with a gesture of importance. "Peace be with you."

"And peace be with you, Judas Iscariot."

Then the disciple turned and walked away through the trees. Simon gazed after him, saw the sun rays illumine him and the shadows claim him in turn until the bank of the brook of Kidron hid him from view.

Simon walked in the same direction for a short distance. Then he stopped. He saw the milling crowds on the road from Bethany, in the Kidron Valley, and on the highway to the city gate. They were the rear guard of the pilgrims that came from that direction for the Passover in Jerusalem.

Simon went back to the storehouse and saw the jar that Judas had forgotten there. He lingered at the wine casks.

When he looked up again, Deborah was standing at his side.

"You have returned, my wife. Where is Ezekiel?"

"Still in Jerusalem. I have everything for the Passover meal. But we haven't got the paschal lamb."

"I will get a lamb," he said, and a smile softened his eyes.

19

Simon did not leave immediately. He tapped his fingers against the vats to hear how full they were. He looked up to the sky. "Summer must come," he said cheerfully. "The vats will soon be empty. I will press wine and olives and make a vegetable garden for you." He turned to Deborah. "What did you see in Jerusalem?"

"Jerusalem is full of people. It is almost impossible to walk in the streets. It is pilgrims, pilgrims, pilgrims. They press around the merchants so much that one really can't get near."

"What do you hear of the Nazarene?" he asked with eyes averted.

Deborah looked at him in surprise. "Nothing. Why do you ask?"

Simon gave a short laugh while he tightened a bung. "One of His disciples was here—a Judas Iscariot."

"A disciple?" Her eyes brightened. "Did you speak with him?"

"He spoke with *me*."

She looked at him, attempting to conceal her expectancy. But he was silent. "Where is he now?" she asked.

"Gone. It seems he intends to betray the Nazarene. I think he is going to inform Caiaphas where he can lay hands on this Nazarene tonight."

"But why?"

"His own disciple does not believe in Him," Simon said with a sneer.

Deborah sank down on a bench. "But He has harmed nobody. Why do they betray Him?"

"You have yet to understand, my wife," Simon said irritably. "You seem quite in the dark. Here is a disciple who has kept company with Him all this time, and even *he* does not believe in Him. How can this man be the Messiah if His own people do not believe He is?" He stepped out of the shadows and looked up at the sun. It was getting late.

Deborah was looking at him and trying to see him as he used to be, but failed. There had been a transformation deep within him. He did not seem to be as big, as powerful, as assured as he once had appeared. And when her eyes searched him, he could not look at her for long. His hands fidgeted and he peered around at the trees, restless, searching, and uncertain.

"I shall have to fetch the lamb from Joseph's flock," Simon said.

"Whose jar is this lying here?" Deborah asked as she got up.

"That Iscariot left it here." He gave a short laugh. "He came here to buy some wine for the Nazarene and His disciples . . . for their supper tonight."

"Did he forget it here?"

"If a man suddenly discovers that for years he has been following the wrong man, he can easily forget a jar, wife. I'm going now. The flocks must have been rounded up by now. Please put the Nazarene out of your head and get everything ready for the Passover." He walked away quickly, following the Kidron in the direction of the Damascus Gate, and her gaze followed him until he vanished among the distant trees.

Then she looked toward the jar, approached it, bent down, and touched it. Her dark eyes were tender and yearning as the tips of her fingers caressed the jar. She pushed the cork in firmly, lifted the jar by one ear, and placed it carefully against a tree trunk. She picked up her goatskin bag and started to walk toward the house. But then she stopped, looking at the jar in the shadow. *Wine for the Nazarene,* she thought. And as she stood there, the desire to see Him came to her again, and to serve Him in some manner, no matter how trifling it might be. She turned around and peered through the trees but could not see Simon. She went quickly to the house, deposited her shopping bag, and went back to where she had left the jar.

She lifted it quickly and swung it onto her head. With a hasty look back toward the trees, she turned and went quickly down the road to Bethany. She was certain that He would be there with His disciples. She had heard that He always rested there . . . and perchance she might set eyes on Rufus.

When she reached Bethany, she went up to the door of Lazarus's house. It was closed. Then she heard the voice of her son.

She turned around and saw Rufus, Mary, and a tall, red-bearded man emerging from the garden.

"Mother," Rufus greeted her and lifted the pitcher from her head. Mary took both of Deborah's hands in hers.

"What is this?" Rufus asked.

"A jar of wine for Jesus. A disciple came to buy it from us . . . and left it there."

"You are very kind," the tall man said, smiling at her.

"This is my mother," Rufus said. "Mother, this is the disciple Simon Peter."

"Peace be with you," the disciple said, and Deborah nodded. She looked about her. "I thought I might see Jesus. I . . . there is something I must tell Him."

"He is resting, and praying," Peter replied.

"Come and sit with us in the garden, Mother Deborah," Mary invited her. "Perhaps you may see Him later."

She stood there undecidedly and looked at Rufus. "But . . . but I must go back."

"No, come and rest first," Peter urged. He took her arm and led her to the garden. "I will take you to Jesus later, good woman. You have done Him a kindness."

"It is only a jar of wine that I brought."

"Even the least is worthy of His gratitude. I will take you to Him later. He must know what you have done."

The last light of the day gave a golden glow to the temple roofs when Simon, propelled along by the stream of pilgrims, approached the gate to the temple grounds.

After he had caught the lamb, he had entered through the Damascus Gate and passed through Jerusalem toward the temple, which now gleamed like a precious gem. In common with the other pilgrims, he had brought his offering. All were carrying paschal lambs over their shoulders.

Never before had he seen Jerusalem as she now appeared. The streets were like rivers rising above their banks. The city swarmed with Roman soldiers, for Pilate knew that if any rebellion was brewing, the chances were that it would burst out here during the Passover, when the religious fervor of the Jews ran highest. Simon looked the other way whenever he saw the red-plumed helmet of the oppressors.

But while he was walking toward the temple—and even now while he was thrust forward by the crowd—he constantly looked about cautiously, for he knew that the happenings in Cyrene had not yet been forgotten.

The pilgrims were converging in great numbers: a rough contingent from Galilee, babbling their dialect; Jews of the Diaspora, drawn to Jerusalem by the attractions of the Passover; Pharisees, decorous and grave, with phylacteries on their foreheads and arms; Syrians seeking work; wealthy Jews from Egypt, conspicuous in their rich and flowing garments.

Simon had almost reached the gate when the sunlight died, and its last rays left the roof of the temple. The crowds immediately became silent; all eyes were closed, all heads were bowed. The call of the trumpets cut shrilly and sharply through the air.

The Passover had begun.

The crowds of pilgrims resumed their movement. After presenting the sacrificial portion of his lamb at the temple, Simon hurried homeward. He was filled with excitement, with the anticipation of the Passover. He was looking forward to being together with Deborah and Rufus and the rest. Half unconsciously he had assumed that Rufus and Mary would come to share the Passover supper with them.

Now he stood frowning in the doorway of his house.

It was empty.

"Deborah," he called.

The silence was callous to his ears.

"Deborah," he shouted loudly.

Silence.

He went to the hearth and put down the lamb. Then he turned to face the table and saw only the goatskin bag that she had carried from Jerusalem. Nothing had been made ready for the meal. He turned back to the hearth and looked at the lamb. He had meant to prepare it and spit it for the roasting, but now he had lost all desire to do so.

It was the first time in all his years with Deborah that, arriving home, he had found his house in darkness.

He could not understand her absence. Aimlessly he picked up a wine pitcher. It felt empty. It should be filled. He felt the desire to go outside, for in the house the silence stifled him. He lit the lamp, picked up the pitcher, and went outside; he gazed at the thousands of tiny lights like little earthbound stars that showed where the pilgrims had made up their fires among the tents.

He walked up and down, listening for Deborah's approach. All he could hear was the slight rusting of the trees, for a light evening breeze had risen. It brought with it the mingled murmur from the pilgrims' camp.

He walked over to the little storehouse and paused under the tree where he had last seen Deborah that afternoon. He looked around but did not expect to find her there. He went into the storehouse and filled the pitcher. He stared at the soft ground, his mind empty. It was then that he saw the round mark on the ground. It was the print of Judas's wine jar.

There was no other sign of it. He held the lamp nearer to the ground and looked carefully at the confusion of footprints.

Simon straightened himself. Near the foot of a vat he saw the drinking mug from which Iscariot had taken wine. He felt certain that Judas had not come back again. He looked in the direction of Jerusalem and frowned.

The wine was spilling over the neck of the pitcher when Simon turned back to it at last. He closed the tap, picked up the pitcher, and went back to the cottage. He stopped often along the short journey. Once he stood so sunk in thought that the lamp turned in his hand and the flame licked at his garment. Mechanically he beat out the flame and then walked on. He stumbled over the uneven ground, and his head jerked forward when he stepped into a pothole.

He entered the cottage and put the pitcher down. He extinguished the lamp and went to sit on the threshold in the dark. He was not waiting expectantly now. He sat listlessly, his mouth open, his hands resting on his knees.

He tried to think of what Deborah was doing at that moment, but his thoughts halted at the picture of her leaving the house. Then they broke and faded, and he sat without thinking, mechanically stroking his beard.

He sat silent until he saw a torch flickering in the trees. Then he heard the voices. He saw Deborah, Rufus, and Mary of Bethany. Rufus held the torch high so that the light advanced before them. Deborah, leading the others slightly, was hurrying toward the house.

They came to Simon, greeted him. Deborah bent down and touched his face. "Husband," she said, "I am sorry that I am late."

He did not greet her or the others. "You went to the Nazarene; you took that jar." He said no more.

"I . . . I took the wine. . . . they need it for this evening's Passover."

"No, you followed Him with it—you followed the Nazarene. It is not only the wine." He rose and stood apart with his back turned to them. "It was not because of the wine," he said, and his voice was broken.

Deborah looked at Rufus and then at Mary. Mary came and placed her hand on the arm of the older woman.

"I only thought to take the jar to Bethany. I wanted to see Rufus and Mary."

"You use many words without saying the thing that you should say."

"What should I then say, my husband?" she asked humbly.

"You should say that you pursued this Nazarene to hear Him and to see Him."

She was silent, gazing at his broad back.

"Why did you desire to see him?" Simon asked, throwing up his hands. He took a step forward, further into the darkness, then stood motionless.

No one made reply. Rufus gazed with deep compassion at his father; Deborah saw him through her tears. "Let us go in and make ready for the Passover," she said. She felt helpless, as if with her words she were endeavoring to halt the progress of the night.

It was then that Simon turned toward them. The torch lit up his face. It was deeply calm, expressionless. But his eyes held a light of decision.

He saw Deborah standing there, and she was all he saw. She was standing between Rufus and Mary. They held her tightly, as if to shelter her from danger.

He moved his lips slowly as he spoke. "We have walked together for many years . . . you and I, Deborah. Our hearts were one. But now you have forsaken me. . . . Now I am alone."

"I never shall forsake you. I shall always be with you, though miles may lie between us." Deborah spoke calmly.

"You forsook me for the Nazarene," Simon said.

There was a long pause before Deborah spoke again. "Simon, He is the Messiah." His shoulders shuddered slightly. "This afternoon I saw Him. He spoke with me. Not long, nor did He utter many words. But I know now that He is the Messiah. You must believe me, Simon."

There was no challenge in her words, only love and reverence. And a conviction that flamed as fire.

He did not appear to have heard her. A film had covered his eyes. His hands stirred with uncertain movements. He looked down to the cool dark earth over which the torchlight flickered.

"I shall go back," he said.

They did not understand.

"I shall go back to Cyrene."

Rufus moved quickly toward him, but Simon looked at him so fixedly, with such a strange aversion, that the young man stopped uncertainly.

"I . . . I shall return and give myself up to Sextus Quirinius."

Deborah pulled herself free from Mary's grasp, ran to Simon, and threw her arms about him. "You can't . . . you can't! You will die!" she sobbed.

"I wish to die," he said softly, hoarsely. "My house is overturned. One son is a servant of goddess Rome. My wife and other son follow a man who will wipe out Israel."

He felt her slump against him, for her legs could not support her. She pressed her face against him, flung her arms about his legs, and gripped him fiercely.

"You must not. . . . I shall go with you," Deborah sobbed.

"I go alone. I am alone. I have nothing left—only my faith in the God of Israel, the only God. I shall give myself for my house that has strayed. I shall offer up my blood because I was too feeble to keep my family at the feet of the God of Abraham."

He looked down at her and saw her pale face turned toward

him, her pupils enlarged, her mouth trembling with emotion. Her hair was loose and fell about her shoulders. And even then, at that bitter moment, she was the loveliest woman he had ever seen. She seemed suddenly to have become young again, as when first they met so many years ago. She was Deborah, his bride, again.

Simon swallowed in an attempt to silence his protesting heart. Then he bent down, and with calm strength he loosened Deborah's hands. He lifted her up, looked for a fleeting second into her eyes, then turned and walked away into the darkness.

Deborah stumbled forward but then made no attempt to follow. She lifted her head, and her eyes went with him until he vanished in the darkness. She strained her ears to listen until his footsteps died away.

Then Rufus and Mary led her into the house.

Simon went heavily through the dark orchard. He walked into a pomegranate bush, stepped aside, and wandered blindly onward, following a ridge of the Mount of Olives. He sat down beneath a tree, rose, and, like an animal, went to shelter beneath another.

For a long time he wandered through the trees, awaiting solace from the night. But the night stayed black and silent.

When the stars had wheeled further across the sky, he turned back, swaying through trees and bushes, until he saw the light of his own house.

But he did not go closer, though the light drew him. He cut across toward the Kidron, walking slowly to consume the hours.

It was then that he saw the light among the trees of Gethsemane.

He went toward it. It was coming from a few torches planted in the ground. He glanced at the men who were lying beneath them relaxed in sleep, but his stare concentrated on the tall, strong man who lay close to the torches. Their light blazed on his red beard. Simon felt a sense of shock as he stared at the man. It was the same man he had knocked over a barrel in the Street of the Tanners years ago.

He was a fisherman, from Galilee—Peter, a disciple of the Nazarene.

Simon looked more closely at the other sleeping men. But he

did not see Judas Iscariot. Suddenly a new realization struck him —its impact was so fierce that he began to tremble. "The Nazarene," he whispered. "The Nazarene should be here!"

He stood rigid, and his body contracted as if he stood upon a high cliff where the night wind was blowing upon him. Then he stealthily crept closer, bending forward, moving slowly, examining the sleeping men. It was not the man with the red beard, certainly; nor the swarthy, thick-set fellow; nor the youth with the wavy hair. The Nazarene, they said, was tall and thin. His eyes darted from one to another of the men lying there asleep.

Simon of Cyrene stood slowly upright, his head tilted to one side, his black beard glinting in the torchlight. Pulses were throbbing in his throat. There was a roaring in his ears. His neck seemed to stiffen and grow cold. He straightened up cautiously, like a man afraid of lightning, searching among the dark trunks of trees.

For he had heard a voice pleading in the silence.

He turned around slowly, still peering into the trees. He gasped once for breath, swallowed, and passed his hand over his eyes.

The voice, low but urgent, lingered in his being.

"My Father, if You are willing, remove this cup from Me . . ."

A voice soft and delicate like the weave of Persian cloth.

It seemed to come from sky and stars, from the dark trunks of the trees, from the cold earth; it filled the evening, it sounded through the orchard.

". . . remove this cup from Me."

The soft voice was like an organ in a vast temple. It reechoed from the arc of heaven and, borne on the four winds, returned and gently sounded in the ears.

Then he saw the man.

He took a step forward involuntarily, for his whole being was absorbed by the sight. His great, perspiring hands slipped purposelessly one over the other, repeatedly.

In the faintest light of the torches, on the nearer side of the deeper darkness of the orchard, the man was kneeling at a stump that once had lived and grown. His old brown garment was dull in the soft light and His shoulders were narrow. His face was tilted

176

up in prayer. His hands were clasped before Him.

He struggled there, where the flickering light of the torches wrestled with the onslaught of the dark. He wrung His hands, swayed His head. He leaned His brow against the dead trunk, lifted it again. He flung His hands far forward and fell with his chest against the stump.

"The Nazarene. . . . It is the Nazarene," Simon said in a whisper that barely passed his lips. "The man who has destroyed my house."

Anger drove him a few steps toward the kneeling man. Then he stopped again.

It was the face of the man that halted him. He could only see the profile. But it was as pale as death, and there were queer, dark creases across his brow that looked like blood.

Simon gazed with breathless absorption at the man in travail. He looked for something different in Him, something that might distinguish Him. But he did not find it. He had wondered for so many days: how would He look, this man whose name was spoken in far-off Cyrene, this man who had conquered an old woman's heart in Alexandria, this man who had won over even his own wife and son.

But He was not different from other men. He had unimpressive shoulders, and His hands were narrow and brown and shone with sweat. He wore His hair like anyone else. His garment was old and shabby. His feet stirred restlessly as He struggled with Himself. And for the moment that Simon saw the eyes, he saw that they were closed in fear.

Fear of what? Fear of the first stone flung when outside the city gates the angry crowd encircled Him? Fear of the arms lifted up to kill? Fear of the first onslaught of pain when a stone struck home?

The redeemer of Israel, the Messiah, whose task it was to drive the oppressors over the hills of Judea, crouched praying in the garden of Gethsemane, sweating blood in fear of His outraged people. He was praying God to shield Him from the punishment His own flesh and blood would mete out to Him.

Contempt and anger forced Simon slowly back to the reality of the dark tree trunks and the silence and the cool air of waning winter.

"So you are the Nazarene," he said soundlessly, "the man who hounded me from Cyrene. . . ." He went still closer, saw the trembling shoulders, the head rocking in despair. "The man who broke up the altar of my house. . . . The man who is master of the Sabbath . . . the satellite of Caesar."

For the first time he took his eyes from the praying man. He saw the wooden cudgel that lay like a fissure in the golden gleam that played upon the ground. He looked at it for a long time.

And then, as if a voice were coming from on high, he heard within himself: "Thou shalt not kill."

He stood with legs astride, his head held low. Panting and perplexed, he thought of Vitellius, the Roman whose blood dyed his hands.

"You have estranged my house, my family," he muttered, "but I will destroy you. I go now to give you over to Jerusalem. . . . That which you fear, I will bring down upon you. Tomorrow you shall bleed before the gate."

He gave one last, hostile look at the man, whose shuddering head was tilted back in an attitude of death. Then he turned and walked away, leaving the light to stumble through the dark. He stopped once, turned, and saw the man staggering toward the place where His comrades lay sleeping.

"Your hour is at hand, deliverer of Israel," Simon said.

He hurried on down into the Kidron Valley, splashed through the little stream, slithering on stones, and raced between the tent of sleeping pilgrims, past the red coals of their dying fires.

"Let . . . Jerusalem . . . stone Him," he panted as he ran.

He rushed through the gate, and soon his sandals thudded on the surface of the Street of the Tanners.

At a corner he saw some gossiping men. "Where is the house of Caiaphas?" he asked them, panting, and wiped the sweat from his lips.

He ran in the direction they showed, his gown flapping, his eyes smarting, a searing stitch in his side. Down one street then to the left then to the right again . . . to the vicinity of the temple where the houses were more imposing, among stately cypresses and towering poplars.

In front of a house with an inner courtyard he stopped, sobbing for breath and hunched up with pain and weariness.

There were torches and a group of men. He approached them with lowered head.

Among them was one he sought—Judas Iscariot. Simon clutched his garment, brought him close. "I . . . I know where He is." Simon's wheezing breath made his voice sound strange.

"Oh, you're the man from Gethsemane," Judas said, his eyes glazed with alcohol. The other men came closer, holding their torches high—a handful of temple guards, Pharisees, and other men, nondescript but for their burning eyes.

"The Nazarene is in the garden of Gethsemane," said Simon, still breathing hard.

"Are you certain?" Judas asked urgently, gripping Simon's shoulder.

"I have just come from there. . . . I saw Him. And His disciples with Him."

"We were on the point of going to see whether He was there. Come," Judas said, beckoning to the others. "Let us go."

Simon jogged along in front with Judas beside him. The disciple pulled a leather purse from beneath his flapping garment and held it up to Simon's eyes. "See . . . what they gave me to deliver up the Nazarene," he mumbled. "Thirty silver pieces. I had thought it would be more."

"How will we know Him?" asked a temple guard just behind them.

"I shall approach Him with a kiss," Judas said over his shoulder. "In this way you will know."

Simon looked back. Some of the men held their swords, spears, and clubs ready, high in the air and glinting. The spears looked like gilded reeds in the light of the torches.

Simon and Judas led them through the gate and turned to the left, making straight for Gethsemane.

20

The small procession went briskly back to Jerusalem. Jesus was up front between two palace guards. Although His hands were tied behind His back, His captors walked with weapons at the ready, spears raised, like soldiers victorious in war.

Simon and Judas Iscariot brought up the rear.

Judas was not sober, and he tipped and stumbled as he went. Hanging from his belt was a leather flask of wine. Every time he drank, he offered it to Simon, but Simon refused, and Judas did not press him.

"Where are the other disciples?" Iscariot asked, looking about him.

"Vanished," Simon answered, laughing. "The followers of the Messiah have deserted Him now that there is trouble—this Messiah who allows Himself to be captured without stirring a finger, who let Himself be cornered in an olive grove! This has been the easiest coup I have ever seen. Only that hulking fisherman did anything—cut off the ear of a slave. The king of the Jews taken by a handful of temple guards and civilians—pitiful!"

"They all ran for it—except Judas Iscariot," Judas said, thumping his chest. He pulled out the moneybag from underneath his garment, held it up, shook it so the silver jingled. "They all ran, except Iscariot," he repeated, dribbling. "Even the great disciple Simon Peter has bolted. Only the lackey, Iscariot, still follows his master—good, faithful Iscariot; the one they always humiliated, the one they forced to do the dirty work—only *he* follows the master. But wait, Iscariot is no longer a slave!" he called out suddenly, and stopped, thrust out his chest and brandished his fists. "When this Nazarene shall have been forgotten, they will remember Judas." He staggered forward and caught at Simon's garment. "Judas Iscariot has saved Israel. . . . Hallelujah for Iscariot!" he shouted, so loudly that some of the men accompanying Jesus looked back at him.

"Hosannah for Judas Iscariot!" Simon called out merrily and thumped the disciple on the back.

"Iscariot . . . savior of Israel!" the disciple shouted.

"Judas Iscariot, savior of Israel," Simon repeated agreeably.

"So they all bolted, did they?" Iscariot asked again, his head lolling forward.

"They all bolted," Simon assured him. "That Peter never was of much account—the fellow with the red beard. I once gave him such a thrashing that he toppled over a barrel."

"You knocked him over a barrel?" Judas asked, poking a finger into Simon's chest, his watery eyes widening.

"I gave him a bloody nose for good measure," Simon boasted.

"Maybe he recognized you—that's why he made off so quickly," Judas guffawed, and they continued on again behind the others, zigzagging toward the gate. Some pilgrims were still awake and looked out at them, listening uncomprehendingly to their loud talk and wondering at their merriment.

In the middle of the gateway Judas tugged at Simon's garment, halting him. A beggar approached them. Judas pulled out his moneybag and swung at the cripple with it, missing him completely. Amused by his own poor aim, he doubled up with laughter.

Again he lashed out at the beggar, but lost his balance and fell down. Simon helped him up. Judas stood upright, breathing heavily, holding up the bag of money. "Do you know what I'm going to buy with this money?" he asked.

"A large pitcher of wine," Simon ventured.

Judas raised a finger and held it in front of Simon's nose. He sighed, stroked his beard away from his lips, and said in a sing-song voice:

"No . . . a throne for the Messiah."

"And a crown?"

"Yes, a crown as well . . ."

"And a purple cloak?"

"Ah, yes, a purple cloak . . . and if there is any money over, a large pitcher of wine . . . and a lamb . . . and new-baked bread. So we can fitly celebrate. Judas, the savior of Jerusalem!" he bawled again. His voice reverberated in the narrow gateway and slowly died away.

181

"Let us go," Simon said.

"Yes, come on," Judas agreed, and again they fell in behind the torches of the procession. "Hurry, Simon Peter!" Judas shouted. "Come save your master! Thomas, where are you? Little John, come and weep on your master's shoulder . . . and Matthew, tax collector—Matthew, you may come and wash His feet!"

Suddenly Judas halted and flung the bag of money from him. "He said I would betray Him . . . this evening in front of all the others," he cried. He did not look at Simon, and his shoulders shook. "Why me? Why not the others? Why not Philip, or Thomas, or James? Why me?"

Simon stared in bewilderment at his companion. "The wine has made you mournful," he said lightly.

Judas Iscariot lifted up his head, and his eyes were dull and tired. His face was contorted. His mouth twitched queerly: "He said I would betray Him, in front of all the others, and that is why . . . I betrayed Him. Do you understand? That is why . . . I hate Him now . . . I hate Him!" He screamed and began stumbling away through the moonlit night, his face turned to the sky between his upraised arms.

"If you hate Him, then you should be glad, for He will be stoned for trying to mislead Israel," Simon grunted contemptuously.

Judas lowered his head. "No," he said in a husky voice, "they must not stone Him—they must crucify Him."

"The law says, 'Stone . . .'"

"Crucify!" Judas shouted in sudden fury.

"Only the Romans may crucify," Simon answered hotly.

"Then let the Romans crucify Him."

"He is a Jew!" Simon said with emphasis.

"The Romans must crucify Him," Judas persisted stubbornly. "He must die slowly so that I can go to Him and say, 'You said I would betray You and I did. You never loved me—only the others, Peter and the others, but never Judas Iscariot . . . never Judas Iscariot.'" He had begun to weep bitterly.

Simon seized Judas's garment and pulled him close. He looked into the brimming eyes of the disciple. "Israel must punish him—not Rome . . . not Rome!" he shouted.

Judas closed his eyes. "Pilate must crucify Him," he whispered. "He rejected me. . . . I hate Him!" He remained silent a long time, trembling, his hands pressed to his eyes. "I love Him. . . . I love Him, and yet . . . I love Him."

"You're demented!" Simon burst out. "How can you both hate and love a man? The wine has made you mad."

Judas picked up his moneybag and sat down on the ground rocking to and fro. "That's how it is. That's how it is!"

Simon stared at the disciple for a long time with a dawning realization of what confounded him. He looked around uncertainly. "Come, let us go," he said at last. He pulled Judas by the sleeve. Judas shook himself free and staggered backward. He spoke in a strange, queer whisper.

"I betrayed Him. . . . I gave Him over to His enemies."

"But that is what you wished to do!" Simon said impatiently.

Again the disciple flung the bag of money down. It fell jingling onto the hard street.

"I have betrayed Him!" It was a piercing cry of shame and of despair.

"You are hopelessly drunk," Simon said, picking up the bag and holding it out to Judas. "Take your money. Here. It is the tears of wine that you are weeping now."

"You take the money," Judas said hoarsely. "I don't want it. It is blood money."

"Return the money to those who gave it," Simon replied contemptuously and threw the bag at Judas's feet. He walked away, stopped, and looking back saw Judas standing in the moonlight, bowed and quite alone. He heard his weeping in the empty street, like a child lost in darkness.

Simon made his way to the house of Caiaphas. He did not look back again. He strove to understand what could change a man's heart so quickly. "He hated the man, and he loved Him," he whispered. He stopped, shook his head, and then went on again.

By the time Simon reached the courtyard of Caiaphas's house, Jesus had already been questioned by Annas, high priest before Caiaphas, and then brought into a large chamber divided from the courtyard only by a row of pillared arches. Simon and the others in the inner court could both see and hear what happened.

Caiaphas was seated on a raised chair against the wall. Jesus was brought before him. In a half circle on benches behind Jesus sat the seventy members of the Sanhedrin, hastily summoned by Caiaphas. Here and there latecomers slipped hurriedly into their places.

Simon, standing close to a fire that had been built in the courtyard to cut the chill of the spring night, could see the high priest where he sat, a big man in his priestly crown and white embroidered gown. He could hear the evidence against Jesus and nodded continually in agreement. "It is the truth," he said softly on occasion. He glanced at the man who was standing there motionless without answering one question or accusation against Him.

He cannot answer, Simon told himself with satisfaction. But he did not speak his words aloud, for the presence of the full Jewish council, the leaders of Israel, filled him with awe.

At length, the cold penetrated through Simon's concentration on the scene before him. He shivered and turned around toward the fire. But before he reached it, he stopped. A deep frown cut furrows between his eyes. Sitting among some servants, his hands stretched out toward the fire, was the man with the reddish beard. "Simon Peter!" exclaimed Simon. "One of the disciples of the Nazarene," he assured the others. "I know you. You were always with Him."

The tall man held his open hands protectively between his face and the flames. "I know Him not," he said, and his voice was strong and clear. He closed one eye, turning his face from the warm glow. "God be my witness, I do not know Him."

"But your speech betrays you—you speak with the accent of a Galilean fisherman. You must be one of His disciples," said a temple guard who was squatting beside the fire.

The man rose quickly, stamped his feet, and cursed loudly. "I tell you I had nothing to do with Him. I swear by God that I had nothing to do with Him. I am . . ."

A cock awoke in the garden of the high priest. Its crow at this unwonted hour was loud and lonely.

The eyes of the tall man changed. Resentment fled from them; fear glinted in its place. His features writhed as from a painful wound. He passed his hand weakly over his cheek and chin and let his head drop. Simon could see drops of perspiration shining at his temples and on his pallid forehead.

"You are a coward," the Cyrenian said.

Simon Peter looked up, and his eyes showed only acknowledgment and guilt. His jaw moved spasmodically, and, turning away like some guilty animal, he slunk away through the gate into the chill night. Simon's gaze followed him until the light of the flames no longer held him.

He became conscious of a voice. He heard the high priest saying, "I charge You by the living God to tell us whether You are the Messiah, the Son of God."

The question made Simon turn back again. For the first time Jesus spoke. He stood quite still and looked directly at the high priest. He spoke without fear, calmly, with great dignity—softly, but with a ringing clarity.

"It is as you say. But I tell you this: from now on, you will see the Son of Man seated at the right hand of the majesty of God and riding on the clouds of heaven."

Caiaphas laid his hand on his garment and tore it from the neck. "It is blasphemy," he said. "You have heard His blasphemy. He must die!"

Simon glared at Jesus with a consuming hatred. Only when a temple guard smote Jesus across the face so that He staggered backward, and a slave spat in His face, did Simon come out of his trance. Then a Pharisee struck Jesus' cheek with his fists so that He fell against a guard, and Simon gasped with delight. He struggled to get closer but was thrust back by the guard.

"Let me strike Him just once," Simon begged, and raised his fist. "Just one blow. He is a false prophet—let us stone Him now!"

It was with gratitude that the Cyrenian heard the members of the Sanhedrin say in ragged chorus, "He is guilty. He must die!"

"The Sanhedrin is adjourned until morning," Caiaphas said. "Then the meeting will be resumed in the temple."

Israel's rulers stood up and began to go off in different directions. Simon noticed Joseph of Arimathea walking out quickly and crossing the inner court with hurried strides. Simon turned and followed until he was walking briskly beside his landlord. "He is guilty, Joseph of Arimathea," Simon said. "I . . . I helped to capture Him . . . in your olive grove. I came to tell Judas Iscariot." He gripped the sleeve of the silent man. "He is guilty, Joseph. Why can't we stone Him now, immediately?"

Joseph jerked his sleeve away. "Leave me," he said loudly. "Go away. They spoke Israel's doom tonight. He has no guilt."

Simon halted. He looked at Joseph fading away into the darkness like a ghost. "He believes in the Nazarene," Simon said, overwhelmed. "He has always believed in Him. He never acknowledged it."

He looked around at Caiaphas's house, then up at the stars, which seemed to be swaying in the wind. He could hear the singing and quarreling of drunken Roman soldiers. Far off he could hear the faint sound of Joseph's footsteps. *"Not guilty," he says. The man has blasphemed against God, but "He has no guilt"!*

He shuddered in the chill wind.

Caiaphas had given orders for Jesus to be taken out to the courtyard. He stood there shivering, for His old garment was threadbare. Some of the guards had begun slapping Him in the face until His head jerked with each blow. Then they conceived the idea to blindfold Him. Again He was struck—in the face, and on the stomach, so that He doubled up, groaning softly.

"Come now, You are a prophet, are You not? Then prophesy who it was that struck You," they tormented Him.

The temple guards tortured Him until He staggered on His feet. His face bled, His body was bent with the blows. At last a guard said, "It is enough. Remember, He must be able to face His accusers tomorrow."

They brought water and flung it in His face. Then they removed the cloth that bound His eyes.

Simon walked back toward the gate. He crossed the Kidron and the orchard, through which the wind was sighing. He passed the lean-to and heard Ezekiel's heavy breathing. He reached his house, stood listening in the doorway. He smelled the unleavened bread that Deborah had baked for the Passover. The aroma of her cooking had always welcomed him back home.

Simon entered the bedroom carefully. "Deborah," he called softly. There was no reply. He lay down on the bed. He lay on his back, his eyes wide open in the dark, and listened to the wind go sighing through the trees. And still in front of him he saw the eyes of the Nazarene, so gentle, so devoid of hate or fear.

He saw them so clearly that he pressed his knuckles against his eyes. He tossed restlessly, unable to sleep. Echoing in his mind came Joseph's words denying the guilt of Jesus, and again he heard Caiaphas say, "You have heard His blasphemy. He must die."

21

Simon awoke when day had just broken. The happenings of the previous night came back to him with a vague sense of shock. He looked at the bed beside him, but it was empty. Deborah had not returned. He thought of the bitter moment of his leaving her. In that early light it seemed fantastic and unreal.

He dressed quickly, left the room, and washed himself at the tub. When he looked up again, he realized that all the preparations for the Passover meal had been removed—only a few unleavened loaves remained. He felt bitter. The night before, all of them had probably been together in Bethany—his Deborah, Rufus, this Lazarus and his people. He alone had not been there. For a moment he hesitated, his face dripping with water, his eyes narrow and calculating. Should he not go to Deborah and Rufus to tell them what had happened?

But his bitterness, pride, and obstinacy overcame him. Had they not deserted him?

"I will not go to Bethany," he whispered determinedly and pulled down a big goatskin bag. He put two unleavened loaves inside it, and some dried figs and raisins, a partly consumed tallow candle, a jar of honey, and a bag of dates. In a corner he saw the paschal lamb, untouched. He poured some flour in a little packet and packed it in the bag, along with some other necessaries.

He went back to the bedroom and stood looking at the empty bed. He came out again, took a crooked stick that Ezekiel had brought along on the trip from Cyrene and lay it on the table next to the skin bag. A small wine bottle hung on the wall. It was empty. He took it to the storehouse to fill it from the casks.

He had just filled the bag and was returning with it to the house when he heard the sudden uproar.

There was a mighty shouting. It reached him like the roar of a great wind—a high, reverberating hysteria that seemed to reach the clouds above Jerusalem. He stopped and looked out over the Kidron. Jerusalem lay sleeping like a maiden before dawn. The first glimmering of daylight seemed to bring the temple nearer and made the tower of Antonia gleam like polished marble. He saw a flock of snow-white pigeons in wheeling flight above the city.

Then the yelling rose again into the chill sky, loud and menacing. The frightened pigeons swerved and hid themselves behind the cypresses that grew on the summit of the hill of Zion.

"The Nazarene. . . . They are stoning the Nazarene," Simon whispered, and his mouth felt dry.

Weighing the wine bag in his hand, he hesitated, reconsidering his resolution to go away. Suddenly he could not imagine life without Deborah. It seemed impossible. His resolve of the previous night seemed a far off, fantastic fragment of a faded dream.

And the Nazarene . . . if the Nazarene was dying at that moment? Surely the digressions of Deborah and Rufus would die with Him. Then his house would be made whole again.

Again came the tumult in the dawn.

He returned to the house, hastily put back the wine bag and hurried through the olive grove toward Jerusalem.

Halfway through the grove he stopped. It was the place where Iscariot had put his arms about the shoulders of the Nazarene and kissed Him. A man lay huddled against a tree trunk.

Only when Simon went closer did he see that it was Judas. He bent down and shook him till he awakened.

"You sleep late, Iscariot—I think they are already stoning the Nazarene."

Judas jumped up, staring vacantly across the orchard, his eyes red-rimmed and weary. Then he looked at Simon and drew a sighing breath. "I've returned to Gethsemane," he said, stroking his cheek. He averted his head, his eyes remote. "What are these sounds of celebration?"

"It is because of the Nazarene. The Sanhedrin declared Him guilty last night. He must die."

"Die?"

"He blasphemed against the God of the covenant, the God of Israel. Come, let us go and see."

189

Judas shook his head, pulled the hood of his garment closer about his face, sank down against the tree trunk, and squatted there.

"I'm going—there is no time to waste," Simon said and began to walk on, but near the Kidron he stopped and looked back.

He saw Judas shambling toward him, slowly, wavering like a child who first attempts to walk. He waited for the disciple to reach him. "Come, Judas," he said when Iscariot reached him, "let us go and see how the prophet dies."

"I don't want to be alone today," Judas muttered. They walked on with Simon leading, Iscariot stumbling along behind him.

The tents of the pilgrims were deserted. Fires had been left to smoke, crying children were wandering about, dogs sniffed at cooking pots; only here and there a man or woman, feeble with age, moved uncertainly.

Simon and Judas hurried through the East Gate in the direction of the almost continuous roar that came from the crowds. There was triumph in the tumult and hatred and contempt.

They saw others running toward the noise: women with pitchers on their heads, water splashing over their shoulders; tanners with arms still rusty-red from the tanning waters; peddlers with baskets behind their backs; saddle makers with nails still held between their teeth; harness makers with leather thongs still strung around their necks; beggars, their rags flying.

At the gate of the temple Simon and Judas joined the crowd, a jostling, jubilant crowd. Craning their necks and standing on tiptoe, people pushed and shoved. There were rich merchants from Jerusalem, Alexandria, Tyre, Sidon, Damascus—men whose white gowns were embroidered with rich purple. There were farmers from Galilee with coarse smocks hanging to their ankles. There were Greeks, Persians, Egyptians, Syrians, Samaritans, Pharisees, Sadducees. All who were enmeshed in the colorful throng were straining with curiosity, shouting, looking toward the temple.

For with the dawning of the day the word passed in Jerusalem that there would be an execution, for the carpenter from Galilee had blasphemed in the presence of the Sanhedrin.

A little apart from the crowd stood the few who took no share in the tumult—silent, apprehensive, or whispering, with hands clasped nervously and eyes downcast as if in guilt.

"Bring Him forth!" someone cried out from the midst of the crowd.

"Bring Him forth!" The crowd took up the cry in a crescendo that surged like a wave over Jerusalem.

Simon tugged excitedly at the garment of a youthful Pharisee. "Will they stone Him?" he asked breathlessly.

"We cannot stone Him," the young man said craning his neck without a glance at Simon.

"Why not? He is guilty."

"Only Pilate can pass sentence of death. The Sanhedrin has no authority."

Simon wished to pursue the subject, but the shouting grew so loud that it was impossible to distinguish individual words and voices. Jerusalem's hatred thundered through the dawn, went rolling down the streets, reechoed from the walls.

Tall and dignified, impressive in his white priestly robes, Caiaphas had appeared at the gate of the temple. His face was drawn and pale. He raised his long arms. The hysterical shouting died away, and all became so still that far down the street Simon could hear an oxcart rumbling over the paving. He heard a dog bark, and it sounded so far away that it might have come from Joppa beside the sea.

"People of Israel!" Caiaphas said, his voice sounding small and thin in the feeble light. "Give ear to me, Caiaphas, high priest of all Israel! In the course of the night that is past, we apprehended Jesus the Nazarene and questioned Him."

He fell silent, his arms still raised, his eyes lifted to the hills over which the young light of the new day was pouring.

"The Sanhedrin has found Jesus the Galilean guilty of blaspheming against the All Highest. He aspires to elevate Himself to the right hand of the God of Israel."

The raging of the crowds rose up from the earth and spread out over the multitude. They began to press forward from all sides and seethe closer to the gate.

Caiaphas flung out his arm, enjoining them to silence. "We are taking Him now to the palace so that Pontius Pilate may declare Him guilty of treason and sentence Him to death. The governor has been informed of His claim to be our King."

A double row of temple guards burst through the gate and drove a lane through the frantic throng. Members of the Sanhedrin joined Caiaphas. The high priest led them slowly through the crowds.

Then Jesus came through the gate, His wrists bound with cord. He walked slowly, stooping like an old man. The injury where He had been struck in the stomach kept Him bowed. His bruised face was discolored, His lips were thick and puffy, one eye was swollen and inflamed.

When he saw Him, Judas gasped, clutching Simon's garment.

Jesus looked neither to the right nor left. Bent forward in pain, He walked between a double row of temple guards, who marched with spears at the ready. Their copper-colored helmets glittered; their bodies were inclined forward, like alert hunters.

"King of the Jews indeed," somebody muttered contemptuously near Simon and Judas. "What a sight He is!"

His appearance seemed to disconcert the crowd. The fierce tumult died away. There was only a low grumble like that of distant thunder.

Somebody flung a soft melon at Him. An old sandal flew over the heads of the guards toward Him, striking the face of a guard. A stone hummed through the air, and then a club.

The double row of guards swung around, menacing the mob, and, with javelins lowered, forced it back.

The crowds around Simon and Judas swung in to move slowly along behind the procession, and the two found themselves right out in front of those who followed. Judas continually bumped into people, for he kept his eyes on Jesus, pulling the hood closer to his face.

They had not moved far when Simon heard the cry. "Praise be to Jesus . . . the Messiah . . . the son of David."

Even Caiaphas turned around to look.

A little man had broken through the cordon of guards and was running across the paving stones toward Jesus, his arms held open, his head jerking with the speed of his running.

When he was three steps from Jesus, a guard's spear struck him between the shoulders. He halted in his stride, and his hands clutched for the blade in his back; he swayed, staggered, and fell. Gasping, he cried, "Jesus . . . my Savior."

The guard came up, plucked out his spear. The man turned over, struggled to his knees, and crawled forward, blood frothing on his lips. The crowds stopped and watched him dying, writhing on a paving stone.

Simon saw him die. And he knew the man. He had seen the truncated arm, the broken mouth, the mutilated face of Nimrod, the shepherd.

Simon and Judas moved on with the crowds, and they scarcely knew that they were moving. Simon walked like a man in a dream. He still could see the man who died. He still could hear him calling Jesus' name. And Judas too walked as if asleep, but his eyes were fixed unblinkingly on the bent, suffering figure.

The procession continued toward the palace. The morning sun shone on the bustling chaos of heads and shoulders. Simon looked up at the sun. It was chill and faint in the haze, like a weak moon that had invaded the realm of day. Its light was not like sunlight, but like a queerly luminous veil.

The murmuring crowd followed Caiaphas under the marble arch in front of the great building where Pontius Pilate was staying. Simon looked up at the eagle on the gate, its wings spread wide, just like the eagle on the palace gate in Cyrene. He shuddered. He looked at the palace lying in front of them like a great pair of pincers—two vast, projecting wings joined to the rectangular building behind them. He gazed with admiration at the sumptuous paving of the path they were traversing, the richly colorful flower trellises extending in all directions, the exotic fish swimming in the marble ponds, the long array of climbing roses already bursting into bud, the double row of dark-green trees gracing the lane to the steps before the entrance. Clusters of pigeons pecked on the verdant lawns, and Simon looked with admiration at the graceful portico that ran the length of the palace. "Now we are in Rome," he whispered to Judas, who was silently shuffling along beside him. Judas withdrew his face more deeply into his hood.

Caiaphas and the chief priests climbed the wide marble stairs, and the crowds swarmed along behind them.

Simon and Judas were still near the front of the massed procession. Simon looked back and saw the crowds stretching through the gate, reaching back almost to the heart of Jerusalem.

They reached the huge expanse of marble paving before the palace. Great events were recorded there in black, green, and red mosaic—the great feats of the Romans, battles on land and sea, the might and power of their gods.

They came to the rostrum that Pilate had set up on the pavement between two fountains that threw white plumes of water into the spring air. The Jews would not enter a Roman dwelling—that he knew quite well. On it stood the gilded judgment seat of the governor.

Simon looked at the Roman soldiers, turned his gaze away, then looked at them again—big men with brown faces and strongly muscled arms. Row on row they stood around the chair, like images in stone without thought or breath or feeling—soldiers of Rome, without heart or individuality.

Their helmet plumes flaunted brilliant red in the early light. Their heavy helmets shone. The rows of round shields looked like scales of a long, bronze monster. Their spears rested motionless on their shoulders.

At two corners of the rostrum stood two heralds with long, glittering trumpets. An order was given. They raised the trumpets high, and a blade of sound cut through the air. The soldiers stiffened behind their metal breastplates.

Simon and Judas saw a man appear on the judgment seat. He was short, rather stocky, his shiny bald head supporting a neat laurel wreath. His eyes were tired and puffy. There were lines of pain on his face. His heavy toga was purple. His jaded eyes could not hide his disdain for the scene before him. He looked contemptuously, almost challengingly, at the crowds that filled the whole forecourt of the palace. He saw Jews on the outskirts of the crowd trampling his spring flowers; even, in their eagerness, standing in his fishponds and chasing his sacred pigeons to the highest ridges of the palace roof.

He glanced up at the watery sun, shivered, and pulled his toga closer about his shoulders; he said a few words to the two secretaries seated on either side of him, ready with their tablets and writing instruments.

Beneath his breath he cursed these Jewish leaders, too fanatical to enter the palace. It would defile them! For their sakes he had to sit outside, in the cold air, before this rabble. And his asthma was particularly troublesome just then.

Pontius Pilate, governor of Judea and Samaria, made a listless, arrogant gesture with his hand. Caiaphas and other Jewish leaders walked slowly up the steps. Jesus followed, and four Roman guards, who had taken over from the temple guards, accompanied Him to the rostrum.

Simon stared at Pilate and felt his palms grow clammy.

Pilate calmly looked at Jesus, neither hatred nor pleasure in his eyes. Caiaphas and the Jewish leaders held themselves stiffly, their heads high, their eyes hostile.

Pilate listened to the beehive hum of voices as the people murmured to one another, and he felt the gooseflesh on his arms as he saw how densely packed the people were. He beckoned; a centurion moved closer, saluted, and bent over toward Pilate. He nodded in quick reassurance. "Your Excellency, there are enough soldiers here to deal with any trouble."

Pilate glanced at Jesus again, who stood slightly to one side between the guards, the ropes slack on His wrists. There was something about this prisoner that caught his attention—His calmness, that of a man at peace, devoid of fear.

Caiaphas moved his hands impatiently beneath his robe.

"What is the charge against the prisoner?" Pilate asked. He looked only at Caiaphas and at no other member of the Jewish council standing before him. "Has He done something wrong?" he asked coldly.

"He has blasphemed against our God of the covenant," said Simon, answering the governor's question under his breath.

"If He had committed no crime, we should not have brought Him here," Caiaphas said stiffly. "We have completed the interrogation. He is guilty. It is for you to punish Him."

Caiaphas spoke with bitterness. And that very bitterness gratified the Roman. He hated these Jews. He had been humiliated by them once or twice. But now the high priest was forced to admit he was powerless to do more, though they had found Jesus guilty.

Pilate now felt the urge to provoke them, to belittle them before the gaping multitude. He drew his toga more closely about him. "If you found Him guilty, why come to me? Go and sentence Him in accordance with your law. Must Rome always make your decisions? Why should I punish a man I have not examined?" He looked at the high priest with a taunting smile.

Caiaphas took a pace forward, his beard trembling, his arms extended before him. "You know full well," Caiaphas said, "that *legally* we cannot sentence anyone to death."

Pilate smiled and glanced at the secretary who was writing busily next to him.

"What has this man done that He must die?" Pilate asked and looked away over the heads of the crowds, over the houses to where the sun hung feebly over the Mount of Olives.

Several priests stepped forward quickly and spoke simultaneously, flinging out their arms, hurling accusations against Jesus, until Pilate raised his hands and said, "I cannot hear when you all speak together."

Caiaphas raised his hands and silenced his companions. "He incites the people," Caiaphas said. He had expected the Roman to react strongly, but Pilate leaned forward, showing no sign of interest.

"He represents Himself to be a King," Caiaphas tried again.

"A King?" Pilate asked with a slight smile and looked at Jesus as if it did not mean anything to him. He passed his hand over his face. "And what else?"

A new apprehension stirred in Simon. Did this Roman not know what it meant if the Nazarene said He was a King?

Caiaphas wavered for a moment under the direct question. He knew he could say nothing about blasphemy that would impress Pilate. His answer would be: "That does not concern me. Your God is not the god of Rome. Your religious troubles are no concern of mine."

"This man," the high priest said and pointed toward Jesus, "opposes the paying of taxes to Caesar." He waited for the sign of shock to appear on Pilate's face.

But Pilate was unmoved. "I have heard," he said, "that this man has said that Caesar must be given what is due to him."

Caiaphas looked at the governor, dumbfounded. He colored beneath his beard. Pilate laughed softly until his belly quivered at the discomfiture of the high priest.

But another member of the Sanhedrin came to the aid of Caiaphas. "This man says He is our King. What will Caesar say to that?"

The question quashed Pilate's amusement. He glanced uneasily at Jesus. The counselor standing behind Pilate's chair leaned over and whispered, "Remember Tiberius. It is wise to proceed with caution."

Pilate nodded and suddenly felt drained and defenseless. He looked up into the angry eyes of the accusers and rose suddenly. "Take the prisoner into the palace," he ordered and left the rostrum. Jesus turned His back on the crowds and followed Pilate into the palace.

In the luminous, columned hall Pilate seated himself on a bench built around a pillar and covered with the soft skin of a lion. His counselor and two secretaries stood on either side. Jesus and the guards came to a halt before him.

"You may be seated," Pilate said, and the others glanced at him quickly as he gave this unprecedented invitation. But Jesus did not reply. He remained standing with the ropes about His wrists.

Pilate stared down on the mosaic of the floor, and when he spoke, his voice, hollow and thin in the empty hall, threaded around the pillars, resounded reedily from the far walls. He rubbed his hands slowly. "You have heard the charges. Most of them are not worth considering. Except one: Are you the King of the Jews?"

Jesus made a small movement. "Are you asking Me that on your own, or did others tell you that about Me?" he asked.

Pilate gave him a sidelong glance. He knew that Jesus had put the question like that because He wanted to find out whether Pilate expected an answer from the Jewish or from the Roman viewpoint, and he felt respect for the man. But the question also made the Roman feel impatient. He suddenly leaned over, his elegant sandal sliding over the floor. "Am I a Jew?" he asked loudly, irritably. "Your own people and Your own high priest handed You over to me."

He looked into the gentle eyes of the man before him and saw how this outburst had affected the prisoner. He saw disillusionment, grief, and pain. The sorrow of one who had been rejected by His own people and had been handed over to a foreigner.

Jesus' voice was clear and calm when he answered Pilate's question. "My kingdom is not of this world."

Pilate sat up straight, relieved, his hands on his knees. He need not fear that this man could possibly be a pretender in opposition to Tiberius. The only justifiable reason for executing Him had vanished.

"But He does call himself a King," the old counselor whispered in Pilate's ear. "He mentions His kingdom." Pilate felt obliged to pursue the subject. He asked, "Are you then some sort of king?"

"You used the word. My task is to bear witness to the truth. For that purpose was I born."

Pilate remained silent for a long time, turning the words over and over in his mind, pondering over them, analyzing them. At last he rose, took a few steps toward a golden torchholder against a pillar, and meditatively touched the unlit torch. His face calm, he turned and spoke his thought aloud as he looked at the prisoner. "Therefore, your kingdom is of the soul, of the intangible. You are King of the human heart, while the illustrious Tiberius reigns over the bodies of humans, countries, navies, and armies, over palaces and fortresses. Your kingdom is that of the conscience, of principles, of ideals—is that the difference?" He looked at the prisoner, but Jesus stood silent.

"You say You are a witness of the truth—what is the truth?" Pilate asked suddenly, passing his hand over his eyes. "What is truth?"

"Everyone born of truth hears My voice," Jesus said simply.

Pilate did not attempt to understand the reply, but he was satisfied that he had divined the difference between Jesus and Caesar. All that interested him was that the Jews had no case for treason against the man, and so he left the hall swiftly, his toga swaying, his sandals flapping. The prisoner was led slowly out behind him.

Pilate seated himself on the rostrum with great confidence, straightened his laurel wreath a little, and waited until Jesus was back on the rostrum. He listened to Israel's hatred. Wave upon shuddering wave of accusing yells broke over the forecourt until the soldiers moved forward, forcing the mob to silence.

Once again Jesus stood in front of Pilate, with the guards beside Him.

Pilate looked in triumph at Caiaphas. "I find no guilt in this man," he said. He could see that his words upset the Jewish leaders. "I listened to Him, I questioned Him. He is only a zealous enthusiast with a new kind of idealism—nothing more. He is not an insurrectionist. He believes that He is the King of a kingdom that none of us can understand. The kingdom of the soul, the heart, a nebulous kingdom."

"But He calls Himself a King," burst from Caiaphas.

"King of a kingdom that does not compete with Rome!" Pilate retorted irritably. Then he played his trump card. "Do you want me to act against the policy of Rome? Does Rome not allow freedom of worship? Do they not even in Rome make offerings to Isis of Egypt? For the Greeks at Olympus, is Zeus not supreme?" Pilate flung his words out harshly. He noticed how quiet the people had become, how they listened with open mouths.

"Now this man wants to play at being King—King of the soul. That is your problem. That is religion. As far as that is concerned, you are as free as you always were. It is no concern of Rome. As long as this man does not set himself up against Caesar, I find Him innocent." Pilate rose and turned to descend from the rostrum.

"Idiot of a Roman," Simon whispered.

22

But Pontius Pilate did not descend from the rostrum.

As he reached the top of the steps, a young Jew with the face of a fanatic and wearing the phylactery of a Pharisee shouted up to the governor, "Have you forgotten about the bloodbath in Judea when Judas of Galilee rose during the census? This man will cause such bloodshed again throughout our country. Just like Judas!"

Young Saul twisted himself free from the hands of two Roman soldiers who had seized him, but they caught up with him again and dragged him away. Pilate had stopped in his tracks. The multitude was closing in menacingly, brandishing their fists in the air.

"You must return to the judgment seat. This case is not over yet," Pilate's counselor whispered to him. "You saw what happened that time in Caesarea."

The words struck home. The governor hesitated for a moment, his left hand stretched out at an angle toward the centurion. On the tip of his tongue trembled the command to have the mob driven off with the sword. But he thought better of it. Rome had already cautioned him against any further bloodshed such as that which occurred when first he came to govern.

Pilate turned slowly and sat down again. Caesarea—the place of his humiliation in front of the Jews, the lovely city where he lived beside the sea. The incident in Caesarea came back to him vividly. When first he came to Palestine as governor, he was younger, sterner, far less tolerant. He had moved the army from Caesarea to Jerusalem for the winter. The Roman phalanxes had marched into Jerusalem with their banners high. Each bore the head of Caesar.

"You are defiling Israel's holy city!" shouted these same fanatical Jewish leaders.

Pilate had refused to yield. Countless Jews marched to Caesarea to speak to him. Five days they wrangled, until Pilate threatened to put the deputation to the sword. But the Jews laid themselves down on the ground, bared their necks, and said, "We would rather die than have our city defiled."

What was he to do? He had to give way and have the banners brought back to Caesarea.

He flushed as he remembered his defeat and humiliation. These were the same men who had humiliated him then. It was now his strength against theirs. He could destroy them if he wished—it would be easy. But what could he then tell Rome?

While Pilate listened to the clamor of the Jews, his thoughts dwelt on a white toga, on the cool restfulness of the grand porticos of the Capitol in Rome. That was where he longed to be—not in this ghastly country where a band of fanatics set fresh traps for him every day. He wished to relax in the sublime tranquillity of Rome, not be subjected to continual tension in this rebellious place where he governed but where the spirit of Israel was the master.

He dared not err in this matter. Should he not yield, and allow this man to die? What did he really care about one Jewish religious leader more or less?

He gazed at Jesus, who stood before him with grave dignity —the only dispassionate person in this sea of hatred, doubt, and uncertainty. The continuous uproar throbbed in Pilate's head like the heavy beat of drums. "Silence the rabble!" he shouted at Caiaphas. The high priest turned and raised his hands. The crowd fell silent.

Pilate looked at Jesus in vexation. "Don't You hear what these people testify against You? Why don't You speak?" the Roman asked. He suddenly sounded powerless. He waited for a reply from Jesus, but the prisoner was silent. Pilate looked at the man in wonder.

"This Galilean stirs up revolt throughout our land!" somebody shouted.

Galilean . . . Galilean . . . Galilean . . .

The word hypnotized Pilate. It throbbed through his dulled mind, and suddenly he saw a way out.

He looked at Caiaphas, standing there insolently now that he knew he had the upper hand. "Is this man from Galilee?" Pilate asked, and Caiaphas nodded. "Then take Him to his royal highness Herod Antipas, Tetrarch of Galilee. He is here in Jerusalem, and this man comes under his jurisdiction. I find the man not guilty, but Herod can sentence Him if he so desires. Take this man to the Palace of the Maccabees."

Pilate quickly dictated a message to Herod and handed it to the centurion in charge of the Roman guards who would accompany Jesus to Herod.

Orders were given, the soldiers drove a wedge through the multitude, and once more Jesus was led from the rostrum. He passed along the crowded street toward the white palace of Herod Antipas, followed by most of the crowd, among them Simon of Cyrene and Judas.

Pontius Pilate, the procurator of Judea and Samaria, sat bowed on the edge of the gilded bed in which his wife had just awakened.

"You sleep late, Claudia," Pilate said lightly.

"I'm so bored with Jerusalem," Claudia replied, yawning delicately as she looked through the window at the pallid light of day.

Pilate touched his temples with the tips of his fingers. He stood up, walked to the wall, and poured wine from a Grecian pitcher. He sipped slowly. "There is a crisis. Every time I come to Jerusalem, it seems, there is a crisis."

"A crisis?" Claudia asked as she unplaited her hair.

"This time it is this new prophet—a man named Jesus. The Jews are thirsting for His blood."

Pilate looked at the faces of the figures depicted on the Greek vase—they represented the gods of the Olympian pantheon, and all stared back at him vacantly.

"A man who preaches and who is said to work miracles?" Claudia asked, tossing a loosened plait over her shoulder.

"Yes, a Galilean."

Claudia looked at her portly husband and realized suddenly that some anxiety had driven him to her. At first she had thought it was boredom that brought him to her bedroom at this early hour.

Now she knew better. She sank back on her embroidered pillows. "What do they want you to do?"

"They want me to convict this man . . . to have Him executed."

Claudia sat up quickly, her eyes alert and bright. "No, you must not . . . you must never convict Him!" she said sharply.

Pilate turned his head and gave her a sidelong glance. A smile made two deep furrows in his cheeks. "Do not tell me that my lovely wife has become a follower of some Galilean holy man," he said lightly. Looking at her he became once more conscious of her beauty. He went to her and kissed her throat. But she remained aloof and tense, ignoring his caress. As he looked up in surprise at her, he saw that she had turned her face away.

"I had a dream," Claudia said.

"About me?" Pilate asked facetiously.

"No, it was about this man . . . this Galilean. He is innocent."

"I know He is innocent."

"Therefore, you must not sentence Him."

"They demand a conviction."

"You are the procurator. Your word is law."

"My word is the law of Rome—not of Israel. You know these Jews. They will complain to Rome about me." He stood up quickly. "I don't want to vegetate here for my remaining years . . . or be sent to some remote outpost of the Empire just because these Jews have complained to Tiberius. Tiberius is a bad-tempered old man these days . . . and doddering. He won't tolerate trouble in the Empire. And if I free this man, there will be an uproar in Judea."

"My dream is an omen."

"I don't need omens. My common sense tells me that this man is entirely innocent. He does not desire violence. He plans no revolt. He is an idealist, a prophet, a teacher—that is all."

"But you have the authority."

"Authority is not everything," he said impatiently and turned toward her, his eyes stern. "Cool judgment is necessary as well—that, above all, is what is needed. I can quite easily put His accusers to the sword, but that would not be wise. I can drive them away and free Him, but that is poor diplomacy. If I did that, I would light a fire that might consume me . . . and you as well."

Perturbed, she looked at him. "If you free Him, you will have freedom . . . in your mind. If you stain your hands with innocent blood, your conscience will always torture you. Tiberius will understand."

"Understand . . . understand! He understands nothing—nothing except lust. If I set the Galilean free, there will be an uprising. They will ask me only one question: Why did you act against the will of the local people in this matter? What will I be able to reply? Violence is old-fashioned. The new policy of Rome is compromise."

Claudia looked at a large pomegranate on the plate beside her bed. "You cannot compromise with your heart."

"Perhaps not, but I have no desire to become an exile."

"Give me a hut in the forest of Gaul and a clean conscience, before a villa on the Appian Way and the knowledge of blood on my hands," she said softly, caressing the pomegranate with her dainty fingers.

She realized from his long silence that she had hurt him. So she asked swiftly, "Where is this man now?"

"Since He is Galilean, I sent Him to be judged by Herod—"

"Herod—that clown? " Her eyes widened slightly. "I thought you were on bad terms with him. Since when have you been asking Herod Antipas to make your decisions?"

Pilate was embarrassed. "This was an excellent opportunity to settle our differences," he said, but she was not impressed.

"Herod will not punish Him," Claudia said. "He is a clown, but he has genius. He'll shake the whole thing off his flabby shoulders and pass it right back to you. He likes authority provided it doesn't give him sleepless nights."

Pilate looked helplessly at his wife; he knew that she was right.

Somebody knocked cautiously on the door. Pilate turned toward it and nervously touched his lips. He walked slowly across the room.

"Pontius—"

He stopped, looked back at his wife. She lay back on the pillows, her eyes closed, her fingertips on the cheeks that were as pale as porcelain.

"Yes, Claudia?"

"I thought it my duty to tell you about my dream."

"I appreciate it, my dear."

"I think that if you are strong today, your name will never die."

"Why do you say that?"

"I don't know. It's something I feel, but can't express."

Again they heard knocking. Pilate looked at the smooth surface of the closed door and it suddenly seemed symbolic, as if it were a scalpel dividing his life into a clear-cut past and future.

While he stood hesitatingly, Claudia came to him and laid her cool fingers on his sweating cheeks. She stood on tiptoe and touched his temple with her lips. "Do what is right," she whispered, "and today your strength will surpass even that of Tiberius."

He walked to the door with drooping shoulders. She could see his neck shining above the edge of his purple garment.

Pilate went outside and quickly closed the door behind him. His chamberlain bowed low. "I regret the necessity to disturb you now, Your Excellency," the man said, "but they have returned the prisoner."

A little to one side stood a centurion. Pilate's hard stare made him break into speech. "His Highness, the Tetrarch Herod, sent this, Your excellency," he said, and held out a gold container to the procurator. Pilate snatched it from his hand, pulled out the scroll and read silently:

King Herod to
His Excellency, Pontius Pilate.
Greetings and all due respect!

I find the accusations against the Galilean unfounded, lacking substance and foundation. I believe Him to be merely a mistaken, harmless enthusiast, one of a number of well-meaning people who believe that they are prophets. I am at a loss to suggest measures to deal with Him, except probably to have Him whipped.

To meet the contingency of your considering this course of action, I now send back the prisoner.

Pilate reread the short document, searched for some hidden advice it might yet contain; then, when he found nothing, he hurled the scroll against the granite passage wall. "I thought so," he said bitterly. "He is as slippery as an eel."

He could feel Israel's hatred sounding in his ears as he walked back outside to the judgment seat. He slowly ascended it, seated himself, and looked at Jesus from under lowered brows.

Pilate was conscious of a great flood of people pressing and pushing here and there. The crowds had grown much bigger than earlier that morning. The forecourt was tightly packed, and the crowd overflowed around the wings of the palace. They sat in trees, on walls, on statues. Some were even forcing their way onto the front staircase of the palace. Pilate's glance darted to the Roman guards, and he saw with relief that their stout barrier had dammed the flood.

He looked at Caiaphas, and Caiaphas looked defiantly back at him. Then he looked off over the heads of the people. Pilate recoiled inwardly. In the gateway the masses were swaying like a pendulum in their struggle to get inside, and he could see that the streets leading to the palace were overlaid with a mosaic of human beings.

"Herod too has found this man innocent" Pilate said to Caiaphas. "I will have Him scourged and then release Him."

His words sounded ludicrous, even to himself. He felt ashamed. The prisoner was innocent, and still he would have Him scourged. Finding Him innocent, he had still sent Him to Herod. He was filled with angry resentment that the Jews should have this hold over him and exact such concessions.

"Herod is ruler of Galilee and Perea only," Caiaphas objected. "This man incites the whole of Israel. Most of the people present in this crowd are from Judea, and there are many from Damascus, Antioch, even from Alexandria and Cyrene. This is no matter for Herod; it is the concern of Rome."

The logic of Caiaphas's words brought an added feeling of impotence to the procurator. But a thought occurred to him: it was the Passover, and he remembered that he was obliged to release one prisoner each year at this time. Pilate looked at the seething mob, and then he beckoned to the nearby centurion.

"Who is the most disgraceful ruffian, the vilest scoundrel in the dungeons of Antonia?" he asked.

"A man named Barabbas, Your Excellency," the centurion replied. "Jesus Barabbas."

"Barabbas?"

"He is a highway robber, and he and his gang were the cause of a serious breach of the peace the other day. There was bloodshed. Some Jews were killed."

"Do these people know him?"

"They know him very well, Your Excellency. They fear him and hate him."

"Fetch him here—hurry!"

The centurion ran down the steps. A few priests hastened after him.

"This Roman is up to something," the Jewish leaders whispered among themselves. "He will try anything to free the Galilean. We must prevent him. Whatever Pilate says, Jesus must be executed. Let us mingle with the crowd and make sure they understand that."

The message was carried from man to man. The restlessness of the crowd increased. A new hatred against Pilate was kindled in them. He would not be allowed to have his way! He was a Roman, and his hands were stained with the blood of Jews!

Barabbas appeared between two guards before the judgment seat. He was a big, wild-looking man, his beard unkept and long, his clothing almost in tatters.

"Barabbas!" sounded from a thousand throats, half in admiration, half in contempt. "Barabbas . . . Barabbas!" Even Simon, momentarily caught up in the blind hysteria, shouted the name and from sheer excitement thumped Judas between the shoulder blades. But Judas was silent. His despair had grown with every new development during the day. He crushed his trembling knuckles against his lips.

Pontius Pilate spoke over the noise of the crowd: "According to your custom, I must release a prisoner today. I am going to do that now, before anything else." He pointed to the two prisoners. "Which Jesus must I liberate? Jesus the Galilean or Jesus Barabbas?" He put it that way intentionally, and his voice was strong and sure. There was even a slight smile about the corners of his lips. He was certain they had not been prepared for anything like this.

"Now you have outmaneuvered them," his counselor whispered.

"We shall see if they would like this scoundrel freed," Pilate said complacently. "They'll be forced to let the Galilean go."

A silence had descended on the crowd.

A soldier approached the procurator and placed a large copper basin filled with water beside him on a table. Pilate looked questioningly up at the man. "The Lady Claudia has asked for the water to be brought to you, Your Excellency," said the soldier. He also handed Pilate a small parchment.

The governor glanced at it hurriedly. It was in the handwriting of his wife. "Be free of guilt for the righteous," it said.

Pilate crumpled the parchment and flicked it under the table. Claudia's warning was no longer of any consequence. He had succeeded. He understood why his wife had sent the bowl of water. "I don't think I'll need this water," he said aloud, but to nobody in particular.

He rose suddenly and looked at Caiaphas with contempt.

"I asked of you, whom shall I set free?" Pilate said. "Jesus the Galilean, or Jesus Barabbas?"

This time the crowd answered in a wild, demented cry:

"Barabbas . . . Barabbas . . . Barabbas!"

Judas staggered, his heart thumping. Through his tear-filled eyes it looked to him as if Jesus were swaying where He stood.

"Barabbas!" Simon bellowed.

Pontius Pilate felt weak. He swallowed. The screaming crowds were a swimming blur before his eyes. He stared at the helmet plumes of his soldiers without seeing them. He did not even hear the uproar. He only heard the soft voice of his wife: "If you are strong today, your name will never die."

But then anger possessed him. He flung out a trembling hand toward Jesus. "And what am I do with this man?" he shouted.

"Crucify Him!"

"But He is innocent!" the governor protested.

"Crucify Him!"

"No, no!" wept Judas's heart, and his knuckles were salty against his teeth.

Pilate was looking at Jesus, straight into His eyes. Those eyes were quiet and serene, but something in them made Pilate afraid. He leaned back against the judgment seat. He saw the copper basin, filled with water, pure and glistening.

He dipped his trembling hands into the water. "I am innocent of the blood of this man!" he called out. "Let it be on your hands!"

"Let His blood be on us and on our children," Caiaphas replied, and the words made Pilate stare fixedly at him while an attendant was drying his hands.

"Crucify Him!" the mob shouted.

Pilate sat down wearily and beckoned to the centurion. His chin rested in his cupped hands.

"Let this scoundrel go," the procurator said, pointing at Barabbas. "I must prevent an uprising here. Let this Galilean be scourged, but see that it is done thoroughly. Let it draw blood. Perhaps they will relent when they see Him again."

He rose, descended the rostrum quickly, and entered the palace.

The soldiers took Jesus to a room in a wing of the palace and undressed Him. They bound His hands to a stake, above His head.

Then the lictor entered—a powerful Roman soldier from Syria, his torso bare, in his hands the scourge, a rounded wooden stock with leather thongs ending in pieces of bone and iron.

The lictor stopped in front of Jesus, looked at Him with a contemptuous sneer. He was pleased at the prospect of whipping this Jew with the lash of Rome.

He walked around to the back of the stake and stood there with legs straddled. He glanced at the centurion, who stood to one side, his arms folded on his chest. The centurion gave the signal. The Syrian made a wide sweep with the whip. It whistled dully and curled around Jesus' chest. As the ends of the whip lacerated His flesh, He gasped with the searing pain. His knees buckled, but He remained upright, His head far back.

The lictor grinned. He had known men to collapse with a single blow. Again the whip swung back, and, lashing forward, sliced into His chest. Again and again, with a regular, murderous rhythm.

The centurion looked hard at the prisoner. He had to see to it that Jesus was not beaten to death. He gave a swift order. The lictor stepped unwillingly aside.

The centurion approached and carefully looked at the blood that had started from Jesus' chest and back and ran unevenly down His legs into His weathered sandals. He put His ear to the prisoner's chest.

"It is sufficient!" the centurion said. "Unbind Him!"

The lictor untied Jesus' hands, and the prisoner dropped down on the cold stone floor of the room.

The Roman soldiers knew what had to be done when a man had been given lashes. Someone fetched a pail of water. The cold water descended on the tortured body, and the half conscious man gasped and twitched spasmodically. The water restored Him to full consciousness, and His body was twisted with agony. Again and again they doused Him, and each time He closed His eyes, shrinking from the onslaught of the icy, fiery water.

Two soldiers helped Him up.

When He was on His feet once more, they knew it was time for sport, as was the custom when someone had been lashed. A red cloak was fetched, and they hung it on Him. Soft as the material was, it added to His torture. They had heard that He was called the king of the Jews. Someone pushed a thick reed into His hand. "This is Your scepter," a soldier said, and struck Jesus lightly across the mouth.

"And this Your crown, O King of Galilee," another added. Somebody had plaited a crown from twigs and thorns. The soldier forced it down on Jesus' head, so that the blood seeped slowly across His brow, down His neck, over His swollen cheeks, even into His eyes. A soldier took the reed from Him and struck Him on the head.

He stood there, His whole body shuddering, and every now and again His muscles jerked fiercely with shock and pain. Someone brought a footstool. "Let Him be seated. This is Your throne, O King of the Jews," they mocked.

They stood around Him, searching for hatred in His eyes so

that they could abuse Him because of it. But His eyes were quiet, holding neither defiance nor resentment.

After He had rested a while, they clad Him in his old garment and took Him back to Pilate. Jesus walked slowly. His strength had been broken by the torture. He staggered every now and then, so that a soldier had to lend support to prevent His falling.

Pilate was taken aback at the appearance of the prisoner when they led Him into the chamber where he awaited Him. But the governor was also conscious of a feeling almost of bitter gratitude that Jesus had been so cruelly treated. Perhaps His wounds would instill some feeling of compassion into His accusers—if not the Jewish leaders, then at least the populace. He took Jesus outside immediately.

The crowds fell silent when they saw Him. They gasped, and Pilate noted it. He ordered Jesus to be taken to the top of the palace staircase to be shown to the multitude. Two soldiers held His arms to support Him.

When Judas saw Him, he shook his head and closed his burning eyes. His hand trembled when he held it over his mouth. He darted quick and fearful glances at the prisoner, like someone looking at the sun—he could look only for a moment at the terrible sight before him. He quickly closed his eyes, and his head shook from side to side. Then stifled sobs escaped him.

Simon's eyes glittered, and he breathed slowly. He stared in exaltation at Jesus. "If He were the Messiah, He would not have allowed Himself to be so maltreated," he murmured. "He is an ordinary person, a common man like me. He is no holy one with power over Rome."

Jesus' face was by now so swollen, so discolored, that His features were almost unrecognizable. His hair was soaked with blood. His hands were crossed by bloody welts where the lash had cut into His forearms. Small rivulets of blood stained His forehead and congealed in His beard.

Jesus' head was sunk on His chest. At one time He lifted His head, looked up to the sky, but staggered backward, so that the soldiers had to hold Him.

Pilate stretched out his hand toward Jesus. "Behold the

man," he said loudly to the people, and waited for compassion to mellow them.

The crowds squeezed closer, until the soldiers thrust out their spears to force them back.

"Crucify Him!" the Jewish leaders cried, and the crowds took up the cry. "Crucify Him! Let Him be crucified!"

"You take Him and crucify Him!" the governor declared. "I find no guilt in Him."

"In accordance with our law He must perish, for He has claimed to be the Son of God!" Saul, the young Pharisee, shouted from the bottom of the steps.

Pilate was startled. He looked quickly at the prisoner and then ordered the soldiers to take Him inside again.

"They say You claim You are the Son of God. Where have You come from?" Pilate asked, and now fear was glinting in his eyes. But Jesus made no reply.

"Do You not intend to answer me? Don't You know that it is in my power to crucify You or to set You free?"

Jesus looked directly into Pilate's eyes, and although His face was bleeding and His bound hands trembled, His expression was one of transcendent nobility. Jesus spoke slowly, softly, but with simple clarity. "You would not have this power over Me if it had not been given to you from above. That is why he who handed Me over to you has the greater sin."

Pilate looked intently at Him and then understood the meaning of the words. He turned around slowly and took Jesus outside again, onto the flagstones, while he seated himself on his judge's chair. He looked at the crowds, at the Jewish leaders. He saw their unyielding enmity. He saw the fiery eyes, the scornful, threatening gestures.

He knew that he had lost.

Pilate stood up, raised his arms, and then dropped them at his sides. "Take your King and crucify Him!" he shouted furiously. Then to the waiting centurion: "Take Him away . . . get a cross. Go, crucify Him."

Pilate, descending from the rostrum, stopped suddenly and with closed eyes listened to the jubilation that filled the courtyard like a storm.

23

When Pilate had passed sentence on Jesus and the guards were taking Him away from the judgment seat, Simon Niger looked around for Judas.

But Judas had gone from his side.

Simon was just in time to see his companion forcing his way through the crowds, his head low, his arms flailing. He looked like a man struggling to breast a swiftly flowing stream.

Perhaps it was curiosity, perhaps pure impulse, or perhaps unconscious friendship that drove Simon to follow Judas. Pushing and elbowing his way through the crowd, Simon went after him.

But Judas was some distance ahead. Simon saw him clamber over the outer wall of the palace, for it was impossible to penetrate the gateway—the crowds had filled it like a plug. Simon reached the wall, jumped, and scrambled over at the point where Judas had climbed it. He caught sight of the disciple running along beside the wall some distance away where there was space to move.

Simon jumped down and began to run after him. Judas's garment flapped as he headed toward the temple.

Simon followed him. He hurried through the gate of the temple area. Panting, he saw Judas on the highest step of the temple stairs, talking excitedly to a few priests. His arms waved wildly. Simon walked more slowly. He saw Judas holding out something in his cupped hands toward the priests. He saw them shake their heads.

Then he saw Judas's arm make an angry movement—the disciple's body jerked as he hurled something to the ground. Small discs bounded and glittered in the sunlight.

Simon stopped at the foot of the stairs. A few pieces of silver came rolling and bounding down the steps past him. He stared at the shining coins in surprise.

At the top of the steps the priests were bending down and moving about, apparently picking up the money.

Then Simon saw the disciple dart away. He was leaping down the stairs with hasty strides. The hood of his garment had fallen back, and his hair streamed out behind him.

"Judas!" Simon shouted. The disciple did not look at him. He swung left at the bottom of the steps.

Automatically, Simon ran after him. He pursued him past the temple, toward the west. Judas moved at a furious pace, like one in mortal terror. Simon steadily lost ground, for Judas easily outstripped him.

A caravan of camels was entering at the Water Gate. Simon saw the fugitive slip between the pack animals and flee through the gateway. At last he too reached the gate, exhausted, sweat running into his eyes. He stopped. Judas was a moving speck on the white road that twisted along the slopes toward the Valley of Hinnom.

Simon ran on, his throat parched. As he reached the valley, he saw Judas climbing the farther rise. The disciple seemed to be moving with less set purpose now. Once he stopped and looked around him. Then he swung left off the road and began to run again.

Judas seemed suddenly to have become his responsibility, and Simon pressed on behind him. He crossed the deep valley, climbed out on the other side, painfully, for his breath had given out. He could run no further. At the place where Judas had turned off the road, Simon stopped, looked around, but saw no sign of the fugitive. He cast about on the gentle slope, but could see nothing. He called out to Judas once, but silence was his answer.

He walked in the direction in which he thought he had seen Judas turn. After a while he found himself above a precipitous quarry where years before men had delved for building stones. The walls dropped steeply down to stony ridges exposed by many years of wind and ram.

Panting, Simon walked toward an ancient almond tree that grew with gnarled limbs near the precipice, its weathered branches stretching out over space.

He stood there wondering, and then began to feel he understood. Judas wished to conceal himself in this solitary place. Possibly he feared the vengeance of the followers of Jesus, the other disciples.

It was then that Simon noticed the white wound where a branch had been freshly torn off. The sight of it touched him with fear. The branch seemed to have extended horizontally over the abyss.

The Cyrenian saw the mark on the edge of the quarry, presumably made by the falling branch. He peered over the edge.

Far down below Judas Iscariot lay, like a broken wheel, his arms and legs spread out upon the stones.

"Iscariot!" Simon shouted and his voice reechoed from the pit. He looked quickly around him, saw where the rain water had washed a furrow down the side of the wall. He followed the furrow down, sliding, slipping, skidding to the bottom. He ran across the ridges to the place where Judas lay.

He stopped beside the fallen man and was filled with horror. Never before had he seen a body so shattered. The neck was slackly twisted. The eyes stared at the sun. Bowels had broken out.

Simon bent down and quite unnecessarily felt Judas's pulse. He touched the leather belt that was tight about his neck, the belt with the attached moneybag which he had worn beneath his garment. He touched it without thinking. There was no need to speculate. The belt around Judas's neck was still tied to the broken almond branch.

Simon rose with a sigh, stared up at the almond tree growing high on the edge of the clay quarry, and felt suddenly alone. He thought of the previous night when Judas had been so sure of himself. He saw the disciple take Jesus by the shoulder, and kiss Him. He bowed his head. "The Son of God . . ." he said half-unconsciously, and wondered . . .

Simon shuddered. A force seemed present in that deserted place that could destroy him.

With a slight shudder he looked into the glassy, staring eyes for the last time. It was the Nazarene who had hurled Judas over the precipice, he thought. He began to walk away. But he turned back, briefly, to draw the bloodstained garment over the betrayer's face.

"The Nazarene has vanquished you, Iscariot," Simon said aloud, and started at the sound of his own voice.

Simon climbed the slope, walked back across the valley, stopped on the other side, and looked back at the distant green speck of the almond tree. Then he walked past the royal gardens, along the city walls, past the Pool of Bethesda, back to the gardens of Gethsemane. Every now and again he looked up at the sun and wondered. What a meaningful day it had been!

He was in no mood to walk quickly. He loitered along through the valley, stopping every once in a while, listening for sounds borne on the breeze, looking listlessly at the city wall, then at the Mount of Olives, and back at the white road winding toward Bethany.

He moved like a man reluctant to reach the end of his journey. He sat down on a stone and looked at the soil, stared up at the sun, and found that the source of all light was too dim to blind him. The aspect of the sun was strange. The shade of an olive tree drew him. He walked toward it, touched the cool bark, and peered into the branches.

Simon closed his eyes, and almost angrily shook his head. Judas's eyes stayed with him. Even when he closed his eyes, the image of those glassy orbs remained. Again he saw Caiaphas's beard . . . and Pilate's laurel wreath . . . and the streaks of blood upon the face of Jesus.

Through his weary, seething mind the voices came and went, disjointed, but with great clarity. "I hate Him, and yet I love Him." Judas's words rang out so clearly that Simon opened his eyes. And as he did so, the bark and branches of the olive tree leaped clearly into focus.

"Go away. They spoke Israel's doom tonight. He has no guilt," Joseph of Arimathea's words, spoken hoarsely in the wind of evening.

Caiaphas's strident voice: "You have heard His blasphemy." Simon could even hear the rending of the high priest's robe.

He sank down and, resting his back against the tree trunk, closed his eyes, awaiting peace. It seemed to him as if the whole world swam and swayed about him.

What was it the widow Naomi had said? "I think you are chosen for something. . . . It is destined so. . . . You will go to Jerusalem . . ."

"He is the Messiah. You must believe me, Simon." Deborah's voice, gentle and angelic.

Pilate—"I find no guilt in Him . . ."

"Give to Caesar that which . . ." The emperor, the enemy of Israel.

Lazarus—"It is strange how many refuse to believe that I am living . . ."

Voices and images . . . images and voices. Now loud and clear, now soft and wavering, like whispers in the dark, like ghosts ruling him by night.

And through all, the one refrain: blasphemy . . . blasphemy.

Simon opened his eyes with a start. He must have fallen asleep against the trunk. The man standing before him had dark, quiet eyes. He stood there, his hands resting on the crook across his shoulders, his striped garment loose around his body, the hood pulled far over his face.

"Peace be with you. You are weary, stranger. You were snoring in your sleep."

"Peace be with you. Where do you come from?"

"I come from the hills just north of Jerusalem. I have come to water my stock. Listen. . . . Listen!"

The tall man half turned around, looked in the direction of the Antonia fortress. A great shouting rose above the silence, hovered high, and then drifted away.

"Now they are taking the carpenter on His last journey. They must have brought out the cross."

Simon rose so quickly that he bumped his head against a branch. He walked out from under the tree and looked closely at the man before him. He resembled the Nazarene. Could it be that this man . . .

But Simon's fear subsided, for the shepherd spoke again. "Come, let us go to Golgotha to watch."

The shepherd started walking, and Simon listlessly fell in beside him. "Now the man who said they could break down the temple and within three days He would build it again will suffer the spikes of the Romans through His hands."

Simon stopped. "Did He say that? About the temple?"

"Yes, He did."

"The temple of Israel?"

"The temple of Israel, built by Herod the Great and standing in Jerusalem."

Simon looked, saw the great roofs gleaming.

The shepherd smiled. "Do not fear," he scoffed. "Our temple is still there. The new prophet has little time left in which to accomplish such a deed." The man spoke calmly and with conviction.

"He blasphemed against God last night. He said he was the Son of God." Simon's eyes showed more spirit.

"So I have heard, but I am certain that if we go to the Damascus Gate we will see this Son of God come through it with a cross upon His shoulder." The shepherd laughed softly and began to walk again, Simon beside him.

"How long did it take Herod to build the temple?" the shepherd asked while walking. "Forty-six years and it is not finished yet."

"Forty-six," agreed Simon.

"And our prophet believes that He can build it up again within three days." The shepherd laughed and shook his head.

They walked on for a little while in silence. When at length they reached the Kidron, the question that Simon had for so long kept concealed within himself came bursting forth: "But . . . but suppose He *were* the Messiah?"

The shepherd frowned and stood still. "I think you are another of those who have two hearts today," he said, "one *for* the carpenter, and one *against* Him."

"I don't believe in Him—I merely asked." Simon's voice was weary.

The shepherd leaned on his crook. "I am a simple man," he said. "I am not learned like the Pharisees. I ask myself but one question: Would God allow His Son, the Savior of His people, to be crucified by a Roman heathen such as Pilate? Would the Lord God, who led Israel from Egypt, allow the Savior of His people to die and fade to nothing? If He dies now, He is no Savior. If He dies today, Israel remains in slavery."

"It is true . . . it is true," Simon whispered, his eyes brightening, bloodshot though they were with weariness. "It is the complete truth. Why have I had difficulty understanding it?"

"Why? I think this Nazarene has touched your heart"

"No!" Simon said furiously and took a step toward the shepherd.

The man smiled slightly. He looked long at Simon. He half turned and pointed with his stick toward the temple. "There the temple stands. He said that He could build it up within three days. But He cannot. For He cannot even save His own life."

Simon looked at the great dome, and he suddenly felt free and certain. Bewildered doubt no longer plagued him. His thoughts were clear and simple.

They continued walking. "Shepherd of Jerusalem," Simon said, and looked across the Kidron to where their cottage stood, "you have reassured me of much in a little time, yet why is it that so many believe in Him? Even my master, Joseph of Arimathea, believes in Him. . . . Even my . . ." He fell silent suddenly, looking at the man whose long garment flapped around his ankles.

"There are many fools in Israel," the shepherd answered. "I saw that years ago with the census when Judas of Galilee rose up. For thousands he was the Messiah. But he led them only to death by crucifixion. He is almost forgotten—just as this man will be forgotten once they have taken Him down from the cross."

"They will forget Him?" Simon faltered as he asked, and stared up again into the shepherd's face, but it was Deborah's face he saw before him.

"They will forget," the shepherd said, and swung his staff onto his shoulder. "Time causes you to forget all things—even false prophets."

They walked across the fields toward the footpath that led from the city to Golgotha. They heard the exaltation within the city walls.

24

While Simon and the shepherd were looking toward the Damascus Gate, they saw the head of the procession emerge slowly from it. Simon looked up quickly at the misty sun and then back toward the gateway.

Crowds were streaming through it, and they moved in Simon's direction—not straight upon him, but passing him at an angle. He stared fixedly. He saw the red plumes of the soldiers, but he had no interest in them. He looked at the men in their midst, and then off toward Golgotha. Simon's heart contracted.

"Do you see the crosses?" asked the shepherd.

"I see them," Simon answered. He began to run, cutting across the field. The shepherd followed. Simon stumbled over scrub and stone as he kept his gaze fixed on the men who bore the crosses. He tried to distinguish them, but could not. The soldiers marched in a hollow square, surrounding the three men with the crosses. One, he knew, must be the Nazarene.

At the side of the wide limestone footpath the procession was following toward Golgotha, Simon paused. There he waited for them.

They moved slowly, haltingly. They weren't making much headway. It was some time before they neared him. The shepherd took his stand a little distance away from Simon, who stepped off the footpath, standing to one side. Soon he saw that it was the Nazarene who was slowing the procession. It was He who so often stopped and stumbled. The cross bore Him down almost to the ground. He carried it clumsily, as a child would carry something too heavy for its strength, and whenever He could proceed no further, He would rest the base upon the ground. Whenever He did this, the rabble would jeer at Him and a soldier would draw his short sword and with menacing gestures urge Him onward. Then He would pick up the cross again, staggering as He did so, and trudge laboriously behind the other two who were bearing crosses. But they were obviously strong men, walking along without effort.

Simon moved even farther off the pathway, stopped again, and looked at Jesus reeling and lurching beneath His cross.

"Where is Your power now, Nazarene?" Simon asked contemptuously from where he stood, but his voice was low. "If You are the Son of God, where is Your power now?"

He stood and watched men and women swarm around Jesus every time He stumbled. They yelled at Him and shook their fists. From time to time their behavior was so threatening that the soldiers drove them away. Dogs barked, children screamed, and there was an excited babble of voices. Every now and again a daring child would dive between the soldiers' legs and tug at the hem of Jesus' garment, then run away screeching as a soldier threatened him.

Or somebody would cry out, "Hosannah to the King of the Jews!"

Others would take up the cry, and it resounded over the quiet fields outside Jerusalem. Or men and women would join hands, dance around, and sing: "Hallelujah to the great Savior of Israel . . . the son of David . . . the new prophet." Then they would burst out laughing, run forward, and, gathering handfuls of small lime-pebbles, pelt Him with the stones.

A section of the crowd followed him grief-stricken, but silent out of fear. There were women who wept softly and men who tightened their lips and clenched their fists when each new humiliation beset Him. And there were the "sisters of mercy" of Jerusalem who accompanied every crucifixion procession offering wine mixed with myrrh to blunt the victim's senses against the moment of dire agony.

A big man with a bushy beard strutted insolently on the outskirts of the mob, beating his chest and roaring, "Hear this . . . hear this . . . hear what I say: I am the man who will wash the feet of the King of the Jews when He sits upon His throne." And the rabble burst out laughing. Someone else walked alongside the centurion pleading with mock earnestness, "Let me anoint His feet."

"Let me carry His cross," a young man jeered and, slipping past the soldiers, lurched against Jesus' cross so that He staggered.

Encouraged by the mocking crowd, Simon also shouted out from the side: "And where are His disciples now? Why do they not come to bear His cross? Where is that big fisherman of Galilee?"

The crowds took up the cry: "Where are His disciples?" They shaded their eyes humorously with their hands and searched behind them. And those who mourned shrank back, fearing the anger of the mob.

"They've gone to prepare His throne!" somebody shouted. "To lay out the purple garment and prepare His crown."

Simon felt pleased with himself for having said something so appealing and effective.

"Where are His disciples?" the rabble shouted again. Simon, laughing softly, began to walk along in line with the head of the procession, off on the side of the path.

He looked at the executioner the Romans had brought with them—a man who claimed attention. He was big, with heavy eyebrows, and his bare arms were muscular and hairy. He wore a reddish leather apron, with large pockets. From his satchel projected the handle of a medium-sized hammer and the angular heads of long, thin iron spikes, sharp spikes that would pierce through hard wood easily.

Then Jesus stumbled over a limestone rock and fell. The cross slipped from His shoulder and grated on the ground. He lay on His side, His hands bleeding into the white lime dust of the footpath. A cry rose from the crowds—a cry of disappointment and derision.

Two soldiers bent and pulled Him up, and white dust streaked His garment. When they let go of Him, He collapsed again, falling obliquely backward with His shoulder against the crossbar of the cross.

The centurion looked impatiently at the prisoner. He realized that the flogging had broken His strength completely. Jesus' head sank slowly forward, and the gray sunlight glimmered on the sharp thorns of His crown. Some of the men from the small group of mourners made as if to go forward to pick up His cross, but their fear of the mocking mob restrained them.

"Rise, Redeemer of Israel!" the crowd screamed.

Two soldiers bent down to lift Jesus to His feet. "Leave Him alone," the centurion ordered harshly. "He cannot carry the cross any further."

The centurion stood there in vexation, looking at Golgotha, which was not so far away, and back over the crowds to where the tower on Antonia shone dimly. He shuddered. He found all crucifixions an ordeal. Even if a murderer was involved, he shrank from the task of execution.

He saw the thin hands of Jesus lying in the white dust of the footpath, with blood smears on the knuckles. He looked away quickly.

He saw Simon Niger standing there—big, dark, powerful. The centurion looked intently at Simon, and he was impressed by the strength of this rustic Jew who, impelled by curiosity, had apparently joined them from some adjacent field. He could not stomach further trouble with this cross. They had been wasting time ever since they had placed the cross on the Nazarene's shoulder at Antonia. In a few hours it would be noon, and he did not want to be stuck at Golgotha till the late hours of night.

"You there—come here!" the centurion called to Simon and motioned to him with his sword to approach. Simon grew chill, and his first impulse was to turn and flee. But when the centurion beckoned again with his sword, he walked slowly nearer. His eyes were narrowed, his whole body tensed.

A silence fell over the crowd. All that Simon was conscious of was the barking of a dog somewhere, the scarlet plumes of the soldiers, the glint of their helmets.

He stopped a few steps away from the centurion, his eyes filled with loathing and contempt. He felt the same animosity as on that evening in Cyrene when he confronted Vitellius.

The centurion jerked his head in the direction of Jesus. "Come, carry the cross," he ordered Simon.

Simon did not stir. There was a prickling sensation on his skin and a singing in his head. His breath felt warm within his nostrils. It seemed to him that he was floating in a vast, silent, empty space where nothing could touch him.

"I told you to carry that cross," the centurion commanded again. His steely eyes had become colder, and his chin jutted out from under his helmet.

"Let Him carry His own cross," Simon said hoarsely. "Is he not a man of miracles?"

"I am not concerned with His miracles. All I know is that He cannot carry His cross any further. Come!"

"Look for one of His disciples. I am not one of them."

The centurion stared threateningly at the big Jew.

"You have a lot to say. Do not forget to whom you are talking."

"What I say is the truth."

"You are speaking to a Roman centurion."

"And you are speaking to a free Jew. Nobody can force me to carry this cross. I am only standing here as an onlooker."

"A Roman can compel a Jew to do anything he wishes."

Simon felt pulses beating in his head. The figure of the centurion grew hazy before him.

The crowds forgot about Jesus. They looked at the Jew and the Roman who stood so close to one another, anger the one link that bound them.

The centurion made a small movement with his sword. Simon was only vaguely conscious of the soldiers forming a circle round him, their spears and swords at the ready. He looked at Jesus lying in the dust, utterly exhausted. He looked completely defenseless, His hands limp and motionless, His narrow face reddened with His blood. Simon saw how His wounds had bled into His worn sandals.

Just like any human being. . . . The man was only human.

"Where are Your disciples? Why don't they carry Your cross?" Simon shouted to the prisoner.

Jesus looked up at him, His eyes gentle but filled with pain. He looked pleadingly, as if He thirsted and was begging for water, at the big man who stood menacingly over him. Like any human being, and in pain . . .

But He spoke no word, only gazed at Simon. Simon felt as if the man were staring at him for all eternity. Then the slight body seemed to shudder, and Jesus looked off toward the Mount of

Olives. His head fell forward again on His panting chest. His hands clenched with pain. His narrow shoulders moved, His face contorted—and Simon understood, for he had seen many men whom the Romans had scourged.

"You are a human being; You are no god. You are not even a prophet," Simon whispered angrily, and although he thought that Jesus had not heard, He looked up slowly and the pain had vanished from His eyes. There was only compassion there.

The big man still stood hesitating. He felt the point of a spear in his back—a small center of incipient pain. He heard the creaking of the soldiers' sandals. He heard their breathing. Then he felt, like the point of a heated arrow, another spear touch him, at the junction of his head and neck. Penetration here would bring immediate death.

"Pick up the cross," the centurion said again. His voice seemed to come from a remote place, like a message from the clouds.

Simon shuffled forward, stopped, and stared at the rough wood of the cross. He closed his eyes, seized the cross, and swung it up on his shoulders—swung it with so much vigor that a soldier who had come too close was knocked to the ground.

As he stood upright, he heard the mob's derision. "There goes His new disciple!" they shouted. He turned around, his head bent under the weight of the cross; and because they humiliated him, he spat fiercely at them. They shrieked with delight because he was helpless and looked grotesque beneath the cross.

He turned quickly from them and went forward, defiantly, swaggering, between the two other prisoners. As he hurried past them with bent head, the small limestone pebbles looked indistinct and strange through his tears of anger. He strained on the crosspiece, trying to break it, but it was strong, and the sharp edges of the wood cut into his wrists and the heavy timber chafed the skin of his back and shoulders.

The voices of the crowd became vague in his ears. His fury was drained away in the movement of his limbs, in the knowledge of his strength.

On the fat hilltop of Golgotha he flung the cross from his shoulders, flung it so far from him that it stood momentarily on its base, then fell slowly over, and a dense cloud of dust came drifting from the ground.

He stood there recovering his breath, looking at the dried blood on the stones. Then he turned slowly and saw them coming up the hill, Jesus swaying and stumbling between two Roman soldiers who held Him upright, who almost dragged Him up the hill.

The centurion came up to Simon, fumbled under his armor, and, taking out a silver piece, held it out to Simon.

"This is for your trouble," the centurion said, grinning.

Simon struck the coin out of the man's hand. "Give the money to your emperor," he panted, and spat in the dust. He walked a couple of yards away and felt his neck where the cross had chafed. He shook his shoulders in revulsion.

The centurion beckoned to the executioner.

"The Nazarene," he ordered. The soldiers stood in a dense ring about Jesus. They ripped off His gown and dropped it on the ground. Then they bound a linen cloth about His waist and fastened it behind. Some of the soldiers turned their heads away as they saw His chest, torn and broken by the scourging. Two soldiers seized His wrists, two His ankles, and they laid Him on His back upon the cross.

Jesus lay still, but His breathing came faster in anticipation of this new, this greater pain. He closed His eyes and moved His head, for the crown of thorns tormented Him anew.

The centurion looked toward the executioner. The executioner gave the wine flask, from which he had just taken a deep drink, to someone beside him, wiped his beard, brushed the sweat from his forehead, and came nearer. He looked down at the prisoner, hesitant, as if he could not bring himself to begin his work. The centurion rapped out an order.

The executioner came swiftly forward, squatting beside the crosspiece. Two soldiers knelt down beside him. One gripped Jesus' arm just above the wrist and held it hard down on the wood. The other soldier held the wood itself.

The crucifier took the hammer from his leather satchel, then one of the long spikes, coppery in the strange light.

There was silence. Some shut their eyes or looked away. Others looked at one another, toward Jerusalem, the hills, or up at the hazy sky.

Simon saw the strong hands of the executioner, the sweat dripping from his forehead. Then he looked quickly away toward Gethsemane.

The hammer blows were fast and dull. . . .

The executioner drove the spikes deep into the hard wood.

The crowds gasped, and were silent.

The executioner and the soldiers moved to the other hand stretched out upon the cross, and again the hammer blows were heard.

Then the feet. The soldiers bent the right foot above the left. The crucifier drove the spike through to the wood, and stared at the welling blood that slowly obscured its texture.

Jesus' body shuddered in shock. His mouth gasped, the lips wide open. His eyes shut in a spasm of agony, His face distorted. But He was silent.

The executioner and the two soldiers walked across to the other two prisoners, who already lay whimpering.

Some of the other soldiers gripped Jesus' cross, swung it upward, and set it in position, stamping down the soil.

Simon looked at Jesus. He looked so thin and small, and it seemed as if His arms would tear out of their sockets. The head lay on one shoulder, swung over to the other, then fell on the panting chest. Then the head was lifted. Jesus stared up at the heavens, and His face screamed with pain. But His lips were silent.

One of the other prisoners screamed loud and piercingly as they nailed him to his cross.

Simon closed his eyes, shook his head, turned, and walked silently, blindly, through the quiet crowds. But he did not go far before he looked around again. He saw how Jesus tried to push Himself up the cross with His legs, His head rolling, His body taut, straining, the trembling muscles corded. The open mouth was raised to the sky as if it cried for succor there—but His lips were silent.

Then the remaining prisoner screamed. They swung his cross on high, and his body writhed in hideous movement of agony as if he were struggling to tear himself free from the cross.

When they had raised the third cross, Simon walked away. He looked for the herdsman, but the man had disappeared. He stood a moment looking mechanically at the palms of his hands. He shivered and walked on. He halted once more, staring down at the main road that ran to Joppa, to the sea—to Cyrene.

But he did not walk toward it. The broad white road no longer called him. He understood suddenly—understood that he had been a fool when he thought he could leave Deborah. Before summer was over, this man would be forgotten—forgotten by Deborah, by Rufus, by everybody. Why should he leave if they were going to forget Him? No, he would stay and restore his home. His family and he would live together as they did of old, before this man had come.

He stood still again, looked back to the hill, saw the crowds dispersing, returning to Jerusalem. He saw the bodies writhing on the crosses.

Simon returned home, but when he reached the house, Deborah was still absent. Everything was silent, and the hearth was cold. He looked at his preparations for departure—the crook and the skin bag—all seemed unbelievable. He walked outside, ashamed. All about him he felt new life stirring, thrusting aside the winter. His urge to work reawakened. The past had ceased to bind him, and only the morrow had any meaning. He had always wondered whose land it was that adjoined that of Joseph of Arimathea. It was level, once-used land. He would restore it, work it again.

He would not delay. He would go to Jerusalem and see Joseph. He would talk with Joseph and then go to Bethany to bring Deborah home. He was quite certain she was staying with Mary and her family. He had no desire to spend another night without her.

He busied himself for some time about the orchard and then set out for Jerusalem. His step was light, his heart was free, as he made his way through the trees toward the city gates. He looked up at the sun from time to time, for it still shone strangely. "The wind is beginning to stir," said Simon cheerfully, "and wind brings rain . . . and I am Simon of Cyrene as I used to be."

Wind and rain, sun and soil . . . that was all he now desired. He walked on, and the crosses were far distant from his mind.

25

When Simon called at Joseph of Arimathea's mansion, he found the elder out.

"My master has gone to the palace of the governor, Pontius Pilate," an Ethiopian slave told Simon. Simon frowned and looked searchingly at the man, wondering if he were speaking the truth. "I do not know when my master will be back," the slave added.

"Will he be gone a long time?" Simon asked.

"That I do not know."

"When he returns, tell him that his foreman from Gethsemane called. I shall come back."

The slave gave a slight bow, and Simon left, a little surprised. What would Joseph of Arimathea be doing at the Roman's palace? It was strange. Simon stood irresolutely in the gateway to Joseph of Arimathea's courtyard. Should he go first to Bethany to fetch Deborah, or should he wait there for Joseph's return? He decided to go to Bethany. His longing for Deborah had grown almost beyond bearing. Yet he had only taken a few steps when he stopped. His curiosity prevailed. Perhaps Joseph would not be absent for too long, and he was intensely curious to know the reason for the elder's visit to Pontius Pilate.

He wandered out into the street. He found that he was thirsty. He felt a desire for wine. There were a few shekels in his pocket. The prospect of his new future exhilarated him. The indecision and uncertainty of the past few days had gone. The day had meaning for him again, and his restlessness had disappeared. There were no more questions to which he sought the answer. There were no riddles that teased his mind and body, that stifled his freedom of thought and action. He felt free and happy in the knowledge that a new day had dawned for him and Deborah, for all that he held dear.

He walked on, looking at the young sprigs in the poplars, at the healthy green of the cypresses, and at the pomegranates budding behind garden walls. He stopped and watched a blacksmith shape a wheel while smoke poured from the hub. He looked with interest at an old man who was bringing a basket of ducklings to market, and he toyed with the temptation to buy a well-dressed skin from a merchant who approached him with a laden mule.

He felt at peace. Jerusalem was living its normal life again; the tension and uproar were over.

He sauntered down the Street of the Butchers. He was busy discovering Jerusalem . . . and he hoped to find a tavern. He walked on, pausing here and there, looking at the quartered oxen hanging on their sheltered hooks, at the poultry, scrubbed clean and white, and at the red-brown bunches of lung and liver.

Halfway down the street he saw a signboard with a picture of a drinking cup. "The very place for me," said Simon and laughed lightheartedly. He entered and enjoyed the sounds of voices and of laughter. The shop owner in his linen apron was hard pressed to fill the cups. Simon collared him, showed a coin, and said, "A large cup of wine for a large man!" and laughed. The innkeeper looked up respectfully, for Simon had drawn himself up to his full height, thrust out his chest, and placed his hands on his hips.

Simon paid for his wine and took his seat on a bench beside a table in the corner. He sat and drank in silence, relaxing and sucking his black beard. His thoughts dwelt on Deborah and on his triumph over those who had allowed themselves to be so misled by the Nazarene. He wondered how long it would take before the man was dead.

Close by him some men were sitting at a table against the wall. They talked loudly, gestured with their hands, laughing and thumping the table top. From time to time they roared in unison, holding their drinking vessels high.

Simon ignored them. He looked about to see if there was someone in the wineshop whom he knew. He felt constrained, but curious.

Absorbed in thought, he glanced outside as he slowly sipped his wine. "The sky seems overcast. Perhaps the rains will start soon," he whispered, smiling. "Early rains mean early plowing," he said softly into his drinking cup.

He took the vessel from his lips, and it gleamed strangely before his eyes—dully, as if in falling twilight, or beneath a clouded sky.

"Rain in April," he said. "That means a fruitful year."

He cupped his hands on the table, and the lines of his palms were invisible in the faint light. He took no notice, for his mind was busy. He thought of the piece of land he wished to discuss with Joseph. He had paced it off one day. He calculated its area and the bushels he would harvest if the wheat grew well.

So deep in thought was Simon that he did not hear a man at a nearby table saying, "The Nazarene must be hanging on the cross by now."

Or how someone said, pointing toward him, "That man in the corner looks like one of His followers."

Or how a big, rough fellow shouted at him, "Hey . . . you there! Aren't you one of the wandering sheep of the crucified shepherd?"

Simon heard them laughing, but he was concentrating too deeply to take notice.

He was shocked into attention only when wine splashed over his face. The impact made him look up quickly—into the glowing eyes of a big man in a brightly striped gown, who had planted himself before him.

"That's better," the stranger said. "Now we can have a little talk." He came forward and pressed his hands on the table top in front of Simon, and grinned through his beard. "I asked you whether you aren't one of the sheep of the crucified shepherd," the man said, and his eyes were scornful. "Or has your tongue been cut out by the Romans?"

Simon slowly wiped the wine from his eyes. He could feel his muscles quivering. "Why did you throw wine in my face?" he asked, and the whites of his eyes showed as he looked up at the stranger.

"You look like a strong Jew," said the other. "I want to see if you are stronger than I am." He sat down opposite Simon, laid his big hand on the table. His companions moved closer.

Simon stretched out his hand, then hesitated. "What will the prize be?" he asked.

"A cup of wine in my face," the man said.

Their right hands closed about each other. Simon felt the strength of the fierce stranger, and felt his own strength answering. Their veins swelled, their muscles tightened, their locked hands trembled, their beards quivered from exertion. They groaned and grunted.

With the strength that had always been his pride, Simon, with relentless pressure, slowly forced the hand of his opponent down and over until its hairy skin kissed the surface of the table.

The stranger freed his hand with a grunt, smiled, and pushed his face forward. "Your strength is great," he said. "Now throw the wine."

"My wine is too valuable for your dirty beard," Simon said and rubbed his hand.

The stranger laughed uproariously, throwing back his head. "Bring more wine . . . for this strong son of Beelzebub."

Simon was satisfied. For a few moments he had been Simon of Cyrene once more.

An attendant brought cups of wine and placed them on the table. The stranger pushed one over to Simon. "Drink!" he said, and laughed. "You have earned it. You are the first man ever to defeat the arm of Barabbas."

"Barabbas!" Simon half rose.

"Sit down, man, let us talk."

"You are a rebel and a murderer."

"I am Barabbas. I am an important man. I was supposed to die today. But the procurator set me free."

"Why did you provoke me?"

"I have been locked up in a cell too long. I wanted to see whether I was still strong. I see my strength has lessened. I think I'm getting old. You must come and work for me, strong man. I need your strength."

"Steal and murder for you?"

Barabbas laughed loudly and brought his fist down on the table. "We Jews are a peculiar people" he said. "Today they have let a fox loose among the sheep. Barabbas is free."

He leaned over. His eyes glowed. "We will go to Tyre and

Sidon. There is always something there for the pickings. Don't you want to come along?"

"No!"

"You aren't a follower of the Nazarene, are you?"

"No!"

"I will make you rich. You will be dressed in purple."

"No, I am a farmer—not a robber."

Barabbas looked up, turned his head. "I think a storm is brewing. Look at the light. It's fading fast."

In the tavern, those who were sitting and drinking had become dark, vague forms.

"You must be grateful to the Nazarene," Simon said. "But for Him, you would have died."

Barabbas raised the wine cup to his lips and drank deeply. "I don't know Him." Then he searched for Simon's eyes in the fading light. "What is there about this Nazarene? Why should He die and I go free? Why did they set me free? They hate Barabbas. . . . They fear Barabbas."

Simon looked down at his hands, saw the peculiar shadows, looked up, and shook his shoulders. It felt cold there—cold and close as if they were all contained in an icy cavern beneath the earth.

"They hate the Nazarene more than you," said Simon. "That is all."

Barabbas laughed loudly in the semidarkness in the blue vagueness of evening that was lying prematurely about them. He raised his wine cup and held it high. "We drink to the one man who is hated more than Barabbas! Barabbas is getting old and feeble. He is no longer the biggest rogue in Israel!"

He brought his drinking cup closer, but did not drink. He rotated it slowly before his eyes. "This light is queer. . . . My wine cup looks as if it were tarnished."

"A dust storm," said one of Barabbas's companions.

"There is practically no wind," Simon replied.

That realization silenced them, and made them look outside. "Bad weather coming," someone said, and his voice held apprehension.

"That is good," Simon answered, "I need rain for early plowing."

Barabbas pulled his newly purchased garment closer around his shoulders, shivered. "It's becoming cold. There must be snow on Carmel."

"The wind is west, and not from Carmel," Simon answered.

Barabbas's eyes looked unnaturally large in the mysterious light. "Leave the land alone. Throw in your lot with me. The wealthy ones won't even notice that we shall be sharing in their bounty."

Simon shook his head. Idly he watched the shop owner place a torch in a clamp on the wall. The flame looked like the broad blade of a spear. It burned steadily without flickering, so that it seemed transformed into a glittering, golden stone.

"No, I'm staying on the land," the Cyrenian said.

"Bring more wine!" Barabbas ordered.

Simon pulled his garment closer and rubbed his hands. They continued to drink and talk as the hours passed.

The innkeeper had lit more torches. He placed lamps on the tables.

At last Simon rose. "I think I'll check on the weather," he said. "I want to go to Joseph of Arimathea. Look how dark it is; it seems we are due for a heavy thunderstorm."

"Peace be with you, strong man," Barabbas said. "It grieves me that you will not accompany me. Perhaps we shall meet again one day. Perhaps then you will say, 'Barabbas, the land is not good any more. I want to come with you.'"

"Peace be with you, Barabbas," Simon said simply. The torches were extinguished, and the features of the robber appeared dim and vague.

They all rose. The shop was nearly empty. The few remaining customers all crowded around the door. Only the shop owner remained, bustling to and fro among the empty tables.

In his hurry to leave the shop, Simon collided with a stool and halted in the doorway. He went outside and looked up at the darkened heavens.

There were no clouds in the sky. It was empty, deep blue, dark. Everything was silent—as if he stood in a dead city.

As if all light were dead . . . and the wind.

He stood in the middle of the street. People lined the sides. They stared up at the sky and gestured with their hands. There was only the ineffectual sun that seemed to fuse into purple twilight.

Leaves glinted blue like shreds of steel caught in firelight. The trees themselves were pillars of blue stone.

Simon began to walk along the street, and as he went he felt the silence and emptiness about him. Axes, motionless on butchers' blocks, gleamed strangely. He was alone in the center of the street except for his shadow, thin and ghostlike. Alone in the long street—the ends of which melted into purple shadows.

He raised his hands and stared at them. His palms were pale patches in a blur of surrounding dusk. Somewhere a dog barked —once only, and then was silent.

Simon looked toward the temple. He could not see the walls; only the roofs were visible, large, round, and silvery. They seemed to float on nothing.

He stood motionless and watched them slowly becoming less visible, like the rest of Jerusalem in the afternoon darkness. A cock crowed uncertainly to greet the untimely night.

Far off in another street a child called for its mother. A flock of birds fluttered through the sky, aimlessly circling, seeking for the light. A woman screamed in fear.

Simon rubbed his neck and quickly withdrew his hand as he touched the place where the cross had chafed him.

At last even the quivering gleam of the temple roofs faded away into the strange shadows.

A tumult arose throughout Jerusalem. The cry of the people's fear filled the darkness and rose toward the stars, but even the stars were veiled.

Two horses panicked and ran whinnying down the street. A wagon rocked along behind them until they broke their legs against an unseen wall.

Guiding himself by the dim outlines of buildings, Simon stumbled down the street. He saw the gloom deepen about him. Suddenly he broke into a run, fleeing from his fear.

When he regained his composure, he found himself before

the temple. Dimly he saw the gate. He entered the temple grounds and found the lowest step of the temple.

The earth shuddered.

The darkness became complete. Jerusalem still screamed its fear. He listened for a moment—only for a moment, for the marble step trembled beneath him. He hurried further up. Then he began to run. Before he knew it he had crossed the Court of the Israelites into the Court of the Priests, and found himself on the porch of the temple itself, where none but priests were allowed. But fear broke through discipline. All that he knew was that he looked for safety, and he felt he could find it in the innermost sanctuary of the God of the covenant. The palace guards and priests had not seen him. They stood outside communing in little fearful groups.

In his confusion Simon moved between the mighty pillars into the Holy Place. Only then did he fully appreciate that he had penetrated to a point directly before the Holy of Holies.

He stood alone. All were outside on the temple grounds where they could look out at the night. The light of a seven-branched lampstand glowed dully upon the altar of incense. At the end of the Holy Place was a high opening, covered completely by a massive black veil. In his panic Simon stared at it. He acted as a man who dreams, without will or conscious thought. He had no impulse to flee from this forbidden inner sanctum.

Sunk in the strange trancelike state that had impelled him there, he moved nearer to the veil. Then there came a sullen rumbling. It felt as if the marble was tilting down beneath him, as if the pillars would collapse. There came a vicious jerk, a grinding. The temple rocked and shuddered. Then the tremor ceased.

Simon had ceased to be conscious of himself. His whole being was utterly absorbed in the momentous experience. He was aware only of immense remoteness, of the absolute exclusiveness of the fragrance of the incense upon the altar.

His mouth hung open, gasping. His eyes were wide with awe. And every nerve in him quivered at the sight before him. As he stood there gazing at the dense veil, ancient, black, and heavy, he did not have the slightest idea of what penalty would be meted out to him if he were apprehended there. Contemplation of such a fate had become as void of meaning as every other thing. He stood rooted there, for he sought enlightenment, clarity, and truth. He sought freedom from his fears. That morning he had believed that he understood, but the strange darkness had altered everything. Perhaps he might yet hear a voice speaking to him.

He pressed his knuckles to his mouth. Once again he felt the earth rock as if it were a vessel tossing in a stormy sea. He felt the floor of the Holy Place shuddering under him. It seemed as if the roof of the temple had broken loose and was falling.

His terror died and he was calm, for before him he saw a miraculous event, and for the moment it purged him of human frailty.

The veil swayed, rippled, and trembled, tearing apart slowly.

From the top, downward, it parted, and the sound of its tearing was clear and terrible.

When the tear reached the floor the two pieces of the veil fell asunder.

Simon of Cyrene stood with his hands before his eyes. He stood thus for a long time, as one who had been blinded. Then he looked, his head trembling. The emptiness of the Holy of Holies confronted him. The separation between one man of Israel and the most holy place of his religion no longer existed.

Simon stood for a long time before the realization of what was and what was not forbidden broke through his absorption. The law of the ages penetrated to him, but he had no fear, for he had experienced something greater than the law. He turned and walked away, bumped into a pillar and struck his forehead on the marble. He felt no pain, but stood leaning against the rising column.

Simon's hands moved slowly on the marble. He looked back once again at the rent veil. An overwhelming revelation came to him. He lingered no longer.

He bounded down the flights of steps, through the Court of the Israelites, through the pilgrims whom the darkness had overtaken in the outer court of the temple.

He made for the Damascus Gate through which Jesus had been led that morning. He ran through the gateway, knocking aside a crippled beggar in his haste. Then up the footpath to Golgotha!

Halfway up the rise exhaustion overtook him. He slowed down to a hurried walk. His eyes leaped up to the crosses. They looked gigantic against the sky, seeming to reach up to the gray heavens, where daylight grew and grew.

The crowds had vanished. Only a small group remained beside the crosses—just the devoted few, bowed low and grief-stricken in the dawn of late afternoon.

They were waiting, staring at the crosses. Some looked up at the sky and saw the wonder of the light that restored the glory to the temple.

Simon stumbled nearer, toward the cross of Jesus. When quite near, he ran, his eyes fixed on the cross. His breath whistled as he stopped beneath the cross. He licked his lips. The man's head had fallen forward. The chest no longer moved. Dead light glistened in the eyes.

Suddenly he clasped Jesus' feet. They felt small and icy in his hands. He saw that the blood had dried. Simon's neck and shoulders were bowed, and his tear-filled eyes could scarcely see.

In the light of that strange dawn he turned away. "He is dead. He has died," he heard somebody say. He knew the voice that spoke. He lifted his head and looked into the eyes of Joseph of Arimathea, looking long at him as if he were a stranger.

Simon Niger nodded slightly. He looked up at the cross. "I can see that He is dead," he said, his voice tremulous and husky. And as he looked up Joseph saw tears glittering in his beard. "I thought He would still be living when I reached here. But He is dead. . . ."

His voice rose higher, and an unnatural smile twisted his face as he looked at Joseph: "In the temple I felt He was the Son of God. . . . I . . . I almost believed. . . . When the darkness came, I almost believed in Him." He gasped painfully for breath. "I thought He would conquer the cross. . . ."

He stopped abruptly. Joseph took him by his shoulder, endeavoring to calm him.

"But He is not the Son of God," whispered Simon. In his despair he grabbed Joseph violently by his gown and shook him. "No, He is not the Son of God. He is nothing! He died like anybody else. He was a human being, nothing more. A mortal man

238

like you and me." He staggered and stood with his head flung back, his face raised to the heavens.

"What of the darkness and the earthquake?" Joseph asked.

"I do not know. . . . I do not know. All I know is that God would never let His Son die this way." He turned toward Joseph. He pointed to Jesus with a trembling hand. "Look at Him. He perished. Does He appear to you to be the Son of God?"

"Were you in the temple?" asked Joseph, powerless to answer.

"I was in the temple. . . . I . . . I. . . ." He was terrified at his secret knowledge. He had thought it was a miracle, but now it seemed a menace. If it became known, he might be put to death.

He fell silent, and looked toward the Roman soldiers who stood tensely by. They were looking at Jesus' cross, then at the sky and back at one another. All were ill at ease.

Simon saw the old brown garment lying on the ground. A little leather bowl and dice with black dots had been left upon it. They lay there gleaming—gleaming in the sun.

Simon looked up, and the bright sun dazzled him. Jerusalem looked fresh and cleansed in the new light. The Mount of Olives stood out again . . . and the bright green trees of Gethsemane . . . the meandering curve of the brook of Kidron.

Once more Simon looked up at the cross, saw its long shadow, then turned away and descended the hill.

26

The man from Cyrene did not hurry; he walked along leisurely. As he went he relived everything—the darkening, the happenings in the temple. He wondered at himself for having believed in those moments of darkness that this man was the Son of God, the great Redeemer.

He halted and again looked back toward the crosses. Not at all of them—only the one in the middle, far-off now and faint. The man hung there, just as when he had left the hill.

Only on the other crosses was there sign of life and movement as the declining sun showed the writhings of the bodies.

Simon reached the brook of Kidron at length and stared at the rounded stones, worn smooth by many waters. Again he touched the place where the cross had chafed him. He had to concentrate to remember what had happened. All seemed remote. He gripped the nape of his neck as if to shake himself from a state of fantasy.

As Simon began to walk on he saw a man sitting under a fig tree on the bank, his long back propped against the trunk. Simon walked toward him, for he felt the need of company. Possibly it might be the herdsman who had disappeared so suddenly when the centurion was looking for someone to carry the cross.

But when he reached the tree, Simon stopped. This was not the herdsman. The hood of the man's garment was thrown back from his head. His hair was curled and his beard was red.

"You are Simon Peter, the man who told those lies beside the fire in Caiaphas's courtyard last night," said Simon. "They have crucified your master, and you sit under a fig tree." He spoke softly, and the tone of his voice held no reproach.

The tall man opened his eyes slowly, eyes bloodshot and dreary. There were deep lines across his forehead, and his hand drew slow tracings in the dust. He lifted his right hand and wiped his lips. He pressed his head back against the trunk and looked past Simon into the empty sky.

Simon moved a step nearer. He felt curiously drawn to this tall fellow who was leaning silently against the tree.

"I have just come from where the crosses are. He is dead. The other two are living still, but He is dead. The Nazarene died quickly."

Simon Peter looked at Simon for a long time, a despairing longing in his eyes; then he stared down at the ground and touched a stone with his fingers. But he could not hide the film of tears in his bloodshot eyes, although he had turned his face from Simon. His beard trembled, and it was long before his lips moved, though his eyes still avoided Simon's.

"How did He die?"

Simon shrugged his shoulders, came and squatted beside Simon Peter, thankful that the man had spoken.

"I do not know how He died. I simply threw down the cross and left—"

"Did you then carry the cross?" Simon Peter turned his head quickly and this time made no attempt to hide his tears. But there was more spirit in his eyes.

"They forced me to do it." Simon looked at the ground between his feet. He felt tenderly about his neck and shoulders.

"You have been blessed." Simon Peter spoke with fervor.

"Blessed? I was defiled!"

"His cross could not defile you."

"You still believe in Him although you denied Him three times last night?"

"What can I believe in now that He is dead? What is left? I only wish I could have borne His cross—that would have been my final act of love toward Him. I would that I were you, stranger."

"You could have borne His cross." Simon spoke softly again, not reproachfully. "Then I should not have been compelled to do it."

Simon Peter pressed his hands into the dust and let his head fall back against the trunk behind him. He closed his eyes. The veins in his neck were thick and pulsing. "When you walk with a man for many days and hear His wisdom, you come to believe He

241

is more than man. Then you have courage. Then you will draw the sword. When you hear that man talk of His kingdom, you believe He is a king. So we believed—I and the others. We believed when we saw the crowds in Galilee. Thousands came to hear Him beside the lake. And the day He preached on the mountain, they were in their tens of thousands. That day He became a king." Peter became silent, swallowed, and the slow movement of his Adam's apple awoke strange pity in Simon.

"But if one day you see that men can hurt His body, that He is mortal, then you become fearful. You fear the power in Jerusalem. Last evening as we came through the Kidron, we believed that Jerusalem would be His—if not today, well then tomorrow. We believed that Jerusalem would now belong to Israel."

"So He misled you?" Simon's question was a whisper. He looked at the tears in Peter's half-closed eyes.

"He made us understand He was a king. We thought He was another David—"

"You believed that?"

"Yes, we believed it. We believed Him."

Simon picked up a twig and broke it in his hands. "I heard him say that He was the Son of God." He looked for shock in Peter's eyes, but the disciple stared off toward where distant trees were budding, off through the clear light that made the Mount of Olives loom large and near.

"He said many things—great things. He said that He would rise after He was dead—"

"Rise again? From the dead?" The twig fell from Simon's hands. He sat on the ground and looked toward far Golgotha where the crosses stood. He stared back at Peter with narrowed eyes. He rubbed his temples with his fingers as if to drive the conception home. "Do you believe that?" he stammered.

"Lazarus rose from the dead. He raised Lazarus."

Simon jumped up so quickly that he almost fell. He turned his back on the disciple. "Even after He has misled you, you still have faith in Him! How can a man rise from the dead unless he is awakened, as Lazarus was awakened by God?"

Peter's voice seemed faint and far away. "I no longer know what I believe. We believed in Him, and He abandoned us. I do not believe He will rise again. A king does not die in such a manner. He is gone from us, that is all I know. We are alone, and tomorrow we will be scattered. Within a year or two or three the eleven of us will be strangers. His kingdom is lost. Israel stays beneath the heel. After the Passover I will go back to the lake and repair my boat, mend my nets. I shall take up my old life, for He is gone."

Simon heard the anguish of his words, the bitterness of his disillusionment.

"I shall return to the lake. I . . . wish I were you, stranger, who never knew Him. Then I should not have suffered so. I long for Him, yet I deny him. How shall I ever be free of that sin?" He ceased abruptly; his words failed and died. "I wish I were Judas Iscariot. For he at least is free. . ."

The choking sob in the disciple's voice made Simon turn around, and he saw Peter sitting huddled forward, his head between his knees. "Did you . . . do you know about Judas Iscariot?" Simon faltered.

It was some time before Peter raised his head and looked despairingly at Simon. Tears beaded his eyelids, and his eyes were listless. "I heard about Judas Iscariot," he said. "They found his body. . . . It is only Judas who no longer suffers. Only he of all the twelve. Only he will not return to empty days and nights of longing. Only Judas will have no need to go back to Galilee, to look up at a hill and think of Him, to draw water from a well and hear His silent voice, or pause beside a stone where once He rested. Only Judas will not need to follow in tears the paths His feet have trod."

"Do you consider Him good because he became like a brother to you?" Simon's voice was low.

"He was a good man. If He had not died, I would have been His slave till the last day of my life."

"Where are the others?"

"They are hiding in Jerusalem. Fear made cowards of them, just as it did of me. They have hidden themselves in fear of the fury in Jerusalem."

"And you are here?"

"I had to come. Here to Gethsemane. I hoped that He would

return here . . . that He would not die. That He would triumph. I have waited here, but He did not come. I saw when they led Him to Golgotha."

He stopped speaking and looked up at Simon. He struggled to lift himself against the trunk as if no further strength was left in his big body. He stood there bowed and bent, and it seemed that a single day had aged him.

"Did you see that He was dead, stranger? Were you near Him?"

"He is dead," Simon said. "I touched His feet. He is dead."

Peter shifted his feet nervously, and looked in the direction of the crosses. He walked out into the open and stared toward them.

The Cyrenian looked at Peter's bowed shoulders. The man looked frank and honest. Then Simon spoke, for he could no longer keep his secret: "I beheld a wondrous sight in the temple today."

"In the temple?" Simon looked uncertainly at Peter, and nervously bit his lip. The disciple understood his hesitation. "You may speak, stranger. I shall respect your confidence."

Simon walked to the tree and pressed his hand against the trunk. "When it became dark, I entered into the temple. I was terrified. I found myself before the Holy of Holies."

"The Holy of Holies!" asked Peter unbelievingly.

Simon nodded, and bent his head. His fingers played with the rough bark. "There was a rumbling and shaking." Simon walked out of the cool shadow into the sunlight. As he spoke, he looked toward the crosses. "I saw the veil," he turned swiftly to Peter, "I saw the veil tear—it tore from top to bottom."

The other came hesitatingly up to him and took Simon lightly by the shoulders. "You saw the veil tear?"

Simon nodded. "I saw it tear asunder. By itself—with no one present but me."

Peter released him suddenly, turned, and walked a few paces toward Golgotha. He stared intently at the crosses. After a while he turned around. He saw how widely Simon's eyes had opened. "And you . . . you were up there with Him?" Peter asked. "You are certain He is dead?"

"He is dead. I touched Him."

"And you saw the veil tearing?"

"I saw it tear. It is the truth."

The disciple walked unsteadily to the tree and leaned against it. He stared down at the ground and shook his head.

"It must have been the earthquake that tore the veil," said Simon in the sunlight. "The temple rocked."

"Yes, it could have been the earthquake," Peter answered. "It was so severe that it opened many graves—that is what I heard. But why should it tear the veil and leave the temple intact?" He looked searchingly at Simon. "You are certain . . . you are sure about the veil?"

"As certain as I am that the sun shines on my hands." And he stretched out his hands to the sunlight.

Simon Peter plucked a fig leaf, looked for a moment at the living green in his hand, then let it fall. "I do not understand," he said, helplessly. "The veil tears . . . and He is dead. I do not understand it. I understand nothing anymore. This day is different, stranger. Different from other days. For a moment I thought that *He* had performed that wonder in the temple, but He is dead . . ."

The words between them were exhausted. They stood silent until Peter said, "I am very weary."

"You may come with me to my house . . . it is hidden in the trees of Gethsemane. There you may eat and rest. . . . I can see that you are tired."

"No, I shall go up to the crosses. There it is quiet."

"What will you do there? He is dead. I saw Him dead."

"I want to be beside Him, to touch Him once again. Look, the sun is low. I must be near Him." He came close to Simon. "Farewell, stranger!"

"My name is Simon of Cyrene. We have met before. You may come to my house if you are hungry or thirsty or in need of rest."

"You have a kind heart, man of Cyrene. I am glad I was able to speak with you beneath this tree—my heart is so empty."

Then Peter turned away and went wearily toward Golgotha, where the crosses could just barely be seen above the shadowed hill.

But Simon's voice halted him: "Did He say that He would rise again?"

Peter turned in surprise. "That is what He said, man of Cyrene. That's what He told us. . . . but He died like any mortal man."

Then he went on his way again. Simon stood watching the tall man's shadow gliding along the ground. He stared long and thoughtfully at the still cross in the middle, off in the distance. After a while he too walked away, along the Kidron and in among the trees of Gethsemane. He gazed at the wonder of unfolding leaves.

He came upon the tree stump where he had seen Jesus kneel. He could see the print that Jesus had left on the ground when He had prayed alone. He looked at the piece of wood he had seen the night before. He looked at the torches that had burned down to the end—he looked but briefly, and then he turned away.

It seemed to Deborah, as she worked before the hearth, that the twilight had deepened. She straightened and turned slowly; Simon stood in the doorway, with his hands upon the frame.

She drew in her breath so sharply that he could hear. He stared at her, and she seemed to him to have grown older since he had taken leave of her the night before. Her face was pale and tense and her eyes were sunken in her head.

"Simon of Cyrene," she said in a shrill voice, "you have come back." She sank down on to a stool as if all her strength had left her.

He walked inside and stood looking down at her. "I wanted to go," he said hoarsely, "but I did not." He looked at her in the twilight and saw the question her heart asked. "I . . . I could not leave you."

Deborah stood up, very slowly. "You have come back to me? Did my love and prayers bring you back?"

He walked around the wooden table to her. She pressed herself against him, and her hands gripped his shoulders. He took her face gently between his hands as if it were a flower. He did not speak but looked into her eyes. She saw that his face expressed more than he could utter. He bent quickly and kissed her lightly on her forehead, and then she knew he had come back to her.

He did not know where to begin. Where does one begin a

new life? How does one start speaking of things that are greater than the sun and sea, greater than the growth of a tree, greater than a volcano that can overwhelm a city? He felt uncomfortable beneath her gaze. He searched for what he should say. Pride still sealed his lips, still kept him hesitant.

That was why he suddenly swung away from her and went to the washtub. He loosened his girdle and drew off his upper garment. He bent over and began to wash himself. She came closer, and her nearness made his hands tremble in the water.

All at once he stiffened above the washtub. His hands were cupped and empty, his head was low, his eyes shut in the realization that fate had caught up with him at that moment. For he felt her cool fingertips on the place where the cross had chafed him.

"Your neck . . . your shoulders are sore, my husband. The skin is broken." He stood erect. His beard shone with drops of water. "You have been fighting. . . . Did you fight?"

"No, not fighting." His voice was thick. "I carried His cross." He spoke the words too quickly.

The grip of her hands on his arm hurt him. Her breath was cool upon his neck. He sank onto a stool against the wall, and she came and knelt before him. He took her face gently between his hands.

"Carried His cross? You carried His cross?"

He nodded. "They forced me to," he added hastily.

"They forced you?"

He felt the disappointment in her voice, felt her hands slip out of his. He looked down into her dark eyes, thankful that he had broken through the tension.

She pressed her face against his knees, held his legs tightly, and lay there weeping. His hands sought her cheek. "Where are the others?" he asked.

"They went to Golgotha, to see the crosses. After the sudden darkness we came here from Bethany. I stayed here waiting, hoping. When I saw your leather bag lying there, I knew our life was not yet over."

"A new life has begun for us," he said, moving his fingers through her hair.

She fetched an herbal ointment and smeared it on the chafed

247

places of his neck and shoulders. "May these marks never disappear," said Deborah as she applied the salve. "I think that one day you will be very proud and thankful that you helped Him."

"Mother, the Nazarene is dead," he said wearily. "Peter, His disciple, says that He claimed He would rise again." Her hands became still. "Do you believe that?"

"I do not know, my husband. I think that with Him all things are possible."

After a while Deborah asked, "Can't we . . . can't we go to the crosses? I have not been there."

"What do you want to see, my wife? He is dead. It is over. A man on the cross is not a pleasant sight."

"I want to see how He looks in death." Her eyes pleaded with him, and he knew that he could not refuse her.

"Come then, let us go," he said.

He cleansed himself, put on a fresh garment, and they set off for Golgotha. When they reached the place, dusk had fallen, and there was but a small group by the crosses.

Joseph of Arimathea was there and greeted them. He had brought a fine linen cloth in which to lay Jesus. The man named Nicodemus stood there too, and he had brought myrrh and spices for the embalming.

Simon saw men struggling to draw the spikes from the cross. He stood at a distance and watched them. At last they loosened them and drew them from the hands. Others, meanwhile, had contrived to free the feet. They lowered Jesus from the cross. They pressed together to touch Him and to help.

The women standing there wept loudly, and even some of the men brushed their hands across their eyes. The body was so limp that it seemed that torment had broken it utterly.

Deborah, who had stood silently beside Simon, moved closer to the body and he saw her touch His face, and stand for a moment bowed above Him. She took His lifeless hand and pressed it to her cheek. It brought tears to his eyes, not because the dead man was Jesus, but because it was death that he beheld.

He saw Rufus, Ezekiel, and Mary also standing by. They stayed quietly among the others, beside the prostrate body.

He heard the women weeping, saw them touch Jesus' body,

take His head in their hands and smooth His beard. They talked to Him as if he still lived and understood.

"My son . . . my son." He heard the wail of a little woman garbed in the black of mourning.

Tears were in Mary's eyes. She had touched Jesus' beard once, but now she stared at Simon. With a little cry she ran to him and flung her arms about him. Strangely affected, he laid his hands on her head, and gazed in turn at Rufus and Ezekiel, who also approached him. Neither said a word, but what they wished to say their eyes spoke for them.

The men took Jesus' body and carried it to a place not far away, where Joseph of Arimathea had carved a sepulcher from the soft sandstone. There they laid the body down, and it was cold and still.

Deborah had taken Simon's arm, and they followed the small procession. They stood with Rufus and the rest before the sepulcher while the women embalmed the body. They worked quickly, for there was little time. Soon it would be the Sabbath.

"I went to Pilate to ask permission to remove the body," Joseph told Simon as they waited. Simon knew now that the Ethiopian slave had spoken the truth.

As they stood in the darkness, Simon's secret moved and gnawed within him. Again he felt he must divulge it. Several times he looked at Joseph, then he clutched the elder's garment and drew him to the deeper shadows beneath a tree.

Joseph's eyes questioned him. "Joseph of Arimathea," said Simon, "you are a good man. There is something I must tell you."

"Is it a good secret that you carry in your heart?" asked Joseph. "I am thankful that you are among those at the burial."

"Man of wisdom, it concerns the veil in the temple," said Simon. "It disturbs me; I must speak to you about it."

"The veil in the temple?" asked Joseph, and he came closer in the uncertain light of the dusk. "What about the veil?" he asked.

"I . . . I saw the veil tearing apart of its own accord—"

"No!" Joseph gasped. "No, Cyrenian, what are you saying? You must be overtired. Perhaps you saw it in a dream."

"I am telling you the truth, Joseph of Arimathea!" Simon's

voice was confident, and Joseph saw the frankness in his face. "It was no dream. I saw it with these eyes."

"What were you doing in the Holy Place? You are not allowed there!"

"But I did see it. . . . I had taken refuge in the temple from the darkness."

"You saw the veil tear?"

"The temple shuddered, and the veil tore—it tore from top to bottom and fell apart I stood before the entrance to the Holy of Holies."

The old man gripped Simon so powerfully by his garment that he looked at him in alarm. For a moment he thought that Joseph would attack him. The elder's eyes had opened wide; he stood for a time without speaking.

"If what you say is true, then you have seen the greatest of His miracles, exalted man."

"It is the truth," said Simon passionately. "Simon Peter said it could have been the earthquake that caused the veil to tear."

"Simon Peter, beloved by Him, sat at His feet so long, yet does not understand. Can you then gather the wonder of this miracle? He brought you from far Africa to give you this revelation, there in the place of His Father's shrine. Do you not see, Simon?"

"It was the earthquake!" said Simon shortly. "The earthquake uncovered graves and tore the veil."

"No . . . no!" cried the elder. "We have had greater earthquakes in Jerusalem and the veil has never torn. It is He who tore the veil. . . . It is His death that brought about this wonder."

"His death?" asked Simon in bewilderment.

"Man of Cyrene, with His death He tore down the barrier between Israel and her God. Today you, an ordinary Jew, stood where only the priests may stand; and when the veil parted, you saw what even the high priest sees but once a year on the Day of Atonement. The veil between God and His people has been destroyed, and atonement is given to all His people. Truly I say to you that Jesus is the Son of God. Truly He is the sacrificial lamb who has died for Israel."

Joseph remained silent for a moment. "And you saw this miracle and did not understand it. His own disciple did not understand.

250

You saw the meaning of His death, and you had no knowledge." Joseph smiled through the tears that had come to his eyes. "To you, man of Cyrene, who do not believe in Him, He has revealed His greatest message."

Simon looked toward the sepulcher, dumbfounded by the elder's words. Joseph said, "It is only His body that lies there, Simon. It is only His body that has perished. But He lives on."

Simon's shoulders were bowed. His breathing was deep and slow. With his open hand he wiped his lips. He swallowed, and stared into Joseph's eyes. His voice was like a stranger's when he spoke. "Simon Peter . . . says . . . He will . . . rise again. He said . . . He will rise again . . ."

"That is what Jesus said," Joseph of Arimathea affirmed. "And what He says is truth."

Simon looked toward the sepulcher again. He turned away and walked unsteadily through the trees. Joseph watched him go, and there was a father's love in the old man's eyes.

In the shadows of the trees Simon stopped, turned around, and looked back at the sepulcher. He saw the men struggling there to move a stone. There were many men, and they strained to roll the stone into the mouth of the cave. In the dim light he saw Rufus's red head among the others. Suddenly they stopped, for Joseph of Arimathea had joined them and was motioning with his hands. Was he telling them about the tearing of the veil? Simon saw their bodies stiffen as the elder spoke. Then they pushed the rock again. It rolled over slowly and fell into the mouth of the sepulcher.

Simon lingered there for a few moments, and then started back through the trees to Gethsemane. Deborah and Rufus overtook him. Each put an arm about him, for he hardly knew where he was going. He stumbled forward like a man struck blind.

27

When the morning star hung over the Mount of Olives, Simon of Cyrene left the cottage and walked swiftly through the orchard. He walked still more quickly, then broke into a run. That morning he felt strong again. Two nights before, after Jesus had been put to rest in the sepulcher, Simon had slept well, for his exertions and lack of sleep had tired him. The previous day was the Sabbath, and he spent that time with his family. Over and over they discussed the happenings. More than once he had left the house to stare out toward the sepulcher. He also told them about the thing he had witnessed in the temple.

But that night he had not slept so deeply. From time to time he awakened, as if he were being called.

The new day had just met the sky when he entered the small garden outside the sepulcher. The tree trunks were gray columns in the soft dimness of the garden.

A bird awoke, chirped softly, and flew away between the trees. Dogs barked and cocks crowed in the dawn.

A short distance from the sepulcher Simon halted. He took a few paces to the side, and stopped again. He peered through the strengthening light that broke the uniformity of night, parting all things from one another and giving them their character. He craned his neck, turning this way and that to see.

He moved nearer, stopped again. The early light could still deceive.

But it could not subvert the truth of what he saw.

In the body of the sandstone there was a dark rectangle, the entrance to the sepulcher. The heavy stone no longer covered it.

Simon slipped from tree trunk to tree trunk, stealthily, like a hunter who stalks his prey. At last he stood before the opening.

The heavy rock, with which the group had struggled two evenings before, now lay to one side.

Simon walked closer, stopping at the mouth of the sepulcher, his hands on the cool stone, while behind him the light grew stronger.

The scent of balsam filled the sepulcher.

The tomb was empty.

He turned and looked about him, looked up at the gleaming summit of the trees.

Then he gazed into the tomb. He saw the winding cloths they had made from Joseph's snow-white linen. They lay in strips and bundles on the stone.

"He is not here," Simon of Cyrene said, and his whisper was loud in the emptiness. He peered into the grave, at its walls, at the winding cloths again, even at the roof.

The sepulcher was empty.

"He is not here," the Cyrenian repeated, overwhelmed, and bent down and touched a bandage with his fingertips.

A sudden noise made him spring around. He heard the voices of people coming through the trees. He jumped away, slipping in among the bushes. Again he peered toward the grave. He saw women approaching with what seemed to be jars and pitchers. The growing daylight glittered in his eyes.

Simon heard the women scream and saw them running from the grave in terror. He saw a pitcher fall and heard the noise of its breaking.

The Cyrenian felt a cold gust of air pass over his face and neck.

He started to search in among the trees, stopping and moving on again. And while he walked, it was as if every tree trunk was a voice that spoke to him. He seemed to hear a voice from above: *He will rise. . . . He will rise. . . . What He says is truth, like rain, and wind, and sun. . . .* Joseph of Arimathea seemed to speak to him through the silence.

He turned, and with his chest against a trunk he peered toward the grave, watching the light slowly dissolve the dark rectangle.

With a sudden movement he swung around, left the trees, and broke into a run. As the sunlight was brightening the leaves on the Mount of Olives, he reached the yard of Lazarus's house at Bethany and halted.

Panting, Simon tried to swallow to bring a little moisture to his throat. He hid behind a pomegranate bush a little distance from the house and saw the leaves of Lazarus's poplars shining like silver daggers. The garden was silent, and the yard was empty.

Then there was a movement. A young woman—it must be Martha—came out to feed the fowl. She did it quietly, without a glance about her.

Lazarus came out, carried a pitcher to the well, and drew up water. He too was calm, and Simon knew that for these two the day was not eventful.

He looked away, down the white, winding path that led to Jerusalem to see if anybody was coming toward the house. He heard Martha calling to the fowl and the dull squeaking from the well.

Disappointed, he turned and went back toward Jerusalem. He walked along, darting glances to both sides of the road, rounded a curve through an orchard and stared up at the heights of the Mount of Olives. He peered into the faces of the pilgrims returning to their homes with the ending of the Passover season.

When he reached the Kidron, he thought first of turning homeward toward Gethsemane. But then he saw the people crowding around the East Gate. The pilgrims' camp seemed to be buzzing with excitement.

He quickly crossed the Kidron and went in among the pilgrims. Some were busy striking their tents for their homeward journey. But most stood about in excited groups conversing loudly. Others were crowding toward the gate.

"The stone was rolled away from the grave. . . . The guards took fright and fled. . . . Only the winding sheet was left . . ." Such snatches of their talk reached him.

"But where is He now?" asked someone.

"No one knows. The body has disappeared. No trace of it has been found yet."

Simon entered Jerusalem, listening to the spirited chatter about the vanished body. He turned aimlessly into the Street of the Wagonmakers. Everywhere there were groups of people. Arms waved, necks were thrust forward, voices were loud.

"Perhaps He is in the temple."

"Perhaps in Bethany."

"Or maybe gone into the desert."

"You speak as if He's really risen. This is but a trick of His disciples."

At the lean-to of a wagonmaker Simon stopped. Perhaps it was because the smith was a giant with frizzled hair and powerful arms who reminded him of Big Micha. People stood around him.

"I tell you, the tomb is empty," said a small man standing near the blacksmith.

With repeated blows, the smith struck the red-hot iron lying on the heavy anvil, scattering red sparks about him. He did it with a violence that seemed intent on shattering the small man's words.

"Lies! Lies!" roared the smith. "Who says He was ever in that grave?"

Simon Niger burst through the idle crowd and stood before the smith. "I saw Him laid away in Joseph of Arimathea's sepulcher," he said.

"Oh, here we have another witness!" laughed the smith, and straightened up.

"And this morning I saw it empty," added Simon loudly. "I was there."

The smith crossed his arms. In his gray eyes was a light that Simon did not understand. "If He is risen, then where is He?" asked the smith, challenging him. He wiped the sweat from his forehead. "Come, let us go and look for Him. If He hasn't grown wings and flown away, we'll find Him. Perhaps He's preaching in the temple. If not, He may be lying at ease under a tree on the Mount of Olives."

"Those Galilean women saw Him," said the small man next to Simon.

The blacksmith roared with laughter, and the company began to laugh with him. "Women's tattle . . . women's tattle! The Galileans still believe in ghosts. But here in Jerusalem we have no specters."

Laughter drowned the blacksmith's voice.

Simon turned slowly to the small man beside him. "Where did the women see Him?"

"In the garden—just in front of the sepulcher." The small man gestured with his hands.

"That is not the truth," said the Cyrenian hotly. "I was there, and I saw the women flee."

"Well, that's what I heard," said the small man placatingly.

Simon pushed his way through the bystanders. "What did I tell you!" he heard the smith shout triumphantly as he resumed his onslaught on the ringing anvil.

He wandered further, but did not walk fast. He looked closely at the crowds that sauntered in the street. He searched for a tall, lean man in an old brown garment. He looked at hands that went swinging by, at feet in sandals. But the hands and feet that passed him showed no scars of recent mutilation.

At every corner he searched for a group of men—a company of eleven speaking in the accent of Galileans. He kept keen watch for a big, red-bearded man.

He saw no company of Galileans. He went on farther. Perhaps Joseph of Arimathea might know something. He walked to the landlord's big house, but a slave said his master was away. Simon went then to the palace of Caiaphas, but the gate stood open and the courtyard was deserted. He walked through the Water Gate, down the decline, along the deep Valley of Hinnom. Perhaps they had hidden themselves in the clay quarry where Iscariot died. Who knew? He stood beside the ancient almond tree and looked into the abyss. But he saw nobody. There was only the dark stain where Judas's broken body had lain. He looked away across the fields, at the shadows beneath the trees. He visited the Fountain of Gihon, and searched there. But there were only herdsmen watering their beasts.

"Has anyone here seen the Nazarene and His Galileans?" Simon asked of some men who loitered at the spring.

"They must be on the way to Galilee to preach sermons to the fishermen," one of the herdsmen answered, laughing.

Simon walked a little further, looked toward Bethany, and then stopped. Should he go to Bethany again? No, he would not go there again, he decided. He went back into Jerusalem, and listened intently to those walking in the streets or gossiping in groups. But the conversations were still the same. Most were exchanging guesses about what had happened to the body. Nobody seemed to know what had happened to the disciples.

Simon could not keep his eyes from the people about him. It seemed to him that any moment he might see the man in the brown garment pass by him.

He visited the temple. Strange, that he had not thought of going there before. It was quite possible that they would have learned of something there. The temple and the Antonia—those were the places he should go to.

He passed through the gate to the temple grounds. He looked at the massive structure, stone piled on stone, vast, with the stillness of eternity. He saw the mighty pillars, so lofty that he was obliged to lift his face to see their topmost point. He saw the golden roofs, proud and mighty in the sun.

Countless years Herod and his successors had labored to build the temple, and this man had said he would rebuild it in three days . . .

He saw again the dark eyes of the herdsmen.

"Yes, Herod built for many years," whispered Simon on the marble steps. He climbed to the top of the steps and stood there looking north over Jerusalem where the hills of Galilee must lie.

He saw three scribes coming up the steps. He approached and stood respectfully in their path. "The Nazarene . . . has anybody heard what has happened to the body of the Nazarene?" Simon asked.

The three scribes looked at him, smiled, and drew their gowns closer about them. "Are you also looking for the Nazarene?" one asked good-naturedly.

"I . . . I was at the grave. . . . The grave is empty."

"Naturally, the grave is empty," said another scribe.

Simon looked questioningly from one to the other, searching for the truth in their eyes.

"Has no one told you yet?" asked the third scribe.

Simon shook his head. "No, I have not heard yet where the body is," he acknowledged.

"The disciples stole the body away and hid it."

"Stole the body? Hid it?" Simon's question was scarcely audible.

257

"That is what I said. They stole the body to make the people believe that the Nazarene has risen. Those Galileans know they are marked men in Jerusalem. That is why they are trying to deceive the people in this manner."

Simon stood and watched them going into the Court of the Israelites. The sun shone on their headcloths. His eyes followed them into the dimness of the temple interior, to where the Holy of Holies must be. Then he wandered down the steps and lost himself among the people of the street.

People bumped into him. He collided with others, who rebuked him in anger and astonishment. But he went on heedless of anything, sunk in confusion and doubt.

Simon Peter's eyes had seemed so honest. He had seen no guile in those open eyes—only the ravages of grief.

Driven by a compulsion of which he was barely conscious, he went back to the garden where the sepulcher lay. But he could not enter the garden. The people gathered there filled it, pressing and treading one another to get closer to the sepulcher.

Simon made no attempt to see it. He turned and made for home, threading his way through the pilgrims returning to the countryside.

When he appeared in the doorway, Deborah came running toward him. "Have you heard . . . have you heard that He is risen, my husband? He is risen!" She began to cry and laugh together.

"I have heard that His disciples stole the body and hid it away," he answered, pressing past her into the house.

"Simon Niger," Deborah said sharply, "how many miracles must you witness before you will believe?"

He made no reply. "Where are the rest?" he asked.

"They have gone to Bethany. They expect that He will visit there."

"I was there. He did not appear."

"Were you at Bethany?"

"I was there this morning. If He has risen, where is He?"

"Some say He has gone to Galilee. But I am certain He's still in Jerusalem. I am certain He and His eleven disciples will go to Bethany to rest and talk together."

He sat down on a stool, his head bowed.

Deborah's voice came to him gently. He felt her fingers touch lightly on the chafe marks of the cross. "You saw His great miracle in the temple, husband—why cannot you believe in Him?"

He stood up quickly, anger once more flaming in his eyes. "Believe? What must I believe? They say His disciples have stolen the body away. If it be not so, if He *has* risen, where is He? Why does He not appear in Jerusalem? Then everybody would believe—everybody. But He has vanished, and His disciples are gone. What must a man believe?"

Deborah looked at him in grief and had no answer.

28

Rufus and Ezekiel returned long after nightfall. Simon had stayed at home that whole afternoon, although he had stepped outside every once in a while, merely to stand looking about him. He was waiting for Rufus and the others, hoping to see Joseph of Arimathea—anybody. But nobody had come.

When Rufus and Ezekiel at last appeared in the doorway, Simon rose to his feet. "Did you see anything . . . hear anything?" he asked in a strangely loud voice. Deborah also stood up.

Rufus, followed by Ezekiel, entered wearily, dragging his feet. They glanced at each other, hesitant.

"Did you hear anything?" Simon asked again even more loudly.

Ezekiel replied. "He did not come to Bethany. We waited the whole day."

"I want to know if the body has been found," Simon insisted.

"Nobody knows where Jesus is, Father," Rufus replied. He looked pale and distraught.

"Did you . . . were you at the cave in Lazarus's back garden?"

Ezekiel nodded.

"There was nothing there?"

"Nothing," Ezekiel confirmed.

"And the disciples?"

"They have vanished," Rufus said. "Nobody knows where they can be. Mary went to Jerusalem to look for the women of Galilee. We did not see her again either."

Simon looked down at the ground. "I am convinced that they used a pack animal to take the body to Galilee," he said with a sigh. "I am sorry I did not keep watch at the grave last night; if I had, Jerusalem would not have been confronted today with yet another riddle."

"If only we knew where He was," Rufus said wearily.

"They removed the body," Simon said positively. "I heard that in Jerusalem. Some scribes said so."

Rufus looked up at his father. "How could they, Father? How could they have rolled the stone away and removed the body without the guards awakening?"

Simon rubbed his brow, weighing the matter in his mind. In his bewilderment that aspect had not occurred to him. He sat down on a stool, looking at his hands.

"Is it certain that the women from Galilee saw Him?" Deborah asked.

"They could not have seen Him—I saw them fleeing from the grave," Simon said with loud decision. "There was no one there. I tell you, no one."

Their complete silence made him look up. He saw that all were staring at him, Deborah with her hands to her checks. "Then you were at the sepulcher, my husband?"

"I was there, early this morning. I think I must have been the very first."

"Then you expected Him to rise?"

"I went there from curiosity," Simon said casually, "idle curiosity, that is all."

Ezekiel interrupted him loudly, stepping forward as if in accusation, his eyes bright and alert. "But the Galilean women came back to the grave," he said. "It was when they *returned* that Mary of Magdala saw Him, and not the first time, according to what we heard."

"That is right," said Rufus softly. "It was the second time."

Simon directed upon them a look in which astonishment and excitement combined. "When they came back . . . they saw Him then?"

"Mary of Magdala went to call Peter and John when they found the sepulcher empty," Rufus explained. "They came and saw that the body was no longer there. They went back to their homes, but Mary stayed. It was then that she saw Him. That is what we heard."

Simon stood up. "By then I was no longer at the sepulcher." His eyes seemed to be attempting to bore through them. He turned to Deborah. "I had gone by then," he said. "I went to Bethany."

"Then you could not have seen everything that happened, my husband." Her words caused his eyes to fall. It was as if he felt a sudden spasm of pain.

"Perhaps not all," he said. Out of the corner of his eye he saw Deborah stir, but he dared not look at her. "But if it is true, where is He now?" asked Simon huskily. He licked his dry lips. "Where is He hiding?"

His question hung in silence.

When he looked questioningly at Rufus and Ezekiel, he saw that they were looking away from him, their eyes withdrawn.

"Someone is coming," said Deborah suddenly.

Simon heard it too, the footfall of one who ran swiftly through the night. He had scarcely distinguished it when Mary of Bethany stood in the doorway.

Rufus called her name sharply when he saw her frightened eyes.

She looked at each in turn, but said no word. She gripped the doorpost, and her head fell forward. Her breast rose and fell with her panting.

"Mary . . . what is the matter. . . . What is it?" asked Rufus anxiously.

She stumbled through the doorway, staggered sideways and leaned her back against the wall, her hands clasped behind her, her head thrown back, her eyes shut tightly. Her lips trembled uncontrollably. She tried to speak, but it seemed that some shock had locked up speech with her.

Simon took a step toward her, and Deborah came hurrying around the table. Mary rocked her head. They saw the tears springing from her eyes, her cheeks growing paler. Then her words came slowly as if she tore each free from the utter depths of her being.

"The . . . disciples . . . saw him . . . tonight."

Her face shone palely, and tears glittered on her cheeks. With one vehement movement Simon seized her shoulders, lifted her from the ground and held her there. The young woman looked at the Cyrenian with dilated eyes.

"Where?" he shouted. "Where . . . where . . . where?"

Mary's head hung down again, her dark hair brushing his eyes. "By the . . . house of . . . young Mark's father . . . where . . . they supped together . . . last. . . . The women of Galilee told me."

"Is it true what you tell us, Mary of Bethany?" Simon asked softly. He set her down on the floor, and with his fingers he gently smoothed the hair clear of her glowing eyes.

"It is the truth."

Simon pressed Mary into Rufus'sarms, leaped over the threshold, and ran into the night.

Simon hammered with such force on the outer gate that the slave sitting in front of the brazier in the courtyard took up his sword before he came over to peer through the gate.

"I wish to speak with the disciple Simon Peter," demanded Simon, his words tumbling over one another.

"He isn't here."

"You lie. I know he's here. And the others too. All the disciples are here."

"Who are you?"

"I am a friend of Simon Peter. Open the door!"

"I must not open it—I'm not allowed to."

The Cyrenian's hand shot so swiftly through the gate that he had seized the man by the collar of his garment before the poor fellow realized what was happening. Simon jerked the slave's head against the door, twisting his garment tighter about his throat. The slave choked; Simon tightened his grip slowly.

"Open up, unless you want to die, son of Cain!" Simon threatened.

As he heard the sliding of the bolt he thrust the gate open. He released the slave, slipped inside, shut the gate behind him, and bolted it. "Call your master!" he commanded. The terrified slave hurried away, tenderly nursing his throat.

It was only a few moments before an aged Jew stood before Simon. "Who is the man who breaks through my gate in the night hours?"

"I intend no harm. I only beg to speak with the disciple Simon Peter."

"Who are you, stranger?"

"The man who carried the cross. I am Simon."

The old man looked at him for a long time. Then he turned and went into the house.

Simon stood listening in the silence. Inwardly he trembled. He clenched his jaws to stop his teeth chattering, and twisted his hands together to calm their trembling. He turned slowly and looked into the courtyard, searching for he knew not what. But the courtyard was empty. There was only the solitary slave squatting by the brazier.

"Ah, the Cyrenian. . . . Peace be with you."

Startled, Simon turned quickly. Before him stood Peter, big and calm, his eyes tired but alight with joy and happiness. The light of the lamp at the door drew reflections from his reddish hair and beard.

He clasped Simon's shoulder, and while he looked into the Cyrenian's eyes, there was a radiance in his own.

"Man of Cyrene," Peter whispered, "this evening He revealed Himself to us in His divinity." Without saying more, Peter took Simon's arm and led him toward a bench under a spreading vine in the corner of the courtyard. Silently they sat down.

"Mary of Bethany said you had seen Him," Simon said curtly. "I heard the scribes say that the body had been removed. Where is the Nazarene?"

Peter looked at the man next to him, and his face loomed larger in the scanty light. "Cyrenian, He has risen from the dead. This evening I touched Him with my hands. He is the Messiah. I know it now." He got up, supporting himself by the branch of the vine, but even so he rocked unsteadily on his feet. "He . . . He is the Son of God." Peter shook his heavy head. "He told us that, and we would not believe. We did not understand. We thought He should dwell in a palace, but now we know that His home is in the heavens."

He looked down at his visitor, but Simon sat there silently, his head bowed, his elbows on his knees. He clasped and unclasped his hands aimlessly.

"You don't believe me, man of Cyrene? You are as I was when I denied Him?"

Simon swallowed and moved his hands. His skin felt unduly

264

sensitive where the cross had chafed him. His ears and neck burned as though with fever.

"If only I could have seen Him once," he said, and passionately beat his fists together.

"It is better not to have seen and to believe, than to have seen and not believe. Truly, it is better."

Peter sat down again, and the bench groaned under their weight. "Perhaps you will see Him, man of Cyrene. I think He will appear to us again. He has bid us meet Him on a mountain in Galilee. We are going there tomorrow."

"Did . . . did He talk to you?"

"He came among us. He came to us this evening, and He spoke to us just as we two sit here and speak."

Simon, looking in astonishment at Peter, saw the serenity that beamed from his eyes.

Peter spoke calmly, but with emphasis. "We remained here today because the people became disturbed when they heard the sepulcher was empty. This evening we partook of the evening meal in the upper room where last we ate together before He left us. His place was still there, empty. No one aspired to it. Judas Iscariot's place was empty. No one desired it.

"We ate very little, for we talked much—about His death and suffering. We were sore of heart, because we thought we had lost Him forever, that death had taken Him irrevocably, that we would never hear His voice again or see His eyes.

"We spoke about Mary of Magdala who said that she had seen Him. We could not believe her. 'She saw a vision,' said James.

"'Or dreamed a dream,' John added."

"You did not believe it?" Simon asked.

Peter laughed shortly, as if baffled at his unbelief. "No, we did not believe it . . . yet. Even by this evening, we still did not believe." He looked almost pleadingly at the Cyrenian. "Is it easy to believe that one has risen from the dead? Is it easy to believe?"

"It is not easy," Simon answered.

"Truly, Cyrenian, it is greater than many things, greater than all that human reason can encompass. The vast sea and sky and all things that have their being are as nothing beside this wonder.

265

"But I must tell you," the disciple continued with the enthusiasm of a child. "While we were talking of Mary of Magdala's vision, Cleopas and his friend came in. We saw that they were tired and breathless, too. Their eyes were large, their faces pale as death. Then Cleopas, that good man, told us how, late this afternoon, they were walking to Emmaus. As they went, they spoke of all that had happened in Jerusalem, His death and everything, and a man walked beside them in the dusk. They looked at him without surprise, for they were deep in sorrow over our master's death.

"Then the stranger said to them, 'What is it you talk of, and why do you grieve so?'

"Cleopas looked at the stranger and said to him, 'Are you then a stranger in Jerusalem? Do you not know what happened there during these last few days?'"

Peter bent forward eagerly. "This man accompanied Cleopas and his friend and even sat down to eat with them in Emmaus. He broke bread and of offered thanks. And then . . . they saw that it was Jesus."

He looked intently at Simon and strove to fathom the expression in his eyes, but the man from Africa sat still as a statue, completely without motion. His hands were limp above his knees, and he moved not a finger.

He turned his head at last and looked at Peter. The disciple knew the question he did not ask.

"He did not come here with Cleopas and his friend. Before their eyes, He vanished there."

Simon looked at the dark earth. "Then did you believe?"

Peter shook his head. "Even then we did not believe. James said, 'Cleopas, you saw a ghost.'

"And Nathaniel said, 'It is because you long for Him that you fondly think you saw Him.'

"'But how does a ghost break bread?' Cleopas asked.

"'And did you see His hands?' asked Philip. But Cleopas said that in his fear he did not notice them.

"Then my brother, Andrew, said, 'If it was a ghost that appeared to Cleopas and his friend, why is His spirit not at rest? Why does He wander, when He should be at rest?'"

266

Peter stopped speaking, stroked his beard, and seemed to be reliving something too momentous to be expressed.

Then at last he spoke. "We all looked at one another, not knowing what to believe. Then Matthew said, 'If it be His ghost, where is His body? Did you not see that His body is no longer in the sepulcher?'

"Not one of us could give an answer, Cyrenian. No, not one."

The disciple paused. When Simon looked up questioningly, he saw that Peter's eyes were wet with tears. His broken voice struggled with his words. "But He Himself gave us our answer. . . . We were still sitting and wondering when we heard His voice, 'Peace be with you.'"

Peter shook his head rapidly, gasped for breath, and rose to his feet. He walked a pace uncertainly, then returned and sat down by Simon.

"His voice . . . His voice . . . it was miraculous to hear His voice again. When I came to myself, His hands were on my shoulders. I, who had denied Him. We scrambled up so hastily that the benches overturned. Poor John stumbled over one and fell; James ran to the door.

"'It is a ghost!' John screamed. We were so terrified that we shrank from Him against the wall.

"'Spirit, be gone from us!' Philip cried out.

"He stood by Himself at the table. He stretched out His hands. He smiled at us, man of Cyrene, but I think there was sadness in His eyes. He said to us, 'Why are you troubled, and why is there doubt in your hearts? Look at these hands. Touch them. Behold Me, for a spirit has neither bones nor flesh.'

"We all looked at one another, and sweat covered our brows. John sobbed with fear. Only His eyes were calm. His beard shone in the light of the lamp. He did not scold us for being afraid of Him even after all our days of knowing Him."

Peter gripped Simon's garment, and his face shone with ecstasy. "James and I approached Him, slowly, because we were still afraid. Who would not be frightened, man of Cyrene, if he saw one who had risen from the dead?

"Each of us took His hands, and looked at them. We could hear the others gasp behind us. His hands—there were deep pur-

ple punctures where the spikes had entered . . . there and there."
Peter showed with his own hands. "I turned His hands to see."

Simon's eyes were thoughtful, and he sat bent forward. Without knowing it he had stretched out his hand, gripping Peter's garment. Slowly he twisted it to and fro.

"He raised His garment and showed His feet. We bent and touched them with our hands.

"Then James put his arms about His knees, lay weeping against Him, and cried, 'Rabbi, you are indeed the Messiah. . . . You are truly God's anointed.'

"I looked up into His face, but then I looked away because shame overwhelmed me. But, Cyrenian, He gently touched my cheek, and I knew I was forgiven.

"James and I knew it was He, but the others still held back. Then He said, 'Have you food, that I may eat?'

"Andrew went to Him and gave Him a portion of grilled fish that was left over and a piece of honeycomb. Cyrenian, He took the food and ate. He held it in his fingers, and before our eyes He ate.

"When they saw this, they all believed. They ran to Him and touched Him. He stretched out His hands to bless us, each in turn.

"Then He said to us, 'This is what I told you about when I was still among you, that all that was written regarding Me in the law of Moses, in the prophets, and in the Psalms might have fulfillment. So it was written, and so the Messiah must suffer, and on the third day rise up from the dead.'

"At that moment He opened our eyes and we believed in Him. After He had spoken those words, we feared no longer, but believed.

"He looked at us and told us we must go forth and in His name preach redemption and forgiveness of sins to all nations, from Jerusalem to the end of the earth."

Peter stroked his beard. He looked tired, as if the words he had spoken had taken part of his strength from him. "That is how it happened, man of Cyrene."

Simon rose with the slow, stiff movements of an old man. He moved to an almond tree and leaned there, his face against the cooling bark. The night wind rose and murmured in the dark leaves, carrying upon it the scent of far-off blossom. The night was growing cooler.

"Can you believe this great wonder, Cyrenian?" Peter's voice seemed part of the whisper of the leaves. "Now do you believe that He has conquered death?"

Simon felt the tree tremble with wind-borne life, closed his burning eyes, and tasted the salt of tears on his parted lips.

"I believe," he said slowly. "I believe you, man of Galilee. There is no deceit in your eyes, and your lips speak truth. I believe that He has risen. . . . I believe He tore the veil. I know now that He showed me His great miracle in the temple. I know now that He called to me to bear His cross. How could I do other than believe in Him?"

"This night He has redeemed you, man of Africa. He has made you free."

"For a long time I fought Him. I was a fool."

"Fools there have always been, but after this night fools shall enter His kingdom because they have belief."

"If I had known, I would have carried His cross to Galilee and back again. I know now that He is the Messiah. For a man who is greater than death is greater than Caesar, greater than all. . . .And I refused to acknowledge Him. Now it is too late."

"You can labor in His vineyard. Then your sorrow will heal like a clean wound in a branch." Peter approached him, laid his hands gently on his sore shoulders. "The cross is of the past," he whispered. "His message is more than the cross. You bear His message. You can help light His torches throughout Israel. We may grieve no longer, man of Cyrene. We must rejoice because He is among us. We must carry His word—from Jerusalem to beyond. We must fear no longer, for He has conquered death. He has given us eternal life, just as He Himself is eternal. And the life He has given us we must bring to all those who still fear and do not understand."

"But He forgave *you*—*I* haven't even seen Him."

Peter looked at the man, who leaned there as if his bones were water. "Why would He have shown you His great miracle in the temple if He has not forgiven you? Why would He have led you to Golgotha if He did not want to cleanse your heart? He would not have brought you to belief this night if He had not forgiven you. If His wrath were on your head, He would not have caused you to believe in Him."

Simon of Cyrene looked at the disciple with a new understanding. As if in a trance he sank down against the trunk and squatted there, looking up through the darkness at the wheeling stars.

"How can my scorn and derision be atoned for? How can I remove the shame of Golgotha?"

"You can serve Him, for you believe in Him. Faith is more than offerings."

"Serve Him? I do not know Him, nor His teaching."

"The day I left my nets beside the Lake of Galilee, I also did not know Him."

"You walked with Him for many days, sat at His feet."

"He will reveal Himself to you—for He has called you."

"I have not the gift of speaking."

"He will put the words into your mouth. He will fill your soul, Cyrenian."

"I am not worthy . . . ."

"You are more worthy than I, who saw the beacon on the mountain and turned back into the dark valley."

Simon rose and stood for a moment, holding Peter by a fold of his garment. "I shall serve Him," he said humbly. "Even if in a little way, I shall serve Him. Even though my light be faint, I shall carry it; for He is the Messiah, the Anointed One."

"Cyrenian, you shall be a light in His temple, a leader of His flock."

They fell silent and listened to the soft whisper of the wind in the night until Simon said, "It is late. I must go to those who await me."

They gripped each other by the shoulders, looked long and wordlessly at each other, for words could no longer express the wonder in their hearts.

"Go in peace, man of Cyrene, chosen of Jesus," said Peter at last. "You are the fortunate one who carried His cross and who saw His great wonder in the temple."

"No, I am nothing. . . . I am grateful, Galilean . . , and I am ashamed." He turned his head and looked away into the night so that Peter could not see his eyes. "I am grateful," the big man got out, and Peter saw his shoulders heave. "Through you He has shown me the wonder of His love—I who hated and derided Him, saw His miracle and was the last to serve Him. I am only grateful that He did not pass me by."

"His ways are wonderful, Cyrenian, as the passage of the sun and the eternal wonder of the sea. Go in peace, for your heart is free."

They embraced, and Simon walked away through the empty courtyard. The place seemed strange, as if he now saw it for the first time. At the gate he turned. Peter stood under the lamplight beside the door. He waved his hand.

Simon appeared silently on the threshold, and those sitting within looked up at him. He looked slowly from one to the other —at Deborah, Rufus, Mary, and old Ezekiel, whose cheeks seemed so sunken.

And as he gazed at them, they saw that he had changed, like a tree freed from winter in a night. Deborah rose, but the rest stayed seated. Apprehensive of his mood, none broke the silence.

"Children of Israel," Simon spoke to them, "your faith was greater than mine. He is risen. He is the Messiah. Truly, He is the Son of Almighty God."

He entered the room, went to Deborah, took her quiet face in his hands. "Blessed wife," he murmured, "you will be in His paradise one day, because you saw the day while night was still with us. You heard His voice when He was still far distant."

He gathered her to himself, holding her face against his neck, while he looked to the rest. He turned his head slowly, and his words came hesitantly. "There is nothing I can say," said Simon of Cyrene. "You all heard His voice while I was deaf."

His heart filled as he saw their thankful eyes. He closed his own and turned his face away.

Part Three

29

The dank stone surface shone like the gold of Solomon in the wavering light of the torch. The light hovered lazily over the dark brown stone that had rested deep beneath the earth for aeons.

Simon shifted his aching body on the straw and looked at the light that flickered into life again each time it seemed about to die. The overseer had struck him that day for talking to another man. Was it that afternoon? Or during the night hours? He did not know, for there it was always night.

He looked at the row of sleeping men in the stone passage where the water, dripping ceaselessly from the rock, collected in small furrows along the sides and flowed away. He edged his hand carefully beneath the straw and took out the half-completed stone figure. It still needed many hours of patent scraping and rubbing smooth before it would be completed. He searched under the straw again, took out his planing-stone, and with deep love and concentration resumed work on the figure: the shoulders had already begun to take shape—and the head that hung askew.

Suddenly he stopped work. He sensed that he was not the only man awake. He lay quietly and stared at the light on the glinting stone above him, listening to the thud of picks in the bosom of the earth.

He thought of Deborah, of sunlight and the sea; his hands clutched at the straw. He closed his eyes, and a vision came of furrows in fresh-plowed land. He saw a temple glitter, grapes swelling under leaves, flamingos tinging a blue sky with palest rose, the reddish beard of Simon Peter, the glint of sunlight on Paul's bald head, the enthusiastic eyes.

Groaning, he turned over on his other side.

For a long while he lay silent before he saw that two eyes were fixed on him. Two quiet eyes—like all the others there, sunk deep in apathy, without hope or expectation, without character.

That face was pale and narrow, like all the faces there. Both hair and beard were unkempt, and the hands lay slackly on the straw like the broken wings of a pheasant.

The man lay on his side. He was like a lion grown feeble in the arena.

"I know you." The thin lips moved almost unwillingly. The voice was hoarse. The man coughed from deep down in his lungs.

Stealthily, Simon pushed the stone figure under the straw, but he could see by the stranger's eyes that his secret was out.

"How far are you with that figure? You've been working on it ever since you came here."

"I do not know you," the Cyrenian said briefly.

"Yes, you know me."

"No, I do not."

"Have you forgotten the tavern in the Street of the Butchers in Jerusalem—the day they crucified that Galilean?"

Simon raised himself on his elbow, and his lips trembled so much that he could not utter a word.

"Lie down or you will be lashed. You must lie and rest; lie down for Rome—she needs you."

"Barabbas. . . . You are Barabbas, the criminal." Simon sank back on the straw. His body trembled with the recognition.

"Barabbas . . . the man who should have died," the man said.

"You . . . you have changed so much. . . . I did not recognize you."

"The years will change you too. Winter gnaws the strongest cedar."

"Why are you here?" Simon asked.

"They captured me in Tyre. I was busy relieving a Greek importer of a small portion of his wealth. And why are you here? I have not asked you this before because the strength of sunlight and of freedom was still inside you. A man doesn't talk then, for he is certain that he'll get back into the sunlight. But now I ask you, for I know you have accepted the darkness here to be your heritage. I know you know that there is no return."

Simon did not answer. He looked down the long gloomy tunnel dug out by those who had gone before him. "What are we mining here?" he asked, and the fragrance of fresh straw brought Cyrene to his mind.

"We mine silver for the Emperor. The silver horseshoes of Caesar's stallions come from here. By my sweat I have brought a silver bracelet to many a Roman beauty. You may yet dig out enough to fashion a vase for a Roman villa . . . or a lamp, or a brazier. . . . Who can tell? You see, friend, here we do not die in vain. We supply the world with beauty."

"How long will we be kept here?"

Barabbas coughed briefly, pressing his wasted hands to his chest in an attempt to check the irritation there. "It depends on how strong you are. If you are strong, a long time; if you are weak, not so long. They keep you here till you die—or till you can work no more. Now and again they take us to the surface to lie in the sun and stare at the horizon, which we shall never cross again."

"Where are we? They brought me here by night."

"I think we're near the border of Mesopotamia. Do you know how high Mount Sinai is?"

"I have seen Sinai."

"That's how deep we are beneath the earth."

Simon put a yellow straw between his lips, chewed it, and tasted its sweetness, wondering how high the corn was standing in Cyrene.

Barabbas smiled slightly. "You're not as strong as I thought," he said. "Not as strong as I thought you were that evening in the tavern. They broke you in more quickly than I expected. There is no spirit left in you. And see how strong you are."

Slowly Simon Niger shook his heavy head. "I do not resist. I accept—"

"I accept as well, but I can hate. Your eyes are gentle and have no hatred."

"There is no hatred in me."

"Not even for Rome?"

"Not even for Rome. I hate no one . . . not even Pilate."

Simon's words shocked Barabbas to silence. At length he said, "You are a Jew, and you don't hate Rome?"

"Hate and love cannot live together. The one destroys the other. I have cherished love. It is the greatest strength that remains to me. I received it from the man they crucified. I gave Him hatred, and He returned me love. Because of this, I can never hate again. Only love and understand and forgive."

"Understand and forgive? How do you understand and forgive this?" Barabbas pointed to the grim confining walls within which men twitched and dreamed of sunlight, clouds, and trees.

"When a man understands it is *His* will, then he is free, even though he has to die."

Barabbas stared into the straw. "You believe so deeply in this Nazarene that they crucified? You didn't believe in Him the day you beat me."

"Yes, I do believe. He has made me free."

The criminal lay on his back, watching a drop of water on the rock ceiling grow like a bubble of gold, tremble, fall, and vanish in the straw.

"He must have freed you very thoroughly to have freed you this way from Rome," he said at last. They lay in silence until the prisoner asked, "Another thing—you've not told me how you came to be here."

"When Jesus had ascended to His Father, I went with the others to teach His good news in Jerusalem. But Saul the Pharisee instigated a wholesale persecution. He had the believers tracked down and flung into prison.

"Simon Peter, who had become our leader, sent us out with instructions to go to other regions where Saul could not reach us and preach the good news there. This we did, and another Cyrenian, Luke, and I went to Antioch in Syria, and taught and preached there for many years. Our work was greatly blessed. Later I sent for my good wife and my workman, Ezekiel, who came there as well."

Simon looked at Barabbas with shining eyes. "While we were teaching there, I witnessed *His* wonderful power again. That same Saul who had persecuted us in Jerusalem was converted on the road to Damascus."

"Does he also believe now—this Saul?"

"He is no longer Saul. He is called Paul. He has become the greatest of them all, greater even that Simon Peter. He travels through the empire and spreads the word of Jesus. We sent him from Antioch on his first journey. We laid our hands upon him, ordained him, and sent him forth. That is how His wonders work. Now the infamous persecutor has become a famous preacher."

"And your family? Have you no loved ones? Where are they?"

Simon played with the straw. "I have two sons. One works for the Romans—the other, Rufus, was sent to Rome by Peter to carry the good news there."

"To Rome?"

"There are many believers in Rome. My son went there, even though he was still a youth." He looked at Barabbas and saw the question in his eyes.

"My wife . . . I do not know what has happened to my Deborah. There was a Jew, Joseph bar Jonas, in Antioch who did not love our teaching. He incited the Jews and the heathen there against us. One day while I was preaching they took me prisoner. They delivered me to a Greek. He was a recruiting agent for these mines. That is how I came here. And that is why I do not know what has happened to my wife."

"This new king of yours has delivered you to your enemies, and yet you still believe in Him? Here the Romans are slowly extinguishing your life as if it were a candle, and you have no hatred for them?"

"Barabbas," said Simon, "that day when the darkness came, the day they put Him to death, you too saw His miracle. I have told you how the venomous Pharisee Saul was converted to His service. Why then do you not believe? You are no longer Barabbas. You are old and weak and ailing. Your days are few. Why do you still show hatred?"

Barabbas closed his eyes against the light that was a substitute for, a mere memory of, the great light of the sun. "Why do you waste your breath on me, my friend? I am a rogue and a villain."

"I talk to all men, because I work for *Him*. You were a villain, but Saul was a persecutor. He flung the innocent into dungeons because they had belief. If Saul could behold His light, you can. I hated the Nazarene, and even I was shown His glory. Nothing can set you free again—except faith in Him."

Barabbas laughed, and began to cough. "With what can my soul hold communion except with that which is foul? A life is not purified in one night, my friend."

"He changed my life in a moment, a fraction of time."

"And did He cleanse you?"

"He cleansed me. I became another man. In the beginning I desired to destroy. But that is changed. I have found peace. Do you not understand that it was not your good fortune or your goodness that preserved your life that day?"

"I've always tried to understand it—from that day on. Even as I lie here, I still can't understand why I didn't die."

"It is because *He* willed it so. It is because He had to die so that you could live. The prophets told us that. He had to die. That is the reason they freed you."

Barabbas raised himself with difficulty, leaned on his bony elbow, and looked hard at Simon. "Is that the truth? Do you really think that?"

"It is the truth. He died for you as well."

"But He didn't know me. He didn't even know my name."

"He died for you . . . He died for me. He died for the whole world."

"I wish I could understand it. I can believe the things I see: the sun, the sea, the stars, good wine when I taste it . . . a lovely woman when her hair is lying on my face. What you're saying now is too deep for me. It is beyond me. I am a simple man, my friend." Barabbas sank back on the straw, his heart racing from excitement. "How can it help? This great man of yours is dead."

"He is not dead," said Simon loudly.

Barabbas warned the Cyrenian with his eyes to moderate his voice. "Not dead? Did they take Him from the cross before He died?"

"He rose again. After three days He rose again."

Barabbas scorned the words with a little gesture. "You're talking like a child," he said staring at the roof again. "My friend, you're talking like a child."

Simon's voice was soft but urgent as he spoke again.

"Barabbas, look at me," he said. "Look into my eyes."

Barabbas looked uncertainly, almost timidly, into Simon's eyes.

"Do you see deceit there, Barabbas?"

"I see no deceit in your eyes."

"Then you must believe what I shall tell you now, because it is the truth. He rose again, as truly as I am looking at you now. I stood in the empty sepulcher. I touched the winding cloths."

"Perhaps . . . perhaps they removed the body."

"I was there when they laid the body in the sepulcher, which Joseph of Arimathea himself prepared. He rose and appeared to His disciples—He spoke with them."

Barabbas thrust his face forward and stared. "How can a man raise himself from the dead? You are talking nonsense."

Without another word Barabbas turned over onto his other side, with his back to Simon. Simon looked at the thin body that had once been so powerful, at the unkempt hair, once so black but now gray and lifeless. He waited for a long time before he spoke.

"Barabbas," said Simon Niger, "I know how difficult it is for you to believe what I say, because you never knew Him. An animal accustomed to the night has fear of the day. But you must do one thing—you must listen to me. Will you listen, Barabbas?"

Barabbas moved restlessly in the straw. He emitted dry, hacking coughs. "I am weary, friend, I want to rest now. Perhaps I've still a year to hear you—possibly even longer. Or it may be only a few days."

The torch against the wall flickered and died. Simon rose to his knees. He prayed long and earnestly, and then lay down again, his eyes wide open in the darkness. He saw the image of Deborah's face before him.

Just as he was about to fall asleep, Barabbas's voice came to him again. "And after He had risen, as you say, what did He do then?"

"He ascended to heaven . . . to His Father . . . to intercede for you and for me."

Barabbas snorted derisively in the darkness.

But for a long time Simon heard him stirring in the straw, tossing from side to side, continually coughing.

Barabbas listened to Simon for many months. When the work of the day was over and they returned to their wretched beds of straw, Barabbas listened while Simon strove to reach the inner heart of this strange criminal.

Not only Barabbas listened, but many of the rest as well. Simon taught them to give thought to the man who died in Jerusalem, to hear Him, taught them even to pray on the straw in the tunnel that dripped with water deep down beneath the earth. One day when they sang together and the Roman overseer came filled with anger to find out what they were doing, Barabbas told him, "We are singing out of joy of labor. Our songs are in praise of Rome." The overseer went away relieved, and naively told the superintendent that the slaves were being converted to love of Rome.

When he talked to them of Jesus, Simon always watched their eyes, seeking a familiar light there. He could see who believed him and who did not. He knew that Barabbas was not one of those who believed.

He was a strange man, this Barabbas. Through all those months he knelt with them in prayer, joined in their singing. He had picked up an old file somewhere in the tunnels and had brought it to Simon. With it Simon had completed the stone figure—the image of the crucified Savior. It was Barabbas who had found some rough slate and polished the figure until it gleamed smoothly. Again it was Barabbas who labored with infinite patience and determination to cut a deep recess into the rock in which to place the statue.

Finally, it was Barabbas who fearlessly outlined the figure of a fish against the damp rock wall, because they had heard from recent captives that the sign of the fish was now the emblem of the Christians. Barabbas did this not as a sign of faith, but as a token of rebellion against the Romans.

This fearlessness and daring on Barabbas's part led to their all being mercilessly flogged. Even the scrawny back of Barabbas came under the heavy Roman lash, so that for days he could scarcely move, and he spent long nights groaning softly.

But again he did it. And again they were flogged, because nobody would admit responsibility. "We suffer together" became their motto.

After one such mass flogging Simon lay staring at Barabbas in the dark. He did not believe, in spite of everything, that Barabbas had been converted.

He looked at the back on which the bloody welts stood out,

at the emaciated shoulders that stirred with the man's slow breathing. Barabbas lay on his stomach with his face turned toward Simon.

Simon could see death beginning to come to the half-closed eyes.

"Why do you harden your heart, Barabbas?" he asked through the waiting silence.

Barabbas's hands moved in the straw. With his outstretched arms he looked like a man crucified against the rock. He wheezed and coughed. "I'm finished. I want to rest." Pain shook his broken shoulders. Weakness silenced him again.

"I will give you rest . . . through all eternity . . . if only you will believe."

"Your heaven is too remote for me, Simon of Cyrene."

"The heaven of Jesus the Messiah is close at hand—you have only to enter it. His light is here. The eternal peace awaits your heart."

"I am blind. I cannot see this light. I've walked so far toward hell that I haven't the strength to turn."

"The man who has traveled farthest through the desert is nearest to the green spring."

"I am in the middle of the desert and time is running out and there is no turning back. . . . Has it been raining on the surface? Listen to the water dripping."

Simon Niger sank back helplessly on the straw and listened to the steady drip of water. With the faint impact of each drop his discomfort grew, for he knew that with each tiny interval the soul of Barabbas slipped further from his hands.

"Greet the sun for me if you ever get out of this," Barabbas said. "Wave to the sea and embrace the wind. In the valley before the gate of Jericho there is a well of sweet water. Go drink of it and think of Barabbas. . . . I long for the icy winds of Carmel and the sultry heat of Sinai. . . . Life is so short. . . . Only yesterday I was a child."

"Don't talk like this. Rest a little."

"Rest? What will it do for me to rest? Can you hear the water dripping? Can you hear eternity? It's coming closer. I can't wait to meet your new prophet in the sun." He gave a reckless laugh. It brought a rending cough to his ruined body.

283

He saw the pain in Simon's eyes, the disappointment, the disillusionment.

He fell silent. He thought about the darkness that had veiled Jerusalem that day. He shuddered. He thought of the night when Simon held cool water to his lips after he had been flogged for taking another slave's food.

The darkness of Jerusalem . . . the shuddering of the earth . . . He shut his eyes, and his soul sought among the stars . . . and fell back helpless.

Barabbas looked at Simon's black beard and tightly shut eyes, more sunken than on the day he came. A man in whom there was nothing of deceit. Simon had seen the empty sepulchur —touched the winding cloths.

Barabbas watched the steady rise and fall of Simon's chest. He had seen the rending of the veil.

A man without deceit.

He had seen Lazarus, the man who had died and was no longer dead.

Why should Simon lie about these things? A man lied if there was a future—and there was no future here. Here even the moments of the future belonged already to the past.

The pain came, and it was like a broad sword twisted in his chest. He coughed again and blood spattered his lips.

Barabbas's cry woke Simon from his sleep. He looked quickly and saw Barabbas lying there, his face shuddering against the straw, his hands quivering. His cry hung for a moment in the long tunnel, faded, then echoed back to die at last in the drip of the water.

"Say something that I may believe!" The cry woke them all. "Say something that I may believe!"

It seemed to Barabbas that Simon's voice came to him from the far sunlight beyond the rocks. "What is there left for me to say? If I had the tongue of an angel, I could utter more. But I am human. I can bear testimony only to the things I saw and the things I know. I have long sown the seed in your heart, Barabbas—but only its soil can put forth the shoots."

"I'm trying . . . I'm trying," whispered Barabbas.

"If you are willing, that is enough. If your heart is open, it is sufficient. Keep your heart open."

Barabbas buried his face in the straw. He remained silent, and Simon spoke no further word.

Hours later Simon awoke as the overseer's trumpet sounded far down in the tunnel. He jumped up, not because of the trumpet call but because of Barabbas.

The criminal lay so strangely. His breast was raised against the sloping rock, his head lolled against the stone. His left hand was limp in the straw. The fingers had released the Roman file.

The right hand still held the crucifixion image in its clasp.

The others came up and looked in wonder at the dead man. Simon bent down and pried Barabbas's fingers from the image. Then they turned him over on his back. Simon fell to his knees and gazed at Barabbas's hollow chest.

He looked at the thin red line upon it.

"The sign of the fish," he whispered.

"He cut it into his chest with the handle of the file," someone said, and raised the piece of metal high in the torchlight.

Simon of Cyrene stood up, stumbled to a dark corner of the tunnel, and wept with his face against the rock.

"Lord, I thank You," he whispered, "that You have delivered him!"

30

The afternoon lingered over Jerusalem. It was in the tenth year of the reign of Nero. A little old man sat in the shade and looked out at the distant hills to the north where the Roman road ran to the far-off world of Tyre, Sidon, Damascus, and Antioch.

His eyes were weak, for he had witnessed many things, had many times seen the sun return, seen evening work its magic on the sea.

He looked searchingly again at the white road to Bethany that flanked the Mount of Olives. How many times had he stared along the high road and along the road to Bethany, he wondered. But still he hoped. One day, of this he was certain, one day he would have to look at them no more.

He sat hunched up and quiet for a while, gazing at the ground with his hands upon his knees. Then mechanically, he lifted his eyes again to stare along the high road that led past Golgotha to the highlands of Samaria and beyond.

He saw a man approaching whose shadow stretched far before him, for the sun was becoming low in the west. There was no firmness in his step. He came as if he were searching for his way. His shoulders were bent, his head bowed, his gait shuffling and uncertain.

It was clear that his years had demanded heavy toll. He halted once, raised his head, and looked at the fields stretching far away, the vineyards, orchards, and then the cottage, dwarfed by the poplar tree that stood so high above it.

The man who sat there before the cottage struggled to his feet, his hand trembling against the wall. He rubbed his eyes and stared again. He tried to grasp the full meaning of what he saw, but his understanding served him as slowly as his body these days.

He faltered a few steps forward. The tall stranger came nearer, and they stood before each other, close in the fading sunlight.

They stood there wordlessly and tried to bridge the years that had cruelly parted them, to live again those distant days when their eyes had been bright and clear.

The eyes of the man who had waited seemed to capture the bygone days—joy flickered in them. But the dark sunken eyes of the taller man were quiet and yearning. His beard was snow-white, like the breast of a swan.

"Simon of Cyrene," said the smaller man with a sob. "God has spared you. . . . He has brought you back again."

"Ezekiel . . . Ezekiel. . . . I find you living!" said the wanderer, his voice hoarse and brittle. He gazed for a moment into Ezekiel's eyes, and then with uncontrollable longing at the open door of the cottage, which he had seen so often in the dreams of countless nights.

Ezekiel grasped Simon's wasted hands and kissed them. When he looked up again, tears were shining in his eyes. "You have come back at last!" he said, sobbing and laughing in the fullness of his emotion. "All these years I've watched and waited!" He put out his hand and touched Simon's beard. "You're back in Geth-semane, and your beard is white, Simon of Cyrene."

Simon stumbled past him into the house. Ezekiel followed him inside and saw his old master standing in the middle of the room. He was listening, searching with his eyes. He raised a trembling hand. He looked at all that suggested Deborah. The hearth . . . the washtub . . . the flour bag against the wall . . . the low chest he had made for her linen.

Then he turned to Ezekiel, and his weary eyes fearfully asked their question.

"She isn't here, Simon," the foreman said.

The shock did not cause Simon's eyes to waver. They remained calm and thoughtful.

"She is in Rome. When you disappeared in Antioch, we came back here. Later Rufus sent for her. She had waited for so long . . . all those many years. She left me here to wait for you."

"She is in Rome?"

Simon sat down on a stool and looked down at the floor that

she had swept so often. "Then she's alive?" he asked, clasping his hands together.

"She lives . . . she lives and waits for you, Simon of Cyrene."

It was long before Simon slowly rose to his feet. He shuffled to their room, stood in the doorway, and looked about him. It was empty and half dark. Then he turned around deliberately, looked at Ezekiel, and smiled. "The years have shrunk you, my faithful friend," said Simon Niger. He shook his head slowly, and there were gentle tears in his eyes.

"And the years have made you look like a patriarch of Israel, Simon," said Ezekiel. "Your beard is white. Your face is the face of a prophet."

"I'm glad to see your face again, Ezekiel . . . and to hear your voice."

"I've longed so much for the sound of your voice, Simon . . . and for your strength. Wait, there is something."

He hurried quickly into the bedroom and took something out from beneath the bedding. He came back and placed it in his old master's hand. Full of expectation, he laughed. Simon looked at the small porcelain box in which one generally kept myrrh. But it had no meaning for him.

"Open it," commanded Ezekiel.

Simon raised the lid and saw within the raven lock of hair.

"She left it here for you," said Ezekiel excitedly, and tapped Simon on the shoulder. "She said I should give it to you, a keep-sake to remember her by."

"My Deborah," whispered Simon, stroking the ringlet with his fingers.

"She said that you must kiss it twice when I gave it to you, and at that moment she would know that you're alive."

He took the lock from the box and pressed it tremblingly to his lips.

"I'll make a fire at once. You must be dying of hunger," said Ezekiel, and bustled quickly across to the hearth.

He made the fire and prepared a meal. While the food was cooking, Simon seated himself at the able. Ezekiel brought cups and wine, and sat beside Simon. Both lifted their cups, unsteady with emotion.

"To our reunion!" said Ezekiel, laughing. He peered at Simon over the rim of his cup as they drank. "We drink the wine of Gethsemane."

Simon smacked his lips. His eyes brightened. "You make a wine beyond compare, Ezekiel," he said and smiled warmly.

"Have you heard from her since she left?" he asked suddenly.

"She sent word when the chance offered itself, asking whether you had returned home. She is full of trust and love."

"May the Lord bless her and keep her until I see her again."

"Tell me . . . tell me. . . . You have told me nothing yet," Ezekiel said urgently. "What happened to you?"

Simon looked down at his drinking cup, seeking to still his shaking hands by clasping them about it.

"It's been so long. I just want to listen to you," the old foreman said.

Simon's face became quiet, his eyes shaded by sad memories. "It has been many years—fourteen years in the mine," he said, and rubbed his hands against the cup.

"Years of darkness."

"Dark years indeed, dark years from the day they took me in Antioch. They carried me away to a place near Mesopotamia, to labor in a silver mine. All these years I worked below the earth."

"All this time in a mine?"

Simon looked down at his bony knuckles. "All this time."

"We were certain that they'd sent you away. That is why we never would believe that you were dead."

"You were sure I was living?"

"We were sure. That's why I've waited here. We were certain that our Lord would bring you back."

"I served Him deep down in the earth. And He allowed me to return to freedom. When they found that my working days were past, they let me go. For one whole day I rested in the sun, and saw the sky, the clouds, the trees, the mountains. I lingered there, letting the sun soak into me."

Ezekiel stared at him wonderingly.

"I saw, and thanked *Him*. . . . I did nothing else. I looked and touched leaves and earth with both my hands. At such a moment a man becomes a child. He sees through the eyes of a child. Even in the beauty of a cloud I found a thing forgotten."

"Rome has made you old." Simon nodded slowly and was silent. Ezekiel touched Simon's hand. "And the mine was bad?"

"How can I describe it? There was only suffering, labor, and loneliness. Day after day we dug out silver ore for Rome."

"And when you came out?"

"I was like a child. I could not walk in the sun. The light was too sharp. I had to screw up my eyes. A caravan driver took pity on me. He let me ride a camel. I was with him almost all the way to Jerusalem.

"All the long way from Mesopotamia?"

"All the way . . . to here."

They looked at each other, and it seemed again that they were seeing each other for the first time. "You have come back!" Ezekiel whispered.

"What has happened in the world . . . all these years?" asked Simon.

Ezekiel hesitated for a moment. "I've seen Alexander."

"Alexander? My eldest?"

Ezekiel nodded, searching for anger in Simon's eyes, but there was neither hatred nor resentment there. "It was during the great famine, when the crops failed in this area. Twice I helped drive caravans to Joppa. It was there I saw him."

"Has he become a big man, my Alexander?"

"A big man, black-bearded, just like you. He is your son, Simon, cast in your image."

"I have forgotten what he looks like," said Simon, slowly shaking his head.

"He is an important man in the service of Rome. Commander of a large vessel."

"Commander? No longer a slave driver?"

His old foremen shook his head. "No longer a slave driver. He asked a thousand questions about you, and Deborah, and Rufus. He is a man of worldly knowledge, calm and strong.

"Did you tell him all . . . ?"

"I told him everything that had happened."

"And he? How does he live?"

"He has traveled much; he has sailed many seas. He has gathered wisdom and experience."

Simon looked at his old servant and could not ask his next question.

Ezekiel looked out into the evening that was darkening the trees. "No, I do not think that he believes in our Lord," he said.

Ezekiel rose, lighted a lamp, and returned to the table. He looked silently at Simon, at his silver beard shining in the light, at the wasted hands, the bowed shoulders. "How they made you suffer!" he exclaimed with anger.

"I suffered," said Simon, but his eyes smiled calmly. "I suffered for Him." He looked at the darkness that had crept to the door. "I can work no longer, but I can still speak." He looked down at his hands, so gnarled and hardened. Then he asked suddenly, "What is the news of Rufus? What have you heard of him?"

Ezekiel leaned forward, clasped Simon's hands, and said with shining eyes, "He's a great man in Rome . . . a true man of God. They have a good following there."

"Just as Simon Peter foretold of him."

"Just as Peter said. Mary of Bethany followed him to Rome. There they were married."

"Man and wife. That is good. And Lazarus, the potter?"

Ezekiel rose and busied himself about the fireplace, stoking the fire and keeping his eyes averted as he maintained a careful silence. But he could feel how Simon watched him through his silence.

"Lazarus has died again," he said at last. "He died in the famine. His sister Martha has become an old woman, though she is still not old in years."

Ezekiel carefully turned around. Simon sat bowed, staring at the flame of the lamp.

"And the brethren? How fares it with the brethren in Jerusalem?" Simon put his hand on the warm lamp.

"The community is strong. Paul was here again, and Peter and the others have done good work. They are noble men." Ezekiel smiled, for he saw the interest in Simon's eyes. "Paul has traveled lengthy journeys—to Athens and to Corinth. He is the greatest of them all, this Paul. A worthy man of God."

"Paul," said Simon, and his mind traced back through the lengthy years. "Paul, who repudiated Him so. Where is he now?"

"He goes on traveling, visiting communities, and working for the master. They persecuted him here. He was long held in custody by the Roman governor. But he appealed to Caesar, and he was sent to Rome. Caesar found him innocent. Then he went off on his travels once again. Some say he is in Greece, some say in Syria—I cannot tell."

"And Simon Peter? "

"He is working among the brethren in Babylon on the Euphrates."

"It is good to learn that the Lord has spared them."

"It is good that the Lord has spared you, Simon Niger—even though you suffered."

"We have much to endure still before His kingdom conquers here on earth! And Joseph of Arimathea? Has he passed away?"

"He died, and they laid him to rest in the very sepulcher where they laid Jesus. He gave all his wealth to the community of the master, everything except this land, except Gethsemane."

Simon could see that Ezekiel had not told him everything. It looked almost as if he wished to hug some secret to himself for a while longer.

"You have something else to tell me, Ezekiel."

Ezekiel nodded. "We have had so much to say that I haven't been able to tell you yet. This land is yours, Simon Niger."

"Mine?"

"This land in the valley—the arable land, the orchard, the wine press, vats, and all. Joseph gave it to you and Deborah."

"No, it cannot be!"

"It's true. I tried to work. All these years I labored here. I sowed, I harvested, and sold, and sent the money to your Deborah. And she wrote to say they were using it for the community in Rome."

"But why did he do it? Why this great generosity to us?"

"At the end it was Deborah who cared for him. Just as she looked after Paul, Peter, Mark, and the others whenever they were here. She tended them like a mother. Through all these years she was a light in the community of Jerusalem . . . through all the years while she awaited you. Every day she hoped that you would come, Simon—every day and every night. She never gave up hope."

Ezekiel saw that a change had taken place in Simon. He saw his old master before him, the man he once had been. In one moment he seemed to have regained his old strength, almost his youth itself.

"We will go to Rome," said the Cyrenian. "We'll go to Deborah and Rufus and Alexander." He tried to stand up quickly, forgetting how the years had weakened him. He sank back helpless on the stool. His weakness wrung Ezekiel's heart.

"Where do we get the money? It costs a great deal of money to sail to Ostia."

"We'll sell this land. We'll sell Gethsemane. It is now ours to sell. We'll pay our passage, and what is left we'll give to the community."

Ezekiel sank down beside the table. "Sell Gethsemane?" he asked, dumbfounded. "Its fertile land? . . . The presses? The orchards? All are yours . . . forever. It is your home, Simon of Cyrene. Here you and your family can grow old. When you're strong again, we can sow crops and reap rich harvests. You have returned to the land, and now you wish to sell it?"

Simon rose slowly and walked over to the door. Even in the darkness he could feel the summer bringing all to fullness. In his mind he saw the rippling wheat and smelled the old lees in the vats. He pressed his hands hard against the doorframe to still their trembling.

"You believed before I did, and yet you do not give yourself completely to the Lord, Ezekiel," Simon said. "The wheat, the vineyards, the orchards—the whole earth belongs to Him."

"You have changed even more than I thought, Simon Niger. To you the lands and orchards have no meaning now. Did they kill your heart and spirit in that mine?" Ezekiel's voice was high and wheezing. "If anybody had ever told me that Simon of Cyrene would deliver up this land, I'd have told him he was an idiot."

"Nothing has meaning without the Lord. He gave life to everything. Wheat cannot be wheat if He doesn't make it grow, and the grape would not be the grape if He had not created sun and earth and light."

"Does the land mean nothing to you now?"

"It has meaning for me, Ezekiel—but a different meaning. First I loved it because it promised riches, a victory with the reaping of each harvest. Now I love it because it is one of His wonders."

He turned and smiled at Ezekiel. "The day you really come to know Him, that day you will see it this way as well. Then you will understand that a swelling ear of wheat and an olive heavy with oil are this way because He made them so."

"But I do believe in Him," said Ezekiel defensively.

"To believe is to believe wholly, because He is in everything, and all belongs to Him . . . and He is all."

"I'll see to the supper," said Ezekiel, and as he turned back to the hearth Simon realized for the first time how really old he had become.

"Who rules now in Rome?" he asked.

Ezekiel stirred their lentil soup. "Caesar Nero."

"Nero? "

"He calls himself Nero Augustus. Nero the exalted, so they call him. He came after Claudius, and Claudius followed that young fool Caligula, who tried to be a god." Ezekiel's hand ceased to stir the pot. "Nero. . . . They say that he has blood of ice and a heart of stone." He turned around and looked into Simon's eyes. "They say he holds a flame in each hand, and the wild stallions of his chariot have no bits in their mouths. I don't think we should go to Rome. I think Deborah, Rufus, and Mary should come back here. . . . I fear Rome under Nero."

"When does the next ship leave Joppa?"

Ezekiel sighed and his arms hung limply, for he knew that he could not stop Simon. "I cannot say," he answered. "But there are many ships. It's now harvest time. Many ships sail from Ostia at this time of the year, taking away the grain to the bellies of the beggars of Rome. Just as they always have, as they did when we were in Cyrene."

Simon patted his old servant on the shoulder. "The old Ezekiel has not vanished," he said smilingly. "He is as proud and fierce as ever."

"It is you who have turned to water, Cyrenian."

"It is good if part of a man dies—the part that is bad. You do not have to go to Rome."

"Where you go, I go with you. Why did I wait for all these years?"

"Then you go because you love me, for I am no longer your master—I am a servant, just as you are."

"That I know. I don't ask for payment. I want to be with you, Cyrenian."

There was resolution in Simon's eyes. "Let us eat, my comrade," he said, and slapped Ezekiel so hard between the shoulder blades that he almost fell.

Simon laughed. "You are older than I thought," he said. "Even I have greater strength than you."

Ezekiel made no reply. He hurried to the table and filled their drinking cups.

31

The morning star had barely risen above the dark sea when Simon awoke on the afterdeck. He listened to Ezekiel snoring beside him and heard the oars creak as the straining galley slaves dragged the vessel through the water. They were progressing slowly, for the wind was contrary and the sails could not be hoisted. They had been so long on the wilderness of waters—when would the journey end? It seemed to Simon that a year had passed since they left Joppa. And still there was no sign of the destination. As his excitement grew he had slept but little. He could scarcely believe he was going to Deborah. He stood up, stretched, and walked to the side of the vessel.

He looked to the north and searched the darkness before them, but the horizon eluded him. He gripped the railing of the galley, with his gaze turned to the north. The sea spume moistened his beard. Then he drew a sudden breath, closed his eyes, and leaning outward opened them to look again.

His eyes had not deceived him.

He heard the slaves talking excitedly. They must be seeing what he saw. Simon walked back and shook Ezekiel. Together they went to the side and stood watching the horizon to which the prow pointed.

"It seems as if the sun were rising in the north," said Ezekiel uneasily.

"Yes, it is a widespread glow."

"Aren't we mistaken about the direction? Perhaps it is the rising sun."

"See how low Venus lies?" said Simon. "That cannot be the sun."

"Yes. It is still dark—we are in the small hours," agreed Ezekiel. "I wonder what that light can be?"

Simon stared at the fiery crescent that rose slowly from the sea. "Perhaps it's a volcano erupting," said Simon. "It might even be Vesuvius."

"But look how high and wide the glow is."

"Let us go and ask," Simon said, and they walked forward.

Captain Festus and some of his officers stood watching at the prow. Even two of the slave drivers had joined them, their big whips idle.

"Is that a fire, captain?" asked Simon as they joined the group, "or is it Vesuvius erupting?"

"Vesuvius doesn't lie in that direction," said Festus indulgently, and the others laughed at the ignorance of their white-bearded passenger.

"A forest fire perhaps?" asked Simon undaunted.

"If that's a forest fire, then all the seven hills of Rome are burning."

"Is that where Rome lies?" Simon asked with lips suddenly gone stiff.

"That's where Rome lies," answered Festus. "That fire can be either this side of the city or behind it—but, as the eagle flies, that's where Rome lies, sure as I'm living."

"Suppose it *is* Rome burning," said the first mate, a young Roman with a keen expression.

"Suppose the sea dries up—then we'll both be out of work, Sergius," quipped Festus. The others laughed, and the mate flushed in the darkness.

"Perhaps the rabble has set fire to the granaries at Ostia," one of the slave drivers ventured.

"No, I'll tell you what it is—probably some spirited young damsel has applied a torch to Nero's ginger beard," said Festus contemptuously. The group burst out laughing, and Simon and Ezekiel wondered at the lack of respect. "That would be sufficient to send the whole Empire up in flames," the captain added.

"The old dragon," said Sergius bitterly. "They should sew him in a calf skin and throw him to the lions." The north wind snatched their laughter and swept it across the sea.

Then they fell silent, while all stared to the north. Simon stood watching until the dawn began to deaden the distant glow. As the sun rose, all went to watch again, and some of the slaves dragged their oars in the water as they tried to see.

A dull brown smudge, hanging on the horizon, marred the blueness of the sky.

"A cloud of smoke," said Simon to Ezekiel as they stood at the prow.

"The captain seems ill at ease," replied Ezekiel.

"He has paced the deck all morning," Simon agreed.

The captain came and stood beside them, hands behind his back. "That heavy bank of smoke," he said, "would you say now, that is Rome?"

Simon shrugged. "That's where Rome lies, captain—you told us so this morning."

"What else could show such conflagration?" Festus muttered into the wind, "except a burning city. And I've a wife there and four sons."

"I too have a wife there," said Simon. "And a son and daughter-in-law."

Festus looked at him quickly. "I thought you said this was the first time you'd traveled to Rome."

"That is true. They are Christians. They work in Rome. But I have been in the silver mines all these years."

"Christians?" Festus said it softly. "Followers of that Jewish prophet they once crucified in Jerusalem?"

"That is right. Jesus the Christ is His name."

Festus looked away toward the smudge of smoke. The name meant nothing to him. He turned and hailed the chief mate. "Sergius, tell them to hurry up the slaves!"

"I have another son," said Simon. "Alexander—he's a ship's captain, like yourself. Alexander of Cyrene."

"Alexander of Cyrene. I know him," said Festus without removing his eyes from the horizon. "A good man. We sailed together. . . . He's off to Alexandria. He'll be back one of these days with a cargo of wheat."

He turned and walked away. "Get more power behind those oars!" he shouted. The heavy whips cracked, and the boat shuddered as it began to move faster through the water.

During the course of the day they watched the smoke grow

darker. When night fell again, the glow was still there, but it seemed less fervent in the sky.

In the middle of the first watch, Festus came to Simon and Ezekiel in the prow.

"That glow is weaker," he said, and his voice sounded much relieved.

"The fire is burning out," Simon answered.

"Perhaps it was only some cargo sheds. Did you notice anything the night before last?"

"Now that I think of it, there was something to the north," said Ezekiel. "I think I did notice a dull glow. But I can't be certain."

"If you're right, it would be more than sheds," Festus remarked. "But I hope you're mistaken."

"When do we reach Ostia?" asked Simon.

Festus looked up at the stars. "Early tomorrow morning, but, if the wind turns, before that hour."

Simon slept little that night. He rose early and prayed for a long time, giving thanks that he had been able to come to Deborah and his family once more. Then he rolled up his bedding and packed his possessions for the landing. He let Ezekiel sleep on and went to the prow.

Then he smelled the smoke.

As the light increased, they saw it: a thick pall that hung from the distant hills far across the sea.

He saw Festus pacing up and down the deck uneasily. He came to Simon. "That smoke rises from the hills of Rome," he said. He sprang around, seized one of the whips from a slave driver, and leaped in among the slaves. He was breathless when he returned to the prow. "There lies Ostia," he said.

With bleeding backs the slaves forced the heavy galley through the water. It was early in the morning when the helmsman carefully turned the heavy tiller and they moved in toward a berth that fronted one of the large warehouses.

When the heavy line was flung out to moor the galley, Simon and Ezekiel stood ready with their bundles.

Festus stood nearby. They looked at the hurried activity on the quay. Wagons were hastily loaded and rumbled away. Slaves ran along bent over with bags of grain. Orders were shouted, and many soldiers moved among the throng. It looked almost as if they had taken control.

"What fire was it we saw from the sea?" shouted Festus to an overseer on the wharf.

"Three-quarters of Rome is burned to the ground," shouted back the overseer.

Simon almost dropped his bundles.

"What did you say?" yelled Festus, astounded. "How can three-quarters of Rome be burned?"

"It's true—hundreds dead . . . thousands homeless. . . . For more than a week there was nothing but flames . . . a red sea of fire . . . homes, temples, everything destroyed. For a whole week the wind blew from the north—they couldn't halt the flames. Warehouses, everything destroyed—there's no food."

"But how . . . how did it happen?" shouted Festus.

"The Christians did it—they set fire to Rome."

Simon sat down on his baggage, for his legs buckled under him.

"But Caesar means to punish them," said the overseer. "They put a number of them together yesterday, sewed them up in skins and fed them to the starving dogs. They've crucified others . . . and some have been crushed by the war chariots. Caesar drove one himself—you should have heard them screaming." The overseer's laugh rang out clearly above the clamor of the harbor.

Festus did not listen further. He came to Simon and Ezekiel. His face was white and beaded with perspiration. Simon looked at him uneasily. "You heard what's happening in Rome," said Festus. "You said you're Christians. I'll take you to my house . . . if my house still stands."

Simon stood up slowly and picked up his bundles. "Captain Festus," he said, "the God you do not know and in whom you don't believe will bless you for this. For you have shown a kindness to two of His humblest followers. But we cannot accept your kindness. We must go directly to my family."

"In Rome there is great danger—"

"We must go; we are not afraid." Simon's voice faltered, and his eyes were misty. "I have waited for many years and traveled far

300

to see my dear ones, Captain Festus." He held out his hand in farewell to the Roman, then passed quickly with Ezekiel down the gangplank. At the warehouse stood a wagon loaded high with grain. The driver was engaged in adjusting the harness of his team of horses.

"May we ride along with you to Rome?" asked Simon.

"My wagon is heavily laden," said the Roman driver. Simon took out some money and offered it to him. "Climb up," said the man.

Simon and Ezekiel climbed to the top of the grain bags and began their journey to Rome. On the way they saw masses of fugitives on their way to Ostia.

They entered the smoking heart of the Empire from the west and found it a black, smoldering ruin. The wind drove the heat in scorching gusts before it and smothered them with smoke as the wagon rumbled up the burned-out street where even the trees had died. They saw the corpses of a dog, a goat, a man lying with outflung arms, a cow with distended belly.

In the ruined squares they saw the people gathered. Far off against a hill white buildings gleamed, far from the chaos that was Rome. The stench of putrefaction swirled about them. In the distance they saw a tower topple slowly and in its place black fumes rise into the blue smoke-haze. Flocks of pigeons flew in bewilderment above them. A thousand columns of smoke spiraled upward from the ruins, to be tattered by the wind and driven to the sea. A long colonnade had crashed into the street, and the broken pillars blocked their way so that the driver had to make a detour. Two calves walked in front of them in the deserted street, lowing mournfully, their eyes red and the hair shriveled from their hides.

Out of a side street came a swaying wagon, the horses rearing and snorting as they turned. Ezekiel gripped Simon's hand. They looked at each other in bitter understanding. On the wagon was a cage filled with silent men and women. Four Roman horsemen rode behind.

"What is happening?" Simon asked the driver.

"It is some of these Christians they've caught. They're being taken to the arena." The driver pointed with his whip at a hill toward the northeast.

"Where are you healed for?" asked Simon.

"To the neighborhood of Mars. The homeless ones are there. I am going to unload the wheat."

"Then we'd like to be set down here. We want to go to the arena."

The driver held up his horses, and Simon and Ezekiel alighted. They started immediately to walk on through the black wilderness, but they did not go to the arena. They followed an eastward course as quickly as they could.

"We must go east," said Ezekiel. "Deborah said they lived on the other side of the main road in the east." He took a piece of parchment from his clothing and examined the rough drawing Deborah once had sent him.

"The crosses," said Simon as they walked, "where would they be?"

Ezekiel only shook his head and stamped his feet to get rid of the black ash. They walked for a long time before they crossed the main road and came to the eastern hill where the houses of those who did not belong to the upper classes of Rome huddled together under lofty trees.

This part had not been touched by fire. Probably the broad main road had acted as a firebreak.

But it was silent there.

They halted, and Ezekiel looked at the plan on the parchment.

"It must be in this vicinity," he said. "She wrote that we should look for a cypress taller than all the others."

"There it is," said Simon, pointing.

"Truly, there it is," answered Ezekiel, and they walked toward it.

32

Simon stumbled as he walked, for his eyes were fixed on the small white house in the shadow of the cypress. His heart thudded, and his lips felt dry and stiff. He searched the yard for signs of movement and looked at the closed shutter in one wall.

And then they stood before the door.

It was open, but not in welcome. The wooden door had been torn from its frame and lay to one side with a broken spearhead deep in the wood.

"They've been here," said Simon hoarsely and with a sob stepped over the door into the house. "There has been fighting," he shouted to Ezekiel, who had followed him.

They stood silently in the middle of the door, looking at the table, flung against the wall, the overturned washtub, the broken stool. Abruptly Simon bent down, picked up the heavy staff that lay there, held it and looked at the fresh bloodstain upon it. "They were fighting," he muttered again.

They walked fearfully into the other rooms. It was the same there—beds overturned, cupboards broken open. A lamp was lying on the floor, a bronze lamp fashioned like a swan. The oil had made a dark patch on the floor. Simon picked it up and held it in his trembling hands. He turned it over and over.

"This is the lamp that Alexander gave her in Cyrene," he said in a low, choked voice. Then he saw lying over the side of a broken chest the purple silk dress that Alexander had given Deborah that evening in Cyrene so many years before.

He shuffled over to it, stumbled over a wooden stool, pressed the dress to his eyes, and stood there bowed—an old, gray man clinging to a memory. A faint trace of myrrh lingered and for a moment he saw Deborah again beside the canal in Alexandria where their love began.

He heard Ezekiel's voice, soft and broken: "Let us go. There's nothing here." He felt the respectful touch of his old servant's hand. He let himself be led away, and he walked as one feeble-minded, with the purple dress beneath one arm and the swan-lamp in his hand. He collided with the lintel and Ezekiel had to help him through the door.

Outside stood a ragged man who looked almost like an animal, for he was one of the beggars from the nearby catacombs. His face was small and bloated, and a huge hump deformed his back. His empty hands hung open.

Only his eyes were alive. He looked silently at the two men who stumbled from the house. Ezekiel looked at him, and he spoke.

"The soldiers came for them at daybreak," he said. His strong voice contrasted with his hideous body. "I came too late to warn them."

Simon leaned back against Ezekiel, who braced himself to take the weight of the once heavy body.

"There were three," said the beggar. "There was the woman who had grown old so beautifully, the young woman with auburn hair, and the big man with a red beard. Three." He held up three fingers. "I know them. Sometimes they gave me food."

"Where . . . where have they gone?" asked Ezekiel.

The beggar turned slightly, lifted his head, and thrust out his hand. "To the arena—there . . . on the hill."

Simon broke out of Ezekiel's grip, leaving their bundles where they had set them down before the house, and walked away, stumbling, swaying. Ezekiel followed him and caught his garment. "You can't go to the arena," he pleaded.

"I must go there," Simon panted, jerked himself loose, and struggled further, his legs trembling. He remained erect by pure willpower, and saw nothing before him but the gray outlines of the arena.

Simon forced his feeble body faster. He began to trot.

"You can't go to the arena," screamed Ezekiel. "We shall both be killed."

"I want to die with them!" Simon answered as he ran.

But he stopped abruptly. A thunderous roar reached his ears, the yelling of vast crowds, as on that day in the courtyard of Pilate's palace.

"It is too late," shouted Ezekiel.

Simon began to trot again, his feet half-dragging.

He did not stop till the roar of the crowds swept about them. He stumbled on, sweating and sobbing, the lamp and the dress clutched tightly. When they were close to the arena, he stopped so suddenly that he almost fell.

There came the onslaught of new sound. They heard the roar of lions, full-throated, as when certain of their prey.

Ezekiel bowed his head, shook the tears from his eyes.

The earth trembled lightly beneath their feet. There came the snarls as the lions sprang, and the high-pitched screams of terror that rose and quavered into silence.

Simon's own scream was lost in the roar of the spectators. The cries from the arena cried to the skies even above the yelling of the crowd.

Simon and Ezekiel reached the solid wall of people who had not been able to gain admittance to the arena. It seemed as if the whole of Rome was present.

Ezekiel seized Simon's garment again and tried to hold him back, but with a furious jerk Simon freed himself and bored into the crowd—pushing, elbowing, wrestling. The strength of desperation drove his weak body. "Where is the nearest gate?" he screamed. "Where's the nearest gate?"

Ezekiel followed on his heels, saw him reeling through the crowd, then being repulsed and flung back by the rabble that refused to be thrust aside.

When a lion roared again in the arena, Ezekiel saw Simon fall. He collapsed slowly, and sank on his face with his white beard in the trampled soil of Rome.

Ezekiel squatted beside him, lifted his head, and held him fast, trying to protect him from the mob that pressed about them like a flood.

News passed from mouth to mouth above Ezekiel's head, called from the upper tiers of the arena down to the crowds below.

"It is done . . . finished. . . . It is over. . . . All are dead," the men above reported. "Some tried to climb out over the walls. . . . The crowds in the arena thrust them back again. . . . There are forty lions in the arena."

The rabble below shouted their approval.

Ezekiel took Simon under the arms, clutched the lamp and the dress, and began to drag him back. Fortunately they had not penetrated far into the crowd. The excitement in the arena was ending. The people outside would soon leave and await the next entertainment that Caesar Nero had to offer them. This one had been stimulating, even though they had seen nothing. It was better even than the crucifixions, or the scenes of starving dogs tearing at the flesh of Christians in Nero's well-kept gardens! The bellowing of the crowds and the roaring of the lions were in themselves a splendid entertainment.

Ezekiel dragged Simon to one side and propped him against the trunk of a poplar tree. The Cyrenian lay against the trunk, his head bowed, his eyes closed, his mouth hanging open. His lips moved slowly, for he was praying.

"It's over . . . over," he whispered at last, and moistened his lips with his tongue.

Ezekiel laid the lamp and Deborah's dress on Simon's lap. "Yes, it's over," said the old workman. "Now they've no more fear . . . and no more pain."

"No, they're in paradise with Jesus. . . . I was too weak, Ezekiel. . . . I could go no further. My breath failed me. I wanted so badly to see them all again, just once—Deborah and Rufus and Mary. I hungered to see her face just once again . . . to die beside her. I would have died so willingly. . . . I wanted so much to hold her, for she was so alone. Did you hear her scream? I think I heard her scream—the last scream just before it stopped. I know her voice, Ezekiel . . ."

"You're imagining things. I think she died in silence."

"Do you really think so?"

"I think so, Simon."

Ezekiel brushed the dust from Simon's beard. "You must rest," he said. "Don't talk any more. Just rest . . . and don't think about it any longer. It's over. . . . They are saved. In this moment we must be close to the Lord. It will make them happy."

Simon was silent He drew deep, whistling breaths.

The crowds streamed from the arena, noisily content. Suddenly a woman came rushing at them and snatched the purple dress from Simon's hand. He made no attempt to hold it; he did not even lift his head. Ezekiel tore furiously after her and seized her by the throat. He struggled to pull the dress from her grasp.

But the Roman rabble were united, and like the dogs of Nero they turned on Ezekiel.

A hungry boy came past and wrenched the lamp from Simon's hand. He let it go as well. He slowly opened his eyes and saw Ezekiel lying limp and still.

With the aid of the tree trunk he lifted himself and went to kneel beside his old servant. He saw the blood trickling from the corners of his mouth. He saw the fragment of purple cloth in his clenched fist, took it, and hid it under his garment. He felt Ezekiel's pulse—it beat slowly, very feebly.

Painfully, with frequent stops for rest, he dragged Ezekiel back to the tree. He rubbed his wrists. He listened to the passing crowds, the cracking of whips as the lions were forced back into their cages.

When all were gone and they were alone, Simon rose and looked toward the arena, at the dark entrances below, the high walls above. He saw the slinking beggars searching for fragments of food to keep body and soul together. He took out the piece of silk he had removed from Ezekiel's hand, looked at it, placed it again beneath his clothing, and sank back against the trunk. He stared at the arena and listened to the lions rumbling in their cases.

He remained there, hardly breathing, until beyond the smoke of Rome, beyond Ostia, the sun dipped below the sea. At his waist he felt the pouch of money he had brought for the community in Rome.

Simon stood up and looked at Ezekiel lying so still beside him. "We must go, Ezekiel," he said. "There's nothing left for us in Rome."

Ezekiel stirred a little. Blood bubbled on his lips as he spoke. "I am hurt. Let me die here. You go . . . and look for Alexander. . . . Let me die here. I am old and done for."

Simon made no reply.

He rose to his knees, and with long and patient effort he propped his old servant up on his shoulder. He struggled to his feet and slowly staggered away beneath his burden. He stopped once and looked back at the arena where the shadows and stillness mingled.

"Peace be with you, my Deborah," he said, and the words sighed in the still air. "Peace be with you, my Rufus. Peace be with you, Mary, brave young wife."

The arena grew dim before him; the massive walls seemed to melt, move, and tremble, its entrances to waver and fade away.

He gripped Ezekiel more tightly and staggered down the hill, toward the dark glint of the Tiber. He did not wish to go through Rome again.

He was weak. Every few steps he had to rest, for Ezekiel's weight seemed to break his back. He longed for his vanished strength. But just as he had forced himself against the crowds, so now he drove himself to struggle forward.

Twilight had fallen when at last he looked down at the brown waters of the Tiber that wound their sluggish course toward the sea. He had to sit and rest often to get Ezekiel this far. The time had been when he could carry a full sack of wheat beneath each arm. Those days had gone. Now even Ezekiel's wasted body had sorely tried him.

On the grassy bank he laid Ezekiel down. "We're beside the Tiber, old comrade," he said. "We'll walk along it to the sea."

He looked at the face of his old servant, at the eyes that stared but did not understand. He gripped both wrists in his hands.

"We're going to the sea . . . to Cyrene, Ezekiel," said Simon loudly. "There's nothing for us here . . . Ezekiel! We're going to the sea."

His voice echoed above the silent waters. Ezekiel made no reply. For him Cyrene had neither meaning nor any prospect.

Simon waited for the darkness; then he took Ezekiel into his arms like a little child and slid him into the water. The great Tiber received him gently, folded him into itself, and bore him to eternity.

"Peace be with you, old servant," said Simon and waved a

trembling hand. "Thank you for traveling so far with me."

He lingered there for a while longer. He looked up at the early stars. He listened to the water. Then he turned and followed along the banks toward Ostia, toward the sea that would bear him away from Rome, the city that taken all and offered nothing.

33

To the bustling harbor of Ostia the galleys came from distant places like fat geese for plucking. There Simon of Cyrene sought work from the Romans, and felt no humiliation. He had to live and be patient.

It was not easy to get work. They laughed at him in the big sheds at the waterside where they took on laborers. "You couldn't lift a roll of hides," said the official. "You're old and your beard is white. You'd collapse under a sack of wheat, or a bunch of dried fish, or a bundle of silk."

"Go and pick olives in the mountains or mend nets in the fishing harbor," said another official.

He did not talk back or feel humiliated, because humiliation was an emotion for those who had something to lose—and he could lose nothing more. In the arena he had lost everything, except faith and strength of soul. He simply bowed his head and left.

"Perhaps there is something you can do after all, old fellow," said the second official as Simon was about to pass through the door. When Simon turned and faced him, the man said: "There are a great many horse-drawn wagons here. Why don't you hold the horses while they load the wagons. Petty thieves are common here. Most drivers want their wagons watched while they're being loaded."

"Thank you," Simon said as he left the room.

So it came about that Simon of Cyrene held horses for the Romans while the wagons were being loaded.

The work paid little in Ostia harbor, for it was usually performed by a broken-down old freedman who had ceased to be good for anything else; but it was enough for Simon, because his needs were few. At night he gathered together remnants of the hay fed to the horses and made a bed for himself against a wall, slept there and dreamed of Deborah. Often he started out of slumber because he saw her so clearly in his dreams. One night he heard Rufus's voice so plainly that he rose, walked a few paces, and stood listening in the darkness.

Sometimes as he stood dreaming beside the horses, he would take the scrap of purple silk from underneath his garment and gaze at it. Or he would caress the porcelain box that contained the lock of Deborah's hair. He loved to take out the glossy lock and put it to his lips.

Unceasingly, he watched each vessel enter the harbor. On these occasions he would give a hungry old freedman a coin to take his place before the horses while he went closer to see what ship it was and who commanded it.

So it was that he was standing on the edge of the wharf when a big galley came in, riding low in the water and with a stallion's head high on the bow. He drew his shoulders back, tried to stand upright, combed his beard with his fingers, and pulled his shabby garment more tightly about him. He felt a little uneasy, for he knew that he seemed a ragged slave awaiting some menial task.

He saw the big dark man standing on the foredeck beside the rail, his shoulders powerful, his beard black and shining. He shouted orders right and left, and what he commanded was performed.

It was his own Alexander.

He moved unconsciously nearer to the edge of the wharf, till someone gripped him and pulled him back.

"Do you want to fall into the water and be crushed against the wharf, old man?" asked the young Roman who had pulled him back.

Simon smiled confusedly, stood back, and kept his gaze fixed on the prow. The plank was lowered, and he went and stood beside it.

The crew made way for Alexander, and he came slowly down the gangway.

Alexander looked once directly into Simon's eyes and looked away again. He brushed by his father.

Simon turned, and for a moment he was at a loss.

"Alexander!" he called softly to his son, and he wondered if it was the right thing to do.

Alexander stopped, looked around for the person who had called him, saw nobody, and was about to walk on.

"Alexander!" Simon said again, more loudly, and walked toward his son.

Alexander frowned at him. "Why do you address me this way, old man?" he asked. "You are a slave, are you not?"

"You could call me that," said Simon and looked down at his clothes and then back at his son. He longed to touch Alexander's hand with his own, to be alone with him somewhere so that they could talk. He smiled, and his hands trembled at his sides.

"What do you want?" said Alexander, and threw his mantle back from his shoulders so that it hung by the gold neck-cord behind his back.

"The years have made us strangers. You've been away for so long. I can see you've forgotten Simon of Cyrene."

Alexander came a pace nearer, and his frown made a deep cleft between his eyes. "Simon of Cyrene," he whispered. He looked searchingly at Simon, tried to fathom the gray face before him.

Then it flashed upon him. "Simon of Cyrene," he exclaimed. "My father. . . . You are my father!"

He gripped Simon hard by the shoulders. He crushed Simon hard against him, and Simon pressed his face to his son's shoulder, and stood quite still. They remained this way for a long time, not knowing what to say to each other. Then Alexander held his father slightly away from him. "But you've changed so much, grown so old," he whispered. The tone of his voice showed how deeply he was moved and Simon looked fondly up at him. But he could not say much. He nodded a few times. "I've grown old," he acknowledged, "old and weak," and he smiled.

"Have you seen mother and Rufus?" Alexander saw a shadow veil his father's eyes, and he tightened his grip on Simon's shoulders. "We can talk about that later . . . when we're alone—not here."

"I can't believe that it is you, Alexander, that I've found you after all these years."

"I can't believe it myself. . . . It's . . . it's a miracle."

Alexander took his father by the arm and led him away.

"I just have to clear my cargo," Alexander said. "Then we'll go home. I've a house here in Ostia. You must bathe and eat, and then we'll talk. We must discover everything that's been lost between us in all these years. . . . The catastrophe in Rome, have you seen it?"

"I was in Rome," Simon said softly.

"We heard it at sea—two days out from here."

They arrived in front of a large building. Simon plucked at his son's arm to halt him. "I came here to ask you something, Alexander."

"Simply to give you one meal would be a tremendous privilege."

"I want you to take me to Cyrene when next you go there."

"Cyrene? " Alexander took his father gently by the shoulders and looked deep into his eyes. "Not Cyrene. You can never go back there. Didn't you hear what happened that time? The crucifixions, the uprising and all? No, it's too risky."

"That's my last wish, Alexander. It was so long ago. . . . They've assuredly forgotten all about it. And I've forgotten fear."

"They'll kill you, father."

"When a man's as old and tired as I am, then life has little meaning left. I want to spread the teaching of Jesus there. By doing so, I'll repay my debt to Cyrene."

"The teaching of Jesus? The Nazarene? Do you believe in Him too?"

"I am a follower of Jesus, a proclaimer of the Messiah." Simon turned his head unconsciously toward Rome. His face told of a bitter recollection.

"What are you hiding from me?" cried Alexander.

The Cyrenian turned his head and looked steadily at his son, his eyes calm. "There is nothing I wish to hide. I desired to wait for the right moment. Now we are alone. I can tell you now—your mother, Rufus, and his wife died in the arena."

Alexander clutched at his father. "No!" he whispered hoarsely. "That bestial Nero. . . . Was it the lions?" Simon nodded.

"No!" cried Alexander with passionate loathing. Shaking his head from side to side, he staggered back against a stack of wheat.

313

"I was too late. I wished to die with them."

"When I saw them last they were so full of hope and fervor," said Alexander with his back to Simon. "They never ceased hoping that you would come back. That mad dog Nero! One day Rome will cut his veins and dogs will drink his blood!"

Alexander turned to him. Simon saw that his face was drained and white. "Let's get finished here," he said. "We can talk later, Father."

Alexander looked down at the smooth, cobbled paving, and the veins swelled on his forehead. Simon could sense his struggle.

"What do you want to say, my son?"

"I want you to rest in my house. . . . I am married to a Roman girl."

"I have forsworn hatred," whispered Simon, and Alexander looked at him in surprise and gratitude. "A Roman can be good or bad, and so can a Jew. It is not heart against heart—there is only good and evil between man and man. The years have taught me this."

"Thank you, thank you, Father," said Alexander. "She is kind. She will be good to you, because you are my father. You must stay with us for the years ahead. You are alone, and old."

"No. I must go to Cyrene. I have work to do there. When I was still a fool, it was there that blood dripped on my hands. Only *His* love can clean them. I must go and work for Him. I must pay my debt . . . to Him and to Cyrene."

34

It was a still summer evening, and the silence was broken only by the rhythmic splashing of oars as the great galley glided over the surface of the water.

The lamp in the captain's cabin hung almost motionless as it shed its yellow, friendly light.

"When do we arrive?" asked Simon of Cyrene.

"We should be in Cyrene just after daybreak, Father," answered Alexander. He looked wistfully at his white-bearded father, who sat across from him at the small table on which lay a basket of fruit. They had been together for such a short time after all the years of separation. His father had lived in his house at Ostia for less than a month.

Alexander rolled a pomegranate between his hands. He felt compelled to speak. He had said it often before, but as the coast of Cyrene grew nearer, he made his final effort. "Father," he said, his eyes pleading, "there still is time to change your mind. You can stay on board and return with me. You don't have to go ashore."

Simon, looking like a prosperous citizen in his new white garment, touched a cluster of grapes. "My son, we've talked this over many times, and there's no changing now. I am assured of your love for me, and of your good wife's esteem. We have found each other again after all these years. Your heart is good, and I am grateful. But I must go to Cyrene. There is no changing that. His service calls me."

"But they haven't forgotten about the uprising and the bloodshed. Rome's memory is long. It may mean your life."

"I do not fear death, Alexander. In Him, death is the gate to paradise."

"But why won't you end your days at home with me?"

"No, in Cyrene lies my life and destiny . . . in His service."

315

"Why can't you do this in Rome . . . or in Judea? Why return here where they'll have your life?"

"Rome is still seething. . . . I cannot work there. Judea has many excellent teachers. No, my work lies in Cyrene. I have a duty here. I must try to conquer Cyrene in His name."

Helpless against his father's resolution, Alexander saw the zeal burning in his eyes. "It would be such an honor to have you spend your last days beneath my roof, after all those years we were apart."

"I can't be idle. I must go on working for Him . . . to the very end. I have suffered for Him, but He has not taken all my strength. And I have done so little for Him. Can you understand this, Alexander?"

Alexander looked up at the gently swaying lamp. "I do try to understand, Father," he said with a sigh. "I've been trying ever since I saw the same spirit in Rufus . . . and in Mother, and Mary of Bethany. I wish I could share it. For I can see that it frees a man and makes him feel at peace. But I do not know its working, for I never knew *Him*. I know but Rome, and the ways of Rome."

"His teaching is for all—for you as well. Even the way of Rome can be the right one if His light guides. I haven't spoken much about this with you, Alexander, but tonight is probably our last night together. I am an old man . . ."

"You must not speak thus."

"Flesh is but mortal."

"We shall meet again," said Alexander, determined not to accept this as their final evening together.

"Before we part, I should like to feel that my elder son is not altogether without His light."

"Speak then—there is little time."

"What can I say, but that His is the true light? I have seen this, and I know. If you can believe in nothing else, you must believe in this." He closed his eyes, and Alexander saw the rapture in his father's face. "You must believe that He came and died, for you and your house, for Rome—He died for the whole world. You must believe it, for it is truly so. When He died, I was there. I witnessed it. I saw the veil tear in the temple. He opened the way for you and me to the All Highest. He showed me that great wonder."

He ceased to speak and looked at his son. "I know He is a stranger to you, my son, just as He was to me. He was a stranger to Barabbas the robber, and to Saul the Pharisee, but in the end He won all three of us. Saul is today His greatest servant, where once he was His bitter enemy." Simon folded his hands. "I too hated Him." Slowly he shook his gray head. "But now I'm ready to die for Him, because I know He is the Life."

"I wish . . . I wish I felt as certain as you do."

Simon talked gently. "I saw the man Lazarus, whom He raised from the dead. How can I not be certain?"

"You have lived it all. Where must I search, if I want to be a stranger no longer? Where must I walk to see His light?"

"You are asking that which Barabbas asked me in the mine." Simon smiled gently at his son. "It is enough simply that you search. If you open your heart, He will come to you and change your life. If your soul is willing, He will touch you with His hands."

"Will it be enough—is it enough if I simply search?"

"It is enough. He does not ask for offerings; He asks an open heart."

Alexander looked at his father. "You have forgiven me that I serve Rome?"

Simon seemed to be looking at his son from deep within himself. "A man can be good in Rome, and evil in Jerusalem," he said softly. "In the days when I blamed you, I did not know this yet. His love can open any heart. That I saw among the heathens of Syria."

Alexander stood up abruptly and walked over to the porthole, to see if the coast of Africa were yet visible. Above the creaking of the oarlocks, he heard his father's voice. "You can become a great man in Rome if only you will believe, my Alexander. What will end for me in Cyrene can be the beginning for you in Rome."

Alexander stood silently for a long time, and finally spoke while still looking out to sea. "My heart is open. I shall try to understand Him as you understand Him."

Simon rose, went to Alexander, and touched him lightly on the shoulder. "If you can find Paul, He will bring you to belief. Or Peter. I should have liked to do it. But I am a simple man. And they have a power I don't possess."

"You have power. You have made me understand that there is another life besides that which I lead."

For a time there was silence between them. Then Alexander turned to face his father. He was surprised to see tears in Simon's eyes.

"I am content," Simon said, smiling. "I know that He will speak to you, and you will listen."

"I have yet to find Him," Alexander said quickly.

Simon looked into his son's eyes. "He once spoke of that," Simon said, and his eyes glowed. "He said, 'Seek and you will find, knock and it shall be opened to you.' Can you understand that, Alexander?"

Alexander nodded, and his dark beard glistened in the light. "I think I understand it, Father. I shall try to remember. Seek and you will find, knock and it shall be opened to you," he repeated.

Simon looked through the porthole at the dark sea, and said, "It is enough. I know now that He will lay His hands upon you. You only need patience. . . . It is late. Let us rest. I want to see the sunrise over Cyrene."

Alexander watched his father turn away and climb into his cot. He felt the burning in his eyes, the pounding of his heart. He went out on deck and stood listening to the silence of the sea; he searched the horizon, but the night was thick. "Seek and you will find, knock and it shall be opened to you." Suddenly the words took on an imperishable quality for him, and he smiled in the darkness.

He went back into the cabin, stood silently beside the cot, and watched Simon stirring in deep sleep. He put his hand out gently, touched the white beard, and whispered, "I shall seek."

Simon rose at daybreak, washed himself, and went up to the deck. He went to stand beside his son.

Alexander pointed. "There lies Cyrene, Father," he said.

"I see it," said Simon, deeply moved, and walked slowly to the railing. "City of my youth, and city of my old age. I wish you were with me, my Deborah," he whispered across the sea.

"See how the rooftops glitter," said Alexander, who had come to stand beside his father, "and how green are the terraces!"

"There are our poplars."

"I can see them. They too have grown old. How tall they are. . . . It is more than thirty years."

Alexander pointed to the little beach below the terraces. "Rufus and I used to play there in the old days."

"Everything has a beginning and an end," said Simon as he gazed at the green orchards that rose from the sea to the plateau. "But the end may be its own beginning."

Alexander made no answer, but he understood.

The wharves, on which great stacks of wheat were piled, came nearer. The city, emerging from the night, towered above them, white, proud, and gleaming.

"Where will you go when you have landed, Father?" asked Alexander.

"I'm going to look at our land—just once again—to see the Lord's work on the soil. Then I shall go to the synagogue to begin my work. Perhaps they have better teachers than I, but I can help."

"I want to see you again before I leave."

"No. We say good-bye on the wharf. You have your work, and I have mine. . . . And my time is short." There was deep finality in his words.

"Will you return to Rome with me one day? I often visit here. Today must not be the end between us, for I have known the light of your wisdom for too short a time."

Simon smiled gratefully. He looked at the white-walled majesty of the palace, where once long ago he had stood in chains. Then he said, "When my joints are stiff, when my flesh is feeble and the years have dimmed my senses, then I shall return with you to Rome, because then my work in Cyrene will be over."

He fell silent and looked at his son, the virile image of his youth. Then he took Alexander by the shoulders, and his grip was as light as a child's. "I say good-bye to you now, my firstborn. Here are the wharves of Cyrene. You have your work. I shall pray that He brings His light to you. Peace be with you. May your years be long and fruitful. Peace be with your good wife. . . . Peace be with your children. . . . Peace be with you all."

"Peace be with you, my father," said Alexander, and his eyes filled with tears. "There is something you must believe—this journey has its meaning for me. I shall hold my heart in readiness."

"Jesus bless you, my son," said the old man simply, his face calm, with a strength beyond his years. Then he embraced his son, turned away, and stood gazing at Cyrene.

A little later, when Simon walked down the gangway, Alexander watched him go, gazing after him as if to store in his mind forever the image of the lone figure. On the wharf Simon turned, raised his hand, and waved. Alexander saw that he was smiling. Then he walked away and vanished from sight among the stacks of cargo waiting to be shipped to Rome.

Simon walked slowly up the terraces, stopping every now and then to rest and look about him. And from the forgotten past memories returned again.

He was breathless when he reached the place where his old lands lay. They were more or less as he had left them. Only the living things were older, bigger—his olive trees, his vineyards, the lanes of fig trees, the pomegranate bushes. New vineyards had been laid out, new orchards flourished. Everything looked well tended. He walked farther along the path and stopped again. The poplars where his house had stood were tall and thick and gnarled, bigger than all the others in the neighborhood.

But the house that he and Ezekiel built was there no longer.

Where Deborah and he and his two sons had lived stood a large Roman villa, with rambling roses on the walls, verdant lawns, sequestered walks, and beds of flowers. Simon closed his eye and saw Deborah coming lightly through the trees, his luncheon basket in her hand, the sunlight on her hair.

"I am back in Cyrene, my beloved," he whispered. "I am back on our lands again. Only the sun is still the same, the sun and the soil."

He opened his eyes and looked away through the sunlight to the place where he had set fire to the wheat stack, but there the Roman had built stables . . . and slave quarters.

For a little while longer he lingered there, leaving many footprints on the soil. He looked at everything, but without bitterness; he looked and he remembered.

He bent and picked up a handful of soil. It was as dark and rich as it used to be. He brought it tremblingly to his face. Yes, it was the soil of Cyrene, the same as when he, Deborah, and his children drew their sustenance from it.

"What are you doing on this property, old man?"

Simon looked up startled.

The Roman overseer saw with surprise the tracks of tears on the cheeks of the old stranger.

"I just came to look. Once this land was mine," Simon said.

"It belongs to the nobleman Brochus now. Everything here is his. We can't have people trespassing."

"I understand," Simon said. "I'll go at once. I only came to look." He let the soil trickle from his hand. Then he turned and walked away, with a last look at the olive trees.

He went then to the synagogue. There he found Gabriel, the head of the synagogue, and Gabriel was older than himself.

Gabriel stared at the gray stranger for a long time.

"You know me no longer, Gabriel of Cyrene?" said Simon. "It is many years since last we saw each other. Peace be with you."

Simon's voice stirred something in the old man's eyes. Shakily, he drew nearer.

"Surely not Simon . . . Simon of Cyrene?" asked Gabriel, his old voice trembling.

"Yes, I am he."

"The man of the uprising."

Simon saw the change in Gabriel's eyes. There was not only amazement in them now, but fear too. "You have come back to Cyrene?"

"I have come back."

"Peace be with you, Simon Niger." Gabriel smiled and took Simon's hands in his.

"You are a brave man to come back to Cyrene. The children of those who died have not yet forgotten."

"I am not afraid, Gabriel. . . . I have come to serve the master, here in the synagogue."

Gabriel sank down on a bench. "The master? Jesus?"

"There is but one master."

"Sit down, and let us talk," said the old man, making room for Simon to sit beside him. Simon thanked him, for he was weary.

35

Simon looked at the full synagogue with gladness. Not all could get inside. Some stood in the doorway, others sat in the windows, for Gabriel had caused it to be known among the congregation that a new teacher had come from Jerusalem and would expound the doctrines of the prophet who had died.

Gabriel raised his hands for silence.

When quiet had fallen Simon began to speak.

"I have come to Cyrene to proclaim the word of the Messiah. I have come to speak of the miracle of His suffering and His resurrection, by which He redeemed us from our sins. I saw it all, and what I tell you is the truth. I was in Jerusalem when they crucified Him—"

A middle-aged Jew, who had been staring at Simon with furrowed brows, forced his way to the front of the congregation, gesticulating and wild of eye. When he reached Simon and Gabriel, he shouted, "But this man is Simon of Cyrene—the man who caused the uprising years ago!"

There was a stirring in the crowd and the deep murmur of many voices. People whispered together, wide-eyed at the news.

"He made Cyrene bleed in that uprising!" shouted the man before them. Other men pushed their way closer to the front.

Gabriel raised his hands again and called for calm.

"Let us not hate!" he begged them. "Let us this day hear the teaching of the Redeemer of Israel."

"My father died in that uprising!" someone shouted, thrusting himself forward.

"My two brothers were killed that day!"

"I became an orphan."

"When they put up the crosses, he had gone!" screamed a woman.

"He ran away!" they roared.

Hatred rumbled through the congregation. They pushed and stamped and struggled.

"He filled the street with blood, and now he wants to preach about a new prophet. . . . Let us bring him before the governor!"

"Yes, take him to the governor!" many cried.

"Let him speak!" Gabriel implored them. "He is one of the elect. . . . Let him speak. Do not make the shame of Jerusalem the scandal of Cyrene. His sin is of the past. He has returned to make amends."

"He can make no amends for the bloodshed he brought upon Cyrene!" yelled one, and the others took up his cry.

In the middle of the congregation a man raised his hands. "Brethren of Cyrene, listen to me . . . listen to me!" he pleaded, and his great voice stilled them.

"Big Micha," whispered Simon. "It is he!" But the man no longer resembled the big blacksmith that Simon had known. The years had cut deep grooves into his face, and his hair was as white as snows on Carmel.

"I know this man," spoke Big Micha. "That day when he set fire to the wheat, he struck a blow for freedom. We all fought for freedom that day. He fought for the freedom of Israel. . . . I lost two sons, but I do not hate him, for we were all one on that day. Touch him not, for he is the messenger of Jesus."

"We have peace here now!" shouted the man in front. "He'll bring another bloodbath to Cyrene and flee just as he did that day our fathers, our mothers, our brothers, and our sisters were mowed down."

"Take him to the governor!" bellowed the congregation.

"We'll have nothing to do with this new teaching."

"He is a Jew. How can you give him over to the Romans?" shouted Gabriel, waving his arms in anger.

But they would not listen to him. They pressed closer and laid violent hands on Simon. Gabriel caught him by his garment and tried to hold him.

"He is an enemy of Cyrene!" they shouted.

"He is a man of Israel!" Gabriel cried in answer.

"My brother in Jesus," said Simon to the aged Gabriel above the tumult, "let them have their will. In Jerusalem Israel put to death a greater man than I. I do not fear. If I still have a debt to pay Cyrene, let me pay it with my life."

They forced Simon away and dragged him through the crowd.

"Do what is good, and bear witness to His light," shouted Simon over his shoulder to Gabriel, who stood there weeping, wringing his hands.

Big Micha forced a path through the milling, demented crowd. He beat arms away, flung men down, thrust an arm around Simon's neck, and held him. In that brief time of meeting, they forgot the fury that raged about them. They looked into each other's eyes in their moment of contact.

"I shall not let you die!" shouted Big Micha, and held Simon firmly by his gown.

"Let them be," said Simon. "If I must die, it is His will. . . . Big Micha, I am thankful to have met you once again."

Once more the crowd seized Simon, but Big Micha fought them, dealing blows at the assailants, trying to fling them back.

But the years had undermined his strength. He was no longer invincible, as he was when young. The crowd thrust him away, beat him to the ground, trampled over him, and dragged Simon out of the synagogue to the palace of the governor.

When they brought him within, the great hall looked so familiar that it might have been only yesterday that he stood there before Quirinius. He walked alone between two guards. But it was not Quirinius before whom they took him. The man who stared at him with a strange anger was unknown to him.

"So you are the anarchist who once tried to burn Cyrene to the ground?"

Simon made no answer.

"After all these years your crime has driven you back to Cyrene? Now do you realize that an offense against Rome never ceases to pursue the evildoer?"

Simon shifted his feet.

"The punishment of a rebel is death. Rome never cancels a debt, however old it is. Do you hear me?"

"I hear Your Excellency's words."

"Are you prepared to die without saying anything in your defense?"

"There is nothing that I can say to Your Excellency."

"I understand you are one of these . . . these Christians who devastated Rome."

"I am a Christian, Your Excellency." Simon's voice was loud and clear.

"You are not afraid to tell me that . . . after what has happened in Rome?"

"A Christian has no fear, Your Excellency. Who believes in the Lord is not afraid even of the might of Rome."

"Take this madman away and crucify him," ordered the governor with an angry gesture. "They are all demented, these Christians."

Simon stood in the cell again. It was strange that they should have brought him to the same chamber to which he had been taken that night long years before.

He looked at the scarred walls, where hundreds of the condemned had left their names and their thoughts. There was little room left.

Slowly he raised his hands and looked at the heavy manacles. He felt a great desire to inscribe there the name of his Master, here in the same prison from which he had been delivered so long ago.

Simon tried to dig into the granite with the wristbands of the manacles. But the manacles were smooth. They had no edges. His hands began to bleed from scraping against the stone. All that he achieved were faint marks on the stone, signifying nothing.

As the dusk deepened those marks faded.

When the darkness came, he sank exhausted, hearing the straw rustle under him. He lay quietly, awaiting death.

His wrist felt sore and broken. Before exhaustion cast him into broken slumber, he touched the palms of his hands and his wrists, and he wondered how the pain would be when they hammered the spikes through his flesh.

Deborah came to him in his dreams, her eyes glad and laughing. He saw Rufus in the fields, Alexander on his deck. Mary of Bethany smiled at him and offered him cool water. He took the cup and drank deeply.

But that was yesterday. The night had passed. Now evening was falling again.

Out of his black agony Simon raised his shuddering head and turned his sweating face to the wind that blew in from the desert.

"Thank you, master, for the cool wind, thank You for evening," he whispered.

He knew that he was alone on the hill where so many had died before him. Here was only the cross and the Roman guard as witness of his torment.

Are Gabriel and Big Micha the only ones in Cyrene who believe in Him? was the thought that he wished to utter. But he could not utter it.

A belt of pain tightened the cramping muscles of his chest and drove the breath from his body. "If it be Your will, deliver me," he said, so loudly that the Roman soldiers looked up at him.

"I am alone," he muttered, and tried to draw himself up by his tortured arms, to force himself up with his shuddering legs, for it felt as if the edges of the iron spikes were tearing through his hands. He threw his head back with a sob and tried to ignore the agony where the spikes had pierced his feet. He raised his body slightly higher; his face contorted, but he endured, for now he could breathe more easily.

It was only for a moment. Then his body sank and dragged again its weight on his hands.

"How long, master? How long must I endure? I am alone. Does Cyrene not yet know You?"

His head fell sideways. For a moment he stared up at the sphere of heaven where the soft purple of the evening hovered. Dimly he saw dark shapes of birds flying high toward the desert. Then once more pain possessed him.

"Let me be silent. . . . Let me not cry out. . . . You suffered this, and You were young; my strength is small. . . . Let me be silent."

His head swayed on his breast. He saw white stones grow shadowy in the dusk; the earth grew darker.

He lifted his head, and sought the sea. The sea was empty, empty as the sky now that the dark birds had vanished.

That morning he had seen the wheat ship gliding slow and deep in the water. Then his strength had been greater. He had shouted, "Farewell, my Alexander. . . . Bear His torch. . . . Peace be with you."

But now the sea was empty.

He looked toward the horizon, but the sun was gone, and the horizon was slowly coming closer. It lay just beyond Cyrene, on the sea. Steadily it came, and soon would lie about him, about him and the Roman guards. Then all else would be far away, beyond the circle of his agony.

He could still see Cyrene—how lovely it was in the evening. But not for long, for soon Cyrene too would lie beyond him. It would be as distant as everything was distant now.

Over on the terraces the tops of his poplars waved, waved their last farewell, for when the sun rose in the morning there would be no wind.

The road to Cyrene—that too was empty. No one came along it with garment swaying in the wind.

Only his poplars called and sighed.

"Cyrene is as Jerusalem was the day You died."

The wind grew cold against his sweating breast.

Cyrene melted into the evening that came from beyond Jerusalem.

The sweat of death lay in his eyes, and it was hard to see. But he could still discern the white splendor of the palace. The prison lay there.

The Cyrenian tried once more to lift his body against the cross, but it did not help him. His strength had faded. He rolled his head in the wind, shut his eyes, and waited . . . waited for the horizon to close about him.

When he opened his eyes again, he looked for the day beyond the desert, but the night was with him still.

Strange, it was night and yet there was light about them.

"The pain," he muttered. "How long must I endure it?"

Through his swoon he felt against his trembling lips the sponge they had dipped in a drugged wine. He sucked at it, and it dripped down on his chest.

"It is night . . ."

"It is night. . . . The sun has gone." The second voice sounded like an echo of his own.

Why was there some cool release to his pain? About his wrists, about his feet? Why was it only his bones that still shrieked in agony?

"Alexander has sailed with an open heart." It was his last consciousness, which slowly flowed away. These were the last words welling from his heart.

His body arched and then sank back.

His eyes opened, and he looked for Cyrene. But Cyrene was lost to him.

"I am . . . alone. Cyrene does not . . . heed . . . Your voice."

"No, you are not alone, Simon of Cyrene. Look round about you."

"I hear . . . Your voice . . . master."

Eyes in which death hovered searched dimly through the dusk. But it was Gabriel's face that was near his. Gabriel had climbed a ladder and leaned across the crosspiece. He held the moist sponge in his hand and pried it into the mouth that gasped for life.

"Gabriel—"

"Cyrene lives. We waited for darkness before we came, man of Cyrene. But now we are here. Look round about you. You are not alone. Cyrene is not lost."

His head swung slowly as he looked. The lights of many torches jeweled the night. He saw them standing silently about him, a multitude of white faces raised to his.

"Do . . . they . . . believe . . . Gabriel?"

"They have heard His voice, man of Cyrene. They believe as you believe, as I believe."

Simon raised his face. For a moment it seemed that his smile transformed his pain. "The wind . . . blows cold . . . upon my pain."

"It is the women of Cyrene wrapping cloths with vinegar about your wounds. Suck this sponge. It will ease your pain."

"Big Micha?"

"He is preparing the grave, where you will rest in the earth of Cyrene."

"Gabriel . . . I . . . I think . . . I'm dying."

328

"Can you still see, Cyrenian? Look down, then. Here is one who would speak to you before you go."

His head fell forward and he looked for the man who touched his legs. He saw him standing close beside the cross.

"You are . . . blind."

"I am blind, man of Cyrene. You blinded me with a torch."

"You . . . are then . . . the Roman?"

"I was a Roman soldier until the night Vitellius died."

"Tonight . . . I suffer . . . also . . . for that night."

"I do not hate you."

"You . . . have no hate?"

"I am your brother in Christ."

"I shall see you . . . in His paradise . . . good Roman."

Simon lifted his shuddering head again. Vaguely he saw the red plumes. He saw the faces of those who stood about him. His eyes were wide and staring, but no more from pain or fear. Something that seemed like happiness brought a last rapture to his body.

"Jesus . . . Savior," he cried, and those last words broke his body.

He still heard those about him singing a hymn in Jesus' praise.

Then his body jerked wildly, and it appeared as though he would tear loose from the cross. A spasm drew back his head, his white beard moved in the wind.

"He is going," cried Gabriel from the ladder, and the others pressed closer, trying to touch his dying body.

Suddenly that body was still. His head lay on his chest; his weight hung on his hands; his knees sagged motionless.

"He is delivered," said Gabriel and touched his forehead.

"Is his suffering past?" asked the blind Roman, staring up with sightless eyes.

"He has paid his debt," answered Gabriel. "He is in paradise."

Thereafter they fell silent. One by one they came and touched his feet, looked up at him, saw the night wind stir in his hair.

They all could see the smile that had not died with death.

Then they turned and went back facing the wind, except for those who stayed to take the body to its grave.

As they went, the wind assailed their torches, but the driven flames were stronger than the gusts.